Uneasy Allies

Uneasy Allies

ANGLO-PORTUGUESE RELATIONS, 1642–1662

T. Bentley Duncan

VANTAGE PRESS
New York

FIRST EDITION

Published by Vantage Press, Inc.
516 West 34th Street, New York, New York 10001

Manufactured in the United States of America
ISBN: 0-533-13585-0

Library of Congress Catalog Card No.: 00-91501

0 9 8 7 6 5 4 3 2 1

CONTENTS

MAPS AND TABLES

MAPS

TABLES

ABBREVIATIONS

AHU	Arquivo Histórico Ultramarino, Lisbon
Ajuda	Biblioteca Nacional do Palácio da Ajuda, Lisbon
Arq. Dist. Angra	Biblioteca Pública e Arquivo Distrital de Angra do Heroismo, Terceira, Azores
Arq. Dist. Évora	Biblioteca Pública e Arquivo Distrital de Évora
Arq. Dist. Funchal	Arquivo Distrital de Funchal, Madeira
Arq. Dist. Ponta Delgada	Biblioteca Pública e Arquivo Distrital de Ponta Delgada, São Miguel, Azores
Bancroft m/f	Bancroft microfilms or the *Portuguese Empire in America* microfilm collection in the Bancroft Library, the University of California at Berkeley (cited only where the Bancroft *caixa* numbers differ from those used by the AHU in Lisbon)
BM	British Museum, London
Cal.S.P.	*Calendar of State Papers,* the *Domestic Series*
CU cons.	Conselho Ultramarino, *consulta,* always followed by a specific date; refers to the official signed and dated memoranda of the Overseas Council of Lisbon
HMC	Historical Manuscripts Commission
PRO	Public Record Office, London

DATES

In the seventeenth century England used the Julian or Old Style calendar and Portugal used the more accurate Gregorian or New Style calendar, with a difference of ten days between them. Thus, when it was 1 July in London it was 11 July in Lisbon. Where reference has been made in the text to English events or to the dates of English letters or documents or to the time kept aboard English ships, a double date has been given, thus: 1/11 July 1650. Otherwise, the Gregorian or New Style date alone has been used. Where only one date is given, the Gregorian date is intended.

1
ANGLO-PORTUGUESE RELATIONS AND THE 1642 TREATY

The Anglo-Portuguese alliance, in its modern form, was an arrangement that provided Portugal with political and military protection in return for economic benefits for England. This type of alliance dates back to the treaties of 1642 and 1654, which were confirmed by the dynastic agreement of 1662 and further extended by the political and economic arrangements of 1703.

An earlier form of the Anglo-Portuguese alliance goes back to the dynastic treaty of Windsor in 1386, which brought to Portugal the Princess Philippa of Lancaster, who became the mother of Prince Henry the Navigator and the direct ancestress of seven Portuguese kings. Even before 1386 there were a number of commercial agreements between England and Portugal that extend at least as far back as 1294.

Yet the earliest of all contacts between the English and the people who inhabited the land later called the Kingdom of Portugal occurred in 1147, when Afonso Henriques (d. 1185) sought to create an independent state under his rule and thereby laid the foundations of the Portuguese nationality. In 1147 the city of Lisbon, long held by the Moors, fell to the victorious Afonso Henriques. An English Crusader, often called Osbernus, left a lively Latin record of how a mixed band of quarrelsome Crusaders, comprising Englishmen (or Anglo-Normans), Rhinelanders, Flemings, Scots, Bretons, and Galicians—a most virile and energetic group—interrupted their journey to the Holy Land, to help the first king of Portugal capture Lisbon, which the Moors surrendered on 22 October 1147.[1] The English contingent took a leading part in storming the Lisbon walls, and on 1 November 1147 an Englishman, Gilbert of Hastings, was chosen to be the Bishop of Lisbon.[2]

During the next two hundred years the kings of England and Portugal had little direct contact with one another, although a brisk trade must have flourished between Portugal and the south of England ports, if only because Italian ships were commonly seen in English harbors and undoubtedly called at Portuguese ports on their journeys to and from the north.[3] Close commercial and political relations between England and Portugal began during the fourteenth century and have continued, with several interruptions (i.e., 1585–1604, 1625–1630, 1650–1651, etc.), until the twentieth. England made a commercial agreement with Portugal at the end of the thirteenth century (1294), but its terms had to be renewed annually.[4] In 1353 the two nations signed a fifty-year treaty of commerce (London, 20 October 1353) to the mutual benefit of "les bones Gentz, Marchauntz, Mariners, & les Comunaltes de la Marisme" of both countries.[5]

Toward the end of the fourteenth century, when John of Gaunt, Duke of Lancaster, made his bid for the crown of Castile—while another John, the Portuguese master of the order of knights of Saint Benedict of Avis, struggled against Castile for the throne of Portugal—English and Portuguese interests began to run in parallel channels.[6] A detachment of English longbowmen helped the Portuguese to defeat the Castilians at the decisive battle of Aljubarrota (14 August 1385), and the treaty (9 May 1386) that followed provided for the marriage of John I, founder of the house of Avis, and Philippa, daughter of John of Gaunt.

During the fifteenth century the English merchants trading in Portugal received many grants of privileges from Portuguese kings (in 1401, 1405, 1427, 1433, 1448, 1454, 1458, 1491, and 1497).[7] Ships bearing Portuguese produce sailed to English harbors, and the port books of Southampton recorded such items as the arrival of 1,810 *pieces* of fruit[8] from Lisbon (in 1428) and the export of English cloth. These books contain such shipping entries as: "Entre j Neif de Luschelne, Mestre John Fernand" (Enter one ship from Lisbon, Master João Fernando) and "Entre la Trinite de Luschebonne, Mestre John Affons" (Enter the *Trindade* of Lisbon, Master João Afonso).[9] On the whole, an English economic historian is probably right in her sweeping judgment, rendered over ninety years ago, that "the Anglo-Portuguese alliance . . . is almost unique in the history of the Middle

Ages for the care with which it was maintained, for its popularity in both countries and for its beneficial results to both parties."[10]

The two countries maintained amicable relations until 1580, when Portugal was annexed by Philip II of Spain. Elizabeth of England at this juncture made an effort to help the unfortunate Dom António, the prior of the monastery of Crato and pretender to the crown of Portugal, but, even with English help, Portugal could not evade the rule of Philip II. Spain expelled the English merchants from Lisbon, and the Portuguese fleet supplied the Invincible Armada of 1588 with its finest galleons. Peace came only after the accession of James Stuart to the English throne in 1603, when a treaty of peace and commerce between England and Spain encouraged the chartering of a new trading company called the President, Assistaunts, and Fellowshippe of Marchaunts of Englande Tradinge into Spayne and Portugale. This company, chartered on 31 May/10 June 1605, was patronized by the highest officials in the government and by the Earls of Dorset, Devon, Northampton, Nottingham, and Salisbury.[11]

Some English merchants moved to Portugal, and the old trading connections were slowly restored, only to be interrupted, once more, by the Anglo-Spanish war of 1625–1630. The peace of 1630 returned conditions to the *status quo ante,* and previous treaties of friendship and commerce were formally reconfirmed in 1634–1635.

The decisive moment in the history of seventeenth-century Portugal was fast approaching; it can be dated with astonishing precision: when the bells of the Lisbon cathedral church struck the hour of nine on the morning of Saturday, 1 December 1640, a group of conspirators overpowered the palace guard of Margaret, Duchess of Mantua,[12] who was in charge of the government of Portugal, and proclaimed John, Duke of Bragança, king of Portugal. The forty or more conspirators acted with notable secrecy, efficiency, and dispatch; the smoothness, speed, and success of the revolt exceeded all expectations. A distinguished contemporary, Dom Francisco Manuel de Melo, penned the classic description: "In two hours the city, in seven days the kingdom, in six months the overseas possessions changed masters; doubtlessly resistance was lacking; sixty years of Spanish dominion exercised by three princes was forgotten in an instant. The peoples submitted, not without wonder, to a lord whom those who were near had never seen, and those who were afar had never even heard of."[13]

Four English merchants in Lisbon—John Mules, Peter Middleton, Francis Hanbury, and Richard Beare (perhaps acting as representatives of the English merchant community)—drew up a report on the situation in Portugal and sent it to London. The report noted the sensational murder of Miguel de Vasconcelos, the hated secretary of state, who was the one man in Portugal the conspirators were determined should not outlive the revolt, but went on to add that within three hours all of Lisbon was calm. "To us there resident it seemed but a dreame."[14] On the day of the revolt twelve English ships were in Lisbon Harbor. Agents from the new government approached the English merchants and assured them that they would not be molested; in fact, they would now be able to trade more freely than before. This was good news, because the English merchants in the months prior to December 1640 had been seriously harassed by port officials acting on orders from Madrid.[15] The new king, John IV, well understood the value of commerce to the nation; by a decree of 21 January 1641 he allowed wide freedom to foreign merchants to trade in Portugal.

Apart from getting rid of Spanish officials, John IV made few immediate changes in government personnel. In Portugal and in the colonies the same officials carried on in the same jobs, while the new king calmly and authoritatively took on the functions of a chief of state. December 1640 was an excellent time for a Portuguese revolt against Spain. France and the United Provinces made war on Spain by land and sea. The policies of Philip IV's favorite, the Count of Olivares, had provoked (or so his critics asserted) a dangerous revolt of the Catalans, who had accepted Louis XIII of France as their prince under the title of Count of Barcelona. One Spanish army was permanently stationed in Flanders, and another was committed to a winter campaign against the Catalans. There were no troops available to send against Portugal, nor would any become available before the summer of 1641. John IV had at least four or five months to prepare the land defenses of his kingdom. In the meantime, he dispatched the Jesuit Inácio de Mascarenhas to the Catalans to assure them of full Portuguese support. Mascarenhas arrived in Catalonia in time to witness the battle of Montjuïc (23 January 1641), fought outside Barcelona and won by the Catalans.[16]

The Portuguese could also take some comfort from the fact that the Spanish fleet, having suffered a serious defeat in English waters in the Downs on 21 October 1639, was not at its normal strength in December 1640; and even if it had been, the Spaniards would probably not have attempted winter operations against the coast of Portugal. As for the small squadron of Portuguese and Spanish galleons normally stationed at Lisbon and used for convoy and patrol duties in adjacent waters, it had already been laid up for the winter. By 1 December 1640, these ten or twelve ships were only half-manned (with 418 seamen instead of 803) and were not in fighting condition. In the circumstances the rebels were able to capture three Spanish galleons on the Tagus with ease.[17] Then they set about outfitting a strong fleet for the operations of the spring and summer of 1641.

By the midsummer of 1641, John Chandler, English consul at Lisbon, made a cheerful report to Charles I on Portuguese prospects. As for the Spanish army, he wrote, "no forces of consequence have appeared, neyther is it feared that the K. of Spaine wil bee able to gather any considerable force this present year, to effect any thinge of consequence in the reducinge of this Kingdome." Although the Portuguese fleet was small, Chandler said its ships were excellent: "As for the 9 Portughese Gallions they are well appointed shippes, as hardly cannot bee seene better, the least of them about 800 tonne, and 3 of them about 1000—all exceedingly well mounted with brasse artillery."[18] For additional strength, John IV hired two English ships for four months of service (a London ship of 450 tons and one from Dover of 250 tons) and, more important, persuaded both France and the United Provinces to send out fleets to help him. Meanwhile, on 4 July 1641, a French Mediterranean fleet defeated a Spanish squadron off Catalonia, thus giving the Portuguese some valuable indirect help. A joint Portuguese-French-Dutch fleet took to sea in the autumn and engaged the Spanish fleet in an indecisive action off Cape Saint Vincent.[19]

Strength at sea was important to the Portuguese rebels or "restorers" (*restauradores,* as the Portuguese historians prefer to call them), not only for the protection of the Portuguese coast but also for maintaining contact with the North African garrison towns and with the islands of Madeira and the Azores. The acceptance of John IV in the islands and the African garrisons was a matter of some difficulty. Ceuta and Tangier were only a few miles from the coast of Spain. The Spaniards sent troops to Ceuta, removed the Portuguese governor (Dom Francisco de Almeida), and made certain that the town remained loyal to Philip IV; and thus Ceuta—so rich in Portuguese associations and sentiments as the first of the Portuguese conquests—became a Spanish enclave and so remains, even today. In Tangier the local governor (Dom Rodrigo Lobo da Silveira, Count of Sarzedas) refused to recognize King John, but a general uprising on 24 August 1643 forced a change of governors and the renunciation of the Spanish allegiance.[20]

In the Madeiran and Azorean archipelagos the transfer of sovereignty, with one exception, was swift and uncomplicated. The citizens of Madeira are proud of having been the first in the Portuguese possessions to acclaim John IV as king. The earliest official communication from John IV reached Madeira on 10 January 1641, and the very next day the chief civil and ecclesiastical officials swore allegiance to their new king and drew up a legal instrument (*auto*), signed by the leading citizens of Funchal,[21] which witnessed and confirmed the fact. In the festivities that followed, the English merchants, on instructions from the municipal chamber of Funchal, built a triumphal arch over the street called Rua Direita, in the heart of the cramped commercial section of the city. The contingent of Spanish soldiers in the Funchal garrison was split into small groups and reassigned to various scattered forts and outposts, where they could be watched.[22]

The process of proclaiming John IV as king was almost as smooth in eight out of the nine islands of the Azores; although some officials felt qualms about breaking their oath of allegiance to Philip IV, the general enthusiasm for the change usually led to a quick acceptance of John IV. But on the island of Terceira, a strong Spanish garrison, under Spanish officers, manning an extraordinarily large fortress that had been built specifically to overawe the capital city of Angra, made any move to support John IV both difficult and dangerous. In the end the new king was proclaimed by the islanders of Terceira, but the great Spanish fortress had to be invested and an improvised series of walls and forts built on the exposed ground that separated the city from the Spanish garrison. Curiously enough, the English merchants at Angra took arms in support of the Portuguese and, at their own expense, built a redoubt on a high point of land, wherein they placed five long-range guns that cannonaded the Spanish fortress. The English merchants William Ray, John Mallory, William Searchfield, and Timothy Townsend were particularly prominent in this activity. After a siege of over eleven months, the Spaniards were starved out and surrendered on 6 March 1642.[23]

The short-term prospects for the survival of Portuguese independence looked good in mid-1641; the long-term prospects appeared far less bright. On the question of Portugal, Spanish opinion was intransigent: Portugal must be reconquered. In the circumstances of 1641, the dangerous situation in Catalonia claimed the first attention of the Castilians. But once the Catalans had been suppressed and their French allies checked, then the full power of Spain would crush Portugal and the king of Castile would confiscate the enormous estates of the usurping "duke of Bragança." Events did not take so simple a course, and the reconquest of Portugal became more troublesome and problematic, but the passage of years did not alter Spanish opinion. Eight years after John IV's accession, a Spaniard wrote about Portugal that "it is impossible that she can maintain herself separate for very long."[24] Eighteen years and five months after the Restoration—with John IV's son, Afonso VI, sitting on the throne of Portugal—Sister María de Jesús de Ágreda, a correspondent and confidante of Philip IV, wrote to him that the time had come to make peace with France and, afterward, "it will be easy to conquer Portugal."[25]

In the many centuries of Portuguese independence, the sixty-year interval of the Spanish "captivity," the result of a dynastic accident, was an aberration; but the Castilians thought of the sixty-year united monarchy as the norm and considered the other centuries as a long period of preparation leading to a natural result—peninsular unity, under Castilian hegemony (of course). It was essential for Portugal during the years 1640–1668 to have strong allies, especially allies who were powerful on the seas. As long as Lisbon, Oporto, Setúbal, Faro, and other ports were secure from the seaward side, then the Portuguese, with defensive and Fabian tactics, taking advantage of their rugged hills, might successfully resist overland attacks. But if ever the Spanish navy were to gain control of the seas of Portugal and were able to supply Spanish troops at Portuguese ports, then Portuguese independence might be close to extinction.

The first weeks of John IV's government were filled with diplomatic activity. Foreign rulers were officially informed of the change of status in Portugal and requested to recognize the new king, whose adherents sent declarations to other countries setting forth the legitimacy of the claims of the house of Bragança to the Portuguese crown. John IV chose distinguished persons to be his ambassadors. On 8 February 1641, three English ships left the Tagus carrying Dom Francisco de Melo and António Coelho de Carvalho to France, Tristão de Mendonça Furtado and António de Sousa Tavares to the United Provinces, and three men—Dom Antão Vaz de Almada, Francisco de Andrade Leitão, and António de Sousa de Macedo—to England. On 18 March 1641 Francisco de Sousa Coutinho embarked for Denmark, and in April 1641 the Bishop of Lamego, Dom Miguel de Portugal, began a long, circuitous journey to Rome (which he did not reach till 20 November 1641).[26]

This simultaneous diplomatic assault on the papacy and on four leading maritime powers produced one quick, practical result: on 1 June 1641, in Paris, representatives of Portugal, France, and the Netherlands agreed that each of their countries should contribute twenty warships for joint operations against the Spanish fleet.[27] This agreement saved Portugal from naval attack until the end of 1641, when the French and Dutch ships returned to their home bases and the cooperation came to an end. The French thereafter did little to help the Portuguese, while the Dutch, who mounted attacks on Portuguese territories in Angola and India, eventually became open enemies, in spite of a ten-year truce concluded between Portugal and the United Provinces (The Hague, 22 June 1641). Denmark and the northern powers expressed little interest in Portuguese questions; and the pope, under heavy pressure from Spain and Austria, refused to recognize John IV as king of Portugal.

In these circumstances, perhaps too much was expected of the embassy to England, even though its emissaries had been carefully selected. Dom Antão Vaz de Almada was one of the leaders of the revolt of 1 December 1640 and his letter of credence said that he was descended from the "old nobility of England."[28] Francisco de Andrade Leitão was a distinguished lawyer and professor at Coimbra—while the embassy's secretary, António de Sousa de Macedo, was at the beginning of what was to prove a brilliant political career. After a stormy passage, the envoys arrived at the Devonshire coast. From Exeter, on 6 March 1641, Ambassador Almada sent Secretary Macedo to London with a request for admission to the English court. Charles I was happy to receive the envoys and became, in effect, the first sovereign in Europe to recognize John IV as the legitimate king of Portugal—a fact that the Spanish government was slow to forget, especially since Charles I had attempted to negotiate a Spanish alliance a few months previously and had admitted Don Alonso de Cárdenas to his court as Philip IV's resident ambassador (August 1640).[29]

English commercial interests and Portuguese political needs drove both parties toward a treaty of friendship and commerce that was hammered out with reasonable dispatch and signed at London on 29 January/8 February 1642. Article 1 of this treaty[30] established perpetual peace and amity between England and Portugal, and both sides promised to make no treaties prejudicial to the interests of the other. This article has been confirmed and reconfirmed many times, even as recently as 14 October 1899,[31] and is still supposed to be valid in international law. Article 2 recognized the right of both parties to trade freely—to have free passage and buy and sell at will—without any special licenses and paying only the customary tolls and fees in all places in the territories of the two countries where such trade had been customary.

Several commercial articles (3, 4, 5, and 6) reaffirmed the ancient privileges of the English merchants in Portugal, protected English shipowners against the compulsory loading of unwanted cargoes, and directed that Englishmen could collect debts from persons whose estates had been confiscated by the Inquisition.[32] Other articles touched on religious questions. By the terms of article 7, English seamen deserting their ships and claiming to be Catholics were not to sue their former employers, in Portuguese courts, for the recovery of wages and possessions. If the king of England appointed a Protestant consul (article 8), his powers were, nevertheless, to be fully recognized by the Portuguese. If a Protestant merchant died in Portugal (article 9), his estate would be settled by the other English merchants, under the supervision of the Judge Conservator.[33] Article 17 stipulated that Englishmen in Portugal could practice their religion in private provided they gave no cause for scandal.

The question of free trading in the Portuguese colonies, a demand pressed by the English but resisted by the Portuguese, caused some difficulty. In Portuguese Africa, the Portuguese would allow English trading only in the "customary places" (article 13)—unnamed places where the English had traded for a long time. In Brazil the Portuguese would permit no English trading, a position the English would not accept—so, by the terms of article 16, the issue was left to the decision of a group of commissioners to be appointed by both sides. As far as relations in the East were concerned, the Portuguese agreed to accept an old Anglo-Portuguese agreement that had been reached at Goa on 20 January 1635.

English ships in Portugal were not to be seized for the king of Portugal's service without the consent of their owners (article 10), nor were goods to be taken without fair payment. In the event of any future quarrel between England and Portugal, merchants on both sides were to be given two years' grace during which to sell their goods and leave (article 18). Individual acts of violence on either side should not be allowed to prejudice the general peace (article 19), and each side would punish its own offending nationals.

There were several references in the treaty to third powers. Article 11 directed that the treaty was not to be construed so as to damage the traditional English trade with Spain. English merchants were to enjoy whatever privileges the Portuguese had conferred on the Dutch in 1641 (article 14) and to have the same immunities from arrest and confiscation as were given by the Portuguese to any other nation (article 15). Nothing in the treaty would be interpreted as damaging any previous treaty made by Charles I with other powers (article 20). The last article (21) promised that the two kings would exchange ratifications of the treaty as soon as possible.

January 1642 was a singularly unpropitious time for a foreign power to sign a pact of friendship with England. When the treaty was signed, Charles I was still in London; by the time it was ratified and ordered published (22 May/11 June 1642) the king was at York raising forces to suppress the London parliament. The Portuguese ambassadors, who in the spring of 1641 had treated with Charles I for their admission to London, one year later had to address themselves to Parliament, and not to the king, in arranging to leave. Parliament supplied a ship[34] for Antão Vaz de Almada, Francisco de Andrade Leitão, and their entourage, which included three English Catholic ladies from good families on their way to join the English convent at Lisbon, who traveled incognito, pretending to be the wives of three Portuguese. Secretary António de Sousa de Macedo, who was left behind in London as Portuguese resident, was amused by the improbability of the deception, for he considered it unlikely that any Englishwoman would ever marry a Portuguese: "Englishwomen are so impressed with the plight of women in Portugal, that it would be difficult for a Portuguese here [in England] to find one who would wish him for a husband."[35] The ship cleared the Downs on 25 July 1642, arrived at Lisbon on 16 August, and there made arrangements to pick up Macedo's wife (Dona Mariana Lemercier, reputed to be a New Christian) and bring her to England. The House of Commons issued a pass to Macedo allowing him to go to the coast and convey his wife and her goods ashore, which he did late in October.[36]

By the end of 1642 and from thence until 1649, the two monarchs, Charles I and John IV, were so weakened by their own difficulties that neither was able to give the other effective assistance. The Portuguese wanted Charles I to send them strong ships to assist in keeping the Portuguese coast secure and the sea lanes of the empire open and wanted him to grant them ready access to supplies of English guns and ammunition. In turn, Charles I requested of Portugal munitions, supplies, and, above all, money. The two demands, springing from weaknesses, cancelled each other out: neither king was strong enough to assist the other. John IV, aspiring to be the founder of a new dynasty, a king for but eighteen months and faced with powerful foreign enemies, was, curiously enough, stronger than Charles I, who came from an ancient house and had been king for seventeen years, but whose fortunes now began their long and fatal decline. As the years passed, Charles I was unable to help himself, let alone send help to Portugal; while John IV, having enemies enough of his own, could not afford to embroil himself with the English Parliament simply to preserve Charles I's friendship.

The Portuguese resident Macedo, in attempting to end the inertia in Anglo-Portuguese relations, pursued his own policy, a policy that was more personal than national and more hazardous than politic, and which consisted of keeping on good terms with Parliament while secretly deceiving Parliament at every turn and doing everything to further the cause of the royalists.[37] From first to last, Macedo had little appreciation of English manners and institutions and never developed genuine insight into the English political and religious struggle. His sympathies for English royalism and for the English upper classes were genuine and deep-rooted; he chided the royalists only for what he thought was their failure to close with their enemies and destroy them—a failure he was prone to attribute to native English cowardice.[38] His dislike for the House of Commons and for the Presbyterians and sectaries was immediate and instinctive. In the early days of his residency, his eagerness to see the parliamentarians defeated sometimes outran his judgment, and his intelligence reports to Lisbon recounted inflated or fictitious royalist victories.

Repeated disappointments, however, made Macedo more critical of the royalists and very wary of believing any claims, whether made by the royalists or their adversaries—for lying, he thought, was a characteristic English trait.[39] Moreover, Charles I was surrounded by pro-Castilian Catholics, who regarded the Portuguese church as in a state of schism and who advocated close ties with Philip IV of Spain. When Charles I seemed to be casting himself into the arms of the Spanish king, a chill fell on Macedo's royalism, and he sometimes expressed almost contempt for the English king: it did not matter much, he wrote in one letter (25 September 1642), whether Charles I made a compact with the Castilians or not, "for it is certain that, whatever chances, the King of England will never be in a condition to do harm or good."[40] At about the same time, Macedo expressed a desire to remain on good terms with all the English factions,[41] but this was an intention that he never really carried into effect.

Macedo's chief service to Charles I lay in permitting the royalists to send their mail in the Portuguese diplomatic pouches that went between London and Paris every week, from Macedo to the Portuguese ambassador in France and back. This allowed King Charles to communicate with his agents on the Continent and with his wife, Henrietta Maria (who had sought refuge in France), by means of a channel that was fairly safe, although none too rapid. It should be stressed, nonetheless, that Macedo was highly reluctant to render this service, at least in the beginning, and the royalists were not able to avail themselves of this means of communication, on a regular basis, before the middle of 1644. Macedo's career as a smuggler of royalist correspondence began modestly, in December 1642, when the Portuguese resident visited Charles I at Oxford, to find out the truth about the royalists' dealings with Spain. Charles asked him, as a special favor, to convey a letter to France, and Macedo agreed to do so. But once back in London, when Macedo received a second such request, on 22 January 1643, he refused.[42]

Gradually Macedo's activities as a royalist courier increased until, eventually, he transmitted letters almost every week, and the House of Commons began to be very suspicious of the resident. In the summer of 1645 Charles I's correspondence was captured (with his baggage train after the battle of Naseby) and the king's letters were read aloud in the House of Commons. The extent of Macedo's dealings with the royalists became clear. On 23 June/3 July 1645 the Commons appointed a committee to consider what was to be done with the Portuguese resident while, in the meantime, Macedo's next bundle of correspondence was intercepted by Parliament. The Portuguese agent had anticipated this move: he filled the letters with jeering observations, fictitious and absurd ciphers, old newspapers, and a drawing of a person offering the reader a pair of spectacles with which to read the letters. According to his own perhaps exaggerated account, Macedo was summoned to Parliament and this burlesque correspondence was solemnly opened in front of him, to his amusement and the great discomfiture of the Englishmen. Whatever the truth of this may have been, the English merchants in Lisbon, who were perhaps apprehensive about possible Portuguese reprisals, intervened with Parliament to allow the free passage of the resident's letters. In August 1645, Macedo reported that "the storm against me has already passed."[43]

Macedo was also active in other ways. He plunged into the pamphlet controversy concerning the legitimacy of the Portuguese Restoration and eloquently defended the claims of John IV.[44] Although he himself was only a lukewarm Catholic or possibly even a crypto-Jew, Macedo—like other Portuguese residents or ambassadors in London—felt it was his duty to extend consolation and protection to English Catholics, then suffering persecution at the hands of the Puritan parliament. The Catholic masses[45] held regularly at the Portuguese embassy in Lincoln's Inn Fields[46] catered to the spiritual needs of not only foreign Catholics in London but also English Catholics. The embassy, in order to accommodate English coreligionists, celebrated holy days in accordance with the English calendar (Old Style), even though the Gregorian calendar (New Style), observed throughout Catholic Europe, would have suited the Portuguese better.

Macedo also did what he could for the missionary priests in England. In February 1643 he persuaded Parliament to release a

Scottish Franciscan friar who had spent thirteen months in prison and arranged for his safe conveyance out of the country. When John Duckett, priest, was hanged at Tyburn on 7/17 September 1644, Macedo accompanied him to the scaffold. During Macedo's residency, the embassy gave shelter to various friars, including a discalced Carmelite who wanted to join another order (Macedo kept a close watch on him because he suspected that his guest actually wanted to abjure Catholicism) and two French Capuchins belonging to Queen Henrietta Maria's household.[47] Parliament ordered the arrest of the French Capuchins in April 1643; five of them were seized and soon sent to France, but another two escaped to the Portuguese embassy, where they remained in hiding. One of these Capuchins managed to reach Calais after two months spent at the embassy, but his companion remained with Macedo for nearly a year.[48]

While the queen's Capuchin friar was still concealed at the embassy, some parliamentary soldiers, at 11:00 P.M. on Sunday, 11/21 June 1643, attempted to break into the building to conduct a search, but Macedo managed to stop them. The next day the Englishmen apologized, saying that they had been issued orders to search the entire area and the Portuguese embassy had been included by mistake; but at the same time Parliament lodged a strong protest about the attendance of Englishmen at the Portuguese Catholic mass. Macedo replied that he was not aware of any Englishmen at the services, that he could not identify them among the foreigners who came to mass, that, in any event, he could not turn away anyone who sought spiritual help, and that it was up to the Parliament, not the embassy, to regulate the comings and goings of Englishmen.[49]

It is hardly surprising that the following month (July 1643), when Macedo asked for a passport to visit King Charles at Oxford, the House of Commons made difficulties and gave him a passport that contained "two clauses that were very unusual and almost offensive."[50] The resident refused to accept the document and applied again, only this time to the House of Lords, who quickly issued a safe-conduct allowing him with seven other Portuguese and two English servants to pass to Oxford.

Macedo's official diplomatic activities, whether at Oxford or London, were either trivial or inconclusive. Late in 1644 certain royalists in Oxford proposed an agreement involving England, Portugal, and France. The king's son, Prince Charles, would marry one of the daughters of John IV (either Dona Joana, then ten years old, or Dona Catarina, then six years old), and the Portuguese would supply Charles I with ships and with a dowry of hundreds of thousands of pounds. The French would send some ships to help Charles and would, presumably, assist the Portuguese more effectively. In return for all this, Charles I would break with Spain. The proposal was curiously naive and unequal in its terms; it presupposed some enormous, imminent victory by Charles's troops over Parliament—otherwise the king of England's friendship would have been worthless to France and Portugal. On 20/30 January 1645, Macedo asked Speaker Lenthall of the House of Commons for a pass to Oxford, which was duly granted. During February 1645 the Portuguese agent spent eighteen days at Oxford with Charles I.[51]

Macedo did not encourage the match with Prince Charles and, at times, even ridiculed it (though it is curious to reflect that the Portuguese marriage, then prematurely suggested, actually took place seventeen years later). He pointed out to the English how ill-treated Henrietta Maria of France had been and asked what fate another foreign Catholic princess could expect at the hands of a Puritan parliament. Instead, Macedo presented some counterproposals of his own, which he put forward in a letter to Secretary of State Edward Nicholas (Oxford, 6/16 February 1645).[52] These proposals concerned Prince Edward (or the Infante Dom Duarte), brother of John IV, who had been traveling in Austria at the time of the Restoration and who had been seized by Emperor Ferdinand III and sold to the emperor's kinsman Philip IV of Spain on 25 June 1642. John IV moved heaven and earth to secure his brother's release. The Portuguese offered King Charles £50,000 in cash, £50,000 in arms and munitions, and £50,000 in salt, wine, ginger, oil, figs, etc.—or £150,000 in all—if he could persuade the Spaniards to release Prince Edward. Charles wrote to Philip IV but obtained nothing.[53]

Macedo's prejudice against the parliamentary party ran deep. In one of his letters (London, 5 August 1644) to the Portuguese ambassador in Paris he jeered at the candlemakers, farmers, shoemakers, taverners, and other base persons then running the government.[54] On another occasion, Macedo seriously proposed moving the Portuguese embassy to Oxford, but Lisbon vetoed the move.[55] When Parliament prohibited all trade with ports held by Charles I, Macedo protested that this violated article 2 of the Anglo-Portuguese treaty of 1642, which guaranteed Portuguese access to English ports, although he admitted that "the Ships of Portugall come not from beyond sea ordinarily on this Coast and that few Portugall Merchants send their Merchandizes for their Accompt."[56] Macedo warned Parliament about any infringement of the rights of John IV and indicated that it was in the interests of both countries that the treaty be inviolably observed. Parliament no doubt understood the protest for what it was: not a bona fide complaint based on a genuine Portuguese grievance but an attempt to meddle in English quarrels on behalf of the royalists.

How well did Macedo serve Portugal's interests? Perhaps not very well. Portugal's interests would have been best served by the cultivation of a flexible neutrality, creating links with both sides in the English Civil War and profiting no matter who came out victorious. Macedo, except in his personal contacts with certain London merchants, identified himself too closely with the royalists and, in effect, severed the connections between Lisbon and London. After the defeat of the royalists, the Lisbon government found that all its main diplomatic contacts with Englishmen were with discouraged and exiled Cavaliers—instead of with the powerful, and potentially dangerous, new administration in London. John IV, in 1650 and 1651, was to pay heavily for this breakdown in communications. Thanks, perhaps, largely to Macedo, it was years before the revolutionary government in London looked on Portugal with anything but suspicion.

Macedo made plans to leave England as early as the spring of 1645, when his three-year term of residency was nearing its close. From Oxford, on 27 February/9 March 1645, Charles I wrote to Macedo and asked him to remain in England. Macedo may have agreed to stay a little longer, but four months later he wrote to the king from London (on 4/14 July 1645) saying that he had to leave and had asked Parliament for his passport.[57] This letter (written in French) is partly in cipher, in itself showing how close was the connection between Macedo and Charles I. Another nine months were to pass before the actual departure of the Portuguese resident. In order to maintain the royalist communications with John IV, Macedo persuaded Charles I to appoint an agent in Lisbon. This agent was Sir Henry Compton, who went to Portugal in 1646—but he was unable to help Charles I from Lisbon. Compton quarreled with the local English merchants and was recalled in 1648 because it was felt he had too little do to.[58] Macedo, after grumbling that "for five years I have not seen the sun as God made it," and after clashing with Parliament once more over his handling of royalist correspondence (February 1646), left Dover for Lisbon aboard a Dutch merchantman[59] at the end of April 1646.

By the time Macedo left England, the royalists had been completely defeated, the country was almost entirely at peace, and moves were being made to settle the contest between king and Parliament by compromise and negotiation. Two years later, in May 1648, the duplicity and stubbornness of the king had plunged England into a second civil war, and the more radical of the parliamentary leaders were determined that Charles Stuart should pay with his life for having deceived them. On that fatal Tuesday, 30 January/9 February 1649, Charles I was beheaded at Whitehall and the parliamentary government was transformed into a truly revolutionary and republican regime.

Anglo-Portuguese relations had no part in this great drama; Portugal, unlike the United Provinces, had no envoy in London to protest the execution. John IV, to be sure, was personally interested in the fate of Charles. In September 1648, he expressed satisfaction at what seemed to be an improvement in Charles's case,[60] and in December 1648 he took steps to censure a certain Father Cornélio de São Patrício, who had written a book attacking England and insulting Charles I.[61] But the desperate plea that Charles, Prince of Wales, sent to John IV (and to other kings) from The Hague, 25 January 1649, to save his father's life could never have been answered in time.

In summary, the period from December 1640 to February 1649, despite the flurry of diplomatic moves that led to the treaty of 1642, was a time of quiescence for Anglo-Portuguese relations. But the period that followed, or the thirteen years that extended until the arrival of Catherine of Bragança in England in May 1662, was a time of great Anglo-Portuguese activity—naval, military, diplomatic, and commercial activity. This activity, during the years from 1650 to 1662, can be divided into three general phases: (1) from 1650 to 1651 there was open war between England and Portugal; (2) from 1652 to 1656 the two countries engaged in a long and difficult diplomatic dispute over the drafting, the signing, and the ratifying of the treaty of 1654; and (3), during the final phase, from 1657 to 1662, there was growing rapport, marked by unity of purpose, culminating in a military, maritime, and dynastic alliance. In short, these were uncertain years for the uneasy allies—years that began with a war, which gave way, in turn, to a peace that was almost as acrimonious as warfare itself; yet underlying trends worked to bring about a restoration of the age-old amity. The denouement was felicitous: for Anglo-Portuguese relations, at least, the marriage of 1662 provided this epoch with its "happy ending."

2
ENGLISH MERCHANTS IN PORTUGAL

In 1686, when the Catholic James II was reigning in England, the Grand Inquisitor of Lisbon summoned before him Thomas Maynard, English consul, and Dr. Michael Geddes, English chaplain, and informed them that no more Protestant services of worship would be allowed in Lisbon, thus interrupting a privilege that English merchants had enjoyed continuously for thirty years or more. Maynard and Geddes drafted a petition of protest, which they directed to Henry Compton, the Bishop of London and patron of the Lisbon chaplaincy, asking him to intercede with James II and his ministers. The petition, dated 7/17 September 1686, carried the signatures of Consul Maynard and thirty-three English merchants, together with a note stating that *every member* of the Lisbon *factory* had signed.[1]

This petition had three interesting features. First, it is perhaps the earliest extant document about Englishmen in Lisbon in which the word *factory* appears to have been used in a special sense—not merely as a general designation for a group of "factors," but as denoting a particular organization, a formal body, with members. In documents of an earlier date the Lisbon merchants were called "the English merchants trading in Portugal," or something similar. By the end of the seventeenth century the customary designation was "the English factory" (or "the British factory"). Second, the petition seemed to have been an official act of the factory, signed by merchants as members of the factory and not merely as individuals. Third, the statement that every member signed the petition provides a good clue to the number of English merchants active in Lisbon in 1686.

The petition of 1686 bore thirty-four signatures (including that of Maynard); the accompanying documents name one other English merchant, Anthony Jordan, who did not sign the petition; this adds up to thirty-five merchants. Two assumptions may be made about these thirty-five merchants: first, they were all Protestants (because English Catholics resident in Lisbon would not have put their names to a petition attacking the Portuguese Inquisition); and second, they must all have possessed a certain minimum of property or capital, since persons without means would not have been invited to join a merchant factory or encouraged to sign its petitions.

To get a true figure of all Englishmen engaging in trade and resident in Lisbon during 1686 we must add to these thirty-five the names of English Catholic merchants and those of the assistants and agents working under the merchants. If the number of English Catholic merchants can be reckoned, most conservatively, at fifteen, this would add up to fifty merchants. If there were fifty assistants to help these merchants, then the English mercantile community in Lisbon would have come to 100 men. But to get the full number of the subjects of the king of Great Britain in Lisbon in 1686 we must also include: (1) the wives and children of these men; (2) English Catholic exiles who were secular priests in the English college of Lisbon or nuns at the English convent; (3) certain large groups of Irish Catholics; and (4) mercenaries, sailors, and men-of-fortune of English, Irish, or Scottish nationality. This total, could we but reckon it, may have been surprisingly large.

It may be said that at any time between the years 1640 and 1680 there were at least fifty or sixty independent English merchants, men of adequate property and capital, active in Lisbon, and rather more than half that number resident in other Portuguese ports (Oporto, Viana do Castelo, Faro, Madeira, the Azores, and elsewhere). Although the extant sources are scattered and fragmentary, one could compile a list, for the year 1650, with the names of seventy English merchants who were probably residents of Lisbon. Also in 1650, there were at least twenty-two merchants, whose names we know, resident in continental Portugal in places other than Lisbon—and names can be furnished for another fifty-one English merchants, who lived in the Portuguese islands. The total, then, for the year 1650, is 143 names—but many more remain to be unearthed.

Perhaps the most prominent English merchant in Lisbon in 1650 was John Mules (or Miles or Muley). He was born in England but went to Portugal as a young man, about the year 1620. He either was a Catholic by upbringing or was converted in Portugal. He married a

Portuguese lady, and his numerous children were reared as Catholics. Mules was naturalized as a Portuguese and seemed to take little part in any official acts of the English Lisbon merchants. (For instance, his signature does not appear on any of the merchants' petitions to London.) The Portuguese government, nonetheless, always referred to him as "English," and always treated him as part of the English community. About the year 1640, Henry Erbury, an English recusant, arrived in Lisbon, and he eventually married one of Mules's daughters. Erbury became an important merchant himself, possibly with the aid of, or in partnership with, his rich father-in-law.[2]

In 1648 the English traveler Richard Flecknoe went by sea from Marseilles to Lisbon. When he arrived at Cascais, near Lisbon, he was treated by the local governor as a spy, but Mules rescued him and lodged him at his own home in Lisbon. Flecknoe had a lute on which he played well. Mules, knowing how much John IV loved music, took Flecknoe to see the king, who was greatly pleased with Flecknoe's music. Mules, apparently, was welcome at the royal palace, and Flecknoe reported that Mules was "a great Confident of the Kings." Mules took Flecknoe to his *quinta,* or country estate, three or four miles up the river from Lisbon, and the visitor was so impressed that he composed thirty lines of (rather poor) verse on this beautiful place with its orchards of olives, grapes, oranges, lemons, peaches, apricots, mulberries, pomegranates, and figs.[3]

The name of Mules appears often in Portuguese documents. Many times the Portuguese government conferred on him special privileges, including the right to send English ships with codfish directly from Newfoundland to Brazil without passing through Lisbon, in violation of all lawfully established practice.[4]

In the Lisbon disturbances of 1650 Mules took a pro-royalist position; John Randolph called him "a bitter enemie to the Commonwealth." Yet when the pro-Parliament merchants John Bushell and Richard Beare were imprisoned by John IV, it was Mules who went to their aid and furnished bond for their release.[5] After 1652, Mules's name no longer appears in the records; he either retired about that time or died.

Robert Cocke was another royalist merchant in Lisbon, but he was far less fortunate and less wealthy than Mules. Cocke came to Lisbon about the year 1630, probably after the close of hostilities between England and Spain. His brother-in-law John Randolph, another Lisbon merchant, described him in 1651 as "a Batchelor and a good Protestant."[6] Cocke was an importer of sugar from the remote African island of São Tomé. After the Dutch had taken the island from the Portuguese, Cocke asked the Lisbon government for permission to send two English ships directly to São Tomé from England, load a cargo of sugar from the Dutch, and then bring it back to Lisbon. Cocke undertook to pay all customs duties *before* the departure of the ships to São Tomé. This scheme received the king's approval on 21 November 1647.[7] The plan involved a high element of risk and helps to show why Cocke was sometimes disastrously unsuccessful in his business ventures.

While Prince Rupert's ships were in Lisbon harbor in 1650 (see chapter 4), Cocke was the most active of the royalist merchants in assisting the cause of Charles II. In spite of his royalism, Cocke suffered serious losses in the general confiscation of English properties ordered by John IV, even though this measure was intended to affect, primarily, the parliamentary or neutral merchants. Cocke did not suffer imprisonment, nor were his properties in Portugal touched, but he lost heavily in the confiscation of the English cargoes aboard the Brazil sugar fleet.[8]

At the Restoration of Charles II in 1660, Cocke's future looked brighter. He was appointed, along with his enemy, Consul Thomas Maynard, to victual His Majesty's Ships when they put in at Lisbon. But His Majesty rarely paid any bill that could be avoided, and debts owed abroad could be easily avoided. Cocke was forced to inform the navy commissioners in London (letter dated Lisbon, 8 August 1662)[9] that the king's credit had collapsed in Portugal, since no one in Lisbon would accept bills to be drawn on the treasurer of the navy. In the meantime Cocke had quarreled bitterly with his colleague Maynard and attempted, unsuccessfully, to get him removed from the consulship on the grounds that Maynard had been a Cromwell appointee. The English merchants reported at about this time, in a list of complaints against the Portuguese, that the king of Portugal still owed Cocke over 30,000 cruzados (£5,668) from the 1650 sequestrations and that, in answer to his petitions, he received only hard words from the Portuguese officials. In 1663, after over thirty years of work as a merchant in Portugal, Cocke was faced with ruin.[10]

More enterprising than the merchants mentioned thus far were the Bushell brothers of London. The saga of the Bushell family began with the marriage of John Bushell, schoolmaster, and Mary Hutchins on 28 October/7 November 1616. The couple produced four daughters (Alice, Deborah, Ellen, and Mary) and three sons: John (born 1617), Edward (born 1620), and Thomas (born 1621).[11] The Bushell brothers were strong-minded Puritan merchants who had that special talent for commercial and public affairs that often characterized the English Puritans. Starting with very little, they constructed a small family empire whose tentacles stretched from London to Lisbon, Bahia, Jamaica, and elsewhere.

In 1649, John Bushell, then thirty-two years old, was in Lisbon and very active in the Brazil sugar trade, while his younger brothers, Edward and Thomas, managed the London part of the business. The Bushells were ardent supporters of the Commonwealth; when Prince Rupert's royalist fleet sailed into Lisbon, followed later by the Commonwealth ships, John Bushell did everything possible to persuade the Portuguese not to support Rupert. Edward Bushell and George Clarke, in London, supplied the parliamentary naval commanders with bills of credit for £4,000 to be drawn at Lisbon in Portuguese currency; these drafts were met by John Bushell, who furnished the fleet with Portuguese coin at the rate of 1$000 réis for every 10s 11d.[12] The Bushells were also instrumental in persuading Parliament to send an agent, Charles Vane, to negotiate with John IV. Prince Rupert, keenly aware of the activities of these energetic young men, denounced them publicly and by name in a manifesto he published in Lisbon.[13]

When John IV made common cause with Rupert, the Bushells suffered heavily. Antônio Fernandes Picoutos and João Peixoto Viegas, agents for the Bushells in Bahia, Brazil, confessed that they had loaded 181 chests of sugar,[14] consigned variously to John or Thomas or Edward Bushell, aboard certain English ships that the Portuguese had sequestered.[15] This was only a part of their losses. In Lisbon the king's agents arrested John Bushell and other merchants and held them in prison. When word of this act reached London, the Council of State sent harsh orders to Adms. Robert Blake and Edward Popham, commanding the "State's Ships" (as they were called at the time of the Commonwealth) in Portuguese waters. Since John IV had imprisoned the "well-affected" merchants John Bushell, Richard

Beare, and William Milward (the only three to be mentioned in the council order) and Prince Rupert had imprisoned certain other English, the council ordered that "you shall therefore upon all opportunities seize upon all such Portugals,[16] as you may any way lay hold on; and to keep them in prison aboard your ships."[17] The pressure of the London government eventually forced the Portuguese to release the merchants. John Bushell went home to London, leaving William Bird in Lisbon as his permanent representative, with power of attorney in the question of recovering the confiscated properties.[18]

The Bushells did not break off their connection with Portuguese commerce but traded with Lisbon through their factor, Bird. On 4/14 January 1659 the Council of State granted license to John and Edward Bushell to export 1,000 barrels of gunpowder to Portugal.[19] The following year, on 26 October, the Portuguese government permitted "Duarte Buchel" to send an English ship to Bahia.[20] In 1661, Edward Bushell, in association with William Bird, represented the Lisbon-based Brazil Company in a petition addressed to Charles II, which sought action against certain English merchants who had infringed on the company's brazilwood monopoly.[21]

The Restoration of Charles II created difficulties for this antiroyalist, Puritan family. John Bushell emigrated to Jamaica, but Edward—who was on at least one royalist list of "dangerous" men[22]—remained in London, kept up a prosperous trade with Portugal and other places, upheld his religious and political principles in a celebrated trial,[23] and died in London (1694) at about the age of seventy-four. In Jamaica, John Bushell entered into partnership with a certain Francis Bond and took charge of the family business in the West Indies. On 18/28 April 1668 a fire broke out in Bushell's house in Bridgetown, Jamaica, that eventually destroyed 800 buildings. It is not known when or where he died, but he was still living in Jamaica in 1680, when he was sixty-three years old.[24] Descendants of the Bushells have survived in Jamaica into the twentieth century.

The careers of these merchants—the prudent, wealthy, Portuguese-mannered Mules, the erratic, unfortunate Cocke, and the energetic, widely traveled John Bushell—summarize the kinds of activity engaged in by a host of other English merchants in Lisbon. Among the Englishmen who figure more prominently in Lisbon commercial records of the mid-seventeenth century, the following deserve mention: Barnaby Crawford, Christopher Warren, Thomas Kemp, William Bird, William Rolls, Robert Parker, and Richard Beare. Others could be named, but not much could be said about them; and still others, active English merchants in the Lisbon community, are nameless and unknown.

In the 1650s, no other part of Portugal rivaled Lisbon in the number of foreign merchants in residence or in the intensity of commercial activity. In the north of Portugal, in 1650, there were only about twenty-five English merchants in the zone stretching from Viana do Castelo to Aveiro and centered on the Oporto-Douro area. The most important English merchant of Oporto, at that time, was perhaps Rowland Hill, who employed Thomas Maynard in the business of shipping olive oil out of Aveiro and who had enough influence in London to secure Maynard's appointment as consul at Lisbon (in 1656).[25] Maynard's brother, Walter, lived in Oporto during the years 1648–1659 and was a moderately successful merchant. The great days of the Douro area, however, did not begin until after 1680, when a stream of English businessmen moved in to develop the port-wine trade.

In the south of Portugal, along the Algarve coast, there were six or seven fairly busy local ports, running from Lagos in the west to Vila Real de Santo António in the east. Among these Faro was the chief mercantile center, and there an Englishman, Henry Johnson, held sway as the leading merchant in the Algarve for a quarter of a century (1649–1673).[26] About Johnson, Consul Maynard once wrote that the Faro merchant supplied Parliament's ships with wine but was not to be trusted, since he had royalist sympathies (letter from Lisbon, 8 November 1657).[27] Six years later Johnson was in trouble with the Portuguese government for trying to buy some pepper from an English frigate of war anchored at Faro.[28] This was somewhat rash of the merchant, for he was undoubtedly aware of how strongly the Portuguese hated the idea of any foreign ships bringing Asian commodities into Portugal.

There were also merchant communities in the Portuguese islands, at four main harbors: Funchal (Madeira), Ponta Delgada (São Miguel, Azores), Angra (Terceira, Azores), and Horta (Fayal, Azores). In 1650 there were nineteen English merchants resident in Madeira and at least thirty-two English merchants scattered through the Azores. The city of Funchal, capital of Madeira, represents a special case in Anglo-Portuguese relations: nowhere in Portugal, not even in Oporto, during the last three centuries has English commercial and social influence been so prolonged, so pervasive, and so penetrating as in Funchal. In the Azores the situation has been different, for there the small groups of English traders have been dispersed among three or four widely separated islands and the English presence has been less concentrated and far more intermittent than in Funchal.[29]

All the English merchants in Portugal, whether Catholic or Protestant, rich or poor, well known or obscure, faced a common problem: the problem of doing business and making a living as alien merchants in a foreign land and, as aliens, likely to become at any time the target of popular hatred and of official harassment. The position of any particular merchant in the English merchant community could quickly become precarious, even if his colleagues remained untouched. The position of the community as a whole was usually secure, except in special circumstances such as war, times of religious excitement or persecution, and those occasions when the Portuguese government tried to raise tariffs to a level that would have ruined all foreign merchants.

The genuine precariousness of the position of the English merchant living and working in Portugal during the seventeenth century has not been appreciated by Portuguese historians. Portuguese historians during the last century and a half have popularized two assumptions about English commerce in Portugal: (1) that English merchants in Portugal possessed privileges that were unique in their nature, unparalleled in the rest of Europe, and obtained by fraud or coercion; and (2) that John IV, overestimating the dangers from Spain and underestimating Portugal's latent powers of resistance, delivered the bulk of Portuguese trade into the hands of greedy Englishmen who from the outset sought to obtain a monopoly position and reduce Portugal to the status of a commercial colony of Britain. Both these assumptions are false.

English merchant privileges in Portugal were rooted in medieval charters and evolved in organic continuity from them. There was little that was anomalous or artificial in the position of the seventeenth-century English merchant in Portugal. In medieval cities the various trades and economic interests were tightly organized into guilds and companies, each of which had its privileges and responsibilities set forth in legal terms. Foreign merchants, coming into such a city, could meet with overwhelming resistance from the native traders; in effect, they could not do business without special protection. Charters of privileges were often granted to alien merchants, in all the great seaports, by princes and other rulers who thereby sought to obtain reciprocal privileges for their own native merchants trading in foreign parts and who saw in the foreign merchant an easy target for lucrative taxation.

In certain essential respects, the situation had not changed much by 1650. The foreign merchant in Portugal in the seventeenth century was still a prime target for harassment: the city mob, everywhere nurturing a special sense of grievance against the alien, could be induced to ransack the foreigner's warehouse; the foreigner might not be able to collect debts owed to him or have proper redress against natives who broke their contracts, because the native courts instinctively favored their own nationals; and everywhere, at all times, the alien had to withstand the extortions of harbor officials and customs collectors. In these circumstances the foreign merchant sought the protection of the king of the land.

The seventeenth-century merchant, petitioning for privileges, could usually cite precedents going back 150 to 200 years. Certain guarantees were absolutely essential to foreign merchants trading in Portugal; without them, they could not continue in business. John IV understood these matters well. He knew that a vital portion of crown revenues derived from import and export duties. The more trade there was, the more revenue there would be for the king. John IV protected foreign merchants (all of them, not only the Englishmen) because this policy led to an increase in trade. He was quite unwilling to risk making difficulties for the foreigners in the hope that native merchants would take their place. The dislodgement of the foreigner would only diminish and damage foreign trade, to the ruin of the royal finances. The king knew well that the foreign merchant was the goose that laid the golden eggs.

Certain Portuguese writers are obsessed with the idea of the English commercial monopoly in Portugal; the image of the port-wine trade dominates their thinking, colors all other areas, and even casts its influence backward into the period before there was any port-wine trade. Yet the port-wine trade is not a suitable image by which to understand any other aspect of English trade with Portugal. The relation of Englishmen to port wine was most unusual: port is a great wine developed and originated by Englishmen—it was Englishmen, not Portuguese, who conducted the early experiments and first saw its possibilities. Englishmen disseminated and advertised the drink, and Englishmen, to an astonishing extent, consumed it. It is only natural that Englishmen should have held a monopoly position in a product they themselves developed, propagated, and consumed.[30] Yet the analogy of port cannot be extended to cover English activities in any other branch of Portuguese commerce. The great article in seventeenth-century Anglo-Portuguese commerce was sugar, and in the sugar trade Englishmen held a vastly different position.

Portuguese businessmen and government officials in 1650 rarely, if ever, expressed any fears of Englishmen acquiring a monopoly position in Portuguese trade. They would have been amused by the notion that Portugal was an English "colony." In commercial matters, they feared only one nation, the United Provinces, and this one nation was hated and feared by most of the maritime countries of Europe. In 1650, it was not Portugal that was a commercial colony of England; rather, it was England that was a colony of the Dutch.[31]

Seventeenth-century European maritime trade had two great anchors: in the north, the Baltic, and in the south, the Levant. The Baltic produced wheat, copper, iron, and, above all, the essential materials for building and servicing ships: pitch, tar, flax, hemp, masts, and timber. The Levant and the *entrepôt* ports (such as Zante) connected with it were the sources of Asian spices, Chinese silks, Persian carpets, and other luxury products. Between the Baltic and the Levant ran a very long and circuitous sea route that was vulnerable at three points: the Danish Straits, the Straits of Dover, and the Straits of Gibraltar. The Dutch, placed geographically at a midpoint between the Mediterranean and the Baltic, hoped to exercise naval influence over all three straits in defense of their shipping, which vastly outnumbered that of any competitor on this "trunk line" of European sea commerce.

Dutch commercial prosperity stemmed from two main sources: (1) the herring fishing and (2) the export of their manufactures. Dutch herring fishing was done in the waters immediately adjacent to the eastern coasts of Scotland and England, often within sight of land. These fish were preserved by pickling them in Portuguese salt obtained in Setúbal by the large Dutch fleets that called at Setúbal every year. In 1630, for instance, at a time when Spain was at war with the United Provinces, 100 Dutch salt ships appeared off Setúbal, and, to minimize any opportunity for Dutch treachery, they were let into the port only ten ships at a time.[32] The salted herring was exchanged in Spain for Spanish silver and wool and also sent to the Baltic and elsewhere. The Baltic supplied many valuable products but consumed little, and the Dutch were forced to buy Baltic commodities with Spanish silver. Dutch manufacturers depended very largely on imports: the Dutch refined Portuguese salt and Brazilian sugar, twisted and cut Virginian and Brazilian tobacco, processed English cloth, brewed beer, extracted oil from seeds, and made soap. And then the Dutch exported these products to countries that could probably have performed these finishing processes themselves without any Dutch middlemen.[33]

The Portuguese had every reason for hating the Netherlander. The Dutch had ruined the Portuguese in the East, had secured half of the sugar trade by invading Pernambuco, and had made large inroads into the slave trade by capturing Portuguese Angola and dominating the Guinea coast. When the *Lisboeta* looked down on the lovely Tejo and the Londoner watched his rather more melancholy Thames, they were two different men in two different capitals looking at two different rivers, but during the 1640s they saw the same thing: Dutch ships. From a quarter to one-half of the ships in London were Dutch,[34] and about a quarter of the ships in Lisbon were Dutch, without reckoning the large Dutch fleets that visited nearby Setúbal.

Statistics for the port of Lisbon are scarce and unreliable, but entries in the Inquisition books[35] for the two periods 12 August 1641 to 4 January 1649 and 14 July 1677 to 8 May 1685—about fifteen years in all—show the arrival of 1,114 foreign ships in Lisbon, of which: 477 were Dutch, 398 British,[36] 145 German, 22 Danish, 20 French, 18 Swedish, 13 Norwegian, 2 Polish, and 19 unidentified. That is, 82 foreign ships put in at Lisbon in an average year during this period, of which 44 percent were Dutch, 34 percent British, 14 percent German, 4 percent Scandinavian, and 2 percent French. The Dutch and English, jointly holding 78 percent of the total, clearly predominated, but the Dutch surpassed the English even though the Portuguese discouraged the Dutch and rarely chartered their ships. During the seven years 1642–1648, 236 Dutch ships put in at Lisbon, as against only 143 English; that is, insofar as these records are reliable, 33 Dutch ships visited Lisbon in an average year and only 20 English.

Although the Dutch were the preponderant mercantile and naval power of the 1640s, dominating so many ports, markets, and trades in Western Europe, the English were soon to displace them in Portugal's maritime commerce. The Dutch had themselves to blame, in part, for the rise of English shipping in Portuguese trade. The wars waged by the Dutch against the Portuguese and the insistent privateering of the Zeelanders made Dutch ships unwelcome in secondary ports, such as Faro in the Algarve, and in the busy island ports in the Azores and Madeira. Only in the well-protected places, such as Setúbal (where the Dutch monopolized the carrying trade in salt) and Lisbon, were the ships of these enemies tolerated. English merchants and English shipping took advantage of the commercial opportunities created by Dutch-Portuguese antagonism.

At Faro, the chief port on the Algarve coast, the Inquisition books for the years of 1619–1657 and 1663–1683 (there are no figures for the years 1658–1662) recorded the entry of 846 foreign ships, divided as follows: British, 380; Dutch, 168; French, 120; Spanish, 78; German, 45; Italian, 31; Danish, 7; and unidentified, 17.[37] Expressed as percentages, these figures work out to: British, 46 percent; Dutch, 15 percent; French, 14 percent; German, 11 percent; Spanish, 6 percent; and Italian, 3 percent. On the average, English shipping at Faro represented a little less than half of the foreign shipping at Faro between 1619 and 1683; yet English ships were far more numerous in Faro toward the end of this period than they had been at the beginning, and the ships themselves were often larger than those of their rivals.[38] Table 1 shows the movement of British and foreign ships in Faro during 1640–1657. During the nine-year period 1640–1648, out of 97 foreign ships calling at Faro, only 35 ships (36 percent) were British; but in the succeeding nine-year period, 1649–1657, of 108 ships at Faro, two-thirds (71 ships, or 66 percent) were British.

A few extant customs registers indicate the strength of British shipping in the Portuguese islands. The registers of the customs house at Funchal, Madeira, supply ample information about the years 1620, 1650, 1682, 1687, and 1699.[39] In 1620, of 39 ships that called at Madeira, 11 were British, 8 French, 11 Portuguese, and 9 Dutch or Flemish. In 1650 (a bad year for English shipping in Portuguese

Table 1
English and Foreign Ships in Faro, 1640–1657*

Year	Number of Foreign Ships	Number of British Ships	Percentage of British Ships
1640	5	4	80
1641	4	3	75
1642	12	7	58
1643	15	4	27
1644	8	2	25
1645	11	4	36
1646	12	2	17
1647	16	6	38
1648	14	3	21
1649	3	2	67
1650	2	2	100
1651	3	3	100
1652	10	4	40
1653	14	10	71
1654	22	11	50
1655	28	23	82
1656	22	12	55
1657	4	4	100
Totals	205	106	52

*Adapted from Virgínia Rau, "Subsídios para o estudo do movimento dos portos de Faro e Lisbôa durante o século XVII," *Anais da Academia Portuguesa de História,* series 2, 5 (1954): 199–264.

waters), of 37 ships at Madeira, 14 were British, 10 French, 3 Portuguese, 5 Dutch, 2 from Hamburg, 2 Genoese, and 1 a foreign ship of undetermined nationality. The registers for the years 1682, 1687, and 1699, added together, show 239 ships at Madeira, of which 143 (or 59.8 percent) were British, 54 French, 25 Portuguese, 15 Dutch, and 1 unidentified. Hence, in 1620, British ships accounted for only 28.2 percent of the total; in 1650, 37.8 percent; in 1682, 60.2 percent; in 1687, 55.2 percent; and in 1699, 64.2 percent. Although the number of ships calling at Madeira increased from 39 in 1620 and 37 in 1650 to over 75 per year during the last two decades of the century, English shippers still managed to account for an ever-growing share of the traffic. In the textile-and-wine trade of Madeira, not the Dutch but the French were the chief rivals of the English.

In the Azores there are customs registers for the years 1620, 1639, 1640, 1646, 1648, 1669, 1676, 1686, and 1694 for Ponta Delgada on the island of São Miguel.[40] (There are no registers for the other two major ports, Angra and Horta.) The registers for the years 1639, 1640, 1646, and 1648, when added together, show the presence of 120 ships at São Miguel, of which 83 (nearly 70 percent) were British, 12 Dutch, 11 Portuguese, 5 French, 4 Hamburger, 1 Spanish, and 4 unidentified. If it were legitimate to average the figures for these four years and then project them for the whole decade of 1639–1648, the projection would show that slightly more than 300 ships loaded or unloaded cargo at São Miguel, of which over 200 were British.[41]

All the foreign merchants trading in Portugal faced certain similar problems. First there were the problems arising from the risks of the sea itself: the loss of ships because of storms, piracy, or war. Marine insurance (whose premiums invariably became prohibitive when risks were high) and the form of loan known as *cambio maritimo* or sea-hazard (a loan at high interest with a condition that the creditor agreed to abandon all claim to his money if the debtor's ship was lost)[42] eased some of the burdens of loss at sea. Few merchants cared to own a ship outright; multiple ownership was the rule, and if a merchant had the money to buy *one* large ship he preferred, instead, to buy three one-third shares in three large ships or even six one-sixth shares in six large ships. Thus he spread his risk, accepted the probability of a small loss sometimes, but avoided the gamble of a large loss.

The ownership of cargo was a more important matter than the ownership of merchantmen, for, at least in the Portuguese trade, the value of a cargo was far greater than the value of the ship that carried it. Merchants of that age divided their cargoes, even if the cargoes were small, among various ships. In May 1658 the *Golden Lion* came to Bristol with a cargo of olive oil, sugar, and cinnamon—loaded at Lisbon—and no fewer than fifteen Bristol merchants paid wharfage fees on these Portuguese commodities.[43] The 181 chests of Brazil sugar consigned to the Bushell brothers in 1650 were loaded aboard six ships. When a Dutch flyboat[44] loaded at Madeira in February 1650, fifteen persons helped to supply her cargo of sixty-eight pipes of Madeira wine.[45]

The Madeira records reveal that much of the cargo in an English ship was owned by English merchants, much of the cargo in a Dutch ship by Dutch merchants, and much of the cargo in a Portuguese ship by Portuguese merchants. Nonetheless, English merchants often made use of Dutch, French, and Portuguese ships; Dutch merchants had no hesitation in loading merchandise aboard English and Portuguese ships; and Portuguese merchants used the ships of many countries. To this extent, at least, there was a good deal of international cooperation among these business rivals.

Another difficulty facing foreign merchants was the task of supervising the sale of their goods in distant ports. Sometimes a merchant would accompany his goods himself, sailing, for instance, with the Brazil fleet and personally supervising the sale or exchange of his merchandise. This was too cumbersome a method for men with many cargoes and widespread interests; they would place their own agents aboard the larger merchantmen or else pay the master or some officer or passenger to keep an eye on their shipment. Frequently a ship would carry a captain who owned an interest in both the ship and her cargo, who was a merchant in his own right, and who, in return for a fee, would act as a representative for other merchants. An English merchant in Lisbon engaged in the Atlantic trade would have required factors or agents in at least the following ports: London, Madeira, the Azores, and Bahia; and might well have factors in some of the following: Rio de Janeiro, Recife, Barbados, Boston, Bristol, Oporto, and possibly some of the ports of France, Flanders, the United Provinces, and Germany. A Lisbon merchant engaged in the Mediterranean trade may have required factors in Faro, Cadiz, Málaga, Leghorn, Genoa, Naples, Marseilles, Barcelona, Zante, and other Mediterranean ports.

The risks of theft and fraud were very real. Dishonesty was partly checked by the principle of reciprocity: Richard Pickford in Madeira might be tempted to cheat on a shipment from Hugh Browne of Bristol, only to be checked by the thought that Hugh Browne could avenge himself by cheating on Pickford's next cargo to Bristol. One very common method of guarding against dishonesty was using relatives as factors in other ports. The Portuguese Jews were justly famed for constructing their great family networks of merchants, whose members would be resident in such places as Hamburg, Amsterdam, London, Lisbon, the Canary Islands, Recife, Barbados, and (after 1654) New York. Each port would be in communication with the others, and the common family interest was supposed to keep everyone efficient and honest. English merchants followed the same practices, although not to the same extent as the Portuguese Jews.

English merchants generally used other English merchants as their factors. Joseph Dorney of Lisbon was factor for Hugh Browne and Joseph Jackson of Bristol. Henry Eliot of Lisbon served as factor for Richard Vickris and Thomas Clare of Bristol.[46] But in Brazil, English merchants had to use Portuguese factors. António Fernandes Picoutos of Bahia declared, in 1650, that he had handled the business affairs of Richard Beare, English Lisbon merchant, for fifteen years. Picoutos also represented many other English merchants, including the Bushell brothers, William Cart, Robert Cocke, Robert Cart (an English surgeon at Lisbon who also dabbled in commerce), Barnaby Crawford, William Fletcher—all of Lisbon—and Roland Abel of Oporto. João Peixoto Viegas kept accounts with the Bushell brothers and Thomas Hughes of Lisbon.[47]

Much of the English merchants' commerce in Brazil was carried on by means of English ships carrying agents who kept watch on the Bahia factors. Sometimes the local traders in Bahia failed to pay their debts and a visit from the Lisbon merchant became desirable. Between the years 1650 and 1658 the Portuguese government issued at least twelve permits to foreign merchants to visit Brazil, on condition that they were not to stay for more than one year. Thomas Kemp, English merchant in Lisbon, received three such permits and visited Brazil three times.[48]

There was yet another range of problems faced by foreign merchants in Portugal: the difficulties and hazards raised by their very position in an alien land, dependent on the indulgence and protection of sometimes hostile authorities and subject to laws and courts that worked to protect the interests of the native. A long series of Portuguese laws excluded all foreigners and their ships from all parts of the Portuguese empire except Madeira and the Azores. Penalties for violations were as severe as possible: the death sentence and confiscation of all ships and cargoes.[49]

At its most ambitious, Portuguese legislation aimed at excluding all foreign ships (except Spanish ships going to Buenos Aires) from the South Atlantic and the Indian Ocean. Only a very powerful navy could have enforced these restrictions. The strong intrusion of English and Dutch shipping into the South Atlantic and Indian Oceans made the Portuguese antiforeign legislation seem quaint and obsolescent. But the laws were still on the books and could be used to harass the unwary foreign merchant. During the 1640s the Portuguese were anxious to freight capacious and well-armed foreign merchantmen, particularly for the Brazil trade, in order to give better protection to Portuguese shipping itself. Yet if a foreign merchant in Lisbon wanted to send a foreign ship to Brazil, he still had to petition formally to have the laws against foreigners set aside. This involved a complicated ritual wherein a carefully worded petition was presented to the Overseas Council, who then referred it to an important court lawyer (the *desembargador do Paço)* who invariably recited all the laws against foreigners—in a long, droning catalog of restrictions—and the petition went back to the Overseas Council. The councillors discussed the matter and issued a decision, almost invariably in favor of the application, and a formal report of their decision was sent to the king, who usually approved it without question.

Petitions to the king for license to send ships overseas could also be routed through the Treasury Council *(Conselho da Fazenda)*, without having to go to the Overseas Council. Eventually, the king decided (4 November 1654) that the Treasury alone should issue these licenses, not the Overseas Council.[50] In addition, the Brazil Company freighted foreign ships on its own authority, without consulting other government bodies. All these licenses required the king's approval. When the governor of Madeira permitted the comptroller of the Treasury to issue a license (17 February 1645) to the English ship *Patience* to take a cargo of wines to the Cape Verde Islands, the result was that the governor of Cape Verde confiscated the ship and cargo for coming to the islands without the king's own license.[51]

The foreign merchant sometimes had to do something extra in order to obtain his license, such as taking the king's cargoes at no charge or offering free transportation to royal officials going out to the colonies. Capt. Francis Hardidge of the *Mary and John* was granted a permit to go to Angola (in itself a rare concession by the Portuguese government) to take on slaves for Brazil, where the slaves would be exchanged for sugar, and then to return to Lisbon—but on condition that the ship carried ten *quintals* of gunpowder and ten of lead, as well as from forty to fifty soldiers, for the Angola garrison, probably free of charge.[52]

About the year 1657 the Overseas Council again began issuing licenses, and from 1657 to 1659 at least nineteen permits were given to ships (all but two of which were English) to go to the colonies: thirteen licenses to go to Brazil, four to the Cape Verde Islands, and two to Angola and Brazil. On one day alone (26 November 1658) the English merchant Robert Parker of Lisbon received permission to send four English ships to Brazil: the *Sara* and the *Lewis* to Pernambuco, the *Culpepper* to Rio de Janeiro, and the *Frederick* to Madeira and Bahia.[53]

A merchant securing one of these licenses had to post a heavy bond covering all customs fees, which was forfeited if the ship did not return to Lisbon, as she was supposed to do, so that her cargo could be appraised and taxed. In 1658 foreign merchants were charged 600$000 réis (£283) for each license for a large ship.

These licenses had to be obtained every time a ship a sailed for the colonies, since the government would not issue general permits to foreign merchants. If a merchant secured permission to send a particular ship to the colonies and then found that the ship he wanted was not available, but another ship would take her place, he had to apply for a license all over again—and the procedure often took weeks and months.

When a foreign, or even Portuguese, merchant ventured a cargo to a Portuguese colony he was often dismayed to discover that his chief commercial competitor was the local governor. Many a poor *fidalgo* went out to the colonies as a crown official and returned a wealthy man. Indeed, if there had been no commercial opportunities it is difficult to see how official positions in such unattractive places as Mozambique, Angola, Guinea, the Cape Verde Islands, and Maranhão could have been filled. Treasury officials complained constantly of how colonial governors defrauded the customs house and treasury. The governors, in turn, complained of the corruption among the treasury officials. Cheating on customs duties and taxes was everybody's game in the seventeenth century; certainly the English merchants evaded customs charges whenever possible, but they had excellent teachers in the Portuguese officials themselves.

Crown officials of many kinds—whether attached to the customs house, the Treasury, the armed forces, or the law courts—could force merchants to pay bribes, could extort extra taxes and fees, and, what was worse for the merchants, could compete with them on unfair terms in the marketplace itself. In addition, the merchants had to conform to the often quite harsh edicts laid down by the municipal chambers. These chambers possessed extensive regulatory and judicial powers. They set the prices for wines, grains, and foodstuffs and regulated, sometimes in minute detail, the conditions and terms of trade. Since they could compel a businessman to sell his goods (even if he did not want to) and force him to accept a fixed price—and since they could also forbid certain sales—the city chambers, if they were unresponsive to the needs of merchants, could make trade so unprofitable as to be all but impossible. The record books of the municipal chamber of Funchal furnish numerous examples of the disciplining and harassing of merchants.[54]

The foreign merchants in Portugal had many other difficulties. The record books of the Funchal chamber show that foreign merchants paid much heavier fines for the same offense than their Portuguese colleagues. If a Protestant merchant accumulated property, it was difficult for him to transmit it to his heirs. Duarte Zormans, a prosperous Dutch merchant who lived in Madeira for many years, left all his property to Manuel Valente, who was a very busy merchant and also an official of the customs house. After Zormans's death in 1658, a local judge impounded all the Dutchman's property on the grounds that heretics could not make valid wills. Valente's friends in the Treasury then ordered the judge to leave "the king's property" alone, arguing on the grounds that Valente was a royal official. The matter was then referred to Lisbon.[55]

International commercial treaties embodied attempts to protect merchants from unfair dealings. On paper, the English secured many benefits from the Portuguese; in practice, the most carefully phrased guarantee could be disregarded. A long series of agreements protected the rights of English merchants and seamen in Portuguese courts—but these same rights had to be defended tooth and nail by the English merchants in Portugal, because Portuguese judges often acted as if international treaties could not bind them. For instance a certain English ship was freighted by António da Fonseca for a voyage to the Cape Verde Islands. When the voyage was over, Fonseca failed to pay the freight charges. With the help of Barnaby Crawford and other English merchants in Lisbon, the captain of the ship brought suit against Fonseca in a Portuguese court. The suit was heard on 9 May 1658 (less than two years after the ratification of the 1654 treaty, which was most explicit in protecting English rights), and the judge dismissed it almost as soon as the hearing began, on the grounds that the ship's captain, not being a Catholic, could not be sworn and therefore his evidence was legally invalid. When this decision was laid down, the group of English merchants present in the court broke out into an uproar. In the end, as always, the English consul had to petition the king for justice.[56]

The task of regulating the relations between the English merchants and the Portuguese authorities fell to the consul at Lisbon. He was a consul general with jurisdiction over all Englishmen in Portugal, Madeira, and the Azores and had the power to appoint vice consuls for Oporto, Madeira, the Azores, and any other center of merchant activity. The English consuls were supported by a levy of .25 percent on the business turnover of the English merchants. This *consulage* tax was difficult to collect because of the resistance of the merchants. When one English consul wanted to see a merchant's books he was told that this was a demand made "by no prince in the world, nor by the Inquisition itself."[57]

Since the consul was himself a merchant and a competitor, the reluctance of the merchants to pay consulage fees to a rival was quite understandable; and even more understandable was their distaste for furnishing a competitor with exact statistics on the volume of their business activity. Yet without such statistics it is difficult to see how consulage could have been fairly and properly collected. A firm and energetic consul was as certain to make enemies among the Englishmen, on whom he imposed discipline and restraints, as he was to irritate the Portuguese authorities, who received his constant complaints. The position of consul, although an awkward one, afforded excellent opportunities for making money and was often coveted. An English consul in office sometimes found himself opposed by rivals who tried to unseat him.

From 1603 to 1690, six men occupied the English consulship in Lisbon: Hugh Lee, 1603–1619; John Stone, 1619–1624(?); John Chandler, 1631–1643; John Rider, 1644–1648; Fr. John Robinson, 1649–1655; and Thomas Maynard, 1656–1689.[58] The year 1603 marked the end of the war with Spain and the revival of the English community in Lisbon. Hugh Lee was appointed consul and held the post until his death in 1619. He was succeeded by John Stone, who may have held the office until Anglo-Spanish relations again became strained (in 1624) or may have left the office at some other time. From 1624 to 1630 there was war with Spain and therefore no English consul; after the peace, John Chandler was appointed and held the post for about twelve years. In 1634 a patent was issued to John Howe as consul at Lisbon, but Chandler regained the office soon afterward.

Chandler was an ardent Catholic and a target of attack for the Puritan parliament; on 10/20 May 1642 the House of Lords ordered him to appear before them on charges of "Popery" and of seducing the king's subjects from their true religion.[59] He may never have appeared before the Lords, but, in any event, he was replaced by John Rider in 1644. After the execution of Charles I, when all appointments came to an end, the exiled Charles II named Fr. John Robinson of the English College in Lisbon as consul. The appointment was recognized by John IV but not by the London Parliament. One of Parliament's agents in Lisbon during 1654–1655 was the merchant Thomas Maynard. Oliver Cromwell eventually appointed Maynard as consul in a patent dated 27 August/6 September 1656, after the royalist appointees were no longer recognized in Lisbon. At the time of the Restoration, Maynard managed to get his appointment confirmed in letters patent issued by Charles II at Westminster, 27 June/7 July 1660.[60]

Maynard held the Lisbon consulship for thirty-three years. During these years he labored, with some success, to make the position of the British merchant in Portugal secure. In their relations with the Portuguese, great problems faced the English merchants of the 1650s; if the position had improved by the 1690s it was owing to a considerable extent to the indefatigable activities of Thomas Maynard, who—building on the treaties of 1642, 1654, and 1662–erected a firm foundation for British commerce in Portugal. This constructive work, by the end of the century, made it possible for John and Paul Methuen, father and son, to negotiate their celebrated treaties.

3

THE SUGAR TRADE AND THE BRAZIL COMPANY

For a period of about two centuries, from the middle of the fifteenth century to the middle of the seventeenth, the Portuguese occupied a leading position as suppliers of sugar to Western Europe. For a long time the island of Madeira was the chief producer, and up to about 1560 the cane grown on the precipitous slopes of Madeira was sufficient in quantity to meet a large part of a growing European demand. The Portuguese, through colonies of New Christian and Jewish exiles, also turned the island of São Tomé (or Saint Thomas), in the Gulf of Guinea, into an important supplier of sugar. Eventually, in the mid-sixteenth century, the São Tomé planters carried the cane to Brazil, where its cultivation proved so successful that the sugar trade of Madeira and São Tomé was undercut and went into a slow decline.

Sugarcane is a gigantic grass, a perennial of the order *Gramineae*, genus *Saccharum*, with a great segmented stalk from ten to twenty feet long, the inside of which is fibrous and juicy. Cultivated cane, the *Saccharum officinarum*, grows best in a uniformly hot climate, in strong sunlight, with heavy rain during the growing season. A rich soil and abundant water are essential for maximum growth.[1] These conditions can be found in the West Indies and in the coastal areas of Brazil.

The Brazilian sugar trade, like the Portuguese colonies in Brazil, grew slowly. Soil and climate are not in themselves the all-important elements in the production of sugar, for the conversion of the cane stalks into the pure crystals of white sugar required three further conditions: (1) heavy capital spending, (2) the attainment of technological sophistication, and (3) an abundant supply of cheap labor.

The Brazilian *engenho*, or sugar mill, was a costly complex of buildings and equipment. The central piece of equipment was the mill, or crushing machine, itself: three large turning rollers or drums so placed that each stalk of cane introduced into the device was squeezed and crushed twice. The fat, robust stalks put into the rollers on one side emerged, at the other side, as well-shredded fiber. In the middle, a copious and precious liquid poured down into great cauldrons. The crushing of the cane stalks required great strength, and the machinery was turned either by sweeps attached to a team of oxen or by a water wheel. Ideally, the mill was built beside a stream with a strong, swift current, because a mill run by water power could crush twice as much cane as a mill whose rollers were turned by bullocks. The cutting of the cane stalks and their transportation from the fields to the mill required laborers, draft animals, and wheeled vehicles. Adriaen Jacobsz van der Dussen, in a report to the Amsterdam municipal authorities written aboard the *Overijssel* and dated 10 December 1639, said that the ordinary *engenho* in Brazil required from forty to seventy Negroes, thirty to forty oxen, and ten or twelve oxcarts.[2] After the crushing of the cane, the juice was processed in a whole series of buildings: a cauldron house, where it was boiled; a "curing house" (*casa de purgar*), where the sugars were crystallized from the juice; and warehouses where the sugar was dried and stored. The *engenho* also required a supply of wood to make the *caixas* (chests, boxes, or crates) into which the sugar was put. These wooden *caixas*, full of sugar, were trundled off to the seaports in the *engenho's* oxcarts. In addition, there were other capital expenses: the land itself; the great house *(casa grande)*, preferably a rather impressive residence, of the master of the mill *(o senhor do engenho);* and the large slave quarters (*senzala*).

Aside from the large capital investment, the successful operation of a sugar mill required technical knowledge and special skills. The juice extracted from the cane is a fluid of complex composition and requires chemical treatment before the desired kinds of sugar can be precipitated from it. The purpose of this chemical treatment is to neutralize the acidity, remove impurities and colloidal substances that will not crystallize, and decolorize the juice for the making of white sugars. The chemical agent that has a strong effect on cane juice is quicklime (CaO). Quicklime neutralizes the acidity, helps both white and brown sugars to crystallize, and so separates the various elements that they are made much easier to handle. After treatment with quicklime impurities can be removed by ladling scum off the surface, by taking away sediment at the bottom, and by filtration.

The seventeenth-century sugar makers were fortunate to inherit a technology that was already many centuries old. Some unknown genius, probably an Arab in eighth-century Egypt,[3] had developed the process of using clay (quicklime) in the whitening of sugar. As cane cultivation spread from Egypt to Spain to Madeira and to Brazil, it was followed, at a respectful distance, by an esoteric body of technical knowledge. The novice in the trade found it easier to grow cane than to make good white sugar. A basic fund of information was open to all, but the practical application of this information was a difficult matter; only patience and long experience brought to the tyro that expertise with proportions and mixtures and that delicate sense of timing which were the vital arts of sugar production.

In the seventeenth-century process of sugar making, the juice of the cane was mixed with sugar and lime and boiled, and then filtered and allowed to cool overnight. The cooled mass, partly liquid and partly solidifying, was stirred often and then placed in a large earthenware pot and taken to the curing house. These earthenware pots were conical in shape, with the narrow portion at the base. The mixture was now allowed to "rest" for six or eight days, after which the crust at the top was broken with a small hammer and the top of the pot covered with a thick layer of fine clay mixed with water, and the moisture would seep down through the mixture. A small hole at the bottom of the pot let out the molasses, which escaped down gutters into large cisterns. After some time (perhaps two or three weeks or longer), the old clay was removed and a fresh application of clay made. Later there might even be a third application of clay. The crystallized sugar in the middle and upper portions of the pot whitened very slowly, while in the bottom section the crystals remained brown in color.

According to Richard Ligon, in Barbados the pots remained covered with clay for four months,[4] but in Brazil the process may have been more rapid. In any event, the curing house had to be a large place, capable of holding the products of an entire harvest, with rows and rows of shelves, with enough room for from 1,000 to 3,000 pots, each of which was expected to yield about one *arroba*[5] of good white sugar. When the curing process was complete, the crystals were removed from the pots, separated into high-grade "white" sugar (actually, each crystal, if properly refined, is transparent and colorless) and second-class sugars, brown or dirty-gray in color, and then dried. In Brazil the sugars were placed on strips of cloth and put out into the blazing sunlight, where they dried out in a single day.[6]

The liquid that dripped out of the pots during the curing process was not a pure molasses (strictly speaking, molasses is a liquid from which no more sucrose can be crystallized) but could be processed to yield more sugar, a third-class brown sugar. Thus, in the Brazilian trade, there were three classes of sugar: (1) the high-grade white sugars *(açúcar branco),* (2) the gray, ash-colored, or light brown sugars called *muscovado* (Portuguese: *mascavado*), and (3) the coarser, less sweet, dark brown sugars called *panel* or *panele* (Portuguese: *panela*). In Brazil, white sugar was worth over twice as much as *muscovado* sugar and four times as much as *panel* sugar. For instance, the average prices paid to the planters at the great Jesuit *engenho* of Sergipe during the 1643–1644 harvest were: 1$280 réis (or a little under thirteen shillings) for one *arroba* of white sugar, $580 réis (or almost six shillings) for *muscovado*, and $320 réis (or a little over three shillings) for *panel* sugar.[7] In these circumstances, only white and *muscovado* sugars were of real commercial importance in the Brazil-England trade; *panel* sugars were carried only as a supplement, to round out a cargo if nothing else was available. During the harvest season 1650–1651, the account books of the Sergipe mill show that no factors would buy *panel* sugar at any price.[8]

English ships to Brazil in search of sugar carried mainly textiles and related articles (stockings, hats, and ribbons), as well as iron, lead, gunpowder, shot, firearms, knives, mirrors, and a few other manufactures. In Brazil they took on sugar and sugar alone. As a contemporary Englishman put it in describing the commerce with Portugal: "All our trade consists in the bringinge of Sugers to England."[9] The Brazilians were not able to persuade Englishmen to buy large quantities of tobacco (which in England could not compete with the favored Virginia product), hides (for which there were many other sources), or Brazilian hardwoods such as jacaranda (whose large size and heavy weight meant high freight costs and low profits).

There was a large market in England for Brazilian sugar. Foreign visitors to present-day Britain often remark on the extraordinary liking of the natives for chocolates, candies, and sugary confections.

The trait is an old one. Francesco Giavarina, Venetian resident in London in 1656, noted "the fondness of the English for sugar" and reported that England "consumes an incredible quantity" of sugar.[10] James Hart, a physician, wrote in a book published in 1633 that "sugar hath now succeeded honie, and is become of farre higher esteem, and is far more pleasing to the palat, and therefore every where in frequent use, as well in sicknesse as in health."[11]

Hart described the English practice of adding sugar to wine, as follows:

> It is a common custome thorow this kingdome, to adde sugar to all wine indifferently, sweet or sowre, or whatsoever sort. I doe not deny, but sometimes, to help a tart taste, or to inhibit the hot fumes of a vaporous or strong sacke, apt to flie up into the braines, a little sugar helpeth well; but to use it indifferently, with all sorts of wines, and without any consideration of circumstances whatsoever (which is the ordinary and common custome) and that merely for wantonnesse, and to satisfie their lustfull desires, I hold it not convenient.[12]

Hart went on to say that sugar is a good medicine for certain diseases of the breast and lungs but that it ought not to be overused, because sugar "heats the blood" and excess leads to consumption (tuberculosis). In fact, the heavy use of sugar was held to be the cause of the high consumption rate in London.[13]

Merchants engaged in importing Brazilian sugar into England had to pay many customs duties and taxes. An English ship with goods for Brazil had first to go to Lisbon, where a license to trade in Brazil was purchased. Then the shipowners had to pay three taxes comprising, altogether, 23 percent of the total value of the cargo—this was for admission into the kingdom of Portugal. Then an additional 3 percent was collected for the reexport of the goods to Brazil. Thus 26 percent *ad valorem* had been collected on the English goods before their arrival in Brazil, where they were exchanged for sugar. The Brazil sugar paid a 10 percent export tax in the port of embarkation and then was taken to Lisbon, where another 23 percent was collected for admission to the kingdom. In addition, a further 3 percent was charged for reexport to England.[14] On arrival in England the sugars faced further heavy taxes: £5 per hundredweight of 112 pounds for white sugar, and £2-10-0 per hundredweight for *muscovado* sugar.[15]

Until the Dutch lost Pernambuco in 1654, English merchants complained that the Dutch did not have to pay the heavy Lisbon duties and therefore could sell their sugar more cheaply. In the middle years of the century Amsterdam, greatly assisted by Portuguese Jewish refugees, became the leading center for sugar refining. (Hamburg, Rotterdam, Rouen, and London were also important.) "One quarter of the total amount of yearly taxes on goods weighed in the public warehouses [of Amsterdam] was paid by sugar refiners."[16] Some of this sugar undoubtedly found its way to English markets.

By the time the Dutch lost their last foothold in Brazil, in 1654, the increasing supply of sugar from the West Indies offered the English merchants an alternative to the Brazilian market. The English conquest of Jamaica (1655–1660) gave a further impetus to the growing of "plantation" sugar for English tables. Although Brazilian sugar continued to be imported into England until 1671[17] and later, the West Indian share of the market grew progressively larger. In the last two decades of the century, imports of Brazilian sugar had shrunk to the point of insignificance.[18]

It is doubtful whether the English merchants busily engaged in the Brazil trade in the 1650s anticipated the decline of Brazilian sugar. Not only did Brazil, in the 1650s, produce the finest white sugar in the world, but Brazil was also the world's largest supplier, potentially able to meet the needs of every nation. The annual Brazilian sugar harvest must certainly have been very large, although seventeenth-century statistics are vague. Pyrard de Laval, a French traveler who in 1610 spent two months in Brazil, said that the 400 *engenhos* in Brazil produced 100,000 *arrobas* of sugar per year.[19] These figures are suspiciously well rounded. The historian João Lúcio de Azevedo said that there were 246 *engenhos* in Pernambuco, 146 in Bahia, and 136 in Rio de Janeiro—or 528 *engenhos* in all—and that the sugar fleet of 1610 consisted of seventy-four ships, which carried 21,000 chests of sugar containing 735,000 *arrobas* (10,794 metric tons) valued at 1,500:000$000 réis (over 1 million pounds in sterling).[20]

Dussen in his 1639 report said that there were 166 *engenhos* in Dutch Brazil, of which only 120 produced sugar during 1639; but the shrewd Dutchman, noting that production of sugar varied greatly from year to year, refused to estimate the average annual output.[21] Prof. Charles R. Boxer has written that Portuguese Brazil in the 1640s had 200 to 300 *engenhos* with an output of from 30,000 to

40,000 chests (or 600,000 to 700,000 *arrobas*) and that Dutch Brazil had 150 large *engenhos*, of which about two-thirds were functioning.[22] In addition to these estimates, there are those contained in a memorial sent to John IV from Pernambuco in 1650 that said that the Pernambuco to Paraíba area contained 150 *engenhos* which, before the Dutch came, could produce 500,000 *arrobas* per year, and the Bahia to Rio de Janeiro area had 200 *engenhos*, with an annual production of 700,000 *arrobas*.[23] Lastly, it may be observed that the sugar fleet of 1655–1656, an enormous armada of over 100 ships, carried 53,221 chests of sugar, which together with other commodities were valued by the fleet's commander at 9 million *cruzados*[24] or 3,600:000$000 réis—an exaggerated amount equivalent to £1,800,000.

From the comparative analysis of these statistics certain conservative conclusions emerge: Brazil, in the immediate post-Dutch period, contained from 380 to 400 producing *engenhos* with an output of from 50,000 to 55,000 chests per year, or about 1,000,000 or 1,100,000 *arrobas*. These figures are based on the assumption that the average mill produced some 2,750 *arrobas* (or forty metric tons) of sugar of all types and that each chest contained an average of 20 *arrobas*.

The weight of sugar in the chests can be established from three sets of statistics. Ships with Brazil sugar forced into Madeira by stress of weather unloaded from April 1640 to January 1641 the following quantities: 27 chests of white sugar averaging nineteen *arrobas* per chest and 104 chests of *panel* averaging twenty-one *arrobas* per chest.[25] The account books of the Jesuit mill of Sergipe for the harvest 1643–1644 show chests of white and *muscovado* weighing always between twenty and twenty-three *arrobas* and chests of *panel* between twenty-one and twenty-six *arrobas*,[26] and thus the chests with the poorest grade of sugar contained usually some two or three *arrobas* more than the chests with the higher grades. And the chests confiscated from the English merchants in Bahia in 1650 included the following: fifty-eight chests of white averaging fifteen *arrobas* per chest, thirty-five chests of *muscovado* averaging twenty-two *arrobas* per chest, and seventeen chests of *panel* averaging twenty-seven *arrobas* per chest.[27] The conclusion is that a chest of white sugar usually weighed about twenty *arrobas*, although it might weigh a good deal

Table 2
Proposed Price Ceilings on Sugar Purchased in Brazil*
(in *réis* per *arroba*)

	White Sugar	*Muscovado* Sugar	*Panel* Sugar
In Bahia	1$100	$550	$240
In Pernambuco	$ 900	$450	$200
In Rio de Janeiro	$ 700	$400	$160

*Source: paper dated 29 November 1655, AHU, Bahia, Caixa VI.

less; a chest of *muscovado* weighed about twenty or twenty-one *arrobas* and seldom less than that; and a chest of *panel* weighed about twenty-four *arrobas* and sometimes a good deal more than that.[28]

The prices paid in Brazil for sugar fluctuated widely. The account books for the Jesuit *engenho*, which always seems to have run at a loss, show wide variations in prices during the course of a single harvest. The prices for one *arroba* of white sugar fluctuated during 1622–1623 from a low of $470 réis to a high of $740; during 1628–1629 from $800 to 1$020; during 1630–1631 from $550 to $850; during 1637–1638 from 1$400 to 1$480; during 1644–1645 from 1$000 to 1$080; and during 1651–1652 from 1$240 to 1$600.[29] In a petition to the king (circa 1655), the municipal chamber of the city of Salvador da Bahia de Todos os Santos, the capital of the state of Brazil, complained about the lack of buyers for sugar and said that Bahia sugar should sell at the following rates, per *arroba*: 2$500 for white, $700 for *muscovado*, and $400 for *panel*.[30] At about the same time the merchants of Lisbon, in a memorial dated 29 November 1655, asked for price ceilings in Bahia of 1$100 for white, $550 for *muscovado*, and $240 for *panel* and for even lower prices in Pernambuco and Rio (see table 2). The merchants defended these cheap rates as "the most convenient prices," pointing out that foreigners would grow sugar themselves in the West Indies rather than pay expensive prices. The collapse of the Portuguese pepper trade, warned the Lisbon merchants, served as a sinister example of how exhorbitant prices stimulated foreigners to create rival sources of supply.[31]

The Bahia sellers wanted to sell white sugar at 2$500 réis per *arroba*, and the Lisbon buyers wanted to buy at 1$100 réis. There is a wide gap between these two figures—a gap that can be expressed as the difference between nine pence per pound and four pence per pound. English merchants hoped to retail white sugar in London at a rate of twenty pence per pound; if they could buy in Brazil at four pence per pound, it meant that the sugar would have increased in value *five times* by the time it reached the London trade. This margin of 400 percent was enough to cover all expenses—the factor's commission, shipping charges, customs, taxes, and middlemen's profits—and still yield a good profit to the merchant. But if the merchant paid nine pence in Bahia it meant that the sugar, on reaching the London market, would have increased in value by a little more than 100 percent. The merchant's expenses, plus losses suffered at sea, would eat up this increase and leave little or no profit. Naturally the merchant expected to make a profit on the outward voyage, after which his European products would double or triple in value when they reached the colonial communities; and in the exchange of these products for sugar it could be said that he obtained sugar at a cost far less than the quoted cash price. This advantage was counterbalanced by the fact that the merchant did not receive the twenty pence per pound retail price at the London end; that is, in England, most merchants would sell to a middleman at a wholesale price. English merchants may have had trouble during the 1650s when the London retail price dropped to twelve pence per pound and sometimes even lower.[32] If Englishmen were buying Bahia white sugar at a normal price of around five and one half pence per pound (or 1$500 réis per *arroba*), then they would perhaps have felt a squeeze on profits.

Hence, in summary, three general factors help to explain the importance of the sugar trade in Anglo-Portuguese relations: (1) the great amounts of sugar produced in Brazil, ranging normally from 14,000 to 16,000 tons per year; (2) the sizable demand in England; and (3) the opportunities for making a profit in the conveying of sugar from Brazil to England. A fourth factor is that of transportation: the means by which sugar was conveyed from Brazil to England—that is, transatlantic merchant shipping. In this transatlantic merchant shipping, Anglo-Portuguese cooperation could be seen at its most enthusiastic and sincere, with substantial benefits to both parties.

Portugal, faced with many challenges from Dutch naval power in the Atlantic and Indian Oceans, was seriously weak at sea by the middle of the seventeenth century. During the period of Spanish domination, the Portuguese fighting ships declined in number and the merchant marine developed very little, in spite of the considerable increase of the commercial shipping of England and the Netherlands. The Portuguese were outclassed on the oceans by dangerous rivals. Their shipbuilding technology had also stagnated. Portugal for nearly two centuries had held a leading place among European shipbuilders, but this very preeminence, by 1650, made the Portuguese reluctant to adopt the ideas of foreign shipbuilders.

The Portuguese continued to produce the types of ships they had always used: the *nau* (carrack), *galeão* (galleon), *patacho* (pinnace), *caravela* (caravel), and the hard-to-classify *navio* (small carrack?). These five types alone account for nine out of ten references in the extant documents to specific ships in the Brazil trade. The caravel, or *caravela*, the oldest type—a highly successful and long-used design—was a small vessel of between 50 and 200 tons, with two masts of lateen rig (i.e., with large triangular sails). The word *nau* was often loosely used for any large or medium-sized ship, but, more strictly, it referred to the Portuguese carrack, the great ship in the India trade. The carrack was a ship of between 400 and 1,000 tons and sometimes larger, with three or four decks, four square-rigged masts, and an elaborate superstructure.

The English called all Spanish and Portuguese ships of any size galleons, but Spaniards and Portuguese rarely used this word in a loose sense. The galleon, or *galeão*, was a ship much like the carrack,[33] but designed as a fighting ship, although she also carried a large cargo. The galleon had a simpler and less cluttered superstructure, was longer and leaner in its lines than the carrack, could sail a little faster, and carried more and better armament.

The pinnacle or *patacho* was a small two-masted vessel, used as a dispatch ship, as an auxiliary man-of-war, or most often as a cargo vessel. The fifth type of ship, the *navio*, presents certain problems. The word *navio* means "ship," and any ship can be called a *navio*. But *navio* was also used by the Portuguese to designate a special type: probably a ship of medium size, from 100 to 400 tons, designed to transport cargoes, and built like a small carrack.

During the year 1652 the Brazil Company claimed to have sent thirty-seven ships to the Pernambuco area; these thirty-seven ships were described as follows: sixteen caravels, nine pinnaces, eight *navios*, and four carracks.[34] No galleons are mentioned in the list, but otherwise the proportions of different types of ships suggested by this list hold true for the Brazil trade in general: twenty-five out of the thirty-seven, or two-thirds, were small ships (caravels and pinnaces), eight were *navios*, and only four, one-ninth of the total, were large ships (carracks). The majority of ships in the sugar trade were small, running to 100 tons and under. Their guns were few, and they could not offer effective resistance to pirates and privateers. When they got in trouble, their tactic was to hoist all sail and run away from their larger, but slower, opponents; this was effective much of the time, except when the wind was so strong as to nullify differences in sailing quality. If caught, the small vessel would usually surrender immediately, and her crew might live to sail another day. Fr. António Vieira, the Jesuit missionary, called the small ships "schools for cowardice," but this was unfair, for the business of a cargo ship was to carry cargo, not to engage in battle against hopeless odds.

A new type of ship, developed during the 1630s and later, shattered the complacency of the owners of small ships and came close to destroying the Portuguese sugar trade. The new ship was the frigate *(fragata* in Portuguese). The frigate design originated in Dunkirk and Flanders, among professional privateers preying on Dutch commerce, and spread thereafter to the United Provinces, England, and elsewhere but was rare in Portugal until the 1660s. The frigate, in comparison with the galleon, was long and narrow, of medium tonnage (200 to 600 tons), with a simplified superstructure, sometimes without a forecastle at all and with the stern works—whose height gave galleons and carracks a topheavy appearance—much reduced and simplified. Her three or four square-rigged masts gave her, for her day, considerable speed; a Dunkirk privateer, newly tallowed and with a clean bottom, could overhaul almost any Portuguese ship. Her two and a half gun decks contained ample space for guns; the gunports of the lower tier were close to the water, where at point-blank range they could hole an enemy ship at the most vulnerable point, the water line. The lower deck was built strongly enough to support the weight of large cannon. An English frigate alongside a tall 1,500-ton Portuguese galleon looked rather low in the water and small, but her broadside might have been almost as destructive as that of the larger ship.

An English writer, in the language of the time, expressed the matter thus: "Our frigots are built so neat and snug, made long and low, so that (as the make of some women's bodies handsomely concealeth their pregnancy, or great belly) their contrivance hideth their bigness without suspicion, the enemy not expecting thirty, when (to his cost) he hath found sixty pieces of ordnance in them."[35]

One major weakness of the frigate was that her walls were too thin to risk an exchange of broadsides with a "great ship" or "ship of force" (which were terms current in 1650 for what were later called capital ships or ships of the line). This weakness was clearly exposed in the Anglo-Dutch naval wars, during which it was found that the frigates could not take their place in the new tactical formation, the line of battle, but had to serve as auxiliary men-of-war.[36]

Portuguese frigates for the king's service were not built until the 1650s—that is, not until some twenty years after the Dunkirk privateers had developed the type.[37] Intensive building of frigates was not begun before 1663, when two frigates, the *Santo Sacramento* and the *Nossa Senhora da Conceição* (both carrying about forty guns), were laid down at the royal yards, the Ribeira das Naus in the heart of Lisbon; they were launched during the first three months of 1664, and preparations were made for building four other frigates. The third frigate, *São José* (forty-two guns), sailed from Lisbon on her maiden voyage on 31 May 1664. The fourth, *São Bernardo* (thirty-six guns), was launched on 9 July 1664. When the fifth frigate, *São Jorge* (thirty guns), was laid down on 23 April 1664, there were 300 men at work and four ships under construction in the royal shipyards; she was launched on 2 October 1664. The sixth frigate, the *Santo António* (fifty-four guns), sailed for Northern Portugal in September 1665.[38]

The new frigates provided Portuguese shipping with the best protection in years. The swift ships took the offensive against pirates and privateers, stayed out on station in all kinds of weather, and were revictualled at sea. When the *São Bernardo* returned from a North African cruise with five prizes, sailing into the Tagus on 14 March 1665, her crew was given a hero's welcome. Five days later they sailed again, on convoy duty. A Spanish prize from Málaga was converted into the Portuguese frigate *Santa Teresa* and went out on patrol on 12 May 1665.[39]

As far as the situation of the 1640s is concerned, these measures came twenty years too late. The enemies faced by the Portuguese on the seas were the Netherlanders off Brazil and Africa, the Barbary pirates off Madeira and the Algarve, and privateers from Dunkirk, Ostend, Galicia, Santander, and Bilbao, who intercepted Portuguese ships at all points between the Azores and the coasts of Portugal. The frigates from Holland, Dunkirk, and Ostend did the most damage. Portuguese merchantmen were either too small, too lightly armed, or too slow—and they were lost by the hundreds. According to one source, from 1623 to 1638, 547 ships were lost to the Dutch.[40] The Restoration of 1 December 1640 brought Portugal a host of enemies allied to or controlled by Spain, while Dutch attacks on Portuguese shipping were halted for only a short time. The Overseas Council considered the question of shipping losses in a *consulta* dated 2 May 1651 and pondered a muddled document listing the names of 118 ships lost during 1647 and 141 ships lost during 1648. This statement named 146 ships lost on the outward journey and 113 on the return, of which 126 were listed as caravels, 112 as *navios*, 17 as carracks, 2 as pinnaces, and 2 as frigates.[41]

For a long time the governments of Portugal had tried to deal with the question of unsafe shipping by passing restrictive legislation. A law of 3 November 1571 decreed that small ships from 25 to 200 tons were to carry a certain specified minimum number of cannons (from five to fourteen guns, depending on the tonnage of the ship), a minimum amount of gunpowder (from one to three *quintals*), and a stipulated number of pikes, lances, and firearms. Each ship had to carry two men for every ten tons, had to submit to inspection before leaving port, and could not sail without an exit permit. The best-armed ships were to be granted preference of loading and to be loaded first, and a bounty was to be paid to shipbuilders who constructed large ships.[42]

On 19 January 1646, John IV told the Overseas Council that no ship carrying less than ten guns should be permitted to go to Brazil; he also suggested that good ships of some 450 tons each and carrying from twenty to thirty guns could be freighted from Hamburg.[43] Two strange and severe laws of 15 March 1648 ordained that after three years no more ships under 350 tons, or armed with fewer than sixteen guns firing at least eight-pound shot, were to sail to the colonies, on pain of confiscation of the vessel and her cargo, and, furthermore, no ships of under 350 tons were to be built or bought or rented in Portugal. This extraordinary and unenforceable legislation was softened by a new law, 25 January 1649, which permitted ships of over 250 tons armed with guns firing five-pound shot to sail to the colonies, and even smaller ships would be allowed if they first secured special permission. But large ships and their officers were to be given certain privileges.[44]

Legal bans against small ships were unrealistic. There were at least a dozen flourishing communities in Portugal that lived off shipping but whose harbors no large ships could enter. In the seventeenth century the small port, in comparative terms, was more important than it is today. Land transport was difficult and expensive; all along the coasts, if a harbor was found that, however shallow, could accommodate small vessels, it was put to use. A shallow bay or the mouth of a small river became the focus of a maritime community, a center of supply for the adjacent inland villages. Tens of thousands of people in Portugal had an interest in the preservation of small ships and wanted men-of-war on patrol to protect small vessels. The legal elimination of ships with shallow draft would have meant the ruin of many prosperous seaport towns.

Unlike the coasts of Britain, the coasts of Portugal have almost no deep-water harbors, and all the rivers (except the Tagus) are blocked by sandbars at the mouth. Lisbon, of course, has a fine harbor: even at low tide the bar at the entrance to the Tagus, at the shallowest point in the main channel, was covered by six fathoms (thirty-six feet) of water.[45] The three other leading ports—Oporto, Setúbal, and Faro—contained navigational hazards. According to seventeenth-century Dutch charts, the channels leading to Oporto and Setúbal offered three fathoms of water at midtide, while in the dangerous channel leading to Faro the water was only two fathoms deep at midtide.[46] The sandbar at Viana do Castelo was covered by less than two fathoms of water at low tide but could be cleared at other times. The poor and exposed anchorage at Vila do Conde offered, at points, only two fathoms of water at high tide. Caminha, on the River Minho, could only be entered at high tide. The narrow passage into the busy port of Aveiro had a clearance of only two fathoms at midtide. The same limitations, or worse, governed the use of the other ports,[47] namely (from north to south): Esposende, Póvoa de Varzim, Matosinhos, Figueira da Foz, Nazaré, São Martinho do Pôrto, Ericeira, Sesimbra, Sines, Vila Nova de Milfontes, Lagos, Portimão, Armação de Pera, Albufeira, Olhão, Tavira, and Vila Real de Santo Antônio.

When entering and leaving these tidal ports ships had to wait not only for high tide but also for the proper wind in combination with high tide. A ship waiting to enter a river and caught in certain weather conditions might find the waiting itself to be full of dangers. For the fully loaded large ships, the great carracks and galleons, Lisbon was the only truly satisfactory harbor, although Peniche, Setúbal, and Oporto could all accommodate fairly large ships.

Severe shipping losses during the late 1640s brought to a head all the problems connected with maritime commerce, and a single comprehensive solution was proposed: the foundation of a powerful, well-capitalized, semi-monopolistic company to control all trade with Brazil. This company doubtlessly owed its inspiration to the highly successful Dutch East India Company—but the Brazil Company, which was formed in Lisbon in 1649, had its own individual features and problems and was, in effect, a peculiarly Portuguese institution, facing difficulties unknown to Dutch or English companies.

John IV founded the *Companhia Geral do Estado do Brasil* (or *Companhia Geral de Comércio do Estado do Brasil*) in the face of organized opposition from the Holy Office of the Inquisition and loyally defended it, until the day of his death, against a host of enemies. While John IV lived, the "General Company of the State of Brazil" prospered, but a few months after his death its enemies fell upon it and emasculated its privileges and impoverished its treasury.[48]

The foundation of the Brazil Company was inextricably connected with the attitude of the Inquisition toward the New Christians and their property. Fr. António Vieira of the Society of Jesus, in a lengthy memorial to John IV, pointed out that the harassment of the Jews was contrary to the national interests of Portugal, while the use of Jewish capital in the shipping and commerce of Portugal would strengthen the Portuguese fleet, stimulate commerce, increase royal revenues, and enrich the nation. As Vieira indicated, there were Portuguese Jewish merchants in every country in Europe, yet only foreigners derived any benefits from this because no Jewish wealth could

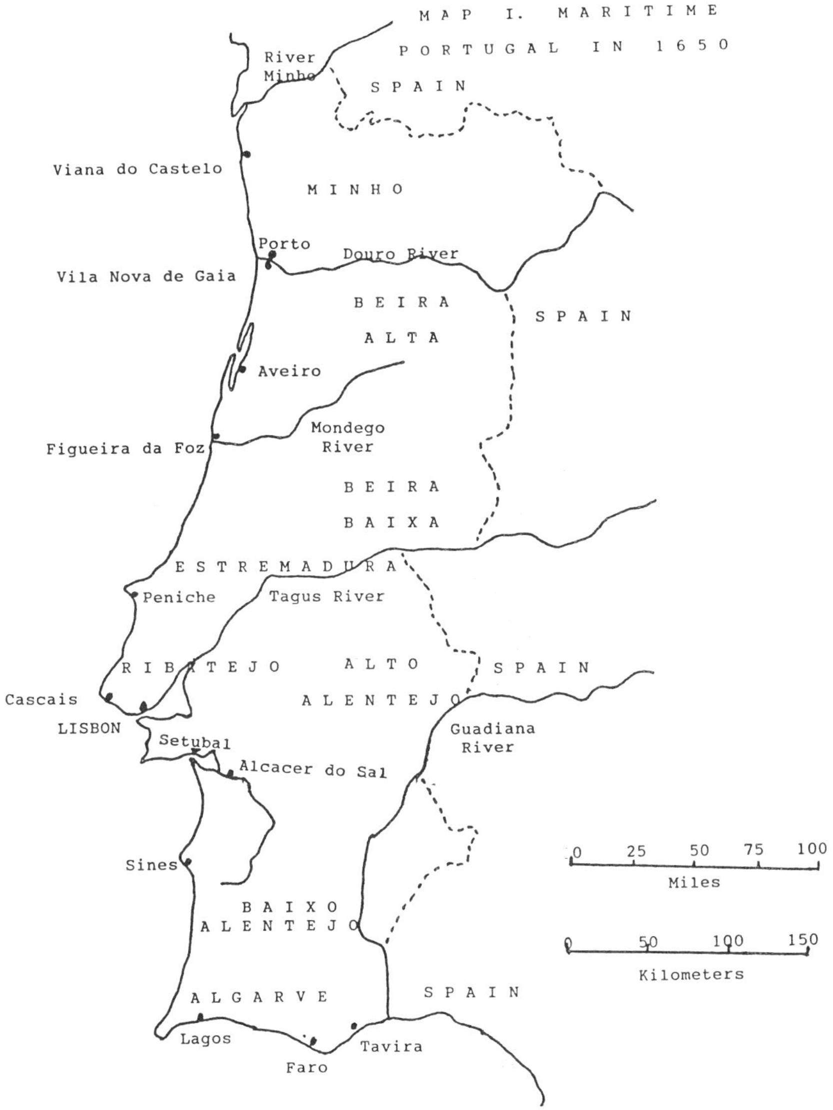
MAP I. MARITIME
PORTUGAL IN 1650
River
Minho
SPAIN
Viana do Castelo
MINHO
Porto
Douro River
Vila Nova de Gaia
BEIRA
ALTA
SPAIN
Aveiro
Mondego
River
Figueira da Foz
BEIRA
BAIXA
ESTREMADURA
Peniche
Tagus River
RIBATEJO
ALTO
ALENTEJO
SPAIN
Cascais
LISBON
Setubal
Alcacer do Sal
Guadiana
River
Sines
0
25
50
75
100
Miles
0
50
100
150
Kilometers
BAIXO
ALENTEJO
ALGARVE
SPAIN
Lagos
Faro
Tavira

be invested in Portugal, where it would risk confiscation by the Inquisition. The Inquisition prevented the New Christians from contributing to the prosperity of Portugal.[49]

In the spring and summer of 1647 the idea of encouraging the New Christians to invest in Portuguese shipping and commerce, on the clear understanding that the capital so invested would be safe from confiscation by the Inquisition, was being discussed in the royal court. Dr. Francisco Pinheiro of the Jesuits' House of Novices (*Casa do Noviciado da Companhia de Jesus*) drew up a statement arguing *against* the confiscation of properties of merchants accused of Judaizing, and over a period of months it was signed by various influential Jesuits.[50] This document was answered in a memorial signed by five Inquisitors (Luís Álvares da Rocha, Belchior Dias Preto, João Delgado Figueira, Martím Afonso de Melo, and Alexandre da Silva)—dated "Lisbon, 28 February 1648"—protesting that confiscation of property was the measure most feared by "heretics" and that, in any event, jurisdiction over the punishment of "heretics" lay exclusively with the Holy See and with ecclesiastical justice and not with the king.[51]

In the early stages the argument concerned the protection of New Christian investments and ways of stimulating Portuguese commerce through such investments, particularly by attracting New Christian money that was held overseas. There was yet no thought, it would appear, of the formation of a commercial company for Brazil. On 5 September 1648, the Overseas Council discussed a melancholy letter from João Francisco Vieira, a commander against the Dutch in Pernambuco, saying that the Dutch were not doing very well in managing their own concerns in Brazil but were sustained solely from the large number of sugar ships they had captured from the Portuguese. The only remedy the Pernambuco commander suggested, to prevent the capture of sugar ships by the Dutch frigates, was to suspend the commerce with Brazil for one or two years. The Overseas Council declared that this was too drastic a measure; moreover, said the council in their message to the king, the Lisbon merchants had made new proposals for the defense of the sugar fleets and these proposals were now under consideration.[52]

The proposals envisioned the financing of warships by the merchants themselves, in return for certain monopolies and privileges. A complete scheme for a company of commerce that would maintain thirty to forty warships at sea and own forty merchantmen armed with at least fourteen guns each was presented to the king on 5 December 1648. One month later, on 8 January 1649, John IV issued an order to the Count of Odemira of the Council of State and to Pedro Fernandes Monteiro, secretary of the Treasury, to call the Lisbon merchants together for the purpose of organizing the Brazil Company.[53] The king had decided to press on with the formation of a powerful new company, on conditions that would be attractive to the merchants, with protection for New Christian properties.

The Inquisitions of Lisbon, Évora, and Coimbra had evolved, over the years, into large-scale, fully staffed, expensive bureaucracies, financed precariously by the confiscated properties that came into their hands. Victims of the Inquisition had all their property seized at the time of their arrest; if they were found innocent, then they were released and their property restored. In the interim, during the two or three years the Inquisitors spent in inquiries and examinations, the confiscated properties remained with the Inquisition. Sometimes the financial pressures of maintaining jails and offices and paying wages and salaries to jailers, servants, and a small army of functionaries and officials created the need for new and wealthier victims and for more convictions. In December 1647 the Inquisition had scored a great coup in the arrest of the New Christian Duarte da Silva, probably the wealthiest merchant in Portugal, a loyal friend of the government—who, in an emergency, is said to have lent the royal treasury 120:000$000 réis (or about £60,000) from his own pocket—and his immense wealth was confiscated.[54]

In December 1648 it was proposed that the Inquisition surrender the property of Duarte da Silva, and of all other New Christians whose cases were pending, to the Royal Treasury, who would restore the goods to their owners on condition that heavy investments were made in the new Brazil Company. The Inquisitors felt themselves threatened, indeed ruined. The Inquisitor General saw King John on 13 January 1649, five days after the order to call the Lisbon merchants together, and asked that the Council of State be given the opportunity to review the whole question of New Christian properties. The king agreed to allow the members of the council to openly and freely express their views on this subject and set a meeting for 6 February 1649. In the meantime, the king's confessor, the Augustinian friar Dionísio dos Anjos, prepared a draft of a decree designed to protect New Christian properties.[55]

The 6 February 1649 meeting was a mere formality; John IV, in his slow and cautious way, had made up his mind and was to prove, thereafter, inflexible and stubborn on all questions affecting the Brazil Company. The king heard all the councillors' objections, one by one; when they had finished, he said simply that the proposed policy on New Christian properties was not a question of choice but of necessity—what was being done had to be done because the national interest demanded it. The king then signed the properties decree and ordered the organization of the Brazil Company—on that same day.[56]

The decree of 6 February 1649, written by the king's Augustinian confessor, was a sophisticated document. In it the king professed the utmost admiration and respect for the Holy Office of the Inquisition, repudiated any intention of invading its jurisdiction, and insisted that heretics must be severely punished and heresy suppressed and, indeed, all heretics who died impenitent were to have all their properties forfeited to the Inquisition. What was decreed was merely a change in procedure, not in principles. Properties of persons accused of heresy were to be delivered to the royal Treasury by the Inquisition; the Treasury would restore the goods to their owners, with whom they had made a binding contract; if an accused person were adjudged guilty, heretical, and impenitent, then all his property would be forfeit. The king and his Jesuit and Augustinian advisers believed that in these changes of procedure there was no violation of canon law and no invasion of the jurisdiction of pope or Inquisitor, but only the proper exercise of the king's secular authority.

The Inquisitors cared little about the intentions behind the royal decree; what worried them were its practical effects. They knew that as soon as an accusation was lodged against a New Christian he would take steps to dispose of his property and have his money sent out of the country. In addition, it was obvious that the Brazil Company, governed by New Christians and protected by the king, would never surrender any money or property within its control. In ecclesiastical terms, the Inquisition's powers to pursue heretics remained unaffected; in secular terms, its existence was threatened by insolvency. By the time a heretic died at the stake impenitent, he would have had no property worth confiscating.

Three weeks after the decree protecting New Christian property, the Inquisition of Évora held a public *auto-da-fé* on Sunday, 28 February 1649, in the presence of the Inquisitor General Dom Francisco de Castro, Bishop of Guarda. At Évora, sixty men and eighty-seven women were publicly penanced, some for bearing false witness or for blasphemy or bigamy, but most of them for performing Jewish practices—ten persons were burned in effigy, but no one was burned in the flesh. Two of the accused had died in jail.[57] The public spectacle was evidently intended, by its timing, to embarrass the king. Five days later the Inquisitors in Lisbon signed a vigorous protest against the properties decree and demanded that the question be referred to Rome.[58] This document was sent to the king on 6 March 1649 but was not answered until 29 March, when John IV replied that all decisions had been made and the matter was to be regarded as settled.

In the interim between 6 March and 29 March all questions had indeed been settled. The king's decree founding the General Company of Brazil was signed on 8 March 1649.[59] On 10 March the king issued another decree, containing a solemn promise that the conditions governing the establishment of the Brazil Company would be inviolably observed and would never be revoked.[60] On 16 March a public notice was issued by the Deputados da Junta da Companhia Geral do Estado do Brasil opening the subscription of capital for the new company and giving Lisbon merchants only thirty days during which to subscribe.[61]

The Inquisition fought back furiously but fruitlessly.[62] All summer long the battle raged and the king would not be moved. The decree on New Christian properties was published and circulated in Lisbon, in spite of attempts to prevent it. On 17 October 1649, the Inquisitor General, ignoring John IV's express prohibition, appealed to Pope Innocent X.[63] This appeal to Rome was made in spite of the fact that the pope did not recognize John IV as king of Portugal or admit the independence of Portugal.

Pope Innocent X issued a brief on 17 May 1650 upholding the jurisdiction of the Portuguese Inquisition over confiscated properties and declaring that John IV's decree or decrees on this subject were "null, invalid, and of no effect, all reasons to the contrary notwithstanding."[64] The king was very angry; his letter to the Inquisitor General contained a strong reprimand, together with an order that the papal brief be disregarded in Portugal. But the king was in a difficult position; for excellent diplomatic reasons, he wanted the goodwill of the pope. When the Inquisition of Évora decided on 26 January 1651, on the authority of the papal brief, to resume the confiscation of property, the king temporized; he resolved on 17 February 1651 that the pope's decision should be respected until such time as His Holiness had been properly informed of the true nature of the dispute in question. In the meantime, the king appointed a special official to watch over the possessions of the Brazil Company.[65]

The truth was that John IV's officials were in a position to block almost all attempted confiscations, and the Inquisition suffered severely. Innocent X's brief was not published in Portugal, nor was its circulation permitted. Only in October 1654 did the Inquisition return to the attack. The General Council of the Inquisition adopted a pleading tone: "We see now that, after the passage of nearly four years [since the king's relaxation of the properties decree], things are in the same state, and the Holy Office is reduced to such straits that, in order to celebrate the *auto da fé,* we have reached the point of borrowing money at interest and on security."[66] The Évora Inquisition, in a strong letter to the king, claimed that the Brazil Company, on whose behalf the decision on properties had been made, was an utter failure.[67] The king's reply of 1 November 1654 was severe in tone; John IV said that the royal Treasury would furnish the Inquisitors with money, if necessary, but that all things must remain as they were.[68] Many months later, the Évora Inquisition, in a letter dated 23 July 1655, had the impertinence to write to the king that "we are not intimidated by the answer which your Majesty gave us on 1 November 1654."[69] But the king, as usual, had the last word: in an order dated 19 August 1655, he affirmed the fact that all confiscated goods were and would remain the responsibility of the Treasury, regardless of whatever happened, and added (with only half-concealed irony) that this would spare the Inquisitors much work.[70]

John IV died on Monday morning, 6 November 1656, and his widow, Queen Luisa de Guzmán became regent for the boy Alphonso VI. Ninety days after the funeral, the Inquisitors posted Innocent X's brief of 17 May 1650, now almost seven years old, on the doors of all the churches.[71] On 2 February 1657 the Queen Regent signed an act revoking the properties decree of 6 February 1649, and this measure was published on 6 February 1657.[72] After eight years the Inquisitors had triumphed over John IV, but only over his dead body.

The Brazil Company created by the decree of 8 March 1649 was to have an existence of twenty years, beginning on Easter Day

1649, with a proviso that an extension for a further ten years might be granted if desirable. The company was to be governed by nine deputies, or directors, who had to be merchants with an interest in the company and who were elected for three-year terms. They were assisted by seven councillors. The company was to have great privileges: it had the exclusive right to sell olive oil, wine, codfish, and flour to Brazil, and it had a monopoly on the export of brazilwood (Brazil's second most lucrative export). The company also had the right to make its own arrangements for chartering foreign shipping.

In return for these lucrative concessions the shareholders of the company assumed exceedingly heavy commitments: they agreed to finance and maintain thirty-six warships, to be divided into two escort fleets of eighteen ships each. The first escort fleet would convoy the sugar ships to Brazil, while the second remained stationed in Portugal; on the return of the first fleet, the second fleet would sail with another armada of sugar ships while the first took up the Portugal station. In theory everyone would benefit: the sugar merchants would have excellent protection for their cargoes; the king would have eighteen more warships off the coasts of Portugal, in addition to the royal armada of twelve or fifteen ships, at no extra expense to the Treasury; the Brazilian colonists would be happy to be visited by two great fleets each year; the eighteen warships that would be present in Brazilian waters for much of the year would keep the Dutch in check; and, as for the Brazil Company itself, the thirty-six warships would also carry sugar for the company, thereby defraying the expenses of their maintenance.

The scheme was visionary: most princes of Europe could not have financed a permanent force of thirty-six warships; the idea that merchants could maintain this enormous private navy out of sugar profits was unrealistic. In spite of its monopolies and privileges, the Brazil Company was never able to support thirty-six men-of-war, nor did it ever send two fleets to Brazil in one year. The critics of the company, of whom there were a legion both in Brazil and Portugal, argued that this failure to abide by the conditions of the contract should result in the cancellation of the contract, with the annulment of all the company's privileges. John IV did not agree; the king defended the company and saw to it that its rights remained intact.

The English merchants resident in Portugal were placed in a perilous position by the formation of the Brazil Company. Extraordinary competitive advantages had been conferred on their Portuguese rivals. The English had been shut out of the Brazil market in the supply of the four commodities—flour, dried codfish, wine, and olive oil—that had been made company monopolies. English merchants had been accustomed to picking up wines in Madeira and selling them in Brazil, and this new prohibition would hurt their trade. Much worse was the codfish monopoly: before 1649 the sale of dried codfish in Brazil had often been an all-English transaction, since fishing boats from southwest England caught the cod, Englishmen in Newfoundland salted, dried, and cured the fish, and English ships transported it to Lisbon and Brazil. Now English ships would have to sell the codfish in Lisbon and allow the large Brazil profits to go to Portuguese middlemen.

The alternatives that confronted the English merchant were either going into partnership with Portuguese merchants who belonged to the company or else joining the company himself. The government not only permitted foreign merchants to join the company, it virtually forced them to do so. The proclamation inviting investment in the company said that any person, whether native or foreign, of any quality, whether resident in Portugal or abroad, could invest any sum of more than twenty cruzados (8$000 réis or about £4) in the General Company—and one-third of the amount should be paid immediately, another third in four months' time, and the last third in eight months' time.[73] The proclamation then went on to make a clear threat: "Foreigners resident in this kingdom who wish to join the company should do so with a sum commensurate with their business and capital, and those not doing so will have to observe the laws of the kingdom and the stipulations of the company respecting the prohibition of [foreign] commerce with Brazil." In other words, foreigners with a large business were expected to invest a large amount in the company, and those who did not live up to the government's expectations would be threatened with the enforcement of the laws against foreigners sending ships to the colonies.

Even Portuguese merchants who elected to stay out of the company must have found themselves in difficulties. The sugar trade was still open to everyone but had been reorganized on a new basis; not only was the independent merchant forbidden to traffic in the four monopoly commodities, but also he had to sail his ships to and from Brazil in the company's fleet—leaving and returning in strict conformity with the company's schedule—and he had to pay a heavy convoy fee (the *avaria* charge) to the company for this "privilege." The Brazil Company, by its contract, had to supply warships for the protection of the sugar ships, and the merchants were compelled by law to accept this protection and pay for it. This also meant that the independent merchant, in every port of call, had to withstand the massive and organized competition of the company's factors, because the ships of the company would always be present.

Lisbon merchants, including the Englishmen, were given only one month in which to make up their minds. Merchants in other parts of Portugal were given ninety days to subscribe to the company, those in Madeira and the Azores had seven months, and those in Brazil and elsewhere had twelve months in which to make their subscriptions. "And after this time has passed the Company may be closed."[74] This threat of early closure denied the foreign merchant a chance to wait and see what would happen before committing his money to a company under the control of a potentially unfriendly government. According to João Lúcio de Azevedo the sum of 520:000$000 réis (£260,000) was quickly subscribed, of which over 10 percent came from three great New Christian families, the Carvalhos (24:000$000), Botelhos (16:000$000), and Serrões (16:000$000).[75]

In spite of these various pressures, English merchants probably did not subscribe very heavily to the company. Whatever assets they may have invested were probably lost, a year later, when there was a general sequestration of English properties in Portugal. When normal commercial relations were restored, the English traders asked the London government to protect them against any attempts the Portuguese might make to exclude them from Brazil. The threats of the Brazil Company against foreign merchants in 1649 may account, in part, for the astringent and detailed articles for the protection of English merchants set forth in the treaty of 1654.

In spite of this unpromising beginning, English relations with the Brazil Company became, for the most part, quite friendly. The English merchants soon realized that the Brazil Company needed them more than they needed the company. Foreign ships were vital for the success of the project, and they could usually be freighted only from France, the United Provinces, Genoa, Hamburg, and England. The French were suspected of harboring a design to found a French colony in Brazil, the Dutch were open enemies, Genoa was too closely associated with Spain—and that left only Hamburg and England capable of furnishing large, well-gunned ships. The Portuguese were interested in Hamburg ships but could never secure them in sufficient numbers. Only England was a reliable friendly source for swift, well-armed merchantmen of the frigate type, to serve as warships in convoying the sugar ships.

On the eve of the formation of the company and afterward, the government still issued licenses to English merchants to send ships to Brazil. On 14 December 1648, John Miller of Lisbon was allowed to send the *Hannibal* to Rio de Janeiro and return with sugar, on condition that the king's cargo of saltpeter, gunpowder, lead, salt, etc., be carried free of charge. On 8 February 1649, John Mules was given a permit to send the *Pilgrim of London* to Bahia, stopping at Madeira for wine on the outward journey, on condition that a royal cargo of ten *quintals* of powder and ten of lead were carried for free. More astonishing still was the permission granted to John Mules by the king on 26 May 1649, some six weeks after the company had begun its legal existence, to send codfish (a prohibited article) directly from Newfoundland to Bahia, although the Overseas Council was reluctant to approve this transaction.[76] Naturally, in all these instances the usual heavy licensing fees were collected by the crown.

On 18 February 1649 a royal order forbade any ship to leave for the colonies without first undergoing an inspection of cargoes.[77] The government enforced the laws protecting the Brazil Company's privileges and monopolies. Manuel Luís Carnoto, master of the *Santo António*, violated the company's prerogatives and was denounced in Rio de Janeiro by João da Silva. The ship was confiscated and, by an ordinance of 28 July 1650, the Overseas Council gave João da Silva, the informer, one-third of the value of ship and cargo.[78] There is little indication in the records of the Overseas Council that this kind of situation ever arose with English ships; there is almost no mention in the council's papers of English ships violating the monopolies and privileges of the Brazil Company. English records contain references to accounts maintained by Englishmen with the company, together with a number of complaints about debts owed to merchants by the company. When the two sets of materials, fragmentary as they are, are brought together, they probably justify the conclusion that English merchants worked closely with the company and solved the problem offered by its enormous competitive strength by, so far as was possible, transacting their business within the company and through it.

It is difficult to discover how many English ships were engaged in the Brazil trade during 1640–1660. Some hints are furnished by the licenses given by the Overseas Council, but English merchants who worked closely with the Brazil Company freighted their ships directly to the company, and no record of these transactions survives. Luisa da Fonseca, working with the licenses in the records of the Overseas Council, reported the following statistics: during the seventy-five years of the period 1613–1687, licenses to go to Brazil were requested by foreign merchants or shipowners for their foreign ships 275 times. This averages out at between three and four licenses per year. Luisa da Fonseca broke down her figure of 275 into categories, according to nationality, as follows: British ships (including Irish and Scottish), 86; French, 40; Italian, 36; Dutch, 17; Flemish, 16; and miscellaneous other nationalities, 32, leaving 48 ships of unidentified nationality. Of the 227 ships classified according to nationality, 38 percent were British and 18 percent were French.[79]

My own tentative figures, based on a wider selection of documents, show that during the ten-year period 1649–1658 at least 56 foreign ships received a license to go to Brazil, of which 46 were English and 10 of other European nationalities (Genoese, Hamburger, and French)—but 9 of these English ships did not actually get to Brazil (because they were detained by Blake's fleet in 1650). If these 9 ships were eliminated from the reckoning, there would still be a large preponderance of English ships (79 percent of the total). These figures also yield a disappointing average: only about 4 English ships per year went to Brazil. The real average, including all the unrecorded ships freighted by the Brazil Company and all the ships licensed by the Treasury Council, may have been anywhere between 12 and 24 ships per year.

An analysis, for instance, of the English shipping in Brazil in 1649 reveals how large the total number of English ships in Brazilian waters may have been. In April 1649, Witte Corneliszoon de With, admiral of a Dutch squadron in Brazilian waters, wrote in his journal that there were 4 English ships at Cape Santo Agostinho (Pernambuco), 8 in Bahia, and 6 in Rio. On the basis of these numbers, Professor Boxer once wrote that "it may be assumed that at least twenty English ships were engaged in the Brazil trade in 1648–9."[80]

The presence of several English ships off Pernambuco was gratefully recorded by Col. João Fernandes Vieira of the army of Pernambuco in a letter (30 March 1649) to John IV. The English ships had brought letters from Portugal, as well as foodstuffs and munitions that had helped to defeat the Dutch.[81]

The 18 English ships listed by the Dutch admiral in April 1649 did not include all the English ships in Brazilian waters during that year, for at least 3 others arrived in Brazil after April 1649. These were: (1) the 200-ton *Newfoundlander* to Bahia with John Mules's codfish; (2) John Mules's *Hannibal* to Rio de Janeiro; and (3) Mules's third ship, the *Pilgrim of London* to Bahia. There was also an English ship in equatorial waters, unnoticed by the Dutch admiral, at São Luís in the state of Maranhão[82] (strictly speaking, not then a part of the "State of Brazil"). There were, if all these accounts are accurate, 22 English ships in Brazil in 1649.

Before the end of the year, 8 more English ships, at least, sailed out with the Brazil Company's first fleet. During the one-year period from April 1649 to April 1650, therefore, there were at least 30 English ships in Brazil.[83] Thirty ships in one year make up one-third of the total of 86 British ships suggested by Luisa da Fonseca's figures for seventy-five years!

On Thursday, 4 November 1649, the first armada of the General Company of the State of Brazil, with 84 ships (the eighteen promised men-of-war escorting sixty-six merchantmen), sailed from the port of Lisbon. João Rodrigues de Vasconcelos e Sousa, count of Castelo Melhor, the newly appointed governor general of Brazil, commanded aboard the flagship, the great Oporto galleon *São Paulo* of 840 tons.[84] The fleet included eight English merchantmen freighted for Bahia and perhaps other English ships as well. Four of the English ships—the *Cyprian, Blessing, Thomas and Lucy,* and *Talbot*—classified by the Portuguese as of from 300 to 400 tons each and capable of mounting from twenty-four to twenty-eight guns, were freighted by the Portuguese as men-of-war and were enrolled as such in the company's list of eighteen warships. The other four English ships to Bahia—the *Sara, Sampson, Three Brothers,* and *Nicholas*—were also large ships and mounted from twenty to twenty-six guns each.[85]

The sugar fleet of 1649–1650 was a visible demonstration of Anglo-Portuguese cooperation. Much that has been said about the sugar trade, English merchants, the Brazil Company, and Anglo-Portuguese relations comes to some kind of logical culmination with the sailing of the first of the Brazil Company's fleets. In that fleet English merchants protected Portuguese cargoes and made a profit for themselves while serving the vital interests of the king of Portugal. English master gunners directed artillery fire aboard the Portuguese galleons. English seamen, particularly skilled men such as carpenters and blacksmiths, served on the Portuguese ships at good pay. However, the English ships often carried Portuguese officers, and occasionally half of the ship's complement were Portuguese (for these were sometimes the terms on which English ships were given license to sail to Brazil). The larger English ships almost always transported Portuguese passengers.

It is unfortunate that Anglo-Portuguese commercial cooperation, so pleasantly and profitably demonstrated at the time of the outward voyage of the sugar fleet, should have degenerated into enmity and conflict by the time the fleet returned. English and Portuguese merchants neither wished for nor brought about this turn of events.

The Brazil fleet's four-month outward journey was slow and troublesome, marked by delays, lack of wind, and skirmishes with the Dutch. Bahia was not reached until 7 March 1650.[86] Before the armada could return to Portugal, the Portuguese government had sequestered all the English ships in Brazil, and the Commonwealth of England's fleet, under Adm. Robert Blake, blockaded the mouth of the Tagus. The affairs of merchants, of sugar and ships, of profit and loss, had been caught up in and superseded by a difficult and complicated international conflict.

4

PRINCE RUPERT IN LISBON

On 26 May/5 June 1648 the sailors of the English fleet in the Downs, who had been loyal to Parliament throughout the civil war, mutinied against their officers. The rebel ships included the *Constant Reformation, Convertine, Swallow,* and *Antelope* and five smaller vessels. After many days of hesitation, the rebels sailed on 11/21 June 1648 to Helvoetsluys at the mouth of the River Maas, in Holland, and placed themselves at the disposal of the exiled Charles Stuart, Prince of Wales.[1]

By the acquisition of the nine parliamentary men-of-war, the royalist fleet, which had consisted heretofore of small numbers of privateers operating out of Dutch ports, became of respectable size and was able to undertake, during 1648 and 1649, offensive operations in the English Channel and in the Irish Sea against English shipping. The struggle between royalists and parliamentarians at sea need not concern us, but a few facts should be mentioned. First, in October 1648, Prince Rupert, Count Palatine of the Rhine,[2] was given command of the royalist fleet. Second, in December 1648 Rupert sailed with his ships for Ireland, where he eventually put in at the Irish port of Kinsale, where he remained for almost nine months, blockaded by the parliamentary navy, whose strength increased gradually during 1649.

After the execution of Charles I the new English government was organized as a Council of State of forty-one members, and they established a subcommittee for maritime affairs, the Committee of the Council of State for the Affairs of the Admiralty and Navy, under the leadership of Sir Henry Vane the Younger, and appointed three colonels of the army—Robert Blake, Richard Deane, and Edward Popham—as commissioners of the navy or "Generals-at-Sea." Blake was given a squadron of ten ships and entrusted with the task of dealing with the royalists in the Irish Sea. He arrived off Kinsale on 21/31 May 1649 and began a long, difficult, and intermittent blockade that was finally abandoned, after a violent storm at sea, early in October 1649.[3]

During the months of the Kinsale blockade, Oliver Cromwell's armies invaded Ireland and marched from victory to victory. Rupert, reasonably safe at Kinsale, nevertheless had to prepare his escape. The problem was where to take his ships. If a safe British port could not be found for the small royalist squadron, then a foreign port had to be sought. Since the Dutch harbors were too close to the Commonwealth fleet in the Downs, the most convenient foreign ports were those of France, Spain, and Portugal.

Prince Rupert had long considered Lisbon to be an ideal port for royalist operations: it was far enough from the Commonwealth's bases to be reasonably safe but close enough to England's main trading routes to allow royalist ships to wreak havoc on the commerce of London. From Kinsale, on 13/23 March 1649, Prince Rupert wrote to John IV introducing a certain Arnauld de Lisle, the prince's agent in Portugal, who was sent to request large privileges for royalist ships in the ports of Portugal, Madeira, and the Azores: the right to enter and leave at will, the right to revictual and to purchase supplies, and the privilege of selling prizes and prize cargoes in Portuguese ports.[4]

John IV's answer to this overture was friendly and generous. In a letter to Rupert dated 18 May 1649 the king said that Rupert's ships were welcome in Portuguese ports, that they would enjoy the same privileges of securing supplies and victuals as the ships of other friendly nations, and that they would be free to dispose of any goods in Portuguese ports in whatever manner they pleased.[5] The emphasis of the letter is on the fact that Rupert's ships would be treated in the same way as other foreign ships, except that they would have certain special privileges in the sale of prize goods.

Two days later, on 20 May, John IV sent a letter of instructions to the governors in the Algarve, in Viana do Castelo, in North Africa (Tangier and Mazagão), Madeira, and the Azores. Each governor received the same letter; its terms are most interesting and ran as follows:

> If the fleet of my good brother and cousin the King of England comes into any port, or any ship thereof, you will receive them and honor

them with every sign of friendship and joy—and if they wish to sell any goods, or buy any, and wish to remain awhile for this, or for any other reason, you will let them stay for as long as they want, accepting their money and furnishing them with whatever they may need. And if Prince Rupert, the general of the fleet, should come with it, or in any ship, in person, you will treat him with the respect due to him and make sure he is so treated and served, advising me of his arrival, or of the arrival of his ships should they come without him.[6]

Nothing in this document authorized a local governor to allow the royalists to conduct forays on English shipping from the sanctuary of a Portuguese port, yet this was the sense in which Rupert seemed to interpret the concessions granted by John IV. The Portuguese government did not invite, or even think about, a struggle with the revolutionary Commonwealth of England; they merely extended what they took to be a temporary courtesy to Rupert's ships. Yet the terms of that courtesy, as expressed by the king to his own officials, invited abuse: Rupert was to come when he pleased, buy what he wanted, sell what he wished without any awkward inquiries into the origins of his prize goods, and stay for as long as he liked.

By October 1649 the growing strength of the Commonwealth fleet had made Rupert's position in Kinsale untenable. On 20/30 October, after Blake had been forced to lift the blockade because of storm damage to his ships, Rupert sailed for Portugal with seven ships.[7] The prince was confident of a good reception in Lisbon, for John IV had even agreed to lighten the customs duties in his favor. Rupert's ships scoured the seas for prizes, and five were taken, three of which—the *John Adventure* (later renamed the *Second Charles*), *Hopeful Adventure,* and *Roebuck*—were brought into Lisbon, which was not reached until about 10 December 1649.[8]

The officials at Lisbon received a shock when they saw Rupert's prizes: the English merchants in Lisbon and perhaps even the Portuguese merchants owned cargoes aboard some of these captured ships. Worse than this, the *Roebuck*—freighted by George Batten, William Bird, and John Burr (all English merchants of Lisbon)—had been employed in the service of the king of Portugal, for she had, at John IV's request, picked up colonists in the Azores and taken them to Maranhão.[9] The ship had been on her way back when Rupert seized her. These misgivings were set aside for a few days while the two princes, Rupert and his brother Maurice, were "receaved and entertayn'd with all possible expressions of love & friendshippe."[10] The royalist ships, originally anchored within the Tagus at the Bay of Oeiras, were invited to anchor closer to Lisbon, at the Tower of Belém, which policed the entry and exit of ships to and from the port of Lisbon.[11] At Belém, facing King Manuel's magnificent Hieronymite church and monastery (*Mosteiro dos Jerónimos*), the princes went ashore.

The royalists, with the help of Arnauld de Lisle, secured certain guarantees from the Portuguese: (1) Rupert was to have sole jurisdiction over the adjudication of prizes; (2) the Portuguese were not to carry out any inquiries into the titles of any prizes; and (3) if any parliamentary ships appeared in Lisbon, they were to be detained by the Portuguese for at least three days after the departure of Rupert's ships.[12] At this early stage both sides, apparently, were thinking of having to deal with two or three Commonwealth ships; neither seemed to anticipate the possibility of having to oppose a powerful fleet. After the negotiations, Rupert, without consulting the Portuguese, ordered some of his ships, under the command of Prince Maurice, to sail out of the Tagus and attack English vessels off the coast of Portugal.

The king's ministers were alarmed, even outraged. The *Roebuck* had been taken within sight of the Rock of Lisbon.[13] Now Rupert was making war on English shipping, frightening away all foreign commerce from the coasts of Portugal, and ruining the Brazil Company's plans for freighting English ships. The prince was behaving with all the irresponsibility of a pirate. On 23 December 1649 the secretary of state, Pedro Vieira da Silva, addressed two sharply worded communications to Rupert. The first said that Prince Maurice's announced expedition to raid shipping from the port of Lisbon could not be allowed and was contrary to the agreement made with Lisle. The princes' use of the port was only that use conceded to all Englishmen; no inquiry would be made into the princes' goods because no inquiry was usually made into the titles of such goods; but *all* Englishmen had the right to use Portuguese ports. English shipping could not be raided from Portuguese ports, because that would involve the ruin of Portuguese trade, would prevent the freighting of English ships for the sugar fleets, and "above all, would compel a very considerable number of English who inhabit the kingdom to abandon it."[14]

Pedro da Silva's second letter concerned the *Roebuck*, explaining why the ship was entitled to John IV's protection: "His Majesty does not wish to damage in any way the rights of the most serene King of Great Britain"[15]—but the ship must be freed. Prince Rupert had his own special way of resolving these issues: aboard his ships he carried the king's Court of Admiralty, who decided the lawfulness of the prize; and since the overriding consideration with the royalists was their chronic shortage of money, their improvised Court of Admiralty almost invariably decided that the captured ship and her cargo were "good prize." Dr. Richard Hart's court ruled that all the prizes taken were lawful, including the *Roebuck*, because the *Roebuck* had refused to salute or acknowledge the royal standard of Charles II flown from the *Constant Reformation's* mainmasthead and therefore must be a parliamentary ship. As for the *Roebuck's* cargo, that portion of it that belonged to the Portuguese, or to "such English as had beene ancient inhabitants in Portugall, and had no trade or commerce with the Rebells of England,"[16] would be released. The royalists composed a letter in Latin defending the decision on the *Roebuck* and sent it to the king.

The royalists' criteria for determining the lawfulness of prize goods made it impossible for the English merchant in Portugal to conduct his business: if he could not trade with the "English rebels," then how could he trade with England at all? And if his ships saluted Charles II's royal standard, the Commonwealth government might confiscate them when they entered an English port.

Rupert's ships, disregarding Portuguese protests, sailed out of Lisbon and attacked a Dutch ship and attempted the capture of another English ship. On 27 January 1650 Pedro da Silva wrote Rupert a letter that virtually invited him to leave Portugal. It listed all the complaints against him, including the violations of the neutrality of the port of Lisbon, and put pressure on him at a vulnerable point: he was told to reload all his cargoes and keep his booty aboard his ships, because prize goods could no longer be sold in Lisbon since merchants with an interest in those goods would prosecute the buyers in the King of Portugal's courts.[17] This threat may have frightened away purchasers of the captured commodities and endangered Rupert's source of income.

Rupert was in no hurry to leave Lisbon. He had many matters to attend to. His prizes had been taken to a point between Belém and Lisbon, where they were cleaned, supplied, and outfitted as men-of-war.[18] After the Portuguese protest of 27 January 1650 the troublesome prince may have promised to behave; if so, he did not keep his promise, but he was allowed to stay. The weeks dragged into months and still the royalists remained. Reports reached Portugal of powerful naval preparations in England. The Portuguese secretary of state, on 18 March 1650, ordered the prince to leave. Nothing in the negotiations with Lisle, said Pedro da Silva, suggested that Rupert intended spending four months in Lisbon with a powerful fleet, frightening away commerce, damaging Portuguese interests, and seizing prizes in Portuguese waters. The Lisbon government reminded Rupert that foreign warships could only be admitted into Portuguese ports in small numbers, no more than four at a time, and then permitted to stay for only fifteen or twenty days, and allowed in solely for the purpose of buying supplies and revictualling. From henceforth these conditions were to apply to Rupert. He was not to bring into Portuguese ports any prize taken in territorial waters.[19]

This protest came very tardily. Two days later General-at-Sea Robert Blake, with fifteen fighting ships, sailed into the Bay of Cascais. The Commonwealth fleet had come to try conclusions with the Palatine prince. Rupert had arrived in Lisbon about 10 December 1649; Blake anchored in the Cascais roadstead on 20 March 1650, exactly 100 days later. During these 100 days, the prince had had every opportunity and inducement to leave Lisbon and escape into the Mediterranean or South Atlantic, but he had not done so. His procedures and conduct embroiled the Portuguese in a war they had not sought, with a power with whom they had no quarrel, and, quite possibly, this was what Rupert intended.

Early in December 1649, London knew of Rupert's presence in Portuguese waters, and Parliament ordered Blake to go to Portsmouth and assemble a squadron with the object of pursuing him. The Council of State decided that Blake's ships should take an envoy to Spain. Spain was the only country in Europe that seemed to be friendly, and that was only because her enemies France and Portugal had become hostile to the Commonwealth. In January 1650 the council appointed Antony Ascham to be the resident in Madrid.[20]

The merchants in London suggested that an agent also be sent to Lisbon—someone who could negotiate on commercial matters as well as on the political issues in controversy. The council saw the wisdom of this suggestion and appointed Charles Vane, brother of Sir Henry Vane of the Committee on the Admiralty and Navy, to be agent to Portugal, with a salary of £800 per year. Parliament decided on 30 January /9 February 1650, the first anniversary of the execution of Charles I, that foreign powers should address the republic under the style "*Parliamentum Reipublicae Angliae,*" "The Parliament of the Commonwealth of England," and Ascham and Vane were instructed to insist on this form.[21]

In the meantime, Blake was furnished with £3,000 in Spanish money, £1,000 in English money, and letters of credit for £10,000. These last were partly arranged through Edward Bushell of London, who instructed his brother, John Bushell of Lisbon, to supply Blake and Charles Vane with Portuguese money. Blake was ordered to destroy the "revolted fleet," and was authorized to engage any foreign ship assisting Rupert; Blake was also to demand that other vessels salute the flag of the Commonwealth.[22]

On 24 February/6 March 1650 the Parliament addressed a formal letter to the king of Portugal protesting the activities of Prince Rupert and making the following appeal: "We again and again request Your Majesty, that you command those Pyrates and Revolters to depart the Territories of Portugal."[23] The next day the Speaker of the House of Commons, William Lenthall, in a letter to Blake, urged the naval commander to make all possible haste. Four days later, on 1/11 March 1650, the fleet sailed from Cowes, with Blake in the flagship *George* (fifty-seven guns) accompanied by fourteen other men-of-war, as well as by some merchantmen on their way to the Mediterranean.[24]

After ten days, on 10/20 March 1650, shortly before midday, the fleet arrived at the Bay of Cascais, six miles west-northwest of the mouth of the Tagus. The Mediterranean-bound ships separated from the main fleet, and Antony Ascham, who was aboard one of them, reached Puerto Santa María in Spain six days later.[25] In Lisbon, some seventeen miles from Cascais, John IV was informed of the arrival of "twenty-four" English ships, and he commanded São Julião and the other river forts to fire on the parliamentary ships if they attempted to enter the Tagus River.[26] Orders not to admit the ships of the Commonwealth were sent to all ports in Portugal. This reception was rather different from that which had been given to Rupert. Blake sent Charles Thorowgood, captain of the *George,* ashore at Cascais to find out if Rupert was still in Lisbon. Thorowgood was informed that the prince's ships were still in the Tagus, so he immediately returned to the *George* to tell Blake,[27] and Blake dispatched a junior officer, together with a merchant, to Lisbon with a letter for the king. This letter urged that piracy should be exterminated and requested permission for Parliament's ships to make a direct attack on Rupert.[28] All of this happened before nightfall. After dark, Blake was visited by Capt. Richard Ell of the merchantman *Prosperous*—one of nine English merchant ships in Lisbon Harbor that were freighted to sail with the Brazil Company's next fleet—and Ell reported that Rupert had eleven ships in Lisbon, some of them in no condition to fight.[29]

The next day Blake held a council of war with his captains and they decided to enter the river immediately, with the first good wind, and—ignoring all Portuguese opposition—attack Rupert's ships at their anchorage in Belém.[30] The most important element in this decision was the factor of *surprise*, for Rupert's ships were reported to be inadequately prepared, and John IV's Armada Real was in no condition to intervene, since many of its ships had been sent to Brazil. The entry into the Tagus would violate Portuguese neutrality, but the Commonwealth could always apologize to John IV *after* Rupert's fleet had been destroyed. If it had been possible to carry out this decision, both Portuguese and English might have been spared much suffering and loss.

The difficulties in the way were formidable. The chief features of the mouth of the Tagus are two great strips of sandbars and shoals that stretch out to sea in two parallel lines, each over a mile long; between these two lines of sandbars (called *Catchoops* or *Ketchoops* in old English naval charts—a curious rendering of the Portuguese *cachopos* which simply means "shoals") lies a broad deep passage that is the Main Channel, and a safe channel, into the river. Between the north shoals and the fortress of São Julião, which juts out into the sea from the north shore, there is a narrow but deep channel, the Cascais Channel, the most direct route between Cascais and the Tagus. Between the south shoals and the south shore there is a narrow and shallow channel, useless for navigation except by small boats.

MAP 2. THE COAST OF PORTUGAL

LISBON-SETUBAL AREA

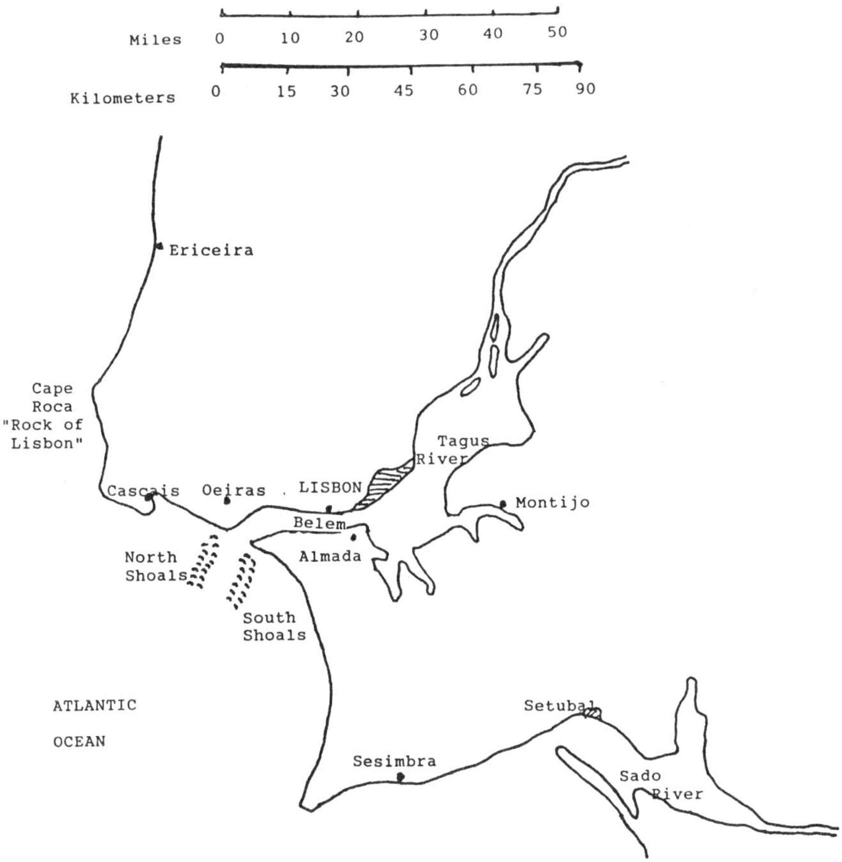

São Julião Fortress, built on a point of land that projects out into the sea and river, commands the northern approaches to the river entrance on three sides; its guns (over one hundred of them, according to Blake's seamen) covered the seaward approaches, the river entrance itself, and a part of the upriver zone and completely dominated the Cascais Channel. The second fortress, the *Tôrre de Bugio*—called the Wooden Fort[31] or the "other fort" by Blake's men—was built on an outcrop of rocks in the southern line of shoals, near the entrance to the river where the modern lighthouse now stands. The guns of this strong fortress covered wide arcs of sea and river, and, in theory, the intersecting fire from São Julião and Bugio should have stopped any ship from entering or leaving the river; in practice, given a good wind, a ship could have entered or left without too much danger.[32]

What damaged the effectiveness of these two forts was the great distance between them: about 2,530 yards separated São Julião from Bugio. A ship sailing down the middle of the Main Channel was 1,200 yards away from the guns of either fort *at the most dangerous point*. The great guns of the seventeenth century had a point-blank or level range of only about 360 paces and a maximum range (almost useless in practice) of under 4,000 paces.[33] At 1,200 yards a siege gun, carefully aimed at the same point, could batter down a wall but could achieve little against a moving ship. To sink a ship, by staving in her hull, point-blank range was required.

Of all the admirals of that day, Blake had perhaps the best understanding of the ineffectiveness of coastal ordnance when used against warships. When his ships sailed up the Main Channel toward the mouth of the Tagus on the afternoon of 11/21 March 1650 he was not greatly apprehensive of the guns of São Julião and Bugio. The "impregnability" of São Julião was an invention of latter-day historians; those whose security depended on these forts knew that they were ineffective unless supported by galleons stationed in mid-stream.[34]

When the English ships approached the river entrance the two forts opened fire. Minutes later the wind had failed completely. The ships drifted out of range and then anchored. São Julião had fired eleven shots and Bugio four—none had fallen near the ships. With darkness coming on, and without wind, the attempt to sail up the Tagus was given up.[35] The opportunity had been lost and could never

MAP 3. TAGUS ESTUARY FORTIFICATIONS 1650

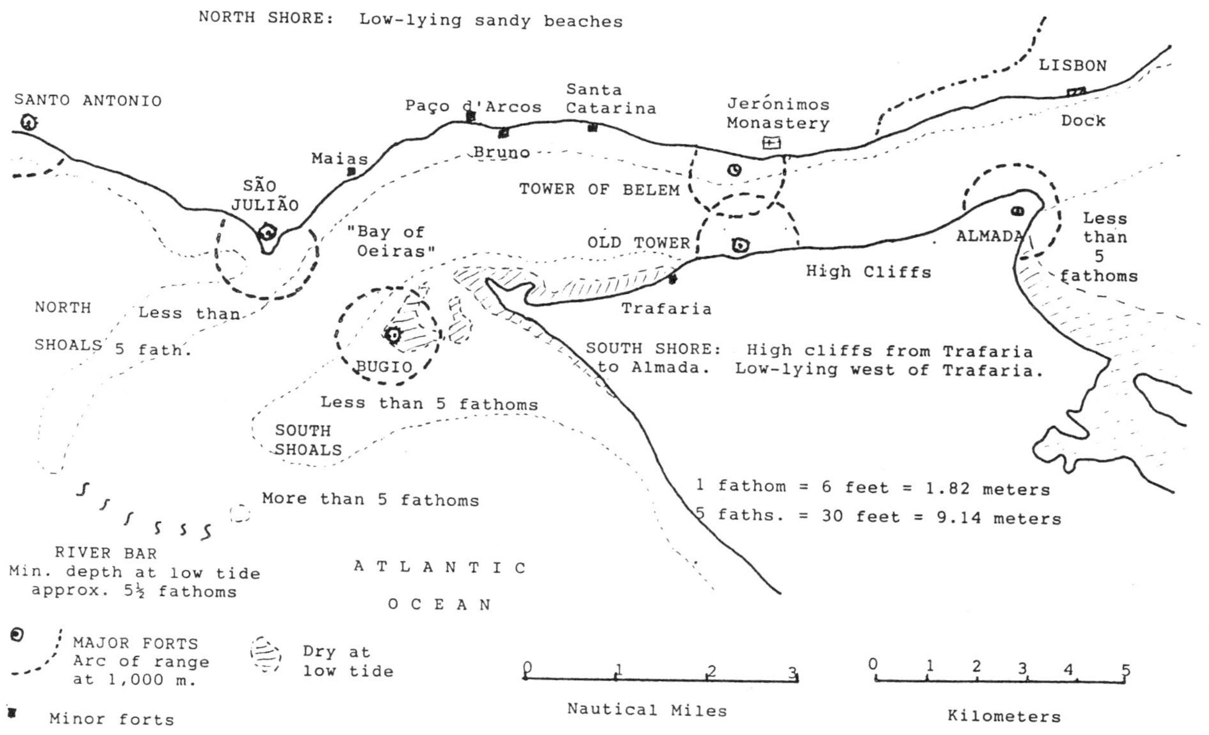

be regained. The attempt could not be repeated because Rupert and the Portuguese had now been thoroughly forewarned: the royalist and Portuguese warships would be armed as quickly as possible, the river forts fully manned and supplied, and small boats could even stretch chains and cables between the Tôrre de Belém and the Tôrre Velha ("Old Tower"), the two forts on opposite sides of the Tagus that guarded the narrowest part of the river (about 1,770 yards wide at that point).

From the unsuccessful attempt to force the Tagus on 11/21 March 1650 until the time of real decision beginning about 31 May/10 June 1650, there were eighty days of indecision and hesitation, during which a "cold war" or a kind of *Sitzkrieg* prevailed, a condition forced on the belligerent parliamentarians by the natural unwillingness of the Portuguese to choose sides in this alien quarrel.

This period of inactivity was preceded by a war of words. Prince Rupert, who at one time had drawn up a Latin memorial accusing the Portuguese of bad faith but had been persuaded not to publish it,[36] issued a "Declaration of Prince Rupert to the Kingdom of Portugal, Concerning the Coming of the English Fleet of Rebels into the River and Port of Lisbon,"[37] which was circulated in Lisbon a few days after Blake's attempt to enter the river. The "Declaration" was a terse and effective statement. It began by denouncing the "regicide" and "the insolent and horrid proceedings of the rebel party in England, commonly known by the name of Parliamentary," suggested that the habit of killing kings might spread to other countries, and warned foreign princes "lest the fire now kindled in England may come to their own doors." After this appeal to the common ground of royalism, Rupert told the Portuguese that the real aim of Parliament's fleet was to help the Spaniards conquer Portugal: "There is some design between these people and the Castilians, against the peace of this kingdom [i.e., Portugal]." Parliament had sent an agent to Spain (so, of course, had Charles II, but this is left out of the declaration); the agent for Portugal was a mere afterthought, brought about through the contrivance of the untrustworthy Bushell brothers, one of whom was in Lisbon and two in London. The declaration went on to denounce John Bushell for having entertained Blake's representatives in his Lisbon house, and Mr. Tatam and Mr. Ell[38] for having visited Blake's ships without the knowledge or permission of John IV. The declaration closed with an attack on Blake for having tried to force his way upriver and denounced the parliamentarians as rebels and sea robbers, who were carrying on a blockade of Lisbon Harbor.

The parliamentarians drafted a reply to Rupert's declaration and tried to circulate it in Lisbon—but it was not a success. The Portuguese were not prepared to listen to Parliament's defense of the execution of Charles I, nor would they allow such a statement to circulate freely in Lisbon. Parliament's reply was couched in the abusive language employed in the controversial literature of the day. Rupert's declaration was denounced as "filthy & scurrilous Rhetorick" and its author called a "vagabond German, a Prince of fortune, whose highnes is nothing else but haughtiness, his Principality mere piracye."[39]

The arguments of both sides, however fiercely phrased, were unlikely to influence the attitudes of the Portuguese government. John IV and his ministers were ruled by one consideration: how to extricate their country from her difficulties with the least possible damage. John IV's policy, in this matter, was in line with his general philosophy of government, which was to temporize, to postpone decision until some new and unforeseen development made decision painless or unnecessary; and if circumstances should eventually force a decision, the king was prepared to commit himself fully and firmly to whatever policy he was driven to adopt.

During these difficult weeks of 1650 the time factor seemed to be working for Rupert and the Portuguese and against Blake. Two circumstances account for this: (1) powerful French assistance, of which the parliamentarians stood in dread, was confidently expected by the royalists, who believed that a strong French fleet might appear in the Tagus any day; and (2) the Portuguese slowly and carefully worked to deny Blake's ships supplies, victuals, and even water, hoping to force his fleet out by depriving it of essentials. The time factor, seemingly so hostile to Blake's plans, in the end began to turn in his favor. For only two French warships actually reached Lisbon to help Rupert, while Blake was strongly reinforced and supplied by a new squadron sent to help him. Moreover, the Portuguese began to be troubled by the difficulty of protecting the returning sugar fleet, which, according to the original instructions,[40] was expected to arrive off Portugal about August 1650. But what would happen if the Commonwealth's fleet was still sailing off the coast of Portugal when the sugar ships arrived? The problem of how to get the Brazil fleet home safely, or of how long to postpone its return voyage, troubled the Portuguese government throughout the spring and summer of 1650. Time became an ally of the Commonwealth: the Portuguese must try to dispose of Rupert before the season for the return of the all-important sugar fleet.

The initial relations between Blake and the Portuguese government were quite friendly. The day after the Portuguese forts had fired on Blake's ships a Portuguese official came aboard the English flagship, the *George*, and apologized for the incident but reminded the parliamentarians that John IV had not given permission for them to enter the river. He also requested the English to move their ships farther out to seaward and stop blocking the Main Channel into the Tagus—but Blake kept his ships anchored in the channel for the next seven days, deliberately threatening the free movement of ships into the river. Four days later, on 16/26 March 1650, the Portuguese again asked the English to move their ships out to seaward, because otherwise, they said, Rupert could not leave the harbor. In reply Blake demanded of King John whether the parliamentarians were to be received as friends or not—and if they were to be received as friends, then Blake wanted permission to enter the river.[41]

On 14/24 March the king had appointed João Mendes de Vasconcelos to negotiate with the English.[42] Dom Francisco de Faro e Noronha, seventh Count of Odemira, president of the Overseas Council, and one of the most important men in the government, intervened in these negotiations with a view to placating the potentially dangerous parliamentarians. On 18/28 March, Vasconcelos and Charles Vane met in Odemira's house and came to a provisional understanding. The agreement they signed had five points: (1) the English ships were not to enter the river without John IV's permission *in writing*; (2) if the weather turned foul, Blake's ships would be permitted to enter the river and anchor at Oeiras, near the mouth of the Tagus, but were not to proceed farther upriver; (3) Blake's ships were not to engage in hostilities except in self-defense; (4) when the weather turned fair the ships were to withdraw to outside São Julião; and (5) the crews of the ships were to remain aboard at all times.[43]

The royalists attacked Odemira for bargaining with "regicides" and accused him of being a tool of the Commonwealth. Warburton, Rupert's biographer, said that the "Conde de Miro" was heavily bribed by Blake.[44] But bribes were hardly necessary: the Portuguese conceded nothing to Blake that he could not have obtained himself with the use of only a little force—and, in return, the threatened blockade of the port was lifted and the Portuguese secured, in addition, Blake's promise that he would not proceed farther upriver without John IV's written consent. Odemira had tried to guarantee, for at least a time, Rupert's safety, but the royalists felt endangered.

The day the agreement was signed was quite stormy. Blake took advantage of this fact, and at nightfall, guided by a Portuguese pilot, the English ships sailed up to the Bay of Oeiras and dropped anchor there.[45] Three or four miles upriver Rupert's ships lay at anchor, huddled for protection under the guns of the Tower of Belém. Two or three days later the king expressed a wish to negotiate with a person of quality to be designated by Blake; presumably Charles Vane was deemed of insufficient "quality" when measured against the Palatine princes on the other side of the argument. Blake summoned his officers together aboard the *George* on 23 March/2 April 1650, and they chose Robert Moulton, vice admiral of the fleet, to represent Parliament and agreed that Moulton should abide by the following instructions: First, he was to demand that John IV deliver up Rupert's ships as property belonging to the Commonwealth. If the reply to this was unfavorable, he was to demand, second, that the Commonwealth fleet be permitted to enter the port and attack Rupert or, third, the Portuguese should set a date for both fleets to leave the Tagus together and, if Rupert refused to leave, then Blake would be free to attack Rupert in the port. Fourth, Parliament asked for the privilege of anchoring anywhere in the river, on the understanding that they would not engage in hostilities unless attacked. Last, Moulton was to assure the king of Portugal of the friendship of the Commonwealth and present the Portuguese government with Parliament's answer to the charges contained in Rupert's declaration.[46]

That same evening Moulton went ashore and had a four-hour conference with Odemira and other officials. The Portuguese wanted Blake to let Rupert's ships leave the harbor and then wait three days before following him, but Moulton would not agree to this. The Portuguese told Moulton that his requests would have to be discussed by the government and that he would receive an answer in due course. No answer had been received by 29 March/8 April when

Blake drafted his reports to London.[47] Charles Vane, writing on 3/13 April to William Lenthall, the Speaker of the House of Commons, also had nothing positive to report. Vane said that he had spent seven or eight days in Lisbon and had seen the king twice and remarked of the Portuguese that "their carriage hitherto is pretty fair, and they seem to grow weary of Prince Rupert's fleet."[48]

These dispatches reached London with remarkable speed, aboard a swift ketch (whose master received a ten-pound reward from the Council of State), and were read in Parliament on 11/21 April 1650.[49] The next day the Speaker wrote acknowledgments to Blake and Vane; in his letter to Blake he regretted that "want of wind" had prevented Parliament's ships from falling on Rupert but added: "Yet we doubt not but a fit opportunity will be offered you."[50] The London politicians were ill-pleased by the lack of activity in Lisbon and busied themselves with preparing a new fleet to be sent to Portugal, under General-at-Sea Edward Popham, who would convey new and militant instructions to Blake. At that moment the Council of State was apprehensive of the possibility of French intervention, and they made speed to dispatch Popham to Blake's relief.

In the meantime the Portuguese had to deal with Rupert. The royalists argued that John IV should carry on no negotiations of any kind with the parliamentarians because they were rebels and because only Charles II represented the legitimate government of Great Britain. The Portuguese reply was obvious: the interests of Portugal required King John to negotiate with whatever government was in effective control of England. This was the kind of answer that Charles I had made to Philip IV of Spain in 1641, when the Spaniards had complained of London's dealings with the Portuguese "rebels." John IV received a memorial from Thomas Eliot, gentleman of the Privy Chamber of Charles II, dated 9/19 March 1650, which made four requests: (1) that the treaty of 1642 be confirmed, (2) that privileges in the 1642 treaty were not to be extended to rebels, (3) that John IV should admit no ambassadors or agents from the London rebels, and (4) that the agreement made with Arnauld de Lisle should be confirmed and enforced. Pedro Vieira da Silva replied from the royal palace, on 21 April 1650, as follows: there was no need for reconfirmation of the 1642 treaty, because it was perpetual and had not been abrogated by the death of Charles I; as to points 2 and 3, the "martyred" Charles I had understood that Portugal must remain neutral in English quarrels and had never favored a Portuguese break with London (hence, by implication, the treaty of 1642 also governed Portuguese relations with the parliamentarians); and as for the Lisle agreement, Pedro da Silva said that it was to be understood according to the modified terms of subsequent arrangements made with Rupert.[51]

The Portuguese case for treating with the rebels was strengthened by the fact that Rupert had behaved irresponsibly, without provocation, *before* the arrival of Blake, whereas Blake—who among the privateering seamen of that day was a model of patience, moderation, and goodwill—had conducted himself with restraint, even in the face of enemy provocations. On Good Friday, 15 April 1650 (by the Portuguese calendar), two French men-of-war entered the Tagus and anchored among Blake's ships in Oeiras, mistaking them for Rupert's ships; Blake promptly seized the warships, but the Portuguese protested and Charles Vane induced Blake to release them—and they were set free on Monday and allowed to join Rupert.[52] The two ships were later used against Blake. On 21 April 1650 the Commonwealth commander allowed the Portuguese squadron to India to sail out of Lisbon unmolested. It consisted of four galleons and one caravel under the command of a new viceroy of India, João da Silva Telo de Meneses, the Count of Aveiras.[53]

Throughout April and May the royalists in Lisbon gloomily debated whether or not they could afford the risk of a sudden attack on Blake's ships. They posted men on the land overlooking his ships and skirmished with parliamentarians who came ashore to get water. The Portuguese began to stiffen their position against both royalists and parliamentarians. In a letter dated 15/25 April 1650 Charles Vane protested to John IV a decision forbidding any more English warships from entering the river, a decision that prevented Blake from being revictualled and resupplied from England. Vane also complained that Rupert's men had seized four of Blake's seamen and carried them aboard the royalist ships.[54] A few days later John IV ordered Rupert to leave Lisbon, on the understanding that the Portuguese would hold Blake's ships in the Tagus for three days. Rupert knew well enough that the Portuguese would never be able to hold Blake for three days against his will. In a melancholy letter written aboard the *Constant Reformation* on 4 May 1650, the prince Palatine sadly thanked the king for past favors and, as always, alluded to the Lisle agreement and its provision for the three whole days in which to escape the parliamentarians, about which the prince wrote:

> Your Majesty's ministers and our enemies deceive Your Majesty. May God dispose of us and of our fleet according to His will, for we are resolved to leave with the first good wind; and if, because of the violation of the said agreement, the fleet should be lost and ruined, I hereby lay at Your Majesty's door (and the respect I have for Your Majesty makes me regret having to do so) the responsibility for whatever loss occurs, maintaining that its cause will stem from the breaking of the agreement by Your Majesty and Your Majesty's ministers.[55]

In his closing sentences Rupert lashed out at the ministers hostile to the royalists and ended the letter with these words: "There is no need to name them, for Your Majesty well knows who they are."

Pedro da Silva sent Rupert a curt reply (6 May 1650) assuring him that John IV *would* hold Blake in the Tagus for the three days: "You may rest easy because you will not be offended on this point."[56] Rupert was told that the king's ministers were not to blame in anything and that a full report would be sent to Charles II. In a letter written the next day Pedro da Silva told Rupert that John IV believed that every effort had been made to assure his safety and that, in any event, the king was not responsible for the security of the royalist fleet, which had been asked to leave long before Blake's ships arrived.[57]

Rupert delayed and did not leave. On Saturday, 10/20 May 1650, at four o'clock in the afternoon, two Negroes and an Englishman in a small boat, pretending to be Portuguese peddlers selling casks of oil, tried to plant a barrel with a bomb aboard Blake's vice admiral's ship, *Leopard.* The men in the boat found the stern ports of the ship closed, so they rowed round to the transom port where, in the act of putting their bomb barrel aboard, the Englishman was recognized as a royalist and the three men were seized. At the same time there was a skirmish ashore (possibly to distract the attention of the ships's crews), in which some men from the *Bonadventure,* while they were getting water, were ambushed by the royalists, suffering one seaman killed, five wounded, and three taken prisoner.[58]

In the middle of May, while still awaiting Popham's fleet, Admiral Blake, if he had lost patience with the royalists, was still restrained in his dealings with the Portuguese. On 21/31 May (or possibly the next day) Blake allowed a Portuguese galleon from the East Indies to enter the Tagus unmolested and pass upriver to Lisbon. For his failure to seize her Blake was rebuked by his superiors in London who imagined that the East Indiaman was worth £250,000.[59]

As the crisis over Rupert became acute, tension gripped the Portuguese government. The king's ministers and advisers split into two camps. The Count of Odemira, in a memorial to the king, put forward the policy of breaking with Rupert, or at least pressuring Rupert to extricate himself from his own dilemma. Odemira argued that neither the 1642 treaty nor the agreement with Lisle obliged the Portuguese government to abandon a course of strict neutrality in its dealings with royalists and parliamentarians. The princes had been well warned to leave the port, they had had many weeks during which they could have done so, and so the king was not obligated to attempt to detain Blake's ships for the stipulated three days. Portugal could not afford to fight both Spain and England; to do so might mean the loss of the sugar fleet, valued at 2 million *cruzados* (about £400,000). Portugal must consider the Dutch danger in Brazil and must assume that France, torn by civil wars (the *Frondes*), might avoid giving Portugal any help. Odemira suggested that the king must ask himself why he should risk everything for princes who were neither of his blood nor of his religion. As for the Stuarts, said Odemira, their restoration in England would not be possible for many years.[60]

This pragmatic and realistic approach—although partly supported by one or two persons, such as the Anglophile José Pinto Pereira of the Overseas Council—was highly unpopular in John IV's court. Against it were ranged Queen Luisa, Prince Theodosius (the heir apparent), most of the clergy, and such influential men as António de Sousa de Macedo,[61] the former Portuguese agent in London. In the center of the argument, uncertain and of a divided mind, stood the king, who perhaps would have preferred to follow Odemira's policy, but in a very cautious way. Odemira's opponents argued from principle: the king could not break faith with Charles II, for that would be an attack on royalty itself, a repudiation of legitimacy and order. The clergy saw the issue in terms of black and white: "There is to be found in our port . . .the purest justice counterbalanced against the greatest evil." If Blake would not agree to the three-day leeway for Rupert, then his ships should be attacked and destroyed. All English merchant ships in Portuguese ports, said the clergymen, should be seized—for it was thought that there were almost sixty English ships that could be taken, and this would increase the strength of Portugal while crippling the English. Such a policy was not immoral or illicit, because the parliamentarians were "outlaws, rebels, semi-pagans."[62]

The sixteen-year-old Prince Theodosius—who was, in Boxer's phrase, "mystical (and probably slightly unbalanced)"[63]—took an interest in the royalists and wrote a Latin memorial in their favor. Theodosius, who was much under the influence of his Jesuit tutors, met Rupert several times but insisted on carrying on religious disputations, with a view toward converting Rupert to Catholicism.[64]

While arguments over policy divided the ministers, the government took practical steps to guarantee the security of the capital. They summoned three detachments of infantry from the army of the Alentejo and 200 cavalry for the defense of Lisbon. Additional forces were sent to Cascais, Setúbal, and Peniche.[65] The important coastal fortifications in the Cascais area were placed under the command of the Count of Cantanhede.[66] The Armada Real was increased and readied for battle. As early as March 1650 the Lisbon Municipal Chamber carried out an inspection of the city walls with its forty gates and recommended that eighteen gates be closed up and two gates rebuilt. The remaining twenty gates were found to be in good condition. The king's decree of 27 May 1650 named Dom Álvaro de Abranches, a colonel in the Council of War, as officer in charge of the repair and construction of fortifications. The city of Lisbon alone spent 7:708$669 réis (about £3,850) from its municipal funds for the repair of walls and forts.[67]

The quarrel between royalist and parliamentarian, so unhappily exported to Portugal, also split the English merchant community in Lisbon. Some merchants were passionately attached to one side or the other; some others were necessarily involved in the business of supplying Rupert or Blake and doing business with the two fleets; one or two others, of great prominence, might have been consulted by John IV, by Rupert, or by Charles Vane; but the majority of English merchants preferred to keep out of the dispute. Unluckily for this neutral majority, when John IV decided to imprison the English merchants and confiscate their property, they suffered the same fate as the strongest parliamentarians, for when the king threw in his lot with Rupert, only *active* royalists were spared.

Charles Vane, in a clumsy maneuver, called the Lisbon merchants together and tried to obtain their signatures to a parliamentary petition to be addressed to John IV. This document, conceived rather late in the day (the end of May 1650), was perhaps watered down to make it palatable to the neutralists and closed with a naive appeal to the king: "Your Majesty . . . in your wisdom find out a way to free your ports of both these fleets."[68] In spite of its innocuous language, only strong parliamentarians could be induced to sign it, and only thirteen of them did so. It can be assumed that the following thirteen merchants who did sign were the most dedicated adherents of the Commonwealth in Lisbon: Richard Beare, William Bird, John Bushell, Barnaby Crawford, Joseph Dorney, George Lane, John Lott, William Milward, Jeremy Onge, William Pennington, John Randolph, William Warren, and John Wilmott.

Of the parliamentarians, John Bushell was by far the most active and important. He helped Charles Vane, provided Blake with Portuguese money, arranged credit for the Commonwealth fleet, and helped to victual it. He was singled out for denunciation in Rupert's declaration and, on his return to England, became closely connected with Cromwell's government. Bushell was assisted and seconded by his close associates Richard Beare and William Bird, both of whom were important merchants in their own right. The young Barnaby Crawford, an assistant in the commercial company run by the ardent royalist Robert Cocke, was a parliamentarian in spite of his employer's convictions. In later years, particularly, Crawford served the Commonwealth fleets as a victualler and an Anglo-Portuguese interpreter. He became one of the more important English merchants in Lisbon. John Randolph, Robert Cocke's brother-in-law, was also one of Blake's victuallers. Randolph, together with William Milward and John Witheridge (a mild parliamentarian who did not sign the aforementioned petition), testified in London in 1651 about the activities of the royalist merchants in Lisbon. The Council of State mentioned William Milward (with Bushell and Beare) in an order to Blake and Popham, and this appears to indicate that Milward played an important part in aiding the Commonwealth. Of the parliamentary merchants, four at least seem to have abandoned their residence in Lisbon after their release from Portuguese prisons: John Bushell, William Milward, John Randolph, and John Witheridge.

Knowledge about the activities of the royalist merchants is contained in a report submitted by the Judges of Admiralty to "The Right Hono'ble the Committee of the Councell of State for Carrying on the Affaires of th' Admiraltie," in October 1651,[69] a report based on the testimony of Randolph, Milward, and Witheridge. It implicated eight Lisbon merchants: William Bennett, Humphrey Burr, John Burr, Robert Cocke, Henry Erbury, Francis Hanbury, James Holcraft, and John Mules.

According to John Witheridge, Robert Cocke was the most active of the Lisbon royalists: "The said Cock was the chiefe man that acted for Prince Rupert." He was "a very violent and disaffected man against the Parliament."[70] He arranged for the sale of the royalist prize goods, revictualled the royalist fleet, and outfitted a fireship and a man-of-war for Rupert. Witheridge's testimony was corroborated, years later, in a letter from Sir John Mennes to Sir Richard Fanshaw (17/27 April 1663), Charles II's ambassador extraordinary to Portugal: "He [Cocke] has always been faithful to the King, and did and suffered more for him when Prince Rupert was at Lisbon than the whole body of merchants."[71]

The great conflict between royalists and parliamentarians split Cocke's own personal associates into two camps. Two other merchants lived in Cocke's Lisbon home: William Bennett, who was an active royalist, and John Randolph, married to Cocke's sister, an active parliamentarian. In addition to this division within Cocke's own household, there was a further division among Cocke's business associates: his partner, Henry Erbury, a Catholic resident in Lisbon for ten years, married to John Mules's daughter, was an ardent royalist; but Cocke's assistant, young Barnaby Crawford, was a parliamentarian.[72]

John Mules was probably as much pro-Portuguese as he was pro-royalist. After war broke out between Portugal and the Commonwealth, Mules seemed to have worked to heal the breach between Lisbon and London. His son-in-law, Henry Erbury, who was an active royalist, owned sugar and tobacco on the *Roebuck*, the ship from Maranhão that Rupert had imprudently seized. James Holcraft, a Catholic mariner and merchant resident in Lisbon for twenty years, was one of Rupert's victuallers and was said to have served as Rupert's pilot when the prince sailed down the Tagus.[73]

According to John Witheridge's testimony, three other merchants—Humphrey Burr, John Burr, and Francis Hanbury—talked against the Parliament and drank the health of Charles II but otherwise did nothing to help Rupert. The deponents at the London inquiry also thought that three captains—Peter Tatam of the *Hannibal*, Edward Wye of the *Sapphire*, and Ambrose Chappell of the *John and Mary* (all English ships in Lisbon waiting to sail to Brazil)—had pro-royalist sympathies. These men, nicknamed "King" Tatam, "Prince" Wye, and "Duke" Chappel by the Commonwealth sailors, were accused of going aboard Rupert's ships, kissing his hand and deceiving Blake about Rupert's naval strength, which they represented as greater than it actually was.

From December 1649 until April 1650 the situation in Lisbon remained deadlocked—the conflicts involving politicians, churchmen, merchants, and seamen were almost always verbal. But during the last days of May and the first days of June, deeds replaced words and the argument was engulfed in the rush of events.

The first new moves came from England, where the relief squadron to reinforce Blake lay at Plymouth, ready to sail. During the afternoon of 14/24 May 1650, General-at-Sea Edward Popham, in the *Resolution*, shot off a warning piece and loosed his foretopsail to signal the fleet to prepare to depart. At three o'clock the next morning, nine ships weighed anchor and sailed down Plymouth Sound, bound for Portugal. There were four men-of-war, four chartered merchantmen serving as warships, and a victualler.[74]

Popham took with him a letter of additional instructions to Blake that urged him to press the case against Rupert more forcibly. The Portuguese must be brought to realize that Rupert's ships were the actual property of the Commonwealth: the royalists "as fugitives and renegadoes have run away with the said ships, and in the same as pirates and sea-robbers they have exercised and made depredations and spoils." They were such persons "as have no place in the world which they can pretend to be their own."[75]

Popham's instructions told him to "make your repair with all expedition, wind and weather permitting, into the port of Lisbon." He was to seize all French ships he came across, as retaliation for French attacks on English shipping. If John IV did not give way,

Popham was authorized to "seize, arrest, surprise, and detain"all Portuguese ships. When he joined Blake the two commanders, as Generals-at-Sea, being of equal rank, could work together or separately, as they pleased. As an afterthought an additional recommendation was added to the instructions: if a breach with John IV seemed inevitable, then Charles Vane was to be taken aboard with his papers.[76] Another order permitted Blake and Popham to borrow up to £10,000 from the English merchants in Lisbon.

Popham took eleven days to reach Portugal. The Berlenga Islands (off Peniche) were sighted between nine and ten o'clock on the morning of 26 May/5 June 1650, and that night the fleet came to "Castcalles" (Cascais), where Blake was then anchored. Five days before Popham's arrival, the Brazil Company's second fleet had put to sea; it contained about twenty ships, of which nine were English merchantmen. Blake, who was still apprehensive of the French, needed more ships; with only ten strong ships he would be outnumbered three to one if the Portuguese joined Rupert. So he ordered the seizure of the nine English merchantmen, apprehended them one by one as they cleared the bar of the Tagus, brought them into his own fleet, removed their captains, and reshuffled their crews, adding some of his own men to each of the ships and distributing some of their sailors among the warships.[77]

Admiral Blake, as the representative of a functioning de facto government, had every right to dispose of vessels belonging to his own nationals in whatever ways his government should direct, especially when armed conflict was in prospect and the security of the nation's warships in hazard. As long as he did not interfere with Portuguese shipping, he committed no act of war. But the Portuguese government was outraged. The Count of Odemira found himself in sudden difficulties and was asked for explanations.[78] The anger of John IV's ministers stemmed from the feeling that they had been tricked: like fools the Portuguese had allowed their naval superiority to be whittled away. On 31 May 1650 the Armada Real and the prince's fleet had to contend with only ten English ships, but on 1 June 1650 they were faced with twice that number, and with Popham's squadron in the offing. The Portuguese were left with the bitter reflection that if they had not been "deceived" by the English, they could have manned the nine English merchantmen themselves or turned them over to Rupert.

The nine ships involved were the *Hannibal* (400 tons, sixty-four men at the time of seizure, under Peter Tatam), *Prosperous* (450 tons, seventy men, under Richard Ell), *Sapphire* (380 tons, sixty men, under Edward Wye), *John and Mary* (300 tons, forty-eight men, under Ambrose Chappell), *Mayflower* (300 tons, forty-eight men, under Thomas Bell), *Success* (260 tons, forty-four men, under William Peach), *Samaritan* (250 tons, forty-six men, under Isaac Stephenson), *Reason* (250 tons, forty-four men, under Daniel Crawford), and *Agreement* (250 tons, forty men, under Nicholas Harwood).[79]

On 28 May/7 June 1650, Blake, accompanied by some English merchants, visited Popham aboard the *Resolution*. The Commonwealth commanders then issued a safe-conduct to an English ship from Lisbon, bound for the Azores, taking a Portuguese governor for the island of Terceira. The next day they received a letter from the directors of the General Company of Brazil asking them to do either one of two things: (1) release the chartered English ships under detention or (2) unload the Portuguese cargoes that were aboard them.[80] The Generals-at-Sea declined to give an answer until they had heard from Charles Vane, who was closeted in Lisbon with the king and Odemira and was now, no doubt, under heavy Portuguese pressure.

While the conferences with Vane were still going on, John IV issued orders to the governors of Madeira, Azores, Setúbal, Aveiro, and Viana do Castelo—dated "Lisbon, 8 June 1650"—to detain all English ships found in their areas, on any pretext, keep an eye on English merchants, and make inventories of all English properties.[81] The Portuguese government made a key issue out of the seizure of Portuguese properties aboard the nine merchantmen. The Brazil Company had at least 11:000$000 réis (about £5,500) in silver aboard the ships, as well as many other goods. The truth was that in questions of seizures of ships and properties everyone suffered—Portuguese, parliamentarians, royalists, and neutrals. Nine English merchants in Lisbon, for instance, owned goods aboard the impounded *Hannibal*. John Mules had a one-thirty-second share of the ship and cargo, and other shares were held by Henry Erbury, James Holcraft, Francis Hanbury, James Cotton, Humphrey Burr, Timothy Shorey, Richard Beare, and John Bushell.[82] This roll of names includes men of all persuasions.

The king probably did not tell Charles Vane that a general detention of English ships in Portuguese ports had been ordered but may have hinted at such an action. Vane was impressed, even frightened, by the urgency of the Portuguese demands. When he saw Popham for the first time, on 31 May/10 June, Vane was dismayed when he read Popham's instructions to demand the delivery of Rupert's ships and attack if the Portuguese refused. Vane despaired, there and then, of reaching a settlement, and he decided not to go back ashore. In Popham's words, Vane, "as soon as he had seen our instructions, resolved to return no more."[83]

Vane's reading of Portuguese intentions was perfectly accurate. By Friday, 10 June, when Vane first heard of Popham's instructions, the Portuguese government had already decided to go ahead with the arrest of English merchants and the confiscation of English properties. For on the next day John IV decreed that all the English merchants were to be arrested on Sunday, 12 June, at ten o'clock in the morning (a time calculated to catch the Englishmen off their guard), an inventory of their properties was to be begun immediately, and only seven merchants (including John Mules, Henry Erbury, and Robert Cocke) were exempted from arrest.[84] On 12, 13, and 14 June orders for the detention of Englishmen and sequestration of their goods went out to Brazil, to the commanders of the fleets at sea, and to Viana, Aveiro, Setúbal, and the Algarve.[85] At the same time instructions went out to all ports that Portuguese ships were not to attempt to put in at Lisbon.

The king accepted the fact that the effect of his actions was to put Lisbon under blockade. Efforts were made to strengthen Peniche, which would be used as an alternative port (Peniche is about sixty miles by road from Lisbon), since the much closer port of Setúbal would also be placed under blockade. On 8 June 1650 the king wrote to Dom Diogo de Lima, Count of Vila Nova de Cerveira and governor of the Portuguese army on the northern frontier of the Minho, to place 200 soldiers aboard small caravels and send them to Peniche. The caravels were instructed to hug the coast and sail in the shallow waters, where the larger parliamentary ships could not come after them. All of this was to be done "without losing a single moment."[86] In reality, the entire month was lost. One month later, in a reproachful letter of 9 July, the king censured Cerveira for having done nothing about the soldiers to Peniche, and now there were two

Commonwealth ships stationed off Peniche. The earlier instructions were repeated even more forcibly.[87] No doubt the Count of Cerveira, with only a few men to protect the northern frontiers, felt that Lisbon could afford to garrison Peniche from among its own forces.

On 5/15 June 1650 the parliamentary commanders held a council of war at which it was decided to confront the Portuguese with an ultimatum: either Rupert's ships were surrendered or the Commonwealth would fight. The next day an officer went ashore with this message; John IV was given until 10/20 June to reply.[88] On 8/18 June a small Portuguese vessel sneaked between the English fleet and Cascais and entered the Tagus through the Cascais Channel. Blake issued orders to the ships *Phoenix, Expedition,* and *Providence* to stop any ships from getting within sight of the Rock of Lisbon.[89] The Commonwealth ships, which had definitely abandoned their Oeiras anchorage sometime before, now patrolled a long semicircular line, about fifty-five sea miles in length, stretching from Cape Roca in the north to the mouth of the River Sado in the south, blockading the entrances to Cascais, the Tagus, Sesimbra, and Setúbal.

The day for the king's reply to the ultimatum (10/20 June) came and went without any reply being received. John IV wrote to "Roberto Blac" and "Duarte Popham" on 9/19 June, but the answer did not get to the admirals until nine o'clock in the morning of 11/21 June, when they were in the middle of another council of war. The king's letter was characteristically mild and rather indirect: His Majesty regretted the sudden and unaccountable departure of Charles Vane, which had left no channel of communication open; he wanted Blake to send him a new representative, with whom the points in contention could be settled; there was no need for the parliamentary leaders to be apprehensive about the safety of their agent, because the king himself would guarantee the security of any parliamentary spokesmen.[90] This answer, "being interpreted delusory or at least dilatory," was considered negative, and plans were made accordingly. The naval commanders decided to send Vane to report back to London. They also decided to maintain a strict blockade and seize all Portuguese ships and fishing boats. The swift frigate *Constant Warwick* was sent back with Vane on 13/23 June. On the day she left, sixteen Portuguese fishing boats were seized.[91] The Commonwealth of England was at war with the Kingdom of Portugal.

The fleet commanders had set themselves a difficult task. The ships had to ride in the open sea, completely at the mercy of the weather. The ships were critically short of beverages. The provisions brought by Popham were found to be rotten. "Of eight months' beef and pork in this ship," wrote Popham, "there was not a fortnight's meat fit to eat."[92] The *Tiger, Providence,* and *Cygnet* were sent northward to the Bayona Islands to get water. A strong force of eight warships—the *Happy Entrance, George, Leopard, Adventure, Assurance, Merchant, Tenth Whelp,* and a ketch—under Rear Adm. Richard Badiley—sailed on the night of 13/23 June (or early the next morning) for Cadiz to obtain provisions. They had to go in strength, because there were reports of French ships in the Straits of Gibraltar and it was Blake's intention to keep the French at a distance.[93]

For a few days the Algarve (that is, the south coast of Portugal) attracted all the interest. On 21 June the king sent António Muniz de Carvalho as his agent to the commander of the French ships in the straits. Three days later John IV warned Francisco de Melo, governor of the Algarve, that eight Commonwealth ships were headed in his direction and added: "If they go there, try to get the French to fight them."[94] Before this letter could be delivered, the Commonwealth ships had met four French men-of-war, who tried hard to escape. The frigate *Adventure* caught the slowest of the Frenchmen, sank her after a fierce fifteen-minute fight, and demonstrated the excellence of English gunnery: "Our Frigat gave him four Broad sides, before hee could give too."[95] Meanwhile, off the Tagus, Blake's ships carelessly let another French ship slip into the river (17/27 June 1650).[96]

In the closing days of June the General Company of Brazil, which was threatened with ruin, made its own effort to reach a settlement with the English. On 19/29 June the company sent a message to the ships calling for an agent to come ashore for a conference. The parliamentarians replied that any conferences could be held aboard the ships. The company then secured the services of William Rolls, an English merchant, who went aboard the *Resolution* (then serving as admiral for both Blake and Popham, since Blake's great ship, the *George,* had been sent to Cadiz) and explained the company's position: the company would send representatives aboard the ships if some officers were sent ashore as hostages. Blake refused (20/30 June), saying that the officers were needed aboard their ships.

The next day the company repeated the same offer, only this time the officers to be sent ashore would be covered by the king's personal safe-conduct. Blake replied that any agents coming aboard the Commonwealth's ships would have *his* safe-conduct.[97]

These comic proceedings, in themselves indications of how seriously Anglo-Portuguese relations had deteriorated in the ten days following the answer to the ultimatum, were interrupted while the company's men consulted the king. Meanwhile, Rolls came aboard the ships with nine English seamen, prisoners at Lisbon but released by the Portuguese; the English then released some of their Portuguese captives. On 2/12 July, Rolls went aboard the *Resolution* at four o'clock in the afternoon with the Brazil Company's propositions, which were as follows: (1) the Brazil Company would buy all Rupert's ships and employ them in the company's service, *only*, and not against England; (2) Prince Rupert and Prince Maurice were to be free to go wherever they wanted; and (3) the nine merchantmen freighted for Brazil were to proceed on their voyage. These disarmingly ingenuous suggestions, so beneficial to the interests of the Brazil Company, met the objects of Parliament's expedition at no point. The proposals, in Popham's words, "we rejected and did not think worthy of an answer."[98] This reaction marked the end of the negotiations. The king rewarded William Rolls by returning all his confiscated properties to him.[99]

The Portuguese Armada Real was now ready to join Rupert. It consisted of thirteen ships (four of which seemed to have belonged to the Brazil Company),[100] supported by fireships, caravels, and other small vessels. Rupert had at least six serviceable warships—the *Constant Reformation, Swallow, Black Prince, Second Charles, Henry,* and *Mary;* the French probably had three men-of-war.[101] At six o'clock in the evening of 20/30 July 1650 these ships moved downriver to the Bay of Oeiras, where they were detected by the Commonwealth ships plying their monotonous station in the open sea.[102] Popham counted twenty-two ships at Oeiras. Blake and Popham had nineteen ships in the vicinity of the Tagus and another four ships away on various missions. Capt. Richard Badiley, with eight ships of the Cadiz squadron, was expected back within a few days.

While Badiley was in the Cadiz area, the Portuguese-royalist-French coalition possessed a slight advantage in ships over Blake, and, moreover, the coalition ships were fresh out of port, newly equipped and supplied, amply manned, and operating in home waters out of adjacent bases. The Commonwealth ships had been at sea for many months and had to be supplied and victualled from great distances, and their crews were weary and underfed and some were ill. Yet the Commonwealth ships also possessed certain advantages: they had superior fighting qualities, had more and better guns (the larger Portuguese ships were, by English standards, undergunned), and had resolute leaders, skilled gunners, and more disciplined crews. In many ways the opposing fleets, on 20/30 July 1650, were evenly matched; if the coalition fleet had been united under a single command, under a vigorous leader, and had agreed on what strategy and tactics to adopt, Blake might have found himself in a difficult, even an impossible, position. But the weak, irresolute, and divided leadership of the coalition fleet and confusion over objectives and procedures made Blake's task much easier.

Blake and Popham had separate and independent commands, but they worked closely together and obeyed a single set of instructions. In the coalition fleet, three nationalities struggled for preeminence. Rupert, as a prince of the blood royal, would serve under no one of lesser rank. The Portuguese, since the operations took place in areas under the jurisdiction of John IV and they furnished the most men and ships, wanted to command the fleet. And the French,[103] as representatives of Louis XIV, insisted on first place (and, in fact, the French commander obtained the place of honor, at the head of the line of ships). The failure to agree resulted in a triple-headed leadership—three commanders in chief, three ships flying the admiral's standard from the mainmasthead, with three vice admirals and three rear admirals—nine admirals for twenty-two ships!

The leadership question was aggravated by John IV's choice of António de Sequeira Varejão as commander of the thirteen Portuguese men-of-war. Varejão was a man of "known valor and consummate experience," to use the words of his friend Francisco de Brito Freire, captain of the *Nossa Senhora da Candelária,* but even Brito Freire admitted that Varejão at seventy-four was too old: "Becoming already decrepit he was more perplexed than resolute" (*passando ja a decrepito era mais embaraçado que resoluto*).[104] Prince Rupert blamed Varejão for the poor performance of the coalition fleet during the first days of the encounter, or nonencounter, with the parliamentarians.

It was easy to see why Rupert and the French did not wish to serve under Varejão; it was also easy to place all blame for failures on the shoulders of the elderly admiral. Yet he was not alone to blame, nor was inept and divided leadership itself the main problem: behind the division of leadership lay a deep cleavage of opinion, between the Portuguese and Rupert, over the purposes and aims to be pursued. The differences in point of view may have been thoroughly discussed in a council of war, held aboard Rupert's flagship *Constant Reformation* and attended by Rupert, Maurice, Varejão, the French commander, and all the captains.

Royalist and Portuguese accounts disagree on what was decided at the council of war. Rupert, the French, and some of the Portuguese wanted to launch a general attack on Blake's ships. If the Commonwealth fleet was to be destroyed or driven away, then all the immediate problems of both Portuguese and royalists would be solved. The royalists came away from the conference convinced that the consensus favored the launching of an energetic and general attack—or so Rupert claimed later, when hindsight, or the desire to evade blame, may have affected his memory of events.

The Portuguese government had a different point of view; the last thing in the world they wanted was a naval war with England or with any other power. King John desired to rid his waters of both royalists and parliamentarians. The king's ships, forbidden by strict orders to sail out of sight of the Tagus estuary, were to "help" Rupert, not in the sense of helping him to fight Blake but helping him to escape. If Rupert would leave, perhaps Blake would follow him, and the sugar ships of the Brazil fleet could return in peace and safety. Brito Freire, who always referred to the Portuguese ships as nothing more than Rupert's "convoy" and who was present at the council of war, reported that the decision of the council was to bring about Rupert's escape, at nighttime, and presumably without engaging the Commonwealth men-of-war. The plan was for the ships to sail out together, in company, and stand out to sea. When darkness fell, the royalists would slip away, without lighting any lamps. The other ships would light lanterns, and enough lights would be visible to represent all the ships, including the missing royalists. The fleet would then sail back to the Tagus, its mission accomplished.

Brito Freire did not explain how a clash with Blake could have been avoided when the ships put to sea or yet how so primitive a ruse could have deceived the parliamentarians or yet how any such plan could succeed without Rupert's cooperation. He merely commented, in a remarkable understatement, that "this correct policy miscarried through confused execution."[105]

On Friday, 26 July/5 August 1650, at 7:00 A.M., the French admiral and Rupert sailed out of the Tagus to do battle with Blake and Popham. The events that followed bore a greater resemblance to comic opera than to naval warfare. The allies had agreed to cross the bar of the Tagus when a favorable wind came in combination with a high tide. The coalition leaders decided that Rupert would be the judge of the conditions of tide and wind, and when he felt the opportune moment had come then his ship, stationed with the French admiral's almost at the mouth of the Tagus, would signal the Portuguese ships in Oeiras to follow him.[106]

The Portuguese pilots aboard the royalist ships complained that Rupert refused to feed them. On Thursday afternoon (25 July/4 August) they went ashore and dined. When it grew dark they decided to spend the night ashore, since they knew that the first favorable daylight high tide would not come until about ten o'clock the next morning. It was after seven on Friday morning when the pilots came down to the Oeiras waterfront and saw that Rupert had sailed out of the river without his pilot. Afterward the officers aboard the Portuguese flagship, the *Santo António de Mazagão,* which was closest to the mouth of the river, swore that Rupert's ship had made no signal to the Portuguese fleet—but since apparently *all* the officers were in the main cabin attending morning mass it seems unlikely that they were ever in a position to see any signal from Rupert. It seems probable that Rupert made some kind of a visual signal but that the Portuguese, not expecting any move until later in the morning, neglected to keep a good watch on deck, were all at their prayers, and never saw it.

The Portuguese never dreamed that Rupert would venture out of the Tagus in a weak and uncertain wind, without waiting for high tide, and without a Portuguese pilot (although the English merchant and seaman James Holcraft, with twenty years' experience of the river, may have been aboard). Nobody on the Portuguese ships was expecting a signal, and no signal was seen. When Rupert's absence was finally detected, there was some perplexity aboard the Portuguese flagship and further discussion and delay. Varejão eventually weighed anchor, started to sail downriver, and signaled the rest of the fleet to follow.

The French admiral sailed out first. Rupert followed but sailed more slowly, deliberately waiting for the Portuguese ships; he delayed for an hour or more, but the Portuguese did not appear. Meanwhile, the French admiral slowed down, because Rupert had fallen about a mile astern. The Portuguese admiral finally came into view near São Julião, and Rupert sailed ahead to join the French, but the other ships had been most confused by Varejão's signals, which they were not expecting, and *did not follow the Portuguese commander.* Varejão, whose ship was dragging her anchor in the water, then waited for the rest of the fleet; by the time the other ships arrived the wind had changed and was blowing directly upriver, so that no more ships were able to sail down the Main Channel between the shoals. Only Rupert and the Frenchman actually got out to sea that day.

Rupert and the Frenchman could not venture to attack the Commonwealth fleet by themselves.[107] Blake's ships had difficulty in getting close to the two admirals. In the afternoon, when some parliamentary ships came close enough to fire, the two admirals retired and placed their ships under the guns of São Julião and Bugio, beyond the shoals. Blake's ships gave up the pursuit when they found themselves, in an ebb tide, in danger of running aground on the shoals.[108]

Later Varejão was accused of timidity, of throwing away opportunities to destroy the enemy, and of failing to support Rupert. Varejão answered that Rupert had acted on his own initiative, heedless of accepted arrangements, without favorable conditions of wind and tide, and quite contrary to all instructions. If Rupert had been impulsive and reckless, as was sometimes his habit, then Varejão may have been telling the truth.

On Saturday, 27 July/6 August 1650, weather conditions were unfavorable and the royalist fleet was inactive. On Sunday, Rupert's ships, accompanied by the Frenchmen and possibly by some of the Portuguese men-of-war, sailed out to attack Blake, but Varejão's flagship, the *Santo António de Mazagão,* with her anchor still dipping into the water, went only a short distance before hauling in her mainsail and then turning aside into the Bay of Cascais. The poor position of the anchor, unperceived by any officer aboard, was indicated to the flagship by Fr. Francisco Cristóvão, a Jesuit chaplain aboard Rupert's Protestantly named *Constant Reformation;* the anchor mechanism was defective, but Varejão was able to have the anchor pulled out of the water. The hauling in of the mainsail was a more serious matter. Varejão later explained that the master, not the admiral, was in full charge of the sails and that the mainsail was not needed, since the distance to Cascais was so short. Evidently Varejão had no intention of following Rupert out to sea.[109]

Brito Freire, captain of the *Candelária*, maintained that Rupert, at nightfall, could have made a safe escape, because there were enough Portuguese ships sufficiently far out to afford the Palatine prince cover and protection—but all English accounts contradict this. The royalists and the French, unsupported and outnumbered, dared not engage Blake. The Commonwealth admiral hauled down his topsails and deliberately surrendered the weather gauge[110] to Rupert, but the royalists would not attack. In the evening eight ships appeared on the horizon: Richard Badiley's Cadiz squadron had returned with victuals and beverage, and the Commonwealth fleet, with thirty ships, was plainly superior to its timid adversaries.

At nightfall on Sunday, 28 July/7 August, the coalition fleet, recognizing its inferiority, retired to the mouth of the Tagus. On Monday, Blake planned to force the bar of the river and attack, but the day was foggy and without wind and nothing could be done. On Tuesday, the coalition fleet retreated farther upriver, to the Bay of Oeiras, and Blake, who had moved back to his old flagship the *George,* returned to his former anchorage in the Cascais roadstead.[111] Ashore at the town of Cascais, John IV, in person, had witnessed some of the weekend's action or inaction (as had many other persons on the cliffs overlooking the estuary); it is possible that the caution displayed by the Portuguese fleet may have owed something to the king's influence.

The king wished to get rid of the royalists without risking his own ships, but it was Admiral Varejão, the target of Rupert's criticism, who took the blame for the failure of this timid policy. At Rupert's insistence, Varejão was deprived of his post, had to answer charges at an official inquiry, and gave way to Jorge de Melo, a younger and more energetic leader. Varejão, who felt victimized, angrily left his flagship and joined Brito Freire aboard the *Candelária.* Brito Freire blamed not the old admiral but princes Rupert and Maurice, who were persistently uncooperative and did not want to leave

Portugal, because they were "too greatly inclined to continue in the splendid hospitality" of the king.[112]

The Anglo-Franco-Portuguese armada was to spend the next three months in the most timid, indecisive, and muddled operations, without developing a clear line of strategy. During three months of sailing to and fro, of going in and out of the Tagus—during three months of "fighting"—the royalists, Portuguese, and French failed to sink or even damage a single parliamentary ship. This backwardness in bellicosity sprang from the Portuguese lack of interest in the result of the royalist-parliamentary quarrel and from their unwillingness to commit their halfhearted grievance to the test of battle.

In the Commonwealth fleet, there was little that Blake could do beyond remaining vigilant and waiting for the situation to mature. On 4/14 August 1650 the *Constant Warwick* returned from England with the latest news and instructions. The *Warwick* had been away for fifty-two days. She had left Lisbon on 13/23 June with Charles Vane and had taken twenty days to get to England. Vane was received by Parliament on 4/14 July and formally thanked by the Speaker for his services in Portugal. Parliament approved of the actions of Blake and Popham in Portugal and promised to conduct an investigation into the victualling abuses that had plagued the fleet. The letters to Blake and Popham contained nothing that was new but did place heavy emphasis on Parliament's concern for the fate of the English merchants imprisoned in Portugal. On this question Parliament was under pressure from the merchants of London who had business associates and kinsmen in Lisbon.[113]

Parliament retaliated on whatever Portuguese were to be found in England. The Portuguese merchants in London—some fifteen or more New Christians or even practicing Jews, most of them refugees from the tyranny of the Portuguese Inquisition—had been arrested in London and jailed in the Marshalsea prison.[114] Unfortunately for the parliamentarians, Lisbon did not greatly care what happened to the New Christians of London (many of whom would have found themselves in the prisons of the Inquisition had they remained in Portugal), and so the Portuguese prisoners were not a useful bargaining counter in securing the release of the English merchants.

In mid-August, Blake made overtures to John IV concerning the release of the English merchants. The king named António Muníz de Carvalho, a royal judge, to negotiate with the English, and suggested that an exchange of prisoners could take place on 21 August. A certain Captain Day was appointed commissioner for the Generals-at-Sea. The English merchant John Mules lent his good offices during the ensuing talks between Carvalho and Day. As a sign of goodwill the Englishmen released a Portuguese prisoner, Diogo Jorge, who was sent ashore aboard a Dutch ship bound for Setúbal. But the talks almost foundered over the Portuguese preliminary demand that the blockade of Lisbon should be lifted before any English merchants could be released. Yet the demand itself was negotiable since the Portuguese, now more anxious than ever over the security of the sugar fleet, were prepared to be more flexible than they had been during the previous ten weeks. On 2 September 1650 the king ordered Jorge de Melo, who had become commander of the Armada Real, to arrange with Rupert for the departure of the royalist squadron. Five days later the king sent a message to Blake and Popham that he was dispatching his emissary, Carvalho, to arrange a general settlement of the major issues dividing Portugal and England.[115]

The anticipated return of the Brazil fleet, which drove the Portuguese to search for a settlement, had the opposite effect on the Englishmen. The parliamentarians had opened negotiations with Lisbon because London had insisted that an effort be made to secure the release of the imprisoned English merchants. The Commonwealth mariners, who sensed that the rich booty of the Brazil fleet lay in the offing, had no wish to go further than reaching some kind of understanding with the Portuguese over the minor question of prisoners. There was no real desire in the Commonwealth fleet at that time for peace with Portugal.

Blake was very busy. On 15/25 August 1650 the nine English Brazilmen were sent home. During their journey to England, the nine merchantmen captured six French ships loaded with fish and oil. When the ships arrived in London, Parliament and the Council of State received petitions from merchants who demanded compensation for losses incurred by Blake's detention of these nine vessels. The petitioners wanted restitution for the freight money owed by the Portuguese; also payment for the time the ships had been in the Commonwealth's service; and, in addition, the petitioners desired a share of the prize goods from the captured French vessels. Edward

Bushell, along with many others, signed a petition claiming an interest in the ships *Prosperous* and *Reason.*[116]

On 19/29 August 1650 the *Constant Warwick* reported having sunk a Portuguese ship off Lisbon, described in English accounts as a "rich" East Indiaman or Brazilman. Actually, she was the galleon *São Francisco,* under Capt. Luís de Ultra Côrte Real, who had sailed in April with the India fleet of 1650, but had abandoned the voyage when his newly built but crank galleon sprang a dangerous leak. When she neared the coast the *Warwick* attacked and drove her ashore at Ericeira.[117] Whether the *São Francisco* was "rich" or not (she may have been carrying some silver to India), the English were not able to board the wrecked vessel or derive any plunder from her.

On 3/13 September, General-at-Sea Edward Popham left the Lisbon area on the *Resolution* accompanied by eight other ships,[118] some of which had been at sea too long and had become unfit. He intended to secure beverages and victuals in northwest Spain but would not remain off that coast for more than ten or fifteen days. If the sugar ships should arrive during that time, then some of Popham's fighting ships might move southward to attack them; if not, then he would lead his squadron back to England.

Blake was left with a diminished force of about a dozen ships, including four large men-of-war—the *George, Leopard, Bonadventure,* and *Assurance*—five or six good frigates, and two or three auxiliary vessels. As these few ships took on the additional responsibility of patrolling the western approaches watching for the Brazil fleet, Blake had to relax the Lisbon blockade. In fact, the parliamentarians began to forget that their chief responsibility was not the capturing of Portuguese prizes but the destruction of Rupert's squadron.

Now, at long last, with a three-to-one advantage in ships, the combined Portuguese-French-royalist fleet grew bolder. The Armada Real left the river and anchored in the Bay of Cascais. On Saturday, 7/17 September 1650, a thick fog, common in Lisbon at that season of the year, covered the approaches to the Tagus. Rupert's squadron sailed out, well hidden in the murk. Out at sea, in thick mist, ship searched for ship in vain. By an odd stroke of fortune, Blake found a small clear patch where he sighted the *Constant Reformation* bearing toward him on a collision course. The twenty-eight-year-old *George,* with her fifty-seven guns and 792 tons, was well matched with the thirty-one-year-old *Constant Reformation* with her sixty guns and 742 tons. Blake was determined that he would not suffer the dishonor of changing course, even if it meant losing the *George* in the impending collision. At the last moment the royalists put the helm about and the *Constant Reformation* veered away. As she passed by, the *George* let fly with a broadside, and a lucky ball shot off her foretopmast. As the mist closed in again, Rupert, with his canvas in disarray, was lost to view. The renowned admiral and the dashing prince had met for the first and last time.[119]

After this curious nonbattle in the fog, during which little damage was done to either side, the Portuguese on both sea and land lost sight of the English ships. In a letter of 20 September 1650 John IV remarked that nobody knew whether or not the parliamentary fleet was still in Portuguese waters; a certain Pedro Velez de Medrano offered to take out a swift, well-equipped caravel and find out. The Armada Real had been ordered not to sail farther than ten leagues (about thirty sea miles) from the mouth of the Tagus, and Rupert, who still showed no signs of leaving, was informed of this order.[120] This decision, which reflected the timidity of government officials concerning the security of the capital, doomed the Rio de Janeiro sugar fleet, which, apparently unbeknownst to the king's ministers, was approaching the coast of Portugal.

During the summer of 1650 there were over one hundred ships in Brazilian waters. From Bahia, on 3 September 1650, the Count of Castelo Melhor, governor-general of Brazil, wrote to John IV that the king's orders commanding the confiscation of all English ships and properties had been received and carried out. The king's further orders, that the sugar fleet was not to return to Portugal until January 1651, would be obeyed.[121] In the safe and commodious harbor of Bahia de Todos os Santos, the seventy-two ships under the command of the returning governor-general, António Teles de Meneses, Count of Vila Pouca de Aguiar and General of the Armada Real of the Ocean Sea, although ready to sail, were prepared to wait for another three or four months, until the Commonwealth had removed Blake's ships from the coasts of Portugal. These timely instructions from Lisbon saved the major portion of the Brazil fleet.

Salvador da Bahia had been warned in time and Vila Pouca's ships eventually sailed to Lisbon in safety, but other ships in Brazil were less fortunate. Eight hundred miles south of Bahia, twenty-three ships laden with sugar from South Brazil had sailed in ignorance of the seriousness of the situation in Portugal. According to paragraph 11 in Castelo Melhor's *regimento*, or official instructions, the Rio de Janeiro fleet was ordered to return to Bahia and join the main fleet before sailing for Portugal. The instructions to the commander of the Rio squadron, Capt. António Temudo de Oliveira, authorized him to sail back to Portugal alone *only* if he encountered Dutch ships in southern Brazilian waters and was seriously delayed.[122]

Paragraph 11 of Castelo Melhor's *regimento* also prescribed that the South Brazil squadron was not to leave Rio de Janeiro later than 1 May 1650. It was impossible to keep to this schedule because of the long delays on the outward journey. Temudo left Rio only on 12 July, ten weeks behind schedule, and thus violated some of his instructions at the very outset of the return voyage. In order to make up for lost time, perhaps, Temudo decided *not* to call at Bahia and *not* to join with the main fleet. This was a clear (and, in the event, quite unnecessary) violation of his instructions and led, ultimately, to the loss of many ships.

Paragraph 19 of the official instructions laid down that if the returning fleet, all of whose components should have rendezvoused in Bahia, expected to arrive in Portugal *before* 20 August 1650, then it should sail well to the westward of the Azores Islands, keeping a northerly course until it reached latitude forty-two degrees and from thence due east until it sighted the coast of Portugal, somewhere between Oporto and Viana do Castelo. There the ships destined for northern ports would detach themselves from the fleet, while the main fleet would sail on to Lisbon. But, if the fleet expected to arrive in Portugal *after* 20 August, it should follow a more direct route, sailing between the Azores and Madeira, taking great care that its presence was not detected in the Azores and proceeding directly to the mouth of the River Sado at the entrance to the port of Setúbal, and from there to Lisbon whenever it was safe.[123] Both routes avoided contact with the Azores, the favorite haunt of pirates and privateers.

The Rio de Janeiro fleet followed the second route, avoiding the Azores and Madeira, and thus lost its best chance of hearing fresh news from Portugal, which would have prevented it from pursuing its voyage. The triangle of sea formed by the lines running from the Azores, Lisbon, and the Canaries was a paradise for pirates; it was difficult for a fleet of twenty-three ships to sail through those waters undetected. News of the sugar fleet drew Blake's ships away from the Lisbon blockade in mid-September. The same news also attracted two or three ships of Popham's squadron from the Bay of Biscay area and two or three Dutch privateers from Middleburg.

Late on Saturday, 14/24 September 1650, Blake's ships made contact with the twenty-three sugar ships. The Brazilmen, who were only between twenty and thirty miles from shore and who had no hope of successfully resisting the powerful English men-of-war, scattered in all directions. It was not possible to pursue all the ships, but each English ship went after one sugar ship. The Armada Real, awkwardly situated at Cascais far to the north of the action, could not intervene until the main damage had been done. On the outer fringes, to the north and west, Popham's men and Dutch privateers sought eagerly to pick up the scraps from this banquet.

Blake in the *George* naturally made for the Portuguese admiral, Temudo, but the *George* was an old ship and too slow; Temudo's flagship and his vice admiral, in the *São Francisco,* made a dash for Setúbal, pursued by two frigates, while the *George*, left behind, attacked the Portuguese ship flying the rear admiral's flag from the mizzenmasthead. The wind was strong and the sea ran high; Blake could not use the lower tier of guns, with its heavy cannon. The lighter pieces of the upper tier fired away for three hours before the rear admiral surrendered.

Early the next morning the Portuguese admiral and vice admiral appeared off "Cape Pitcher" (Cape Espichel), pursued by the *Assurance* and another frigate. Temudo's galleon, with thirty-two guns and said to be carrying 1,500 chests of sugar, still showed good speed in the northeast wind, reached the bar of Setúbal, and luffed up and dropped anchor. She had suffered severe damage to her mainmast, and had three or four feet of water in the hold, and twelve of her men had been killed. The *São Francisco* (a thirty-four gun galleon said to have carried 300 men and 1,700 chests of sugar) had her maintopmast shot down and did not escape. The two English frigates closed in on her; the *Assurance* boarded her and burnt her. The Portuguese refused to surrender, and she went down with her decks "covered with corpses."[124]

In the final stages of this prolonged, complex, and scattered engagement, the ships of the Armada Real went into action. One of the Portuguese warships, the *Nossa Senhora da Natividade,* was captured by ships of Popham's squadron and eventually taken to Bristol, where she was added to the Commonwealth navy and known, successively, by the names *Crowned Lion* and *Marigold.* Another Portuguese man-of-war, the *São Lourenço,* defended the mouth of the Tagus against English ships pursuing some of the Brazilmen that had escaped into Oeiras. Dutch Zeelander privateers moved in to help cut off the escape of the sugar ships and managed to capture two small ships, one with 500 and the other with 200 chests of sugar, "taken hard by the River of Lisbon."[125]

Of the twenty-three ships, eleven were saved: nine Brazilmen reached the safety of the fluvial Bay of Oeiras; Temudo brought his damaged flagship, the *São João,* into the harbor of Setúbal; and another Portuguese vessel, a Peniche caravel with Lourenço Durão as master, while presumably bound for Peniche, was attacked by parliamentary ships off the Cape of Roca well to the north of the Lisbon estuary, and she made full use of the northeast wind, crowded on all sail, and headed not for the bar of the Tagus but for the island of Madeira, which she reached on 27 September 1650 and where she unloaded her cargo unhindered.[126] The Portuguese lost twelve Brazilmen as well as the Lisbon-based *Natividade.* Blake captured *seven* ships and destroyed the Portuguese vice admiral's[127] ship, the *São Francisco;* Popham took *two,* and the Zeeland privateers seized another *two.* Of Blake's seven ships, four—the Portuguese rear admiral's *São Pedro* and the *Santo António, Nossa Senhora dos Remédios,* and *Bom Pastor*—were sent back to England.

The three most valuable prizes were taken by Blake's squadron: the *São Pedro,* valued by the Court of Admiralty at £20,481; the *Bom Pastor,* valued at £19,420; and the *Santo António,* worth £15,360. Blake reported that his seven prizes contained over four thousand chests of sugar and almost four hundred men. Much of the sugar belonged to English merchants who had just had it confiscated by the Portuguese and who then stood in danger of losing it to the Commonwealth government. The merchants of Lisbon who had been loyal parliament men probably obtained, through their associates in London, the speedy return of their cargoes, but those merchants who had not sided with the Commonwealth probably encountered greater difficulties in securing their twice-confiscated goods.[128]

After the victorious action against the sugar ships, Blake found it difficult to hold his station off Lisbon any longer. He needed beverages and victuals and, above all, a safe port where his prizes could be repaired, manned, and if necessary, unloaded. He directed his ten ships, with their prizes, to sail for Cadiz, where on 29 September/9 October 1650 he was well received by the Spanish authorities. The blockade of Lisbon had been abandoned, and Prince Rupert, although not forgotten, was left free to sail where he wished. But if the royalist ships intended to enter the Mediterranean and put in at a friendly port in South France (which seemed to be Prince Rupert's most likely plan), then they would still have to elude Blake's fleet at the Straits of Gibraltar.

In Lisbon, the disappearance of the Commonwealth ships created uncertainty rather than relief, for Blake had not returned to England but had merely sailed southwards and might soon be back. The king ordered Jorge de Melo, the commander of the Armada Real, to put to sea with a strong squadron and shadow the movements of the English fleet. With his customary caution the king instructed Melo to sail no farther than the coast of the Algarve and to return to Cascais as soon as possible. But Melo's brother, Francisco de Melo, was then governor of the kingdom of Algarve, and it is possible that the admiral took a greater interest in the safety of that southernmost province than did the king. In any event, Jorge de Melo, with four good fighting ships (the *Santo António de Mazagão, Esperança, Candelária,* and *Conceição*) sailed south, discovered that Blake had gone to Cadiz, and put in at the port of Lagos, prepared to spend a few days in the Algarve.[129]

The admiral's failure to return within the prescribed time caused fresh apprehension in Lisbon, where the king feared that the small Portuguese squadron might have run afoul of the much larger Commonwealth fleet. On 5 October 1650 the king wrote to the governor of the Algarve that the English ships had returned to the bar of the Tagus and resumed their blockade. This was not correct. The Portuguese may have sighted one or two English frigates or perhaps some English privateers off the coast of Portugal, but there were not enough English ships in the Lisbon area at that time to attempt to renew the blockade. By 8 October the king had heard of Jorge de Melo's arrival at Lagos and wrote to him expressing joy at the safety of the squadron and urging him to return to Lisbon.[130] The king's apprehensions were exaggerated: Lisbon was no longer really threatened, and there were still twenty ships available for her defense, including Rupert's ever-present royalist fleet. After receiving the king's orders the commander of the Armada Real left Lagos, and eventually his squadron sailed into the Tagus on 13 October 1650. The next day the king wrote happily to the governor of the Algarve: "Your brother, Jorge de Melo, arrived here yesterday with all the ships entrusted to him."[131]

The vicinity of Lisbon was virtually clear of parliamentary ships. Melo reported to Prince Rupert that the royalists would face no difficulties in sailing to the Mediterranean until they neared Cadiz, where Blake lay in wait. Even in the Cadiz area there was ample sea room: if the royalists kept toward the African coast they might slip into the Straits of Gibraltar undetected. For the fourth or fifth time the prince made arrangements for his departure. Finally, on the afternoon of 12/22 October 1650, Prince Rupert in the *Constant Reformation,* Prince Maurice in the *Swallow*—accompanied by the *Black Prince, Second Charles, Henry,* and *Mary*—sailed out of the Tagus. For thirty-six hours they bore west or southwest, in the hope of misleading any spies, before bending their course southward toward the straits.[132] In the words of an unknown diarist aboard the ships, these were the feelings of the royalists: "Now misfortunes being no novelty to us, we plough the sea for a subsistence, and, being destitute of a port, we take the confines of the Mediterranean Sea for our harbour; poverty and despair being companions, and revenge our guide."[133]

After almost ten and a half months the Portuguese had rid themselves of their importunate guest. Prince Rupert had left Lisbon at last. As the words of the unknown diarist suggest, the royalists felt that they had been expelled from Portugal, that they were outcasts and exiles, without friends, or refuge, or funds. In truth, since the English "regicides" had filled the seas with fighting ships, royalist prospects at sea in October 1650 were bleak indeed. Yet Rupert and his followers, the forlorn standard-bearers of the "martyred" Charles I, had achieved a great deal during 1650. By their mere presence in Lisbon they had provoked a war between Portugal and the Commonwealth and won to their cause, for a time, the only Continental nation willing to take up arms on behalf of English royalism. They had forced the Commonwealth to spend unprecedented sums on the development of a powerful navy. And they had damaged English commerce by disrupting trade with Portugal.

Unfortunately for the royalists, the Commonwealth came out of these difficulties stronger than ever, while Rupert's Portuguese allies, with their weaknesses at sea made painfully evident, emerged disheartened and apprehensive. By the time Rupert left Lisbon, it was clear that the Portuguese wanted peace with England as quickly as possible, provided they did not have to pay too heavy a price. Rupert's success in Lisbon in 1650 was temporary and limited, although, in relation to his meager resources, he performed a remarkable work of destruction.

After Rupert left Lisbon, a number of his ships, which had become separated at sea, eluded Blake at the straits and spent two months in Spanish and Italian waters, masquerading as parliamentary ships and flying the Commonwealth standard. Their disguise enabled them to capture or destroy about eight English merchantmen, but Blake soon put an end to these depredations. By the middle of December 1650, when Rupert and Maurice retired to the French port of Toulon, they were reduced to three ships—the *Constant Reformation, Swallow* and *Marmaduke* (a prize)—and all their other ships, including the captured merchantmen, had been seized or sunk by the parliamentarians. Blake returned to England at the end of January 1651 and was replaced in the Mediterranean by Adm. William Penn whose squadron anchored within the Bay of Cadiz on 28 February/10 March 1651.[134]

The royalist "navy," insofar as it represented a danger to the Commonwealth, had been reduced to a mere nuisance. In R.C. Anderson's words: "The events of 1650 had shown that the Royalists had no chance of recovering their position at sea. . . . He [Rupert] was able to keep the King's Standard flying at sea for another two years or more, but it was only by moving to waters where it was not worth while to follow him. As a serious danger in European waters he was finished."[135] Rupert's small squadron left Toulon on 7/17 May 1651, evaded Penn's warships, and spent the next two years sailing rather aimlessly, with little success or profit, in the Azores, the Cape Verde Islands, off the coast of Guinea, and finally in the West Indies.[136] In visiting the Portuguese islands and colonies (where he was not nearly as well received as he had been in Lisbon in 1650), he tried to stir up new tensions between the English and Portuguese but was not very successful, if only because his naval force was unimpressive and his crews unreliable.

The Palatine prince's career as a semipiratical royalist seaman, or his "mad wild-goose chase" (as a disillusioned royalist described it),[137] closed with some painful failures. On 1/11 October 1651 the *Constant Reformation,* his strongest ship, was lost in a storm and 333 men were drowned. Other ships and prizes were lost from time to time. In September 1652 Vice Adm. Prince Maurice, by far the less talented of the two brothers, was caught in a hurricane in the West Indies, and neither he nor his ship was ever seen again. It must have been with a heavy heart that Rupert in the *Swallow*, the last of his original ships, left the Virgin Islands in December 1652 and charted his course for Europe.

On his way back to Europe, Rupert put in at the island of Fayal in the Azores, but the Portuguese opened fire on his ship and drove him away. His friendly relations with the Portuguese had come to an end. By the time the prince, with the *Swallow* and four prizes, entered the Loire River in France on 4/14 March 1653, hostilities between the English and Portuguese had virtually ceased, and John IV was making every effort to be friends with Oliver Cromwell.

5

GUIMARÃES AND THE PURSUIT OF PEACE

Rupert's visit to Portugal had far-reaching consequences for Anglo-Portuguese relations. The royalists brought upon Portugal a war that the Portuguese could only have regarded as the wrong war, at the wrong time, and with the wrong enemy. The burden of a maritime war with a great naval power, coming in addition to the struggle against a great land power, placed the small, gallant nation in an impossible position. At the same time the Dutch, angered by the rebellion that was driving them out of Pernambuco (in "Dutch" Brazil), renewed their assaults on Portuguese shipping. Had the Commonwealth chosen to press the war against John IV the Portuguese might well have been completely defeated.

The general sequestration of English properties, accompanied by the internment of English merchants, were errors of Portuguese policy. The wholesale confiscation was an exaggerated response to Blake's detention of the nine Brazilmen and was interpreted in London as an invitation to armed conflict. The Portuguese, if they could not bring themselves to pursue a policy of collaboration with the Commonwealth, a collaboration required by many considerations of expediency and self-interest, should have clung to a strict neutrality in the dispute between royalists and parliamentarians. If, in the end, a war came, then let it have come as a result of English provocations and aggression. In the Anglo-Portuguese diplomacy of 1651–1656 Portugal might have fared much better if she could have represented herself more convincingly as the injured party.

In the event, Portugal seemed to have forced war on the Commonwealth. The sense of injury and grievance was felt much more in London than in Lisbon. Once the state of war between Portugal and the Commonwealth became a fact, with the Commonwealth growing stronger month by month, there was neither the need nor the desire for peace in England. With her merchants imprisoned and their property lost, England had little more to fear from the continuation of the war and not much to gain from the return of peace. Portugal, on the contrary, soon found out that peace with England was essential and the continuation of the war a disaster. These two attitudes, springing from conflicting situations, conditioned all the peace negotiations. England would agree to peace on no terms but her own: complete satisfaction from the Portuguese.

Article 18 of the Anglo-Portuguese treaty of 29 January/8 February 1642 stipulated that in the event of war between the contracting parties, merchants were to be given two years' warning, during which they might sell their goods and make arrangements to leave. London regarded the sequestration of English properties as a clear violation of this article, although the Portuguese argued that the treaty had been made with Charles I and not with the Commonwealth. This was an argument that no self-respecting English government could have accepted. The aim in London was to make Portugal pay for the peace: pay not merely by restoring confiscated properties but also by indemnifying all the merchants for their indirect losses such as the interest and profit that might have accrued to them had their capital not been seized. Moreover, it was London's intention, before agreeing to any peace, to obtain detailed and positive guarantees for the protection of English merchants doing business in Portugal. Not only had there to be compensation for past injuries, but also clear precautions against future misbehavior.

Portugal wanted a return to the status quo ante and tried to obtain peace by the mere promise to restore the sequestered properties. Lisbon was slow to realize how strongly the English government, backed by the London merchants, felt about these matters. In London's view, full restitution and restoration, combined with other guarantees, must come *before* the peace; in Lisbon it was felt that restitution could only come *after* the end of hostilities.

Lisbon may have thought that merely negotiating with the "regicide" government, thereby recognizing it de facto, was in itself a substantial concession. By the end of 1650 no European country, other than Spain, had explicitly recognized the Commonwealth government. By the naval campaign against Rupert and Portugal London intended to give warning to all powers that the Commonwealth government was not to be trifled with and that any country rendering assistance and shelter to English royalists could expect serious trouble. In this fashion the Commonwealth used Blake's expedition to convey an object lesson to European diplomats. At the same time, the events in Portugal helped to confirm the English in their belief that a powerful navy was an essential tool of their diplomacy. With such a navy there was no need for England, no matter what government held sway there, to beg for recognition from the capitals of Europe; recognition could be demanded as a right. Since half the countries in Europe had exposed coastlines and were vulnerable to attack from the sea, England could use her ships to silence insults and avenge injuries. The truth of this was proved and confirmed by England's victory over the United Provinces. Even the powerful naval forces of the Netherlands, led by admirals who were among the most capable ever to be seen, could not defeat the Commonwealth's new navy.

The government that was soon to contrive the downfall of the Dutch could not have regarded Portugal as a dangerous enemy. In the markets of London the Portuguese sequestrations created grievances that rankled. The issues of restitution and compensation were to poison Anglo-Portuguese relations for many years. Even when the Stuarts had been restored to the English throne, the London government continued to demand compensation for the seizures that the royalists had themselves inspired! In 1669, nineteen years after the sequestrations, the English envoy in Portugal, Sir Robert Southwell, was still negotiating with the Portuguese for the compensation of English merchants.[1]

Historians have sometimes depicted the Englishmen's demands on Portugal for heavy financial restitution as oppressive and unjust, amounting even to extortion, backed by a blackmailer's threat to make war on Portuguese shipping. In truth, they did request a large quantity of money and did present their case in the bluntest way—yet four considerations can be advanced in extenuation of London's policies and attitude: (1) the Commonwealth had not sought war with Portugal, nor was the pursuit of Rupert, in its initial stages, motivated by anti-Portuguese feeling; (2) it was no secret that in confiscating English goods John IV had acted for economic as well as political reasons and intended to enrich his own treasury,[2]—and thus

England's "greed" was in response to the "greed" of the king of Portugal; (3) the Portuguese government's imprisonment of almost the entire English merchant community was an unduly harsh measure that exasperated English opinion; and (4) the losses suffered by the English merchants had been severe.

Portuguese policy, as has been described, made no distinction between the merchants belonging to the parliamentary faction and those of the great body of neutrals—only a handful of vocal royalists were spared the effects of the decrees of confiscation and imprisonment. This was a political miscalculation. The Portuguese government might have penalized only the most enthusiastic parliamentarians and left the other merchants unmolested, on the expedient assumption that the neutral merchants were loyal subjects of Charles II. Portugal could then have claimed, with much more reason, that she made war not on the English nation but only on the parliamentary faction. Such a course would not have been any more pleasing to the London government, but it would have antagonized the London merchants less and been far more acceptable to the general English public.

In the formulation of Portuguese policy the short-term economic advantages of wholesale confiscation were allowed to predominate over long-term political interests. Portugal appeared to have gone to war for the purpose of despoiling the whole community of English merchants, taking up arms on behalf of a clique of royalists against the government and people of England. As a consequence, English merchants suffered enormous losses. Compensation for these losses was so grudging and so tardy that many individuals may have recovered little or nothing. It is probably fair to say that twenty years after the confiscations the entire sum paid by the Portuguese in restitution and compensation did not cover the full extent of direct and indirect losses sustained by the English merchants.[3]

Existing records prove the severity of English losses. From a variety of sources a list of at least twenty-two English ships seized by the Portuguese can be compiled, and there were probably other ship seizures of which no record survives. The worst blow fell at Salvador da Bahia, where eight English ships, loaded with sugar, were boarded and taken. In Brazil, the returning sugar fleet of seventy-two ships (including the eight English ships), under the Count of Vila Pouca, left Bahia on 24 July 1650 but met with adverse weather, in which the fleet could make no headway, and returned to Bahia on 5 August, by which time dispatches had arrived from Portugal containing the king's orders that the Brazil fleet was not to reach Portugal before January 1651 and that English ships were to be seized and Englishmen detained.[4] The governor-general of Brazil, the Count of Castelo Melhor, acted slowly and carefully. The order for the seizure was issued by the governor on 18 August and carried out on 23 August.[5] The eight English ships[6] must certainly have been under observation for several weeks and may have been placed under some kind of constraint as early as mid-July.[7] The man in charge of the Bahia confiscations was Simão Álvares de la Penha, High Comptroller of His Majesty's Treasury of the State of Brazil (*Provedôr Mor da Fazenda de Sua Magestade do Estado do Brasil*), who compiled elaborate inventories of the English ships and their cargoes. English captains and officers hampered this task by concealing their cargo registers and other books.

The heaviest losers in the Bahia sequestrations seemed to have been the Bushell brothers, who lost at least 216 chests of sugar, in addition to a great amount of property that went unrecorded. For instance, of the 515 chests of sugar aboard the *Nicholas,* the owner's name was listed for only 30 chests, because the cargo book had been left behind in Pernambuco (i.e., hidden)![8] Ownership was not stated for a single one of the 540 chests aboard the *Sampson*, because the English cargo manifests had been sent to the Bahia customs house for translation into Portuguese and this process took too long for inclusion in the sequestration inventories.[9] Among the merchants possessing property aboard the English ships were Richard Beare, Robert Cart, Robert Cocke, James Cotton, Barnaby Crawford, William Fletcher, Thomas Hughes, and Peter Middleton. Some others—including Robert Abel, Raymond Purdon, and George Sain—owned goods on the Portuguese ships *Nossa Senhora da Graça, Nossa Senhora da Bôa Nova,* and *São Francisco.*

The inventories of each ship and her equipment were carefully drawn up and included even the cooking utensils in the galley. The *Sampson*, for instance, was listed as having four cauldrons, as well as a main anchor weighing fourteen hundredweight with a chain measuring ten fathoms, four other anchors, eight large sails, twenty-four guns, eleven barrels of gunpowder each containing 100 pounds,

294 round shot, seven bronze ladles for loading the guns, twenty-four muskets, and many other items, all of them properly listed, pertaining to the armament and equipment of a ship.[10] In London the owners of this fairly large merchant ship (650 tons) claimed the excessive sum of £30,000 for losses resulting from the sequestration.[11]

In August 1653, Andrew Rand and Company, owners of the ship *Thomas and Lucy,* presented a declaration to the London government claiming losses of £8,734 of which £7,530 was capital lost and £1,204 was the interest lost on the capital. This claim only included a small part of the cargo, since much of the cargo had been owned by other merchants. The owners of the *Thomas and Lucy* said the ship had been freighted by the Brazil Company at the rate of 600$000 réis (or £300) per month to carry infantry to Brazil. She had arrived safely in Brazil, where she had been seized by the king, yet kept in the Brazil Company's service, returned to Lisbon in January 1651, had been discharged by the company in April 1651, and then was permanently seized by John IV in August 1651.[12] The shipowners' principal claim was that the Brazil Company had not paid the freighting charges, which were computed at over £4,000.

Oliver Cromwell in person wrote to John IV in October 1656 on behalf of Thomas Evans, master of the *Scipio*, who claimed a loss of £7,000 from its confiscation and who traveled to Lisbon in an effort to recover the money. After Cromwell's death and nine years after the confiscations, Richard Cromwell, the new Protector, wrote to the new king of Portugal, Alphonso VI, on behalf of Alexander Bence, merchant of London and owner of the *Three Brothers*, to whom the Brazil Company refused payment of freightage.[13]

The ship *Sara,* on which the Bushells had a large cargo, created special difficulties. On 4 June 1648 the Lisbon merchants John Bushell and Edward Baliff had received permission to send the 400-ton *Sara* to Bahia.[14] She went to Brazil, returned to Portugal, and then set out for Brazil again with the Brazil Company's first fleet. By August of 1650 the *Sara* had been constantly at sea for at least two years and began to leak badly. The Portuguese authorities also felt that the ship was overloaded, and they ordered that 200 chests of sugar from her be transferred to the flagship *São Pedro,* an Oporto galleon commanded by Master Manuel Álvares. After the confiscation the *Sara*, on her way back to Portugal and manned by Portuguese, disappeared from the view of the rest of the fleet and was never seen again. Apparently the ship foundered with all hands. Later the English claimed up to £20,000 in damages for the loss of the ship and her cargo. The Portuguese argued that the *Sara* was old and leaky and that she had met with an accident for which the Portuguese were in no way responsible. The English answered that the ship would never have disappeared if she had been manned by Englishmen.[15] As late as 1657 the Portuguese were still refusing to pay any claims arising from the loss of the *Sara.*

Another English ship, the *Mary and John* under Capt. Francis Hardidge of London, was seized in Bahia late in the summer of 1650. She was not part of the sugar fleet but had received a license (9 June 1649) to go to Angola and pick up a cargo of slaves, to be exchanged for sugar at Bahia. After the Portuguese had taken possession of the ship, she was captured by the Dutch. Thomas Gould, merchant of Bristol, claimed to have lost 800$000 réis (or £400) when some slaves belonging to him, aboard the *Mary and John,* were taken by the Portuguese. The captain declared that the ship and cargo were worth 70,000 crowns (28:000$000 or £14,000), of which the Portuguese agreed to pay 25,000 crowns (10:000$000 or £5,000), according to the compounding agreement, but they were very slow in doing so.[16]

Eight English ships were apprehended in Madeira, but the details and even the names of some of them are obscure. Something is known of the *Desire* of London (Roger King, master), bound for Newfoundland, which began to take on a cargo of wine at Madeira on 18 June 1650, that is, almost one week after the general confiscations had been ordered in Lisbon. The loading of the ship was interrupted, and she was seized. By that time the English merchants of Madeira had loaded 285 pipes of wine aboard the *Desire.* Richard Pickford, the merchant prince of Madeira, accounted for 123 of these pipes; Albans Willoughby loaded 74 pipes, and William Ray, 33 pipes. The governor of Madeira, Manuel Lobo da Silva, confiscated 21,000 cruzados (or £4,200) in nineteen sacks of money from the *Desire*, as well as thirteen bars of silver.[17] On this ship alone, English merchants and shipowners probably suffered direct losses in excess of £10,000.

Other ships lost in Madeira included: the *Genoa Merchant* (John Williams, master) with thousands of Mexican silver coins and a cargo of tobacco; the *Roebuck* of London with English textiles; the *George* from New England; and four other ships known only by the Portuguese version of their names—the *Dereito* of London under Capt. John Williams with a cargo of English textiles, mirrors, and ribbons, the *Chapel* from New England, the *Conceição* (?), and the *Patta.*[18]

The disturbances between Blake and Rupert had frightened away merchantmen from Lisbon, so that very few ships were seized in Lisbon itself, yet at least two ship commanders—Edward Witheridge of the *Defence* of London and George Chappell of the *Peter and Jane,* also of London[19]—were careless enough, or unlucky enough, to be caught in Lisbon Harbor in June 1650. The *Defence* had been among the last ships to sail to Brazil before the formation of the Brazil Company's fleets; she returned to Lisbon in April 1650 and was apprehended in June. Her owners put in claims for freightage, demurrage,[20] and cargo amounting to £9,230, plus interest and damage charges of £2,128—or £11,358 in all.[21]

The Portuguese also confiscated English ships in Oporto, the Azores, and elsewhere, but there are only traces of these events in the historical records. Two English ships from Newfoundland, laden with codfish, sailed unknowingly into Oporto in October 1650, four months after the beginning of the confiscations, ignorant of all that had occurred. They were promptly impounded.[22] A ship called the *Barnstable* seems to have been confiscated, possibly in Brazil.[23] Faro and the other ports of the Algarve may not have seen many English ships during the first half of 1650 because of the plague that raged in the Algarve during 1649 and until June 1650[24]—so probably there were not many confiscations in that important commercial area.

Details of one of the Azores confiscations survive in the indignant deposition (30 December 1652/9 January 1653) made by George Pitt, master of the *Jonathan* of Bristol, when he finally got back to England. The *Jonathan* was a small vessel of fifty-five tons, three-fourths of which was owned by Stephen Keech, merchant of Bristol, and one-quarter by Israel Gough Cooper. She sailed from Bristol in mid-April 1650 and arrived at Fayal, one of the nine scattered islands of the Azores, in June 1650. She had barely taken on twelve pipes of wine when the Portuguese seized her, emptied her of cargo, and put the entire crew ashore. The Portuguese then stripped the vessel of her sails, topmasts, yards, and rigging and carried them ashore. After three months the Englishmen were returned to the stripped-down ship, but, naturally, they were unable to sail her. In

April 1651 the Portuguese loaded the vessel with wines and took her to Portugal. All the English sailors were left in the Azores, from whence they presumably found their way to England in twos and threes sometime later, when the Portuguese allowed them to leave. George Pitt declared that the *Jonathan*, without its cargo, was worth £622.[25]

Merchants in England, some of whom may never have taken to sea or ever lived abroad, were also affected by the Portuguese confiscations. Hugh Browne, mayor of Bristol, lost property worth £775, of which £292 had been in the possession of Joseph Dorney of Lisbon and £483 with Richard Pickford in Madeira. Richard Vickris, alderman of Bristol, lost £155 in the hands of Henry Eliot and John Bridger, prisoners in Portugal. The elder George Lane, merchant of Bristol, lost £1,300 through his son George Lane and his kinsman Thomas Nethway, both prisoners in Portugal. The merchants of Bristol, all together, reported £5,630 in direct losses.[26] The total claims of the London merchants for losses of all kinds came to exactly £140,839 10 s. 6 d.[27]

The severity and extensiveness of the Portuguese confiscations and the large numbers of merchants and seamen affected by them are matters that must be grasped before the Anglo-Portuguese diplomacy of the 1650–1656 period can be brought into focus. The persistence with which the English government sought for compensation, even in the midst of the struggle with the United Provinces, can be explained by the pressures that the afflicted merchants, seamen, and their families brought to bear on the London government, in the form of countless petitions.

Historians should not conclude that England's demands on Portugal were unreasonable without first looking at the statistics of actual English losses. The assumption that the Portuguese, a few months after the confiscations, restored all the sequestered properties to their rightful owners is not supported by the evidence. The seizures of English goods began on 12 June 1650; nineteen months later, on 8 January 1652, the Treasury Council advised the king to begin returning the properties, but another five months passed before the king issued the necessary orders.[28] Two years separate the summer of confiscation from the summer of restitution; during the interim, money disappeared and goods deteriorated and dwindled. Such restitution as took place was inadequate and slow, following prolonged processes of petitioning. No effort was made to restore ships to their owners.

From the outset the policy of confiscations involved a mixture of motives. First, there was the fear of the Commonwealth of England expressed in the safeguards that surrounded the sequestrations. If the naval power of England was turned against Portugal then it might be necessary to make full restitution with all speed; for this purpose, complete inventories were made of the confiscated properties, moneys were put into special funds where they could not be spent, and valuables collected in distant provinces were sent to the capital for safekeeping. In theory, all goods could be returned to their owners—or the proceeds from the sale of such goods—with the same ease with which they had been taken. Yet there was also a second motive, a desire to add to the wealth of the Treasury and to the number of ships in the fleet, which worked against the aforementioned safeguards. The well-gunned English ships made a useful addition to the Portuguese merchant marine, and there was never any serious intention of returning them, particularly since the parliamentarians had seized a number of Portuguese ships and sunk a number of others. The merchandise taken from the English had to be sold before it deteriorated. The proceeds were held in trust, and the Portuguese made an honest effort to avoid spending this money. But in financial matters Lisbon could not always hold distant subordinates to a strict line of discipline. The governor of Madeira seems to have helped himself to English valuables,[29] and it is likely that other officials in other places did the same thing.

Financial pressures created a strong temptation to "raid" the protected English funds, even where these had not been eaten away by corruption. On 15 May 1651 the king himself ordered the governor of Oporto to send two ships to Angola (as a precaution against Dutch attacks) and added: "For the expenses of this assistance you will make use of whatever money is there [in Oporto] belonging to the sequestration of the English, making a note of the sum you take out so that it can be replaced."[30] Then less than a month later the king again wrote to the governor, saying that for the Angola ships the governor was to make use of other money, money that had been set aside for the repair of a fortress (the São João da Foz); the governor was "not to meddle with the money from the sequestration of the English."[31] The reason for this change of instructions lay in the demand, then being made in London, that no peace could be made with Portugal until full restitution had taken place.

By full restitution the Commonwealth government meant even more than the return of all confiscated properties, with due indemnity for indirect losses and injuries. London felt that the Portuguese were also responsible for all ships and goods captured by Rupert[32] and disposed of in Lisbon and also partly responsible for the heavy expenses of Blake's fleet, expenses made so much the more heavy by Portugal's sheltering of the Palatine prince.

Whether or not the claims against the Portuguese were excessive or unjust, the Commonwealth government intended to press them. The government, burdened with heavy outlays for the army and navy and hampered by an inefficient system of taxation, had sought relief in such measures as the confiscation of royalist estates and the sale of church lands and were not likely to overlook any opportunity for extorting money from the Portuguese. In August 1650 the Committee on the Admiralty recommended that twenty English ships should be kept in Portuguese waters until Christmas, at which time eight ships should be recalled, leaving twelve ships in that area until April 1651. Sir Henry Vane estimated that the maintenance of twenty ships, and 3,000 men for three months off the coast of Portugal would require £38,656; the further maintenance of twelve ships and 2,000 men off Portugal for another four months would cost £31,730. In addition, the forty ships in service in British waters for six months would require £115,294. In other words, it was proposed to spend £185,680 for the operations of the Commonwealth navy from October 1650 to April 1651. Parliament approved of these arrangements on the condition that the preceding estimates were not exceeded.[33] Of the budgeted £70,386 for the Portugal fleet, £25,000 was for victuals, £23,700 for wages, and £21,186 for all other expenses. On this basis the fleets under Blake and Popham must have cost, before October 1650, at least £100,000. The Portuguese, naturally, had no intention of accepting any liability for these expenditures.

From the sum total of all admitted English claims the Portuguese hoped to subtract the value of all the prizes captured by Blake and Popham. Initially it was the strategy of the Portuguese government to inflate the value of these prizes to close to the level of the total English claim for compensation; in this way the claims and counterclaims would cancel each other almost completely. But the excessive

Portuguese valuations were contradicted by the English judges of the Court of Admiralty, who ascertained the exact value of the prizes. The eleven prizes disposed of in London were worth £106,330. After the deduction of taxes and some other charges, this yielded £81,869 in prize money, which was divided into six parts and distributed as follows: three parts to the Commonwealth, two parts to the English merchants, and one part to the sailors who had participated in the taking of the prizes.[34] The Portuguese sugar ships contained cargo belonging to faithful parliamentary merchants, which was returned to them and which could not be counted as Portuguese losses. Such Commonwealth stalwarts as Barnaby Crawford (fifty-one chests of sugar returned to him), the Bushell brothers (thirty-five chests returned), John Randolph (twenty-seven chests returned), William Pennington, George Lane, and Christopher Warren, among others, had property restored to their London representatives.[35]

The Portuguese also claimed that the value of the nine English ships freighted for Brazil and detained by Blake should be deducted from the total of their liabilities. A large number of legitimate claims from English merchants with an interest in these Brazilmen had to be settled before the Court of Admiralty could dispose of the ships. The proceeds of the nine Brazilmen, therefore, amounted to only £38,214 before taxes; and the prize money to be distributed came to only £20,952. In spite of the small amount involved, London did not think that the nine English ships could be used to diminish the amount of Portuguese liability, since the ships were, after all, English, and not Portuguese.[36]

Lisbon was displeased by this argument but felt at a disadvantage. The breakdown of Portuguese commerce, the shortages of ships, of seamen, and of food, and, above all, the menace of the irreconcilable Dutch—these were difficulties that drove Portugal to make peace with the Commonwealth. Lisbon, like many European cities, lived with a constantly recurring fear of famine. The presence of hostile ships offshore aggravated a situation that was difficult enough in ordinary times. While Blake's fleet patrolled the coasts of Portugal, food supplies in Lisbon dwindled and prices soared.[37]

Food became scarce because grain ships refused to call at Lisbon. The comparative absence of foreign ships meant that the Portuguese could not find vessels to freight for service in the Brazil trade. The Portuguese had depended heavily on English ships, but it was no longer possible to freight them—nor were there enough friendly foreign ships of other nationalities to replace them. In these circumstances the twenty-two, or perhaps twenty-five or thirty, sequestered English ships became important for carrying on whatever Portuguese commerce could still be transacted.

The lack of foreign ships in Lisbon also meant a scarcity of seamen, because the Portuguese regularly recruited foreign sailors for their ships. These seamen were usually skilled men, gunners, carpenters, and surgeons. Gunners, in particular, were in very short supply in Portugal. During Blake's blockade the shortage of seamen became acute. Portuguese shipowners requiring alien sailors for ships bound for Portuguese colonial ports where foreigners were forbidden had to petition the Overseas Council for special permission. The council always allowed ships to carry two or three foreigners but seldom permitted more than that number, especially aboard small vessels, because of the risk of treachery. When João Francisco Baptista, master of the *Nossa Senhora do Rosário e Santo António* bound for Angola, petitioned to be allowed to employ seven or eight foreign seamen—French, Flemish, or Hamburgers—the Overseas Council permitted him to take only four.[38] The council habitually reduced the number of seamen requested, and quite probably captains who wanted three foreigners would ask for six. Occasionally the government allowed the employment of alien mariners in larger numbers. Pierre Stalpart (an important French merchant in Lisbon) was given permission to employ up to fifteen foreigners on each of five ships, or seventy-five aliens in all.[39]

In the selection of foreign sailors, Catholics were preferred to Protestants and aliens who were denizens of Portugal were chosen before those who lived abroad; all were supposed to belong to nations friendly to Portugal. Dutch seamen and subjects of the king of Spain were seldom accepted. Frenchmen and Hamburgers seemed to have been the usual choices. Englishmen had a definite place in this policy: they were employed as master gunners. During the 1650s English marine ordnance and English marine gunners were commonly reputed to be the finest in Europe. The Portuguese shipowner who could induce an English master gunner to enter his service could consider himself fortunate. In 1655 an Englishman even served as gunner in the strategic fortress of Cascais.[40] Salvador Fernandes Gago of Cascais, master of the *Santa Úrsula e as Onze Mil Virgens,* bound for Brazil, asked for and received permission to employ two English gunners and two English sailors on his sixteen gun ship.[41] Simão Luís Roxo, master of the *Nossa Senhora da Conceição e São Francisco Santo*, freighted by the Brazil Company, wanted to employ John Williams, master gunner, a denizen of Lisbon, because "in this Kingdom there is a great shortage of Portuguese gunners."[42] The Overseas Council, as usual, granted the request. The number of English gunners available was, nonetheless, rather small; Portuguese shipowners usually had to content themselves with Frenchmen or Germans.

The many difficulties besetting the Portuguese, sharpened by the food crisis in Lisbon, made John IV anxious for peace with England. On 4 November 1650, a mere thirteen days after Prince Rupert's departure, Portuguese policy underwent a change of direction. The change was from belligerency to reconciliation, from warlike activities to overtures for peace. Events in England had a decisive effect in bringing about this transformation. Throughout the late spring and most of the summer the London government had been very worried about the progress of the royalist movement in Scotland. These worries were ended by Cromwell's victory at Dunbar on 3/13 September 1650.

The Council of State, now less anxious about royalist activities in Britain, considered the Portuguese problem. On 10/20 September the council discussed measures for securing the release of the merchants Richard Beare and John Bushell from Portuguese prisons, and ten days later the council decided to increase the winter fleet in Iberian waters from twelve ships to sixteen (thereby modifying the decisions of August 1650).[43] The new vigor of the government was a direct consequence of the victory at Dunbar, but Dunbar had no impact upon Lisbon until at least a month later, that is, until mid-October. Rupert, who may have been holding his ships in the expectation that Cromwell would be defeated in Scotland, nurturing a slim hope that the royalist fleet could return to northern waters, now saw no chance except escape to the Mediterranean. The Portuguese began to take a serious look at their policy of supporting the royalists; once Rupert had left, on 22 October, Lisbon could initiate the reconstruction of its foreign policy.

A small sign of John IV's change in attitude can be seen in his letter to Dom Rodrigo de Meneses, governor of Oporto, nine days after Rupert's departure, in which he ordered the governor to treat the English crews of two captured codfish ships with kindness but sell the cargoes of dried salted codfish and hold the money in a special fund. Four days later, on 4 November 1650, when there was a general change in Portuguese policy, the secretary of state, Silva, issued somewhat different instructions: the governor of Oporto was to sell the codfish only with the consent of the English captains and at a price that was to their satisfaction; if the Englishmen did not want the codfish sold, then the governor was to hold it for them in a warehouse. Moreover, according to further instructions of 4 November, the English captains were no longer to be arrested and imprisoned but were allowed to go free on bail, provided they did not attempt to leave the kingdom.[44]

During the summer of 1650 the English merchants had endured a harsh imprisonment; many had been taken to places outside of Lisbon, where they could not handle their business and family affairs, even indirectly, through their Portuguese associates. Richard Beare was kept in solitary confinement in a prison in Santarém, fifty miles upriver from Lisbon. Young George Lane spent five months in the convent-castle of the Knights of The Order of Christ at Tomar, ninety miles from Lisbon.[45] The government began to relax these severe measures early in November.

On 4 November 1650 the king signed a number of important letters. A general letter went out to all the ports in the kingdom and colonies saying that the port of Lisbon was now free of all enemy ships and that Portuguese ships could sail to the capital without fear.[46] In a letter to the governor of Oporto, the king communicated an important decision: "I have resolved to send Doctor João de Guimarães, judge of the high court of appeal, to London to remedy the ill-feeling that Prince Rupert's arrival and stay in this port has caused between the English and Portuguese nations."[47] A few days later the king chose Manuel Pinto, a priest, to accompany João de Guimarães to London, so that he could give comfort to English Catholics "and even convert some who are not Catholics, if God allows it."[48] On 23 November 1650 the king made another major decision, of which he informed the governor of the Algarve, as follows: "For good and fit reasons of our service, it is our pleasure to ordain that from henceforth free commerce between these kingdoms and those of England be admitted, and that the ships of that country may come freely to these kingdoms in the same manner as they used to do before the hostilities committed in this port by parliament's fleet."[49]

At the same time, the king took steps to release the Englishmen from prison, provided they posted bond and made no attempt to leave the kingdom and its possessions. All English ships, even the Commonwealth's men-of-war, were to be well treated in all Portuguese ports.[50] Lisbon made an energetic and unilateral effort to bring about peace by refusing to carry on its share of the hostilities. King John hoped that London would forgive and forget and allow circumstances to return to normal—but, in the meantime, the confiscated ships and properties would remain in Portuguese hands.

The hundreds of English merchants hurt by the sequestrations would not allow London to forget anything. Nor would the Commonwealth navy grant peace to the Portuguese just when the sugar fleet was expected back from Brazil. On 8/18 November 1650, Parliament passed an act authorizing the seizure of Portuguese prizes.[51] Capt. William Penn prepared a squadron of five ships to reinforce Blake in Iberian waters. The Generals-at-Sea Edward Popham and Richard Deane instructed him to attack the returning Brazil fleet and then take up his station off Vigo in northwest Spain.[52]

It is hardly surprising that when João de Guimarães, John IV's agent, arrived in Southampton in December 1650 he met with the chilliest of receptions. On 13/23 December 1650 the Council of State issued orders for letters to be written to the governors of Portsmouth and Southampton advising them that "there is a person come from Portugal, pretending to be sent as a public person from the King there to the Parliament here," and asking them to put Guimarães under guard.[53] On 5/15 December the Portuguese agent had sent identical letters, in Latin, to the Parliament and the council announcing his arrival "with full power to treat for the preservation and confirmation of the ancient peace between England and Portugal." He declared that the war between the two countries was the accidental result of the mistakes of ministers and that neither country had wanted it.[54]

The Council of State returned a stiff reply (16/26 December) demanding to know whether the person from Portugal came in the character of an ambassador ordinary or ambassador extraordinary or merely as an envoy or agent and what powers he possessed to treat of reparations.[55] The letters of Guimarães were read in Parliament on

17/27 December 1650 but not discussed. Two days later the letters were read again and a question was put before the house—that safe-conduct be granted to the person from Portugal to come to London forthwith. A motion to consider the question was approved by the narrowest of margins, 27 to 26, with Sir Henry Vane, the leading member of the Committee on the Admiralty, acting as teller of the "Noes." The question of whether or not to issue the safe-conduct was then put to the house, there was a division, and the motion was carried by a margin of one vote, 28 to 27, with Sir Henry Vane again serving as one of the tellers of the "Noes." The council was authorized to prepare a safe-conduct to be signed by the Speaker.[56]

The closeness of these votes was a good indication of the feelings of Parliament toward Guimarães and his mission. At the very outset Lisbon had made a number of mistakes in the handling of its peace overture. First of all, Guimarães had not sufficient prestige in his own person to impress London. Second, Lisbon had refused him the title of ambassador—meaning that John IV had not fully recognized the Commonwealth—and Parliament was quick to interpret this as an insult. Third, the powers of this envoy were very much in question: how could a mere agent commit the king of Portugal to observing the terms of a peace treaty? Guimarães's statement about his powers seemed to imply that he had full authority to confirm the treaty of 1642, but this was of little interest to London—London did not want to treat with any agent who did not have the power to negotiate the question of compensation. For these reasons, Parliament was extremely reluctant even to allow Guimarães to come to London. Also, for exactly these reasons, the Guimarães mission was a failure from beginning to end.

The negotiations were further tarnished by a fault that belonged to the envoy himself: seeing himself as the representative of a great king dealing with republicans and regicides, Guimarães adopted an attitude of condescension and allowed his dispatches to convey a tone of disdainful haughtiness. In revolutionary England, even considering that the agent was only trying to protect the honor and dignity of his king, this was a miscalculation.

The condescension of Guimarães and the reluctance of the Portuguese to send a full ambassador to London contrasted poorly with the friendly overtures of Philip IV of Spain. On 24 December 1650/3 January 1651 Parliament arranged for the Lord Ambassador of the king of Spain, Don Alonzo de Cárdenas, to be received in audience—and the members of the Commons did so without divisions or hard words but with all courtesy.[57] Cárdenas was received by Parliament on the appointed day and made a speech during which he stressed the fact that Spain was the first nation in Europe to recognize the Commonwealth: "His Catholic Majesty being the greatest and first King of Christendom, hath thought fit to oblige this Commonwealth by being also the first who should make acknowledgment."[58] The ambassador spoke harshly of Prince Rupert, who had abused the hospitality of Spanish harbors, and invited the Commonwealth to make free use of the ports of Spain.

The next day, 27 December 1650/6 January 1651, the Speaker read to Parliament a letter addressed to the *Illustrissimo Domino Domino Oratori Parliamenti Reipublicae Angliae,* from Guimarães, and also the Portuguese envoy's letter of credence, of which copies were submitted in English, Portuguese, and Latin.[59] John IV's letter to Parliament stated that Guimarães had power to make peace and to ratify past treaties and even possessed a vaguely defined power to introduce changes in the clauses of old treaties—but it did not refer to him as ambassador and made no mention of any power to negotiate indemnities. Parliament appointed a committee to consider the matter of giving audience to the Portuguese envoy.

The parliamentary committee reported on 1/10 January 1651 that the credentials of the public minister of the king of Portugal did not state that he was either an ordinary or an extraordinary ambassador, but the committee recommended that he be received by Parliament at 10:00 A.M. on Tuesday, 7/17 January 1651, probably with reduced ceremony.[60] Guimarães was determined, naturally enough, that he should be received with exactly the same courtesy, at the same hour, and with the same ceremony as Parliament had extended to the Spanish ambassador, even though the two envoys were not of the same diplomatic rank. Guimarães protested to Parliament that he was not being accorded the customary reception but was being treated as a special case, Parliament having devised a depreciatory formula to be used for him alone and contrived after his arrival in London. Parliament at first rejected the protest but eventually gave way after receiving another appeal from Guimarães. The reception was set for 11:00 A.M. on Friday, 10/20 January 1651.[61]

Parliament appointed a distinguished committee of eleven members to meet the agent, including the Lords Commissioners of the Great Seal Bulstrode Whitelock and John Lisle; the attorney general, Edmund Prideaux; Sir Henry Vane; and various members of the Council of State—but the reception was not a success. The interview was formal, dry, and chilly. Sir Oliver Fleming, the officer who always attended visiting ambassadors, conducted the Portuguese envoy to the parliamentary deputation; everyone removed his hat and then Guimarães was told to sit in a certain seat and address himself to Bulstrode Whitelock, the member in charge of the committee. The men then all replaced their hats. The resolution appointing the parliamentary committee was read to Guimarães, who did not understand English; then Guimarães presented his credentials and read them, in Portuguese; neither side understood anything said by the other. The agent made a formal oration, in Portuguese, invoking the antiquity of the Anglo-Portuguese alliance and the joint struggles against the Moors in the twelfth century, alluding to Queen Elizabeth's help to the Portuguese patriots in the forlorn fight against Philip II of Spain, and closing with the statement that he came with full powers to confer about the preservation of the peace.[62]

The Portuguese acted as if the war did not exist; their strategy was to speak about maintaining and strengthening the *peace,* not about ending the *war.* If they could persuade the English that peace already existed and that it was only necessary to confirm it, then they might win a major diplomatic victory. This pretense did not deceive the Commonwealth government, who realized that substantial financial compensation could not be obtained without keeping alive the threat to Portuguese shipping. The Council of State informed Blake that the Portuguese had sent a public minister to England and added: "notwithstanding which you are to take no notice of it, but prosecute your former instructions."[63] Capt. William Penn had left Falmouth on 20/30 December 1650 and was already at sea, on his way to join Blake.

Penn was supposed to intercept the Brazil fleet but had only five ships, which were soon reduced to three, wherewith to attack seventy sugar ships. The sugar fleet, after a delay of fifty days in Bahia, left Brazil on 24 September 1650, expecting to arrive in Portugal early in January. Off the Azores the fleet ran into severe storms and four ships were lost, including one or two of the largest galleons. Penn's small squadron was too late to meet the main fleet and managed to catch only one tardy straggler, whose capture was recorded in Penn's journal as follows (entry for 13/23 January 1651): "Tooke *Senora* of Lisbon, laden with sugar, some of which put into the *Pellican.*"[64] This ship Penn sent to England. The rest of the Brazil fleet reached Lisbon safely in the middle of January. "Their arrival probably saved Portugal from complete collapse, as the seventy-odd sail which reached port were very richly laden."[65]

Penn made for the island of Terceira, in the Azores, and ransomed a few Englishmen held prisoner there. After a few days of searching for prizes, the English squadron departed for the straits and joined some of Blake's ships. Blake himself had returned to England where he was received by a grateful parliament on 13/23 February. Penn's squadron spent fifteen months at sea (during which the commander never once set foot ashore) and captured thirty-six prizes.[66]

These naval operations were realities, but in London Guimarães conducted his diplomacy on the basis of fantasies. On 8/18 January 1651 he demanded that the sale of all Portuguese prize goods be stopped, and he repeated the demand five days later in a letter to the Speaker of the House written on the very day (13/23 January 1651) that Penn captured the sugar ship. Parliament returned no answer to these protests. On 27 January/6 February 1651 Guimarães again demanded that Parliament suspend the sale of all Portuguese property and demanded an answer to his peace proposals. As always, Guimarães behaved as if he were bargaining from a position of strength, representing a government that was conferring favors on the Commonwealth—and this approach only stiffened opinion against him.

Guimarães's last letter was read in Parliament on 29 January/8 February 1651, along with many petitions of wives and relatives of the English merchants imprisoned in Portugal. Parliament had also read some intercepted correspondence between the Portuguese ambassador in Holland and Prince Rupert, and the members were in no mood to placate Guimarães on the question of stopping the sale of prize goods. Parliament presented Guimarães with a list of English grievances and again required the Portuguese envoy to state whether or not he possessed full powers to negotiate compensations.[67]

The scene then shifted to the Council of State,[68] who were prepared to treat with the Portuguese envoy after he had satisfied the council that he possessed powers to grant compensation. Joseph Frost, a secretary attached to the council, went to Guimarães and asked to see his powers as these were expressed in John IV's *original* instructions to the envoy—and the agent was told that if he refused to disclose the king's private instructions the council would decline to negotiate at all. Frost secured a paper from Guimarães and translated it, and the council appointed a committee to consider the Portuguese question.[69] The agent had hoped that somehow peace could be arranged between England and Portugal without making any commitment to pay compensations; his first line of defense, on this issue, was to affirm that John IV had not given him powers to treat of compensation but only of the peace, which, in any event must come first, since one cannot pay reparations until arms have been set aside. The council weakened this argument by forcing Guimarães to declare, at the very outset, that he was competent to negotiate compensations.

The committee on Portugal—consisting of Sir Henry Vane, Sir Henry Mildmay, Dennis Bond, and Thomas Scott—met Guimarães formally at 3:00 P.M. on 12/22 February 1651, in the presence of Charles Vane (the old envoy to Lisbon) and of the foreign language secretaries Joseph Frost and John Milton. The committee presented a list of Six Preliminary Articles to Guimarães, and the Portuguese agent replied with his own list of Three Preliminary Demands—but the committee told him that his demands would not be considered until an answer had been given to the Six Preliminary Articles.[70]

These Six Articles, which remained the focus of Anglo-Portuguese negotiations for several years, ran as follows: article 1: Portugal must release all English prisoners; article 2: Portugal must return all sequestered ships, goods, and money, render satisfaction for properties that had deteriorated, and compensate the proprietors for damages suffered; article 3: the persons who had assaulted and killed English seamen in Portugal and who had tried to blow up the warship *Leopard* must be brought to justice; article 4: Portugal must compensate the Commonwealth for the expenses of the fleets sent to pursue Rupert, expenses of £214,640 from the autumn of 1649 to the spring of 1651; article 5: Portugal must make restitution or reparations for the English goods seized by the princes Rupert and Maurice; and article 6: Portugal must pay compensation for the English vessels brought into Portuguese ports by Rupert and sold there.[71]

Guimarães acted with speed and replied, the very next day, to the Six Articles, concentrating most of his attention on article 4, in which the Commonwealth laid claim to £214,640 in reparations but agreed that the value of prizes and prize goods taken from the Portuguese should be deducted from the figure. Guimarães claimed that the value of Portuguese prize goods held by the English came to £900,000 (!), or, to put it another way, this was the minimum extent of Portuguese losses suffered at the hands of the English.[72] The balance of claims, therefore, under article 4, left England owing Portugal £685,360, and this sum could be used to defray the amounts for which Portugal was liable under the other articles.

On 15/25 February 1651 the Council of State expressed its great dissatisfaction with the replies of the Portuguese minister and appointed a committee to see Guimarães and furnish him with a detailed exposition of English views. Negotiations went on for seven weeks between the envoy and the council and ended with an impasse. On 18/28 March 1651 Guimarães went so far as to accept articles 1, 2, 3, and 6 provided that agreement on substantial modifications in articles 4 and 5 were reached within fifteen days. The council rejected his suggestions and again insisted on the acceptance of all six articles. Guimarães replied with an angry protest (on 25 March/4 April 1651).[73]

On 1/11 April 1651 the council informed Guimarães, in a chilly note, that "notwithstanding his last paper was fuller of expostulations than satisfaction, yet Council have resolved to report the whole business of the treaty between them and him to Parliament on Friday next" (i.e., 4/14 April). The envoy was asked if he had anything further to add. Guimarães's answer to this last appeal was discussed in the council on 3/13 April 1651 and considered unsatisfactory. The matter now lay in the hands of Parliament.[74]

On 4/14 April 1651 Bulstrode Whitelock, Lord Commissioner of the Great Seal, who had followed the negotiations step-by-step, reported to Parliament on the question of peace with Portugal. Guimarães, in the meantime, had decided to lay his case before the general English public and distributed in London a printed paper titled *A Brief Relation of the Whole Treaty Between the Public Minister of Portugall and the Council of State: Printed for the Satisfaction of All the Members of Parliament of the Commonwealth of England, by Order of the Said Minister of Portugall.* This appeal to English citizens, over the heads of the government, offended Parliament and probably contributed to the angry tone that marred the negotiations during the next five weeks.[75]

The House of Commons held a long discussion concerning the Anglo-Portuguese negotiations (on 10/20 April 1651) and arrived at certain clarifications about the precise meaning of the Six Preliminary Articles. Article 1, concerning the release of English prisoners in Portugal, was not to be construed as extending to persons held prisoner for civil or criminal offenses unconnected with Anglo-Portuguese politics. Article 2, respecting the payment of damages resulting from the sequestrations, meant, said Parliament, that the English "shall not insist upon the greatest extent thereof, but only as consonant with equity and reason, and testifying our propension to peace."[76] Under article 3, requiring the punishment of those guilty of attacking English seamen, only English nationals would be delivered into the hands of Parliament; culprits of Portuguese nationality would be left to the punishment of Portuguese courts. In article 4, the amount claimed for the expenses of Blake's fleet was reduced from £214,640 to £180,000, and the value of Portuguese prizes in the Admiralty Courts was to be deducted therefrom; but this value was to be the amount realized from the sale of Portuguese goods in England and not the inflated values assigned to them by Guimarães. As for article 5, concerning compensation for English goods seized by Rupert, Guimarães had protested that the article was "abstruse and difficult" and that the Portuguese could not be held responsible for Rupert's actions; but Parliament said: "We conceive the demand exceedingly plain and clear," claiming that, since John IV would not allow the English to initiate suits in his courts for the recovery of property seized by Rupert, "nor would the king suffer our ships there to do justice themselves," Portuguese responsibility for these losses was beyond doubt. The same arguments applied to article 6, involving the restoration of ships taken by Rupert.[77]

The Portuguese minister had said that he would accept the first three articles provided there was an immediate cessation of all hostilities. Parliament replied that when the king of Portugal had released all English captives, restored all confiscated goods, and given satisfactory security for the performance of the other articles, then the English government would accept a truce for three months, at the end of which time clear and definite arrangements for the peace must have been arrived at, or else hostilities would begin anew.[78]

After weeks of negotiations London had adopted a clear position: Guimarães must accept the Six Preliminary Articles or else leave England. But he refused to do either. What he wanted was to end all hostilities in return for promises to deal justly with the English in the matter of the Six Articles. He was even prepared to accept the articles in principle, provided that the details could be worked out after the proclamation of the truce. His first aim was to try to silence the guns of the Commonwealth Navy but, unfortunately for him, he could not induce the Englishmen to suspend their maritime offensive.

Since each side adhered to its view, the negotiations foundered. Guimarães's efforts to prolong the discussions were unsuccessful, because Parliament kept setting a time limit for his replies. In one aspect these talks were rather clumsy, because Parliament would make a decision and communicate it to the Council of State, who would relay it to the envoy; Guimarães would then reply to the Council of State, who reported the reply to Parliament. This tiresome procedure was saved from confusion by the fact that virtually the same men handled the Portuguese question in both the council and the Parliament, although the council could not quite control the voting in the Parliament.

The council informed Guimarães of the "final" offers of Parliament on 17/27 April and gave the envoy six days in which to reply. Guimarães answered on 21 April/1 May, agreeing plainly to all the demands in the Six Articles, but this seeming acquiescence was merely a bait that contained a sharp hook. Guimarães claimed that, with his acceptance of the articles, the truce now came into being automatically and immediately, but he carefully refrained from committing himself as to when the articles were to be carried out. In other words, peace would come, but no compensation. The envoy also offered to conclude a peace treaty within a few days—hoping, of course, that the treaty would only consist of declarations repeating or renewing the treaty of 1642.[79] In this way the truce and the treaty would come at almost the same time; the peace would have been won and the Portuguese would carry out the Six Articles at their leisure, if at all.

Dennis Bond reported to Parliament on 22 April/2 May 1651 that the envoy's answer to all the articles was satisfactory "except as concerns the time for a cessation to begin, and the manner of performing the said articles."[80] Parliament instructed the council to issue a brusque demand for a "positive" answer within three days. Guimarães's next communication (24 April/4May) only advanced the deception a stage further: he now alluded to the Six Articles as if they constituted the peace treaty itself, spoke as if everything had been decided with only the question of "ratification" remaining; and, as for the time factor, articles 1 and 2 would be put into execution when Parliament's approval was known and published in Lisbon, on which day there would be a complete cessation of hostilities; the other four articles could come into effect within any reasonable length of time agreed on between the English and himself, by an amicable clause to be inserted in the peace treaty.[81]

These disingenuous proposals reversed the time sequence intended by the council. In the English view the execution of the articles was to be followed by a truce, then by a treaty, then by peace; in Guimarães's view the innocuous articles 1 and 2 would come into effect on the same day as the truce, then would come the peace treaty, one of whose clauses would set a time for the execution of the articles dealing with compensation, which would come into effect not as the first step but last of all, if ever.

Parliament rejected these suggestions immediately and ordered the council to require of the envoy "a positive and clear answer" within three days. The council translated this message into Latin and sent it to Guimarães (on 26 April/6 May), who took *four* days to compose his reply (30 April/10 May), in which he adhered to all his former contentions, with some new supporting arguments. He began by stating that he thought his previous replies had been quite satisfactory; he drew a distinction between the "political articles" (i.e., the Six Articles) and the "commercial articles" (i.e., the renewal of the treaty of 1642)—the former created the basis of the peace, not the latter, which was nonpolitical in character, so that his acceptance of the Six Articles already had brought the peace into being. But if the "commercial articles" were insisted on, then he was prepared to accept the 1642 articles, and perhaps one or two other things, immediately; as for the "political articles," the envoy was prepared to pawn his head and person that John IV would carry out the agreement.

But, above all, Guimarães urged that these matters be settled within the next few days so that news of a secure peace could be sent to Portugal soon.[82]

Parliament did not debate the Portuguese question again until 7/17 May 1651, when Guimarães's reply was rejected after a division. Another division favored continuation of the state of hostilities with Portugal until such time as the articles had been put into effect or indisputable security for their execution obtained. Guimarães sent two papers to the council on 11/21 May 1651, in the first of which he said that he could do no more than consent to the articles and any other question (such as the time of execution) must be referred to John IV; and, in the second paper, he proposed the immediate execution of articles 1 and 2, but had nothing to say concerning the date of enforcement of the other articles. Parliament considered these replies unsatisfactory.[83]

The diplomatic negotiations had now reached a dead end, although Guimarães was still searching for ways in which to postpone a final rupture. On 15/25 May he told the council that he had decided to consult John IV in person, that he required a safe-conduct to leave the country, and that he would return with a reply from his government.[84] This would delay a decision for weeks or months, during which time the English might perhaps be induced not to press the naval war against Portugal.

Thomas Scott of the council informed the House of Commons of this final communication from Guimarães. The House passed a series of hostile resolutions (16/26 May 1651), which ran as follows: (1) all concessions made to the Portuguese in former resolutions were canceled, and Parliament was not to be bound by them; (2) Parliament would issue a pass to Guimarães (through the council), valid for fourteen days and signed by the Speaker; (3) the council was directed to consider measures leading to speedy help for the prisoners in Lisbon; and (4) consideration must be given to ways in which to capture more Portuguese prizes.[85] On the same day, the council ordered John Milton to go to the envoy's house and secure a list of names of persons belonging to Guimarães's retinue, so that they could be added to the safe-conduct. The council referred the question of the Lisbon prisoners to the Committee on the Affairs of the Admiralty and Navy.[86]

Guimarães was horrified at being ordered to leave the country within two weeks. In a note to the council, he demanded a longer time to prepare for the journey. The council's reply was insulting and abrupt; the messenger was told that the council could accept no more letters from the Portuguese envoy, except such as were addressed directly to Parliament.[87]

On 23 May/2 June the agent made one last effort. He informed Parliament that he refused to accept a safe-conduct that was for leaving only and that made no provision for his return. Again he offered to sign a peace immediately and to enforce articles 1 and 2 at once, also to give security for the performance of the other articles. In addition, he wanted copies of all previous parliamentary resolutions and declarations and expressed willingness to hear any new proposals the English might want to make.[88] These remarks went unheeded.

On 11/21 June 1651 the council issued an order that letters should be written to all the commanders in the fleet not to hinder the free passage of "Joas de Guiamaras" and his retinue, who were on their way to Portugal.[89] This is the last mention of his name in the official English records. He sailed for Portugal aboard the *Peter and Jane* of London on 22 June or shortly thereafter. The *Peter and Jane*, under the command of George Chappell, had been confiscated in Lisbon in 1650 but was sent back to London (where she arrived, so it would seem, early in April 1651) with a load of sixty-eight English seamen who had been liberated after imprisonment in Portugal. Chappell promised the Portuguese that he would return his ship and himself to Lisbon without delay.[90] The Council of State paid Chappell £423 for his services and also released the fifteen Portuguese prisoners who had been confined in Marshalsea Prison. On 3/13 June 1651 the council duly authorized Chappell to return to Lisbon, as per his agreement, and the Portuguese envoy went back with him.[91]

The Guimarães mission may be described with complete fairness as a failure; between his arrival in December 1650 and his departure in June 1651 not a single aim of Portuguese diplomacy had been achieved. This failure was caused not only by the clumsiness of the Portuguese envoy but also by English obstinacy on the issue of compensation. The Portuguese reluctance to grant money compensation to the English and the disinclination of London to accept peace on any other terms doomed the negotiations. As the essential prerequisite to the peace London insisted on a transfer of valuables from Portuguese to English hands. Here the issue rested, after the departure of Guimarães, for another year, until the arrival of a second Portuguese envoy.

In Lisbon, John IV had supported Guimarães's policy in whatever ways he could. The official pretense that the war with England had come to an end was maintained. In spite of William Penn's attack on the sugar ships, the king insisted that English ships were not to be molested.[92] When a report reached Lisbon that Rupert's ships were again lurking in the straits, the king wrote the governor of the Algarve, on 25 April 1651, that the princes Rupert and Maurice were not to be admitted to Portuguese harbors, "because of the grave damage resulting to the Kingdom from their stay in this port [of Lisbon]."[93] These instructions were to be kept secret. Two months later fresh orders not to admit Rupert or his ships went out to the Algarve ports and to Oporto, Setúbal, Aveiro, and Viana do Castelo; royalist ships were not to be admitted, or supplied, and no one was permitted to buy any merchandise from them.[94] This time the instructions were not kept secret but publicized widely.

During the first eight months of 1651 the royalists still had hoped for a victory over the armies of Cromwell. Charles II, "King of Scotland" (as he was called), had an army in the Highlands of Scotland, yet unbeaten, with which he invaded England in August. The invasion ended with the complete defeat of their forces at Worcester, on 3/13 September, by Cromwell. The young king escaped from the battlefield and eventually reached the Continent, but the royalists lost almost all hope. Fifteen days later Cromwell went to Woolwich to witness the launching of a new frigate of 660 tons, with room for sixty guns, and christened the *Worcester*—the twelfth powerful new frigate to be built by the Commonwealth.[95] Day by day England grew stronger on the sea.

On 20/30 October the Council of State issued an order to Penn to sail slowly along the coast of Portugal, using his victuals and water as economically as he could, and "as much as you are able distress and straighten the Portuguese, and take such of their ships and goods as you meet with."[96] This order was a fitting epitaph to the Anglo-Portuguese peace negotiations of 1651.

6
THE PEACE TREATY OF 1654

The year 1652 began auspiciously for Anglo-Portuguese relations. On 8 January the king of Portugal signed a decree authorizing the return of sequestered properties to the English merchants,[1] and Lisbon once again, in response to the long-felt need for an accommodation with the Commonwealth, prepared an embassy to go to England. In London, Parliament, having vanquished all domestic enemies, marshaled its forces for a decisive confrontation with the United Provinces. The government could give little time or attention to the problem of Portugal. John IV, in whatever ways he could, had to attract and hold English attention and somehow induce London to end the one-sided maritime war.

Lisbon did not repeat the mistakes made during the preparation of the Guimarães mission. Guimarães had been a relatively unimportant official, endowed with vague powers, insufficiently accredited, and sent to a government that Lisbon had treated as illegitimate. This time the envoy was a magnate, João Rodrigues de Sá e Meneses, Count of Penaguião and Grand Chamberlain or Lord High Chamberlain (as he was sometimes called in London) to the king of Portugal. He was not a mere agent but an ambassador extraordinary, endowed with full powers to negotiate for peace;[2] nor did he approach Cromwell's government in the haughty manner of a royalist deigning to hold converse with regicides and usurpers, but with courtesy and respect. Lisbon surrounded the distinguished envoy with a brilliant entourage and made every effort to attract the goodwill and cooperation of the English.

On 11/21 August 1652 the ambassador extraordinary wrote letters to the Council of State and Parliament from Plymouth, announcing his arrival and requesting a quick answer. The letters were taken to London by Francisco Ferreira Rebelo, secretary to the embassy. The Council of State referred the ambassador's letter to Parliament, and on 17/27 August 1652 the Parliament issued an order welcoming to England the "Earl Lord Chamberlain Lord Ambassador Extraordinary from the King of Portugall."[3] The council instructed the mayor of Plymouth to render all courtesy and assistance to the Count of Penaguião and his party and asked the Committee on Foreign Affairs to confer with Sir Oliver Fleming (the official in charge of foreign envoys) on how to bring this ambassador to London.

In the seventeenth century the first entrance of an ambassador to a capital was a grand and ceremonious business, requiring long and patient preparation. Between the time of Penaguião's arrival at Plymouth and his reception in London, five weeks passed. This delay was not unusual. Even ambassadors who arrived at Tilbury or Greenwich often waited for two or three weeks at the outskirts of London, pretending not to be there, while preparations were made for their official entry. The Council of State arranged to entertain the distinguished Portuguese visitor with nine meals, at the expense of the Commonwealth of England, served on the state's plate, "the Portuguese Ambassador to be allowed a diet of 50 dishes, for first and second course, and 30 dishes of fruits and sweetmeats, for each meal."[4] The first banquet took place on Monday, 27 September/7 October 1652, with six councillors of state—the Lord Commissioner of the Great Seal John Lisle, Sir William Masham, Robert Wallop, Thomas Scott, Henry Marten, and Cornelius Holland—personally escorting Penaguião.[5]

The day after the opening banquet Penaguião sent a copy of his credentials to Francis Lenthall, Speaker of the House of Commons, and requested that he be received by Parliament as soon as possible.[6] Parliament arranged to receive him on Friday, 30 September/10 October, at 11:00 A.M. The ambassador appeared at the time appointed and delivered a persuasive speech in Portuguese. The Portuguese government, said Penaguião, had not been participants in Rupert's activities but judges over them. No English ships had been seized until after Blake had attacked the Brazil fleet.[7] The imprisonment of the English merchants had prevented their being injured or killed by the enraged Lisbon populace, and the sequestrations had prevented English property from being stolen or destroyed. Portuguese actions had not been wrongs inflicted on Englishmen but remedies for the disorders brought about by the parliamentary fleet. The king of Portugal had rendered satisfaction on all claims as soon as possible.

The king's envoy, João de Guimarães, had not been well received in England, yet John IV had given his consent to the Six Preliminary Articles. Penaguião finished by stating that the English in Portugal were now in enjoyment of liberty, property, and their former privileges. The only thing remaining was to conclude the peace, for which purpose he had come to England.[8]

The speech, although effective in its way, adopted the same approach that had failed with Guimarães: namely, that almost all was well with Anglo-Portuguese relations; that adjustments had been made in Lisbon that removed all the "misunderstandings" created by Rupert's presence in Lisbon; that peace had been reestablished and all that was necessary was a formal recognition of this fact. Unfortunately for the Portuguese, the ambassador's speech could not make any immediate impression on the members of Parliament, because few, if any, could understand what he said. A rather poor Latin copy was delivered to the Speaker, together with a copy of the ambassador's credentials. Parliament did not even understand what the ambassador's name was and could make out only the first half of it, which was reported to be "John Roderick——."[9] Since João Rodrigues de Sá e Meneses usually signed official documents, in the Portuguese fashion, with the titles of his highest office—i.e., "Conde Camareiro" (Count Chamberlain)—he came to be known in England as "Count Camara"!

Parliament referred the negotiations with the Portuguese to the Council of State. The council gave audience to Penaguião on 7/17 October 1652 and received from him a Latin paper that was given to John Milton to translate. A more formal meeting took place a few days later when thirteen members of the council waited upon the Portuguese ambassador, including all who had experience in Portuguese questions.[10]

During the next three months, from the middle of October 1652 until the middle of January 1653, negotiations between the English and the Portuguese revolved around two issues: (1) the English insistence that the Portuguese accept the Six Preliminary Articles and carry them out immediately and (2) new and strong demands from the Portuguese for restitution of Portuguese goods seized aboard Dutch vessels.

London's requirement that nothing could be done until the Portuguese had accepted and carried out the Six Articles remained as binding, and was advanced as strictly, as in the days of Guimarães. In the autumn of 1652 the dispute centered on article 4, which required reimbursement for the expenses of the fleet sent in pursuit of Rupert. Originally the English government had claimed £214,640 minus the amount raised from the sale of captured Portuguese cargoes; then the figure was reduced to £180,000, although this "concession" had been canceled when negotiations with Guimarães broke down. In November 1652 the council returned to the figure of £180,000 and agreed to deduct therefrom the sum of £114,246 11s 6d realized from the sale of Portuguese ships and cargoes, leaving a balance of £65,753 8s 6d owed to the Commonwealth. The council demanded this sum of the ambassador and confronted him with an old declaration (17 April 1651) by the king of Portugal in which he had accepted all of the Six Articles.[11]

Penaguião argued that the £114,246 realized from the sale of Portuguese ships and cargoes was too small a figure, since it failed to include such ships as the 500-ton *Nossa Senhora da Natividade,* a captured Portuguese warship added to the Commonwealth fleet. This ship yielded £2,330 to the Admiralty's prize office[12] but had not been included in the reckoning. The ambassador also pressed the question concerning the Portuguese goods seized aboard Dutch ships. On 2/12 March 1652, while leading his squadron back to England, William Penn had seized six ships coming out of Lisbon. These six ships, five from the Netherlands and one from Lubeck, were released after their arrival in England, but the Portuguese claimed considerable losses of cargo.[13]

The Anglo-Dutch war inflicted losses on every European merchant who had goods aboard Dutch ships. Since much of Western Europe's maritime trade was carried in Dutch bottoms, England's assault on Dutch shipping brought a stream of protests, complaints, and demands for compensation from neutral capitals. The Commonwealth pursued its course with considerable resolution and seldom gave relief to neutrals. When Penaguião tried to protect Portuguese goods seized aboard Dutch vessels, the council always referred him to the Court of Admiralty, who took no notice of his petitions. The ambassador appealed to Parliament and secured an order, issued on 16/26 December 1652, directing the council to require the Court of Admiralty to prevent the sale of all Portuguese properties duly proved to be such. Although most of the men who were leaders in the small parliament (then attended on an average by about fifty-seven members)[14] also sat in the Council of State, the council ignored Parliament's directive. The ambassador was forced, once more, to complain directly to the council, who finally sent down an order (13/23 January 1653) saying the following: "that it be signified to the judges of the Admiralty, that proofe being made, in due forme of law, that such goods doe bona fide belong to the said King [of Portugal] or his subjects, that they cause restitution to be made thereof."[15]

The Admiralty judges professed themselves to be much puzzled by this order; had not the policy been laid down by Parliament that all Portuguese property was to be sold for the compensation of the English merchants? How was the council's order to be reconciled with Parliament's previous decree? The judges, "findeing not the necessarie iurisdiction nor such clearnesse in this matter," asked for further instruction.[16] The judges were technically correct: if parliament had not explicitly amended or repealed their former resolutions, then the judges had to obey them, regardless of the council's wishes.

The legal difficulty was genuine but may have been provoked deliberately. The Commonwealth government, which, on occasion, was a model of administrative efficiency, energy, and speed, produced only confusion and delay on this question. They may indeed have acted in bad faith. By the time a further order from Whitehall (2/12 February 1653) was considered by the Admiralty Judges, all the property in dispute, to no one's surprise, had already been sold.

The ambassador had obtained his original order for the protection of the properties a full seven weeks before, on 16/26 December 1652, but Parliament's paper promise, perhaps deliberately, had never been carried out. Yet in return for this promise the ambassador had agreed to settle the question of the Six Articles. Although the protection of Portuguese properties was not officially linked to the discussions about the Six Articles, it is clear that Penaguião would not agree to compensation under article 4 until the English protected the goods seized from the Dutch ships. Penaguião's promise to pay compensation under the articles, at some unspecified future date, was probably as insincere as the promise he had received from Parliament. Three and a half years elapsed before Portugal paid anything to England, and even then payment was made only under the threat of force.

The details of these negotiations possess a certain interest. Initially, during December 1652, Penaguião played his hand with considerable skill. On 8/18 December he accepted all the articles except article 4. The sum of £65,753 desired by the Parliament he considered excessive, but he was willing to submit it to the judgment of a two-man arbitration board (Parliament and the King of Portugal would each appoint one arbitrator) and was willing to pay £25,000 regardless of the decision of the arbitrators—that is, he would pay £25,000 even if the arbitrators decided nothing was owed by Portugal. Meanwhile, Parliament and the council pressed on Penaguião the necessity of accepting all of the Six Articles. On 16/26 December 1652 Parliament received the ambassador at the Court of Wards. Penaguião made a strong complaint about the Portuguese goods in the Admiralty and obtained the order for their release; then he offered £50,000 in settlement of the claims under article 4. Parliament formally accepted this offer, asked the council to arrange for its collection, and authorized the council to proceed with an Anglo-Portuguese peace treaty.[17]

In the circumstances of December 1652, with London virtually under a blockade by Dutch ships, not much attention could be given to the Portuguese question and the English were quite happy to dispose of it for an immediate cash settlement of £50,000. The Commonwealth was critically short of money because of the heavy naval expenses of the Dutch war. On 24 December 1652/3 January 1653, after intensive negotiations, the council arranged that Sir Oliver Fleming and John Thurloe should receive from Penaguião bills of exchange for the payment at Lisbon of £20,000, the first portion of the £50,000. The council declared that £20,000 was worth 42,240,000 "rials Portugal money"[18]—or 42:240$000 réis, at the exchange of £1 to 2$112 réis, a rate that in terms of the bullion content of coins in mint condition was almost mathematically exact.[19] In the meantime, on 19/29 December 1652, the ambassador asked the council to issue a safe-conduct to three or four Dutch ships, which would carry cargoes to Portugal. The council made no answer to this until almost six months later, when the war with the Netherlands had developed favorably for England, but agreed to issue safe-conducts if the Portuguese would furnish complete information about the ships and the goods.[20]

On 5/15 January 1653 Parliament reported that Penaguião had signed the Six Articles and placed his seal on the official copy in Latin. On 11/21 January the Speaker subscribed the same copy and affixed the seal of Parliament thereto.[21] A spirit of concord prevailed. Francesco Bernardi, Genoese agent in London, reported to his government with wild inaccuracy that "the treaty with Portugal has been very successfully completed, and a firm peace and free commerce between this Republic and that Kingdom have been concluded."[22]

The Genoese agent mistook the Six Preliminary Articles for the peace treaty itself. This mistake was deliberately fostered by the Portuguese, who now maintained that nothing more remained to be done except to determine what was owed to English merchants under article 2 (providing for the restoration of sequestered properties) and to sign an additional article reconfirming the Anglo-Portuguese treaty of 29 January/8 February 1642. The mood of amity barely lasted through the month of January 1653, during which month the English merchants busily compiled statements of their claims under article 2.

In February the ambassador complained bitterly about the disposal of the Portuguese goods in the Admiralty Court, saying that "everything that has been done in this matter has been useless."[23] The council had complaints of its own: the £20,000 supposedly set aside by John IV in Lisbon for remittance to London was retained in Portugal. The council expostulated in vain[24]—English unwillingness to accommodate the Portuguese in the matter of the properties seized from the Dutch ships was counterbalanced, neatly and exactly, by Portuguese procrastination in making the agreed payments under article 4.

After the signing of the Six Articles the government called on the merchants of London to do two things: (1) present their claims for compensation for the losses suffered during 1650 and (2) draw up a list of suggestions for articles in the new peace treaty to be made with Portugal. The merchants' financial claims formed the basis of negotiations and quarrels between the diplomats that continued well into the 1660s; the merchants' suggestions for a peace treaty led to a number of new and important stipulations that eventually were included in the treaty of 10/20 July 1654.

Penaguião wanted a treaty drawn up along the lines of the treaty of 28 January/8 February 1642, preferably an article-by-article copy of the earlier agreement. The London merchants, or at least some of them, had very different ideas: they sensed that the moment had come to obtain expanded privileges, increased security, and broad new opportunities for the merchants resident in or trading with Portugal.

The London merchants' suggestions for the treaty with Portugal covered wide and miscellaneous groups of topics, ranging all the way from the opening up of Portuguese India to the English trader to specific proposals on how to settle disputes over damaged cargoes. The merchants' proposals can be grouped into four general categories. First and foremost, they wanted free and unrestricted trade in all parts of Portugal and her empire—including Brazil, Guinea, Angola, Mozambique, and India—without any special or general licenses, with complete freedom to return from a Portuguese colony directly to England or elsewhere without passing through Lisbon.

Second, the merchants wanted special safeguards with respect to the payment of customs duties, taxes, harbor and wharfage fees, and the like. Englishmen should not be required to pay more duty than the Portuguese pay; duties should not exceed 23 percent *ad valorem;* nor should duties be paid twice just because an article had been taken to two Portuguese ports. Harbor fees should be no higher than 5$000 réis (£2.36) for a 500-ton ship, and proportionately less for smaller ships (at 10 réis per ton).

Third, the merchants wanted certain guaranteed personal freedoms for Englishmen resident in Portugal: they were not to be arrested or imprisoned without the consent of the Judge Conservator; they were to be free to buy and sell houses and other properties without hindrance; they were to be allowed to bear arms, to own and ride horses, to disregard provisions in local sumptuary laws, and to decline to be conscripted for the king of Portugal's service. They must possess religious freedom, including freedom of worship, the right to own Protestant books and Bibles, and the privilege of burying their dead in their own cemetery. English Protestants should not be compelled to contribute toward the support of St. George's Chapel, the English Catholic church in Lisbon, and must enjoy full exemption from all the powers of the Inquisition.

Fourth, the merchants wanted a number of concessions respecting ships and shipping. English warships should be freely admitted in Portuguese ports. English ships should not be compulsorily loaded or unloaded, forced to carry a cargo, or seized for the service of the king of Portugal without the consent of the owners. If possible, however, the Portuguese should charter English ships and only English ships. Perhaps English merchants should be granted a ten-year monopoly for the carrying of Portuguese salt. Also, if a third country should bring English prizes into a Portuguese port or Portuguese prizes into an English port, then those prizes should be apprehended and returned to their owners.[25]

These proposals, or most of them, were presented to the Portuguese ambassador during January or early February 1653. Penaguião may well have been stunned by the number and novelty of the suggestions. In a letter written to the Council of State on 17 February 1653 he tried to sidestep the hard bargaining and long discussions that apparently lay ahead: "Many times I have repeated that the purpose of my embassy was to ratify the peace and not to build it up from its first foundations."[26] He claimed, unconvincingly, that he lacked "the powers to make innovations in past treaties,"[27] echoing the line that Guimarães had used so often. Penaguião protested that the Portuguese had offered satisfaction shortly after the opening of hostilities—that they had accepted the preliminary articles—and why should the English now demand new privileges? It was no use claiming, as the English liked to do, that all privileges and benefits were mutual and reciprocal; few Portuguese merchants and ships did business in English ports while large numbers of English merchants and ships were to be found in Portuguese ports, and thus the English alone would reap most of the advantages from the treaty.

In his letter to the council and in other papers, Penaguião replied to the English proposals point by point. The English demand for free trade throughout the Portuguese empire could not be granted, because access to the empire by foreigners was contrary to the fundamental laws of the Kingdom of Portugal. Trade with Brazil was regulated by the statutes of the General Company of Brazil, and nothing in a treaty could abrogate the rights and privileges of the Brazil Company. There was no need to talk much about Portuguese India, since there had been no war between the English and Portuguese in the East and hence that area did not require special mention in a peace treaty. Moreover, the Goa convention of 20 January 1635 would continue in force and would govern Anglo-Portuguese relations in India. As for Africa and the islands, Portugal could admit no more than that the English should continue to enjoy whatever rights of access they had obtained heretofore.[28]

The second group of English demands, concerning customs duties, met with a firm reply. Every sovereign state, said Penaguião, could fix whatever customs duties it pleased. No one compelled a foreigner to trade in Portugal. The English would continue to enjoy their old privileges and would be treated no worse than any other foreign merchants. As for anchorage and harbor fees, the king of Portugal had expressly forbidden all exorbitant charges.[29]

In reply to the demands for increased personal freedoms for merchants resident in Portugal, Penaguião stated that Englishmen would be guaranteed the same treatment as other foreigners in Portugal. But religious freedoms could not be increased without the consent of the pope and the church, since the king of Portugal had no authority in such matters and was bound by canon law.

To the fourth group of demands the ambassador replied that foreign warships were permitted to use Portuguese ports only in the event of extreme necessity—no general rights for foreign men-of-war in Portuguese ports could be conceded. The English demand that only English ships be chartered by the Portuguese ran contrary to the request that no English ship be chartered without the consent of the owner, since there were not enough English ships to supply Portuguese needs unless they were chartered forcibly. The English request for a monopoly in the carriage of Portuguese salt was quite impossible; there was far too much salt to be carried aboard only English ships, and Portugal could not afford to anger other friendly nations engaged in the salt trade.[30]

The differences between the diplomats of both sides were so many and so great that they furnished the materials for months of wearisome negotiations. Notes, memoranda, and proposals—in Latin, English, and Portuguese—by the dozen passed from one side to the other. A continuing dispute over the manner of compensating the English merchants who had claims on Portugal ran parallel with these negotiations. Penaguião informed the council on 16/26 March 1653 that he had appointed three persons—Jerónimo da Silva de Azevedo (secretary of the legation), Francisco Ferreira Rebelo (a Portuguese agent), and the lawyer Vitalem de Sousa—to consider the claims of the English merchants.[31] The council wanted the merchants' claims examined and the extent of their losses determined *in London* by a board consisting of two Portuguese and two English. The ambassador wanted the merchants' claims to be decided *in Lisbon,* where evidence of such claims was easier to obtain and where some of them were already being processed in Portuguese courts.

On 30 June 1653 Penaguião declared that the Anglo-Portuguese treaty was now almost ready to be signed. What the ambassador meant by this, apparently, was that the Portuguese had made all the concessions they intended to make and that the English must accept the proposals as they stood. The ambassador tried to be put pressure on Cromwell's government by informing the council, in a letter dated 6 June 1653, that he was leaving England soon. A few days later he wrote that "I am commanded by the King my master, as I have already declar'd, to return home into my country," and he asked the council to assist him in securing a ship.[32]

On 6/16 June 1653 the council held a full discussion of the Portuguese question in the presence of all the councillors who could attend, and they decided to hold firm to the principal English demands. Four days later they ordered a frigate prepared for the use of the ambassador.[33] The ambassador's attempt to pressure the English government had failed.

The council reported on 13/23 July 1653 that the Admiralty had readied the frigate *Nonesuch,* in the Thames River, to convey the ambassador to Portugal.[34] But the envoy no longer seemed to be in a hurry. At the end of July the ambassador began to give ground on an important question: the 23 percent *ad valorem* ceiling on customs duties in Portugal, as requested by the London merchants. Previously the ambassador had flatly rejected the notion of a ceiling on customs, but, on 30 July 1653, he said he would refer the matter to the king—but if it was to be included in the treaty, it must be a secret article.[35] He boarded the *Nonesuch* at the end of July, sailed a short way down the Thames, and then proceeded no farther. After spending more than three weeks aboard, he disembarked again. On 27 September/7 October the council ordered the unloading of any Portuguese baggage aboard the *Nonesuch,* which had been kept waiting for eleven weeks, because the ship was now to be employed in another service.[36]

The summer of 1653 brought triumph and glory to the Commonwealth. During June 1653, Blake, Monk, Penn, Deane, and Lawson—with 101 ships of force—faced Tromp and De Ruyter, with 98 ships of force, off the Gabbard Sands. It was a contest of giants. In the words of the Venetian envoy Sagredo: "One may assert without exaggeration that the sea never before witnessed more formidable fleets nor more sanguinary battles, contested with so much courage and ferocity."[37] The Commonwealth won an astonishingly one-sided victory: the Dutch lost 30 ships, including 11 taken prize by the English with over 1,000 prisoners; the English did not lose a single ship. The result was that 100 of the state's ships blockaded the coasts of the Netherlands and the Dutch sued for peace.

Hieronymus van Beverning, the first Dutch peace emissary, arrived in London at the end of June, and 23 June/3 July was proclaimed a day of thanksgiving for the victory over the Dutch. A great fireworks display was held at night, with the enthusiastic participation of the Portuguese embassy. The Dutch envoys in London took sour note of the activities of the Portuguese embassy and reported to their superiors in The Hague: "The Portugal ambassador yesterday night, after thanksgiving, did excell all the rest in making of fireworks before his door, to celebrate the victory of this government against our fleet."[38] The Portuguese rejoicing was genuine, because for forty years the Portuguese had suffered greatly at the hands of the Hollanders.

On 4/14 July 1653 Oliver Cromwell attended the first meeting of the Nominated Assembly or Nominated Parliament—a group of 139 hand-picked "saints," known to history as the "Barebones Parliament"—and delivered a moving and eloquent speech that conjured up a vision of the coming Puritan millennium.[39] Despite this initial euphoria, it was not long before the Cromwellians became disenchanted with the parliament of the saints. Meanwhile, the peace talks with the Dutch broke down and the war went on. At the battle of Scheveningen (31 July/10 August 1653) the Dutch were again defeated and lost their great admiral Maerten Harpertszoon Tromp.

The Dutch made fresh proposals for peace, including a cynical suggestion that the Dutch and English fleets should combine in a joint action against the empires of Spain and Portugal and promote the "Protestant Interest" in the Iberian-held territories.[40] Cromwell had designs of his own against the Spanish empire but did not wish to include the Dutch in his plans. He displayed no interest in an attack on Portuguese territories.

In the meantime, during the last five months of the year, little progress was made in the Anglo-Portuguese negotiations. Penaguião, adhering to his disingenuous argument that the treaty had been ready for signing at the end of June 1653, declared that fresh differences had arisen after July.[41] Actually the differences had been present from the very beginning and had given trouble all along. On 9 November 1653 the ambassador required of the council a final statement summarizing all the claims of the English merchants, so that these could be presented to John IV. The council did not wish to handle the matter in this way, and, apparently, they returned no answer to the demand.

The English did make certain conciliatory gestures toward the Portuguese. The council allowed Dom Pantaleão de Sá e Meneses, the ambassador's younger brother, to send 250 horses from England to Portugal; they issued a license to the merchant James Medici allowing him to transport to Portugal 100 horses valued at no more than £20 each; and they permitted the merchant Ambrose Goodwin to send 1,000 quarters of wheat to Portugal, provided the price in England did not rise above three shillings per bushel.[42] Horses and grains were items of strategic importance, and permission to export them was considered a favor.

The council also performed other favors for Penaguião. Between 10/20 August 1653 and 9/19 December 1653 they permitted the ambassador to import into England, *free of all customs charges*, the following items: ten boxes of fruits, sweetmeats, and bacon; twelve boxes of oranges and three of perfume; three cases of bottles of sweet water; two pipes of wine; and seventy-one chests of sugar.[43] It is possible that the embassy, during five months, consumed these rather large quantities of fruits, sweetmeats, bacon, wine, and perfume; but the sugar was obviously intended for resale in England at a profit. The seventy-one chests, at twenty *arrobas* per chest, would have contained some 46,000 pounds of sugar, which at a retail price of 15d. per pound would have been worth £2,875. Either the Portuguese ambassador took advantage of his diplomatic position to conduct private trading or else the government of Lisbon paid the expenses of the embassy in chests of sugar, rather than in specie.

The stalemated Anglo-Portuguese negotiations were interrupted during the last month of the year by a sensational incident that provoked great public indignation in London and eventually brought pain and tragedy to the ambassador's family. Dom Pantaleão de Sá e Meneses, the ambassador's brother and the youth who had exported the horses to Portugal, was the central protagonist in the drama that became indelibly associated with the Portuguese embassy of 1652–1654.

During the evening of Monday, 21 November/1 December 1653, the nineteen-year-old Dom Pantaleão, accompanied by several Portuguese, was walking through the arcades of the New Exchange in the Strand, a favorite place for strolling and shopping in the London of that day. The Portuguese, speaking loudly in French, made some disparaging remarks about England and the English. They were reproved by Col. John Gerrard, a royalist, and the reproof led to a scuffle during which Gerrard was stabbed in the shoulder. A certain Mr. Anstruther rescued Gerrard, who was a small man, from the clutches of the Portuguese, and berated Pantaleão. A crowd of bystanders took up the cry, and the Portuguese retired under a barrage of insults. Pantaleão was extremely angry, especially at Anstruther, and returned to the New Exchange one hour later, with ten or twelve well-armed retainers, but could find none of the persons he was looking for, and so he withdrew.[44]

All the next day Pantaleão, a rash and immature youth, brooded about the injury or imagined injury that he had received, and he decided that he would lead a party of armed men to the scene of the insult, in the hope that he might come across the "culprits" and chastise them. On Tuesday evening, 22 November/2 December 1653, the Portuguese appeared at the New Exchange clad in coats of mail and bearing arms, accompanied by a party of Negro servants with swords. Most English accounts say that there were "fifty" Portuguese at the New Exchange, but this may mean no more than perhaps fifteen or twenty or twenty-five. The Portuguese had come in boats, which had been left at the Thames embankment nearby, and in three carriages, in one of which were found several earthen jars containing gunpowder, stopped up with wax and furnished with matches.

The presence of so many armed men provoked panic in the New Exchange. On seeing the Negroes brandishing their swords the passersby fled in fear or scurried into the shops, where the merchants pulled down their shutters. A short, earnest conversation was held between Pantaleão and a certain Thomas Howard, who urged the Portuguese to leave. Then the Portuguese quarreled with Howard and struck him a blow, wounding him. A certain Colonel Mayo, possibly mistaken for Anstruther, was attacked and critically injured. Mr. Carter and Mr. Libbiter, bystanders, were also hurt.

All of this was bad enough—but these follies were surpassed by the shooting of Harcourt Greenway, a twenty-four-year-old student of Gray's Inn, formerly of Leckhamsteed, Buckinghamshire. Greenway, in the company of his sister Mrs. Frances Clarke and of his betrothed, was shopping in the New Exchange in anticipation of his coming marriage. He was suddenly "pistoll'd in the head: of which wound (the very braine flying out thereat) within twelve houres after, in extreame anguish and torture he most miserably dyed."[45] (These were the words of his sister who was present at the event.)

The alarm went out and the Portuguese fled. Commissary-General Edward Whalley, in charge of the security of the city, led out the Horse Guards from the Mews and surrounded the Portuguese embassy. Pantaleão and some of his followers sought sanctuary in the ambassador's house, but Whalley arrested them and had them confined at Newgate Prison.[46]

The indignation of the Londoners at these events can well be imagined. The newspaper *Severall Proceedings of State Affaires* (17–24 November 1653) announced that "this night was a great mutiny at the New Exchange in the Strand, such, as hath scarce ever been seen the like." *The Faithful Scout* (18–25 November 1653) raged at "the horrid and bloody Mutiny." The story soon spread throughout England that the Portuguese had intended to blow up the New Exchange and murder every Englishman they could find.

Penaguião put in an immediate protest to the council that the arrest of his brother was a violation of diplomatic immunity. The day after the riot the council ordered Whalley to present his prisoners, together with witnesses, before the Lord Chief Justice Henry Rolles, to be proceeded against; the council also arranged an inquiry into the ambassador's allegations concerning a breach of privilege.[47] Pantaleão, Steven Redman (the ambassador's page, who was an Irish Catholic born in Bristol), and three other Portuguese prisoners were duly examined by Rolles of the Court of Upper Bench and lawfully committed to Newgate Prison to await trial.[48] The other Portuguese prisoners were discharged (the government was interested in the principals, not in the Negro servants), including a certain Jorge Vila, considered by the council to have been arrested "in the wrong of the privilege of the Ambassador."[49]

On 24 November/4 December the council ordered the officers in all English ports to prevent the passage out of the country of all Portuguese subjects.[50] On the same day, the "Barebones Parliament" approved a somewhat superfluous resolution directing Rolles to apprehend "all such Persons as were Actors in, or Abettors, or Assisters to, the horrid Murther and Outrage committed by some of the Portugal Nation, on Tuesday last."[51] A few days later thirty-six inhabitants of the New Exchange presented a petition to the council protesting the violence of the Portuguese and requesting punishment for "their more than ordinary wickedness."[52] The council, meanwhile, forbade persons from walking about the New Exchange bearing arms.[53]

While Pantaleão was in jail he prepared a twelve-page memorandum on the riot, which he called an "accident," and this was translated into English and speedily printed under the title *A Narration of the Late Accident in the New-Exchange* (London, 1653). He declared that he had been walking peacefully through the New Exchange on 21 November/1 December, holding conversation with an Englishman lately returned from Portugal, when a gentleman (Col. John Gerrard) obtruded himself between them "with great violence" and then insulted him. Bystanders then intervened and separated the disputants. Gerrard was hurt, but not by Pantaleão, who claimed he was unarmed.

The next day, said Pantaleão, he came to the New Exchange *unarmed*, accompanied by a few *unarmed* attendants. He was followed, he admitted, by many servants who were armed—but they followed him without orders to do so—and their intention was only to protect him, not to offend anyone. Pantaleão claimed no knowledge about the gunpowder in the hackney coach and had no intention of blowing up anything or hurting anyone. At the Exchange he had a quiet talk with an English gentleman, and then the merchants noisily shut up their shops, alarming everyone! He knew nothing about the shot that killed Greenway but said that it could have come from anywhere. At this point, just when a reader might expect a description of what occurred, the narrative came to an abrupt end.

If Pantaleão's *Narration* was intended to placate English public opinion, it must certainly have failed in this object, for it neither explained the circumstances of the riot nor apologized for the violence committed. It did little to mollify English opinion and only increased the anger of Greenway's sisters, Mrs. Elizabeth Worsopp and Mrs. Frances Clarke, who petitioned for justice "according to the Lawes of God and the Nation" and put out *A Briefe Reply to the Narration of Don Pantaleon Sa* (London, 1653). Mrs. Clarke said that her only brother had been wantonly slaughtered. Although she did not know who had fired the pistol shot, she was sure it must have been a Portuguese. She demanded of Pantaleão that if he considered himself to have been injured and insulted, "was there no nobler way of vindication than by a Riot?"[54] Pantaleão had stated he was unarmed; yet if he had no sword, wrote Mrs. Clarke, his servant beside him had two. The sisters affirmed that Pantaleão had never expressed his regrets to them after the murder of their brother. Their seven-page *Reply* to the Portuguese *Narration* was restrained in tone, neither vindictive nor abusive, but it demanded justice.

English justice was something the ambassador's brother would have liked to evade. On 14/24 December Pantaleão escaped from Newgate Prison dressed in women's clothing. He had been visited by some ladies and passed out of the prison yard in their company. He was apprehended later the same day, and recommitted to Newgate under closer guard. Ten days later the council issued an order to the keeper of Newgate Prison to deliver his Portuguese prisoner to the Tower of London (because Newgate was unsuited to the quality of the prisoner and was affecting his health), and this was done.[55]

The extraordinary incidents in the New Exchange came only a few days before some even more extraordinary events that altered the structure of the Commonwealth government. On 12/22 December 1653 Cromwell dissolved the Nominated Assembly, or the "Barebones Parliament," showing as much impatience with the senate of saints as he had shown with the Long Parliament. Four days later, in spite of the opposition of the old radicals who were hostile to government by a "single person," he assumed the title and took the oath of Lord Protector of the Commonwealth of England, Scotland, and Ireland. Hence the Lord General Cromwell—hitherto the head of the army, Lord Lieutenant of Ireland, and a member of the Council of State without legal or titular preeminence over the other members—assumed the style and functions of a prince and head of state.

Cromwell's assumption of the title and style of "Lord Protector" confronted foreign diplomats in London with the difficulty of recognizing, in the proper diplomatic and ceremonial fashion, the elevation of this commoner without reflecting adversely on the honor and dignity of the princes they served. The Dutch and French envoys perceived difficulties in appearing cap-in-hand before the new Lord Protector, but the ambassadors of Spain and Portugal were less reluctant. And, aside from the initial problem of recognizing the Protectorate, the diplomats probably felt more comfortable with the new and nearly princely forms of address, which were more familiar to them than the contrived and awkward styles used to address as the head of state that curious official the Speaker of the House, who was neither royal, nor noble, nor a true head of state—and did not claim to be any of these things—but who, particularly during the early years of the Commonwealth, often fulfilled the ceremonial functions of a chief of state.

The first diplomat to call on the Lord Protector was the Spanish ambassador Don Alonso de Cárdenas, who had audience with Cromwell on Tuesday, 27 December 1653/6 January 1654, and congratulated him on his new dignity.[56] Two days later the Count of Penaguião did the same. The Spanish ambassador, as usual, was the first, but the Portuguese ambassador (according to the Genoese agent) took a more splendid train.[57] The French, who had held aloof from the Commonwealth for so long, now felt that the moment had come to recognize Cromwell in all his new protectoral splendor. On 3/13 January 1654, Paul de Castelmore, Baron of Baas, arrived in London, sent by Cardinal Mazarin to seek a rapprochement with England. The other powers soon fell into line. By the end of the month Cromwell had also been seen and congratulated by the public ministers of the United Provinces, Hamburg, Sweden, Florence, Switzerland, Genoa, and Venice and by an agent of the Prince of Condé (who, at that time, was rebelliously conducting his own French foreign policy).[58]

During 1654 the Commonwealth plunged into the business of making treaties with foreign powers. Treaties were signed with the Dutch (5/15 April), the Swedes (11/21 April), the Portuguese (10/20 July), and the Danes (15/25 September). Spain, the United Provinces, and France were all, at the same time, pressing England to make alliances of one kind or another. If the Dutch or the Spaniards should succeed in their objectives, Portugal might suffer great difficulties. An Anglo-Dutch alliance could bring a new Dutch effort in Brazil; an Anglo-Spanish coalition might encompass the end of Portugal's independence. It was essential, from the Portuguese viewpoint, that Cromwell's new moves should be toward an understanding with France and directed against Spain.

For these reasons, John IV, aided only by an uncertain and unreliable France, had to accept, or pretend to accept, whatever peace terms Cromwell proposed. It was necessary for the Portuguese ambassador in London to work with the English merchants who had an interest in Portuguese trade and to convince them that an Anglo-Spanish alliance would bring about their ruin. The London merchants might have more influence on Commonwealth policy than any Portuguese threat or bribe or argument could hope to have. Yet to obtain the support of the merchants Portugal would have to agree to compensate them generously for their losses in 1650 and might also have to acquiesce to English demands concerning free trade and fixed customs duties. If these concessions were required in order to obtain English cooperation against Spain, then perhaps Portugal's national interest demanded that they should be made.

The fly in the ointment was young Dom Pantaleão, held prisoner in the Tower of London. To Lisbon, the actions of the rash young man had created an untimely crisis involving argument over inessential and extraneous things. Lisbon could not allow any squabble with Cromwell over diplomatic immunity to prejudice the larger issues affecting the relations among England, Spain, and Portugal; nor could Lisbon allow the Portuguese ambassador to fall into the trap of making the release of Pantaleão a precondition for the signing of an Anglo-Portuguese treaty. The situation of Portugal was so pressing that Pantaleão might have to be abandoned and sacrificed to the larger interests of the state.

The unfortunate Penaguião was torn between personal loyalty toward his brother and his responsibility to do the best for his country. The ambassador pressed Cromwell's government on the question of diplomatic immunity: Pantaleão, whose name had not been mentioned in the preceding diplomatic negotiations, was said to possess credentials permitting him to represent the king of Portugal in the absence or illness of the ambassador himself, and therefore he was entitled to full diplomatic immunity, protected from arrest, imprisonment, trial, and conviction in England, and subject only to his own sovereign. The Portuguese declared that this did not mean that Pantaleão would escape the consequences of any misdeeds committed at the New Exchange; rather, the king of Portugal, if the offence was proved, would mete out punishment in accordance with the laws of Portugal.

The Council of State established a committee of distinguished jurists to give a decision on the question of breach of privilege as charged by the Portuguese ambassador. The committee comprised the Lord Chief Justice Henry Rolles; the justices Philip Jermyn of the Upper Bench and Edward Atkins of the Court of Common Pleas; Dr. Walter Turner, the Judge Advocate of the Admiralty Court; and Drs. Walter Walker, William Clark, and John Godolphin, experts in Admiralty and civil law.[59]

On 16/26 January 1654 the committee reported its decision that Pantaleão was not entitled to the diplomatic immunities and privileges that pertained to his brother, the ambassador extraordinary, and should stand trial according to the laws of England. There was some disagreement among the judges as to the form of the trial—whether trial by jury would be lawful or possible—but unanimity on the main points under consideration. They acknowledged that the ambassador, as the representative of his sovereign, was immune from prosecution in England; but only the ambassador represented his sovereign directly, and no one else attached to the embassy possessed complete diplomatic privileges. They said that whatever lesser kinds of diplomatic privilege may have been possessed by Pantaleão, who had never served in any public or diplomatic capacity in England, had been forfeited by his acts of violence against the citizens of the Commonwealth, his inciting of an insurrection, and his subverting of the peace and public order of the Commonwealth—things that they felt were manifestly contrary to the laws and customs of all nations.[60]

Early in March 1654 the council ordered certain legal officials to examine the Portuguese and English witnesses of the New Exchange affair and prepare the case for the Commonwealth. In mid-April this investigation was still in progress, and the trial itself did not take place until July.[61] In the interim, the Anglo-Portuguese negotiations continued. By February or March the English draft of the treaty, with twenty-seven articles and one secret article, had already reached finished form, and—except for some minor corrections—it eventually became the treaty itself. The Portuguese fought a long rear-guard action against a number of the articles, but eventually they gave way, yielding ground word by word and clause by cause.

The treaty, in its final form, contained twenty-eight articles,[62] of which seven (1, 5, 8, 9, 12, 15, 16) merely repeated provisions in the 1642 treaty, while the last three articles (26, 27, 28) were purely formal in character. Five new articles were inserted because of the kind of conflict Rupert had precipitated: three (18, 19, 23) of these regulated access by English warships to Portuguese ports and provided for the recovery of prizes and prize goods; and the other two (24, 25) dealt with compensation for English losses. The remaining thirteen articles either strengthened the privileges that the English had already obtained from the Portuguese in 1642 or else set forth new privileges in matters of commerce, shipping, and religion.

The principal innovation in the commercial sections was a guarantee of English access to the ports of the Portuguese overseas empire in Brazil, Africa, and Asia, "and there to dwell, negotiate, and trade by land, sea, rivers and fresh waters in any kind of goods and merchandise" (article 11). Access to Brazil, however, would be governed by the regulations of the Brazil Company. Trade in Portugal and England, by the ships of either party, was to be free and unrestricted, with liberty to sell and buy, load and unload, in all places, without the need for licenses, permits, or safe-conducts, all local laws and ordinances to the contrary notwithstanding (article 2). Other commercial articles provided that customs duties in effect in Portuguese ports should not be raised in the future (3), at least not for English ships; that no English ships should pay duty twice for the same cargo (10); and that disputes over spoiled cargoes, particularly those involving pickled and salted fish, should be arbitrated by impartial umpires chosen in equal numbers by both sides (17).

There were numerous small innovations in the articles concerned with shipping: English ships were not to be loaded or unloaded by compulsion; cargoes were to be handled speedily; at the unloading of an English ship, only two Portuguese officials were to be allowed aboard at a time (4); in chartering ships, the Portuguese were to give preference to English vessels (11); and the anchorage fees charged by any Portuguese port should not be greater than those collected in

Lisbon (20). Unless caught red-handed in the commission of a crime, no Englishman was to be arrested without the consent of the Judge Conservator of the English (13), who would have jurisdiction in all civil and criminal disputes involving Englishmen. The Judge Conservator must not take longer than four months to decide a case (7).

Article 6, which required Portuguese authorities to return, by force if necessary, all English seamen who had deserted their ships, was intended to protect English shipowners, but it stirred up much religious passion because it provided that the Portuguese were to return such seamen even if the seamen claimed sanctuary in Portugal on the grounds of adhesion to the Catholic religion. English shipowners argued that runaway sailors who claimed conversion to Catholicism were transparently insincere and were only fleeing from debts and obligations—but this provision caused a bitter controversy in Lisbon.

The religious articles, given the temper of the age, caused far more difficulty in Portugal than the commercial articles. The key religious article (14) allowed the English the practice of the Protestant religion in Portugal, shielded them from the Inquisition, permitted the ownership of Protestant Bibles and other religious books, permitted Protestant services of worship, and gave the English the right to bury their dead in their own cemetery. The qualifying "scandal clause" of previous treaties (liberty of worship was permitted only insofar as no "scandal" was offered to Catholics), all-important in the eyes of the Portuguese, was omitted. Other religious provisions required the English consul in Lisbon to be of the Protestant faith (7) and prohibited the Portuguese from compelling English Protestants to support St. George's Chapel, the English Catholic church in Lisbon (21).

Article 25, dealing with compensation for English losses suffered in 1650, established a four-man committee with two Englishmen (John Crowther and Walter Walker) and two Portuguese (Francisco Ferreira and Jerónimo da Silva of the embassy) to adjudicate all claims. The committee was to meet in London on 20/30 July 1654, swear an oath before the Court of Admiralty to decide all cases impartially, summon witnesses and examine records, and make final decisions from which no appeal was allowed. But if by 1/11 September 1654 any dispute over compensation had been left undecided because of a deadlock in the committee, then the Lord Protector was empowered to appoint a member of the Council of State as an extra judge, who would make final decisions on all unsettled cases. This last stipulation was unacceptable to the Portuguese. The Portuguese should set aside one-half of all customs duties paid by Englishmen in Portuguese ports, which would provide a fund to meet the claims as arbitrated by the four-man committee.

The last article (28) in the proposed treaty provided for ratification by both sides within six months. Appended to these public articles was one secret article that limited *ad valorem* duties on English goods in Portugal to the level of 23 percent. Values were to be fairly determined and would rise or fall in relation to price changes. Disputes over exact values would be decided by disinterested referees chosen equally by both sides. Portuguese merchants trading in England would not pay any higher duties than those in force in May 1654.

The twenty-eight public articles and the secret article, as proposed in the spring of 1654, were nearly the same as the treaty signed in the summer of 1654 and ratified in 1656. Although the Portuguese were opposed to many of the details contained in the treaty, English insistence carried the day. On 3/13 April 1654 the Lord Protector received Penaguião, who came to discuss two subjects: (1) the fate of his brother, Dom Pantaleão; and (2) the Anglo-Portuguese treaty. Two days later the Dutch envoys signed a peace treaty in which they gave way to most of the English demands, and agreed to pay £100,000 to the English merchants, and also accepted a demand that the Dutch East India Company should pay £85,000 to the English East India Company, as well as £3,615 to the claimants, or descendants of the claimants, who had suffered as a consequence of the "massacre" of Amboyna, an event that had occurred thirty years previously.[63] These amounts, together with the sums promised by the Portuguese, represented a considerable "profit" for English diplomacy during 1654.

The Portuguese could take little comfort from the Anglo-Dutch peace. If the English could extort so much money from the powerful and stubborn Dutch, how much could they not extort from Portugal? And if the passage of three decades had not erased the memory of the losses suffered at Amboyna, how long would the English continue to remember the losses suffered while Rupert had been at Lisbon?

For their own purposes the Portuguese might have wished for a long-drawn-out war between England and the United Provinces, preferably with both combatants growing progressively weaker.

At the same time, Portugal was apprehensive that Spain would succeed in constructing an Anglo-Spanish alliance. Thurloe wrote to Whitlocke, the English ambassador to Sweden, on 24 February/6 March 1654 that "the Spanish ambassador doth alsoe very much courte his highnesse, and the present government."[64] Giacomo Quirini, the Venetian ambassador in Madrid, reported to his government (27 May 1654) that the Spaniards had high hopes of an English alliance directed against France and Portugal, especially since the Pantaleão affair had made London hostile to the Portuguese.[65] After England and Spain had contrived the downfall of Portugal and her empire, England would be given a free hand in Brazil, where the English might succeed in building a powerful colony where the Dutch had failed. Spain, said Quirini, had offered to pay Cromwell 1 million crowns per year in return for the English alliance.

Madrid was delighted by the Pantaleão affair, but Lisbon, evidently, decided that the incident should not be allowed to embarrass Anglo-Portuguese relations. Late in April 1654 the Portuguese government sent fresh instructions[66] to Penaguião, which ran as follows: (1) the ambassador was to press hard for certain changes in the articles suggested by the English; (2) he was to try to secure the release of Pantaleão and the other Portuguese; and (3) if both these courses of action were to fail, he was still instructed to sign the peace treaty, for it was better for Portugal to have a costly peace with a friendly England than to face a hostile England in a far more costly war.

The king of Portugal suggested fundamental changes in article 11 (the key article on free trade throughout the Portuguese empire), and detailed alterations in the articles dealing with religion and small verbal changes in nine other articles.[67] In his letter (20 April 1654) to the Council of State, Penaguião said that he was prepared to sign most of the articles as they stood but wanted what he called "small changes" in articles 7, 10, 11, and 14 and in the secret article. If Cromwell would accept these changes (which really entailed a considerable weakening of the more important clauses), then the treaty would be signed "without any new approbation from his Majesty, from whome I have powers for this purpose."[68] Both the king and the ambassador failed to mention article 25, dealing with the manner of compensating the English merchants for the losses of 1650, and acted as if it had never been considered.

While the Portuguese and English wrangled over the clauses of the proposed treaty, the drama involving Pantaleão neared its climax. To conduct the trial, the council appointed a Commission of Oyer and Terminer (i.e., a bench of judges to "hear and decide") composed of nine eminent members—three judges experienced in common law (Henry Rolles, Edward Atkins, and William Steele) and three experienced in civil law (Walter Turner, Richard Zouche, and William Clark) and three gentlemen (Sir Henry Blount, Richard Lucy, and Robert Tichborn).[69]

The trial did not take place until July. On 23 June/3 July 1654 the council made three decisions: it (1) renewed the Commission of Oyer and Terminer; (2) approved the finished draft of the Anglo-Portuguese peace treaty; and (3) suggested the insertion in the treaty of an additional clause providing for an extra judge to umpire claims on which the committee on compensation could reach no decision (as per article 25).[70]

On 27 June 1654 Penaguião wrote to Cromwell informing him that the Côrtes of Portugal had just passed an act raising Portuguese customs duties to the level of 26 percent of the value of dutiable goods.[71] The ambassador suggested that the secret article should be reworded to say that the English merchants would pay no higher duties than the Portuguese, which was the wording the Portuguese had wanted all the time. The English disregarded the act of the Côrtes, since they considered that it was deliberately designed to annul the 23 percent agreement before it ever came into force. This was the origin, it would seem, of a statement sometimes encountered in Portuguese books, that the English forced the Portuguese to accept an arrangement in which English merchants were to pay lower customs duties than the native-born merchants.

Pantaleão's trial began on Wednesday, 5/15 July 1654, at the Court of Upper Bench (as the King's Bench was then called) in Westminster Hall, before the nine-man Commission of Oyer and Terminer, called together under the Great Seal of England, with Chief Justice Henry Rolles presiding. The charge was the murder of Harcourt Greenway, late of Gray's Inn; the accused were Dom Pantaleão, the Irish servant Steven Redman, and three Portuguese of the embassy.[72] The prosecutor was Attorney General Edward Prideaux, assisted by John Glyn; the twelve-man jury consisted of six Englishmen and six foreigners.[73] John Bushell, the former Lisbon merchant, served as translator to the court; the accused made use of the translator João Milis de Macedo,[74] the embassy interpreter.

The proceedings were opened in the normal manner by a demand of the prisoners how they would plead. Pantaleão replied by asking for counsel. He was told that he was entitled to counsel, if he so desired, on any matter of law (although not on matters of fact), but only after he had entered his plea. Dom Pantaleão then refused to plead guilty or not guilty to the charge. The judges explained to the accused that if they refused to plead they would be subject to the *peine forte et dure*—that is, that they would be pressed to death under heavy stones, a penalty incurred by prisoners who refused to plead, since such a refusal paralyzed judicial procedures. Pantaleão and the other Portuguese, thus coerced, pleaded not guilty.

The next formality was to demand of the prisoners how they would be tried; the procedures of common law then required the prisoner to answer audibly, "By God and the country!" (or "By God and the king!" in the days of the monarchy). That is, the accused were required to acknowledge, with their own lips, the authority of the court and the justice of its decisions. Dom Pantaleão was most reluctant to make any such acknowledgment, since he still clung to the principle of extraterritoriality, by which the court had no jurisdiction over him. "It being asked how he would be Tryed? it was long before he gave Answer: It was told him that if he did not Declare *By God, and the Country* he must be pressed to death."[75] The required declaration was wrung from him, once more, by the threat of the *peine forte et dure.* The proceedings were then adjourned until the morrow.

The accused defended themselves with three arguments: (1) that no English court had any right to try them; (2) that they were completely ignorant of English law, did not know what was or was not a crime in England, and understood none of the proceedings taking place; and (3) that it could not be proved that the shot that killed Greenway had been fired by a Portuguese and since all of the accused denied having fired the shot they could not be held responsible for his death. Of these three arguments, only the third carried any weight with the court.

On Thursday morning, 6/16 July 1654, the trial was completed. The court declared that the question of the Portuguese ambassador's privilege had already been decided by a judicial committee called for that purpose. The Lord Chief Justice Henry Rolles had determined that the ambassador's privilege did not cover Dom Pantaleão. Rolles had few precedents to guide him, and his judgment on this question contained certain innovations; but the court did not intend to reopen the issue. The court also decided that ignorance of English law could not be admitted as a plea in an accusation of murder, because murder was deemed a crime in all known systems of law and no one was ignorant of this fact. As for whether or not the accused could be found guilty of the murder of Harcourt Greenway in the absence of exact evidence as to who fired the shot, this was a matter for the jury to determine. Yet the presumption of the law lay against the accused: it had been proved that they went to the New Exchange in considerable numbers, clad in armor, and bearing gunpowder, firearms, and swords; it was evidently the intention of the accused to kill or to do grievous bodily injury to citizens of the Commonwealth. The claims that their weapons were for defensive purposes only, that their intentions were innocent, and that they were not concerned in the death of Greenway ran counter to the evidence.

The jury of Englishmen and foreigners took only half an hour to consider their verdict: all of the accused were found guilty. The judges then sentenced all five to be hanged on Saturday, 8/18 July. The condemned men immediately moved for a stay of execution until Monday, 10/20 July, which was granted.[76]

On that same Thursday (6/16 July), in the afternoon, death sentences were passed on Col. John Gerrard, Francis Fox, and Peter Vowell—persons who had been involved in a plot to murder the Lord Protector[77]—and they were condemned to be hanged on the same day as the Portuguese. The eight doomed men (Pantaleão, Redman, Gerrard, Fox, Vowell, and three other Portuguese) had only three days in which to persuade Cromwell to grant a reprieve. A full pardon, as such, lay outside the power of the Lord Protector, because in his oath of office he had sworn not to grant pardons to men found guilty of murder or treason; all that Cromwell could do was postpone the execution of sentence until the new parliament met (it was scheduled to meet on 3/13 September 1654) and then recommend to the Parliament that they pass an act of clemency.

Penaguião embarked on an extraordinary effort to save the life of his brother. He approached all the foreign ambassadors or agents in London to secure their intercession with Cromwell. On the question of ambassadorial privilege, the London diplomatic corps were prepared to present a united front. Later M. de Bordeaux, the French ambassador, said, "I did all that I could."[78] Others, perhaps could have said the same. The condemned men addressed petitions to Cromwell.[79] Penaguião, with tears in his eyes, saw the Protector in person and pleaded for the life of his brother. According to the Spanish ambassador, Cromwell relented and said that a stay of execution would be given to Pantaleão until such time as Parliament had met and resolved the issue.[80] As he left Cromwell, Penaguião came across a deputation from the English merchants trading with Portugal, who had come to add the weight of their petitions to the efforts being made by the diplomats to save Dom Pantaleão. The Portuguese ambassador told the merchants that their efforts were no longer needed.

The agent Bernardi reported to Genoa that Cromwell had ordered a prorogation of the execution of Dom Pantaleão's sentence until the meeting of Parliament.[81] *The Weekly Intelligencer of the Commonwealth* (4–11 July) related that Pantaleão's execution had been postponed until 3/13 September 1654 and said that the decision had been handed down on Friday, 7/17 July, the day after the trial. *A Perfect Diurnall* (3–10 July) agreed but stated that the decision was reached on Saturday night, 8/18 July. Lorenzo Paulucci, the Venetian secretary in London, and the French ambassador Bordeaux both believed, rather optimistically, that Dom Pantaleão would soon be released.[82]

The cases of the other seven condemned men were handled according to their individual merits. There could be no hope for Redman, the ambassador's Anglo-Irish servant: he was a British subject and fully cognizant of English law and had no claim to diplomatic immunity. No reprieve was granted to him. The other three Portuguese of the embassy Cromwell reprieved, since their responsibility for the New Exchange riot had been less than that of Pantaleão. Among the three Englishmen convicted of crimes against the state, Vowell, the schoolmaster, was obstinate and unrepentant; Gerrard was resigned to his fate but firmly devoted to Charles II; and Fox expressed sorrow and repentance. Cromwell confirmed Vowell's sentence to be hanged; Gerrard had petitioned to be beheaded or shot instead of hanged, and the Protector directed that he die by the ax and not by the rope, a nobler death; Fox was reprieved until the meeting of Parliament.[83]

Although the Protector had probably made his decisions on these various matters by Saturday night (8/18 July), legal papers giving effect to these decisions would not be signed, perhaps, until Monday morning, a few hours before the executions. Until a prisoner, who was expecting clemency, had been officially notified of a stay of execution, it was wise for him to conduct himself with the greatest prudence—because the Lord Protector could always, at the last moment, refuse to sign the reprieve. It was during this interim, on Sunday evening, that Pantaleão committed his last, fatal blunder: he tried to escape.

On Sunday evening Lady Philippa Mohun[84] visited Pantaleão at Newgate Prison; she was accompanied by her maidservant, who pretended to be pregnant. When the ladies were alone with Pantaleão, the maidservant slipped out of her dress, beneath which she had on a page boy's costume. Pantaleão put on the maid's dress, with its stuffed protuberant belly, suggesting a pregnant woman. The party almost succeeded in making their escape but were detained at the last gate, where the subterfuge was discovered.[85] The attempted escape was reported immediately, and Cromwell, apparently, was very angry; he may have felt that he had been duped, since to the Portuguese the stay of execution was but a means to give them more time to effect an escape.

Cromwell had good reasons for rescinding Pantaleão's reprieve. The arrogant young man had never acknowledged either guilt or sorrow for his conduct but clung obstinately to his claim of privilege—a claim that seemed to imply a license to murder with impunity. He had twice attempted to evade justice by making his escape. The English public demanded that the ringleader of the Portuguese pay with his head for the outrage at the New Exchange. Perhaps even Parliament, when it met in September, might make difficulties about a pardon. The Lord Protector decided to allow the law to take its course with the Portuguese ambassador's brother, with the proviso that the criminal should not be hanged but beheaded, since he was the son of a nobleman. That same Sunday evening, Cromwell informed Penaguião of his decision.[86]

The situation had now become desperate for the condemned man. He wrote a letter in Spanish to the Spanish ambassador, Don Alonso de Cárdenas, pleading for Cárdenas to use his influence with the English government to secure a stay of execution. Pantaleão now sought "the incomparable clemency of His Catholic Majesty," flinging himself down "at his Royal feet." The Portuguese declared, "I am Spanish" ("*soy Hespano*"). He hinted at future service to the Spanish crown and closed with the words: "Do not neglect to favor my cause with the brevity it demands." The writer signed his name in Spanish, thus: "Pantaleon de Sa y Meneses."[87]

If John IV's ministers had been able to read this letter, they might have concluded that it was a good thing that English justice had rid them of Pantaleão. A man face to face with death may be pardoned if he resorts to extreme courses, but for a Portuguese gentleman to forswear his king, merely for the sake of saving his skin, would only have earned him contempt in Lisbon. Cárdenas honored the young man's request immediately and wrote to Cromwell that same Sunday night. But Pantaleão had miscalculated: the Spanish ambassador had no great influence with the Lord Protector.

Penaguião realized late on Sunday night that nothing could be done to save his brother. As the personal representative of John IV, Penaguião felt that it would be a derogation to the dignity of his king if he were to visit Pantaleão in prison. For the same reason he could not remain in the city of London while the execution was taking place. Yet he could not leave without signing the peace treaty. The only course open to him was to sign the Anglo-Portuguese peace treaty early on Monday morning, 10/20 July 1654, and then leave the city as rapidly as he could. It is probably not true to say, as so many have said (not only historians but also contemporaries who were not close to the center of these events), that the ambassador signed the treaty in a last desperate effort to change Cromwell's mind. By 10/20 July the Portuguese had accepted the commercial parts of the treaty (knowing that the most obnoxious concessions could be whittled away, circumvented, or ignored) and objected, mostly, to the phrasing used in the religious articles. In any event, the signed treaty had no value until ratified by the king of Portugal—and the argument about the religious articles could be carried on during the negotiations over ratification, for the Portuguese were determined that further negotiations should precede ratification.

The ambassador realized that his personal usefulness came to an end the moment the English executed his brother. The treaty had to be signed, therefore, *before* the execution—not in the forlorn hope of saving his brother but in the hope of preventing an Anglo-Spanish alliance. The national interests of Portugal, not the personal interests of the ambassador, determined that the treaty must be signed.

At eight o'clock on that gloomy Monday morning, 10/20 July 1654, the ambassador signed what was to become, perhaps, the most important treaty in the long series of Anglo-Portuguese treaties. Four Englishmen—Nathaniel Fiennes, Sir Gilbert Pickering, Sir Anthony Ashley Cooper, and Walter Strickland—signed for the Commonwealth.[88] The ambassador said his formal farewells and left London immediately, proceeding down the Thames River toward Gravesend. It seems that Penaguião made no further appeals on behalf of his brother. Although in the diplomatic sense the ambassador had departed from the country, he had no intention of leaving England until another few days or weeks had passed. During the interim, while he waited for a Commonwealth frigate to take him to Portugal, he could put his affairs in order.

The interest of Londoners now centered on how well the condemned men would die. Peter Vowell was hanged during the morning at a gallows in Charing Cross. During his last moments he was cheerful and made a speech unabashedly comparing himself to Jesus Christ at Calvary. After floods of tears, the servant Steven Redman was hanged at Tyburn—but Londoners paid little attention to this execution. John Gerrard and Dom Pantaleão were both beheaded at Tower Hill in the evening. Gerrard died after making the usual speech and drinking a cup of sack. Pantaleão was brought from Newgate Prison to Tower Hill in a coach drawn by six horses, accompanied by several members of the Portuguese embassy. He was dressed in a long black gown, and some of his party wore full mourning. The condemned man, although comforted by a Portuguese priest, showed signs of great distress; he was "extreamly dejected in spirit,"[89] "looking as if he would have died before execution."[90]

The Portuguese arrived at the scaffold a few minutes before Gerrard's beheading. Eight and a half months had passed since Pantaleão and Gerrard had exchanged insults at the New Exchange. By some quirk of fortune they had been brought together to share the same scaffold. When the ax fell on the royalist colonel's neck there was silence and sadness. When Pantaleão's turn came, his last words were not understood by the spectators, but he was thought to have blamed the English for the New Exchange riot and to have pronounced himself a martyr to the Catholic religion. "After a few private Words and Passages of Popish Devotion with his Confessor," reported Whitelocke, "he gave him his Beads and Crucifix, laid his Head on the Block, and it was chopt off at two Blows."[91] *The Weekly Intelligencer* (4–11 July 1654) was more grisly and exact: "His Head was cut off with one blow, and a drawing of the Ax too and again, to perfect the Decollation."

The crowd, who had been silent when Gerrard died, greeted the stroke on Pantaleão differently: "They gave a great and general shout, as applauding the Justice of the Portugals death."[92] The critical London spectators thought it a poor performance. One of the more irreverent London newssheets linked Pantaleão and Redman in an insulting couplet:

> Before their deaths they waild and cryd,
> Both lived *Catholicks*, so both dy'de.[93]

Dom Pantaleão de Sá e Meneses suffered death at about 7:00 P.M., some eleven hours after the signing of the Anglo-Portuguese peace treaty.

The issues raised by the trial and execution of Pantaleão have been discussed with much emotion. Edgar Prestage, a knowledgeable student of Anglo-Portuguese affairs, bitterly denounced Cromwell's failure to grant a pardon, a failure he attributed to the "middle-class usurper's" Puritan prejudice against "a Catholic, a noble, and a foreigner."[94] The issue (as we have seen) did not involve a pardon but a reprieve—which was granted and then, for good cause, rescinded. By the standards of the day, the trial had been scrupulously fair, and it had engaged the finest legal talent available to the Protectorate. The evidence, although circumstantial, had been overwhelming and damning. English public opinion supported the verdict of guilt and the sentence of death.

Yet it is probably true that a reprieve from the Protector and a pardon from Parliament might both have been procured if the Portuguese had conducted themselves in a different manner. In seventeenth-century England an appeal for clemency, in order to be effective, required a confession of guilt and some kind of public demonstration of repentance and grief. If the Portuguese had acknowledged their errors, apologized to the injured parties, expressed their sorrow to Harcourt Greenway's sisters, and offered them some sort of compensation, then they would have placated public opinion and greatly strengthened their plea for clemency. Instead they chose to depict themselves as the injured parties, they put out unbelievable and insulting explanations of what had occurred, they blamed their victims for what had happened, they hatched escape plots, and always they denied the authority of English laws, English courts, and English officials. In so doing the Portuguese deprived the Lord Protector and Parliament of the moral and legal support necessary for recommending a pardon.

Officially Cromwell maintained that the New Exchange affair was not a matter between governments; that the delinquents acted as individuals and had been punished as individuals; and that nothing in these events compromised the Portuguese ambassador or Anglo-Portuguese relations. It suited the interests and inclinations of John IV to treat the matter in the same way; it does not appear that the Pantaleão affair was ever mentioned in the diplomatic correspondence exchanged between the king of Portugal and the Lord Protector.

Penaguião and his retinue, when they returned to Lisbon, had some difficult explanations to make; the exact truth was not flattering to their case—indeed, it might have made them look foolish. The muddled accounts of the episode, discussed on the streets of Lisbon, centered on the supposition that young Dom Pantaleão had been sacrificed as the consequence of an affair of honor. Pantaleão had received an intolerable insult from an Englishman and had later replied in the only way possible for a gentleman, although the violence used was technically illegal. In a monarchy (or so the Portuguese argued), where gentlemanly honor was a thing understood and protected, Dom Pantaleão's breach of the law would either have earned a light reprimand or else have been entirely overlooked. But in a country ruled by regicides and usurpers policy was unpredictable, and the tyrant Cromwell had avenged himself on the Portuguese ambassador's brother for a technical breach of the law.

In Portugal this was the simplest and least confused version of the story of Dom Pantaleão and has left its traces in some Portuguese history books. Other versions were more fantastic. The most famous of the seventeenth-century histories of Portugal, *História de Portugal Restaurado,* by Luís de Meneses, Count of Ericeira—a man who was in a position to find out a great deal about Penaguião and his family—said that Cromwell sentenced Pantaleão to death (there is no mention of any trial in this version) in order to get rid of Colonel Gerrard.[95] The truth about the New Exchange affair has never made much headway in Portugal, neither during the seventeenth century nor later. Even the studious Santarém, the nineteenth-century compiler of Portugal's diplomatic records, gave but a tendentious version of the event.[96]

The Count of Penaguião, it will be recalled, rushed out of London on the morning of 10/20 July 1654 but did not leave England. The English law courts were soon presented with actions petitioning for the seizure of the ambassador's properties, because he had left large debts in London. The creditors hoped to prevent Penaguião from taking property out of the country. King John had failed to keep the embassy supplied with money. The Council of State, at its meeting on 12/22 July, ordered an inquiry into the ambassador's debts.[97]

The Lord Protector took a personal interest in speeding the ambassador on his way. On 17/27 July, one week after the execution, Cromwell wrote an order to the Admiralty in his own hand: "You are to appoint a good frigott for the transportinge of the Portugall Ambassador to Lisbon."[98] The Admiralty was instructed to reply the next morning, which they did, designating the *Kentish Frigate* for the task required. One week later, on 25 July/4 August 1654, Cromwell directed that a pass be issued to the ship *Francis,* which had been chartered by the ambassador, allowing the vessel to sail without molestation. Penaguião probably left England a few days later.[99]

Penaguião took to Portugal a letter from Cromwell to John IV in which the Protector rejoiced at the conclusion of the peace: "The peace and friendship which your majesty desired . . . at length we brought to a happy conclusion, and as we hope, as a sacred act, have ratified it to perpetuity."[100] In the letter, the Protector also sang the praises of "the lord John Roderigo de Sita Meneses, count of Pennaguiada." The ambassador's beheaded brother cast no shadow over these sunny lines, although one wonders what the ambassador himself felt about the "happy conclusion" of his embassy.

On 3/13 September 1654 the first Protectoral parliament met in London, and on the following day Cromwell delivered a major address to the members in which he compared the former miserable condition of the Commonwealth, rent by wars both foreign and domestic, to the happy state reached in the summer of 1654, when by God's signal grace and mercy the Commonwealth of England had grown prosperous and mighty. Formerly the nation had been at war with the royalists and with the Dutch and virtually at war with France: "To add yet to our misery, whilst we were in this condition, we were in war, deeply engaged in a war with the Portugal, whereby our trade ceased; and the evil consequences by that war were manifest and very considerable."[101] Yet, said Cromwell, the Lord of Hosts had granted victory and peace to his servants in England. France begged for the friendship of the Commonwealth. The Dutch war, which had cost the Commonwealth £120,000 per month, had been brought to a most successful conclusion. Similarly, there had been a happy outcome to the war with Portugal:

> You have a peace likewise with the Crown of Portugal, which peace though it hung long in hand, yet is lately concluded. It is a peace that your merchants make us believe is of good concernment to their trade, their assurance being greater, and so their profit in trade thither, than to other places. And this hath been obtained in that treaty, (which never was since the Inquisition was set up there,) that our people which trade thither have liberty of conscience.[102]

At this point, the speech was interrupted by loud applause.

These remarks about Anglo-Portuguese affairs show a misplaced optimism. The Anglo-Portuguese treaty, hailed by Cromwell as virtually an accomplished fact, was not ratified by King John until twenty-one months later, and then only under great pressure from the navy. The reason for Portugal's dilatoriness sprang not only from Lisbon's dislike of the provisions concerning free trade but also from the strong opposition of the Portuguese church to that very "liberty of conscience" hailed with so much self-satisfaction in London.

On 10/20 July 1654 the government had signed an Anglo-Portuguese treaty singularly advantageous to the interests of England, but a signed treaty is one thing, a ratified treaty is another—and, indeed, a treaty enforced and executed is yet another.

7

ENGLISH MERCHANTS AND THE INQUISITION

"During the two centuries which elapsed between the time of King João III and that of Pombal," wrote C. R. Boxer, "Portugal was probably the most priest-ridden country in Christendom, and only exceeded elsewhere in this respect by Tibet."[1] In this priest-ridden country of Portugal the news of the contents in the religious articles of the 1654 treaty aroused anger and outrage.

The Iberian Catholic church made universal claims on the inhabitants of the peninsula, claims that involved the control of the spoken and printed word, of conduct, of devotions both private and public, and even of individual thought and belief. The Inquisition, exercising impressive powers of persuasion and coercion, was the instrument of this control. The Protestant merchant resident in Spain or Portugal was a privileged creature, allowed to exist in contradiction to the laws and principles of the nation and permitted to nurture within his brain Protestant ideas, which were regarded by the community as blasphemous and abominable.

The Iberian community had to find some way of living side by side with the resident alien Protestant. Early in the seventeenth century when Spain (whose king also ruled Portugal) made peace with England and a truce with the United Provinces, the problem of normal, peaceful relations with heretics occupied the attention of the peninsula's theologians and specialists in canon law, including those in the universities of Coimbra and Évora, who wrote out their learned opinions during the summer of 1606.[2] These opinions were dug out of the files and reconsidered in 1654 and 1655, after John IV had issued a decree (29 October 1654) calling on the Inquisitors and canon-law jurists to set forth formal opinions on article 17 of the treaty of 1642 and article 14 of the treaty of 1654.[3] The king furnished the Inquisitors and canonists with Latin copies of the preceding articles, and the resulting discussions were exhaustively detailed, although frequently out of touch with events.

In 1606 the doctors of theology of the University of Coimbra held that a heretic could not be punished by the church until he was proved to be pertinacious and impenitent; the ordinary English heretic arriving in Portugal, never having been instructed in the teachings of the true faith, could not be considered pertinacious or impenitent. The English, it is true, had been baptized and thus had once been members of the "true church," but their subsequent heresy was insufficient ground for framing a charge of apostasy. The church had long ago determined that a baptized Christian child, captured and brought up by infidels, could not be an apostate, "because, never having been instructed in the faith, he remains invincibly ignorant"; he did not will to be brought up an infidel, and so "there can be no blame, where there has been no will."[4]

Yet many English heretics must have heard, at one time or another, something about the Catholic church; and a few, reasoned the doctors of Coimbra, might know a good deal about Catholic dogma and practice. For whatever things they had heard and known about, and not believed, they could be held blameworthy; the heretic who knew the least about the "true church" was the least at fault, but he who knew the most was answerable for everything he knew.

English heretics possessed different levels of knowledge. Four separate categories could be distinguished: (1) heretic preachers and educated men, (2) ignorant men of humble station, (3) educated youths just reaching the age of reason, and (4) ignorant and uneducated men who had deliberated on the questions of Protestantism and Catholicism. The first category, comprising heretic clergymen and other educated men, contained heretics beyond all doubt, because they were knowledgeable about church matters. The second category, that of the unlettered men, could be called invincibly ignorant. The third category, that of educated youths just at the age of reason, before they had made a mature decision, might be admitted as invincibly ignorant. As for the fourth category, the men who though unlettered had given the matter much thought, they were true heretics.[5]

If men coming under categories 2 and 3 were arrested by the Inquisition, they could not be proceeded against until after they had been carefully instructed. Once they had been carefully instructed, then their persistence in heresy would call for appropriate punishment. "By the Baptism which these English have received they all are obliged to hold and believe all that the Holy Church of Rome holds and believes." If heretics would not accept the truth after they had been instructed in it, then "they must be judged as impenitent and pertinacious."[6]

The argument by the Coimbra doctors can be summarized thus: if the Inquisition captured an English heretic who was a learned man, they could soon turn him over to the secular arm and have him put to death; if they captured an Englishman who was ignorant, they would instruct him and if, after instruction, he would not recant, then they could have him put to death anyway.

The theologians had been called on to find some acceptable means whereby the church could allow foreign heretics to pursue their business in peace; their task was to discover a theologically acceptable *modus vivendi*. Instead of doing that, the theologians had found what were to them excellent reasons why the Inquisition should continue to put most heretics to death in most circumstances. Their abstract reasoning, thus divorced from the realities of commercial and diplomatic relations, could not be permitted to have any influence on policy; for if the governments of Spain and Portugal were to follow the ideas of the ecclesiastics, they would have to sever all contacts with the Protestant world.

The issue arose again in 1641, after the Portuguese Restoration when John IV worked busily to arrange treaties of alliance with England and the United Provinces. On 22 September 1641 Dom Rodrigo da Cunha, the Archbishop of Lisbon, called together a commission to examine the religious articles in the Dutch and English treaties, a commission composed of Inquisitors, Jesuits, Franciscans, Dominicans, Augustinians, and secular clergy.[7] The commission issued its report after only two days of consideration, setting forth what became a standard principle for the treatment of heretics resident in Catholic countries. This principle, in the words of the commission, was: "It is only legitimate for Christian princes to act negatively in these matters, without allowing in them anything of the affirmative or positive."[8] This meant, in effect, that a Catholic king could *not* say to Protestant merchants: "We give you the right to hold private services of worship," but he *could* say to them: "We shall not disturb you if you hold private services of worship."

Laymen may be pardoned if they fail to perceive the distinction herein set forth. The important point is that the clergy, having played their game of words to its conclusion, had come up with a formula of *positive* and *negative* that permitted a Catholic king, in good conscience, to take *negative action*—that is, which permitted him to act. Under the umbrella of this ecclesiastical authorization, John IV could promise the English, under article 17 of the 1642 treaty, that he would not interfere with their private services of worship held in their houses or aboard their ships, provided they gave no cause for scandal.

It was clear to the English that the Portuguese Inquisition might declare almost anything to be scandalous; thus the scandal clause gave the Portuguese the power to abrogate the religious concessions without violating the treaty. The scandal clause did not trouble the ministers of Charles I in 1642—but the Puritans who succeeded him in 1649 took a different view and thought of religious liberties as possibly the most important of their demands. When the London merchants drew up "A Particular of the Articles of Peace desired by the English Marchants to be graunted them by His Majestie of Portugall," they placed the following at the top of their list: "That the English Nation and all the People of this Commonwealth of England shall have a convenient place appointed or their owne house permitted them . . . for the free Exercise of their Religion and alsoe a convenient place appointed for the buriall of their dead, without being molested or inquietted for matter of conscience or for their English Bibles or other Religious bookes by any person or tribunall whatsoever."[9] Four things, then, the merchants demanded: (1) a place of worship, (2) a cemetery, (3) the use of Protestant Bibles and other religious books, and (4) immunity from molestation by persons, institutions, or courts in matters of conscience.

The Count of Penaguião, in reply to these proposals as later formulated by the Council of State, suggested the following: "Although the King of Portugal doo acknowledge that he hath noe power to determine and dispose of faith and religion, yet for his affection and much goodwill to the Parliaments subiects, shall in the practice and exercise of their religion within the Kingdomes Dominions and Territories of the King of Portugall use and enioy as much liberty as shall be permitted to the suiects of other Prince or Republike whatsoever."[10] The ambassador promised that the English would not be molested in religious matters "where they give noe scandall to others."

The Englishmen regarded these suggestions as unsatisfactory. In place of the ambassador's disclaimer, which alleged the king of Portugal's helplessness in religious matters, they substituted a more positive declaration of their own:

> But since the Rights of Peace and Commerce would be rendred vain and ineffectual if the subjects of the Commonwealth of Great Britain should bee disquieted for their conscience sake . . . the said King of Portugal shall take effectual care that the said subjects of the Commonwealth of Great Britain bee not molested or disquieted by any person, Court or Tribunal for their conscience sake, or for that they have and use English Bibles or any other Books.[11]

These words, which come from article 14 of the 1654 treaty, run remarkably close to the words of the merchants' proposals cited earlier. As a substitute for the limitation contained in the scandal clause, the Puritans proposed a reservation phrased in terms very much more to their liking: "But the English are to take care that they doe not exceed what is granted by this article." A provision for a cemetery was also part of the treaty.

Besides article 14, there were a number of other provisions in the 1654 treaty that touched on matters of religion. From the Portuguese point of view, the most unsatisfactory of these came in article 6, which required the forcible return of runaway seamen to their ships, even if they claimed they had deserted because they were Catholics. Like all the maritime countries, England suffered from a shortage of sailors; each nation tried to prevent its own seamen from entering the service of foreigners. In article 6, the English were trying to close the easiest avenue of escape for a deserter: such a runaway, claiming to be a Catholic or a Catholic convert, would receive the enthusiastic protection of the Portuguese and could institute proceedings in Portuguese courts for the recovery of wages and personal property. The English merchants and shipowners, in addition to losing a man, might be harassed with lawsuits. Article 6 forbade such lawsuits and required the return of the man to his ship. There may have been, to be sure, some element of anti-Catholic prejudice in these clauses, but the religious problem was not central to them: the idea was to eliminate a common secular abuse. The very notion, nonetheless, of one professing to be a Catholic, perhaps sincerely, being compelled to rejoin the company of heretics dismayed the Portuguese clergy, who felt that this provision was impossible and intolerable.

Other clauses in the treaty touching on religion were of lesser importance. The English consuls had to be Protestants; English residents were not to be compelled to contribute toward the support of St. George's Chapel, the English Catholic church in Lisbon; and the Inquisition was supposed to pay all debts owed to Englishmen by persons whose estates had been confiscated.

On 4 July 1654, sixteen days before Penaguião signed the treaty, some Portuguese ecclesiastics met at a Lisbon church and issued a statement on what religious liberties could and could not be permitted to the English. The clerics said that the English might practice their own religion in their houses or on their ships—but they were not to carry Bibles or devotional books, talk to other people about religion, give offense to Catholics in any way, and they positively could not be allowed to have their own cemetery.[12]

The Lisbon Inquisition handed down an opinion stating the same point of view. The Englishmen's religious rites, said the Inquisitors, could only take place within a closed house, with the doors and windows shut; the ceremonies must not be audible to any persons outside; on no condition might Catholics be present thereat; and the English must not be seen carrying Bibles or religious books, whether on the way to their services or not. The proposal for a Protestant cemetery could not be considered under any circumstances, because such a burial ground would be consecrated by heretics, who would perform their blasphemous rites in the open and adorn the place with heretical signs and symbols. Such a visible show of Protestantism would be a standing affront to honest Catholics, a dishonor to God, and possibly a snare to the unwary. Moreover, the idea was unprecedented: "It is a new thing, never seen or heard of" *("he couza nova, nunca vista, nem ouvida").*[13] The Inquisitors concluded that the English should be given only those privileges that they had enjoyed in the past.

The Inquisition also wrote an opinion (13 November 1654) concerning article 6 and the forcible return of Catholic seamen to their ships. They condemned the article completely and exclaimed that it was inconceivable that Catholics should assist the return of Catholic converts to the company of heretics.[14] This opinion was contradicted by certain Portuguese laymen, with diplomatic and mercantile experience, who understood that the article was not an attempt to secure religious advantages for heresy but an effort to prevent the defection of seamen from visiting ships. These Portuguese argued that the English did not propose penalties against Catholic seamen *as Catholics* and that the article could be approved without qualms.[15]

King John found himself in difficult circumstances. On the one side the Portuguese clergy denounced the religious articles with every breath—on the other Cromwell, with a passionate interest in the religious question and with "160 ships swimminge," possessed the naval power to obtain what he wanted. On 22 July/1 August 1654 Cromwell sent General-at-Sea Robert Blake his instructions for a projected expedition to the Mediterranean. Blake set sail from Plymouth on 8/18 October 1654 aboard his old flagship, the *George,* with twenty-seven warships.[16] During the next twelve months, ships of this powerful fleet spent much time off the coasts of Portugal, especially in the Algarve area.

To John IV, English pressure was but one factor in the situation—for the king had to deal with a dangerous domestic enemy, the Inquisition. The king's troubles with the Inquisition were of long standing; some of the higher clergy, like some of the Portuguese nobility, were widely suspected of being Hispanophiles, or Castilianizers, lukewarm in their loyalties to the house of Bragança. John IV's protection of New Christian properties, in the interests of the Brazil Company, had exacerbated relations between the crown and the Inquisitors. The Portuguese Inquisition—which in effect constituted a state within a state and paid little heed to other ecclesiastical or civil authorities—had met its match in the figure of the stubborn, corpulent, phlegmatic, but capable and gifted king. On the question of the New Christian properties, he did not intend to give way, even though in November 1654 he was once again under extreme pressure from the Inquisition. But there was no need, unless Cromwell threatened war, for the king to resist the Inquisition in the matter of privileges for English heretics.

In dealing with the English and the Inquisitors on the religious question, the king had to weigh what effect his acts might have on the pope at Rome. Throughout the whole of John IV's reign Rome pretended that there was no such person as the king of Portugal. The king went to great lengths to placate the Vatican, but without favorable result. During his squabble with the Inquisition, the Inquisitors forged their own contacts with Rome; this move forced the king to tread warily, because the pope, supported by the Inquisitors, had enough influence with the estranged church of Portugal to endanger his authority. His situation was such that, no matter how hard London pressed its demands, he had to proceed cautiously in making religious concessions to the English.

In discussing these problems, the Dominicans of Lisbon raised the question of the relations between king and church. The king, said the Dominicans (in a memorandum written at their Lisbon convent on 29 August 1655), could not issue any guarantees to heretics that were binding on the Inquisition, unless those guarantees had received the approval of the pope: "The Apostolic Ministers of the Sacred Tribunal of the Holy Office can deal with the said English, and punish them, even if they conduct their heretic rites without giving rise to scandal, as long as the Supreme Pontiff has not given them his express approval."[17] Thus no sureties of religious protection given to the English by the king of Portugal had any value unless approved by the pope—and since relations between the pope and the king remained suspended, there was no possibility of obtaining that approval. Moreover, the Dominicans explicitly asserted that the Inquisitors could arrest English heretics even if no scandal had been committed against Catholics—in effect, puncturing the value of the scandal clause that the Portuguese diplomats had tried hard to insert into the 1654 treaty. The Dominicans concluded that "the Church has superior jurisdiction over heretics independent of all secular Princes."[18]

Some Dominicans, in the same document, attacked the 1654 treaty on another level. Portuguese politicians had argued that the Anglo-Portuguese treaty was essential for Portugal because war with England could not be risked, because England might join Spain, and because Portuguese commerce required English support. The Inquisitors declared that these reasons were unconvincing. The Commonwealth was an unstable power, likely to disintegrate at any moment:

"The whole machinery of power and authority in the Englishmen's government rests on the presumption of one tyrant, the murderer of his Natural King."[19] As for Spain, far from joining Spain, England had made war on her. Nor did the interests of Portuguese commerce depend so much on the English; on the contrary, Englishmen participated in Portuguese commerce because it was profitable to them; they would continue to participate for as long as it suited their convenience, since "no tie of friendship with Portugal will oblige them to continue it so much as their own self-interest."[20] The Inquisitors also argued that it was useless to sign the 1654 treaty, because its provisions, heavily slanted towards benefiting the English, would not be kept by the Portuguese, since only treaties with reciprocal advantages are ever kept. With these fairly telling and well-stated arguments—in themselves more likely to influence the king's ministers than the doctrinal points raised by the theologians—the Inquisitors hoped to prevent the ratification of the 1654 treaty. Yet, they added, if their statements about commerce were completely erroneous, it was still true that "the interests of commerce are not to be bought at the expense of Religion."

The Inquisitors weakened their case by understating the power of the Commonwealth. Lisbon was only too aware that the state's ships, in strength, patrolled the straits, under Blake, a most capable opponent. Portugal's position was uncertain: had peace with England been established or not? In a letter to John IV (22 March 1655) the merchants of the Brazil Company complained that "as regards the English, your Majesty knows the state we are in, with neither peace celebrated, nor war declared."[21]

John IV's anxieties about a possible Anglo-Spanish alliance ended when Cromwell sent an expedition to attack the Spanish West Indies. A combined sea-and-land force assaulted Hispaniola in April 1655 and suffered the worst defeat ever experienced by the armed forces of the Commonwealth. The beaten expedition then attacked Jamaica, in May 1655, captured it, and added it permanently to the British empire. Reliable news of these events did not reach Europe until July 1655. Until the end of June the Spaniards made a determined effort to preserve the peace with England but were rebuffed by Cromwell.[22]

Cromwell's attack on Spain meant that England and Portugal would be drawn together, if only because the state's ships, shut out of Spanish harbors, would need to use bases in Portugal. Lisbon rejoiced that the might of the Protectorate had been used against Portugal's greatest enemy. Yet Portugal could not take much immediate comfort from the Anglo-Spanish war, because if John IV refused to ratify the treaty, there was no basis for thinking that Cromwell would hesitate to attack the Portuguese. England had once been willing to fight both France and the United Provinces at the same time; why should she shrink from making war on both Spain and Portugal, illogical as the move might seem?

On 4/14 April 1655 Admiral Blake carried out a successful and well-executed action against a Tunisian fleet at Porto Farino, where he burned nine ships in the teeth of heavy firing from shore batteries. A few weeks later the fleet took up its station at the straits, preventing Spain from reinforcing the West Indies. In mid-July 1655, Blake, aboard the *George,* anchored in the Bay of Lagos, where he found it hard to procure water or beverage wine. On 24 August/3 September 1655 the *George* sailed into the Bay of Cascais. When the English fleet sailed into Cascais, Lisbon felt alarm and the king summoned infantry and calvary units for the defense of the capital.[23]

The Portuguese knew that they would now have to render some kind of explanation for their failure to ratify the treaty, which, by the terms of article 28, had to be ratified within six months, that is, before 10/20 January 1655. The Portuguese were unaware of the circumstances of the Commonwealth fleet: Blake's ships, after a year at sea, were in poor condition, the men in bad spirits, and their commander despondent. Blake's letter to Cromwell (30 August/9 September 1655) described the situation in these terms: "Our condition is dark and sad, and (without special mercy) like to be very miserable; our ships extreme foul, winter drawing on, our victuals expiring, all stores failing, our men falling sick through the badness of drink, and eating their victuals boiled in salt water for two months' space. . . . We have no place or friend, our recruits here slow, and our mariners (which I most apprehend) apt to fall into discontents, through their long keeping abroad."[24]

Blake's melancholy dispatches were taken to England by the frigate *Hampshire,* which also carried the agent Thomas Maynard with letters from the king of Portugal. Maynard, who was to hold the office of English consul at Lisbon for thirty-three years

(1656–1689), thus played his first part in fashioning Anglo-Portuguese relations. Maynard came originally, it seems, from Plymouth, where he was one of a large family of eleven brothers and sisters. He emigrated to La Rochelle, where he set up as a merchant but went bankrupt. He then moved to Portugal, probably in 1641, where he lived at Aveiro, south of Oporto, and worked for Rowland Hill, merchant of Oporto, as an agent in the shipping of olive oil. Hill, who had influence with Cromwell's government, persuaded London to employ Maynard on the state's business in Lisbon in 1655. The following year Hill secured Maynard's appointment[25] as consul at Lisbon. Hill had lent him large sums of money and probably hoped, by securing lucrative employment for him, to guarantee the repayment of the loan.

John IV's letters, carried to England by Thomas Maynard, were read before the Council of State on 14/24 September 1655.[26] The king claimed that he lacked the authority to ratify the treaty of 1654 because it included matters that required the approval of the church; the approval of the church would not be forthcoming until certain changes had been made in the religious articles; the ratification of the treaty depended, therefore, on London's acceptance of changes in the signed treaty.

Most English officials believed that the king of Portugal was using the church and the Inquisition as excuses for his refusal to ratify the treaty; they believed that he could coerce the church if he pleased. There may have been, to be sure, some use of the religious question as a device to discredit a treaty that the Portuguese disliked for other reasons, but as has been set forth, the king's difficulties with the church were genuine, and his letters to London did not exaggerate the problem.

The troubles with Portugal over the ratification of the treaty came at a most inopportune moment for the Commonwealth. The Lord Protector was seriously ill, London was still smarting from the defeat suffered at Hispaniola; and Blake wanted his ships to be recalled from Lisbon, while fresh ships and reinforcements had to be sent to the Mediterranean and the West Indies. The government felt that a firm line had to be taken with the Portuguese—that on no account was the Commonwealth to submit to a renegotiation of the treaty—but London did not feel prepared, in the autumn of 1655, to confront John IV with an ultimatum. Blake was called home and arrived in England on 7/17 October 1655, and the decisive confrontation with the king of Portugal was postponed until the spring of 1656.

In a sense, John IV's policy had proved most successful. Ever since the autumn of 1650 he had been striving for peace with England at no expense to the Portuguese. Portugal had obtained all the advantages of an alliance with England without sacrificing anything in return. England had obligingly inflicted a devastating defeat on the Dutch and, even more obligingly, had made war on Spain—hampering John IV's two great enemies—and Portugal had not compensated any English merchants for the sequestrations of 1650, nor paid to London a single cruzado of the £50,000 so earnestly pledged to the Commonwealth in December 1652, a sum supposed to have been paid immediately! No wonder Cromwell thought England had been ill-used by the king of Portugal!

England's displeasure at the unkept promises and endless procrastination of the astute John IV led to direct naval action in the spring of 1656, when the king was coerced into signing the treaty and paying the £50,000 without further delay.[27] Cromwell would consent to no change whatever in the religious articles, and the Portuguese were forced to swallow the Protestant liberties along with the commercial concessions, without any alteration of language or diminution of meaning in the treaty to which the unfortunate Count of Penaguião had once affixed his name.

Many Portuguese historians have asserted that the "tyrant" Cromwell brutally imposed his will on the "helpless" Portuguese. Such a charge, reducing a complex situation to a single and sensational explanation, does an injustice to King John, who for six years had led London a merry chase and who, in the end, gave up (beyond the £50,000) perhaps no more than some paper promises—for it must not be assumed that the articles of the treaty, clause by clause, thereafter governed the lives of Englishmen resident in Portugal. On the contrary, many things in the treaty were ignored by the Portuguese. In the circumstances, Cromwell's dissatisfaction with Portugal in the spring of 1656 was understandable and possibly even justifiable.

The important question of what kind of religious life was actually led by the English in Portugal in the seventeenth century remains to be considered. Neither the Protestant religious freedoms set forth in the treaty nor the reactions of Portuguese ecclesiastics to them bore a direct relation to the day-to-day practices of the English residents in Portugal. If the ideals expressed in the religious articles had been enforced always and without question, then Protestants would have enjoyed complete security in the exercise of their religion; however, if the king had upheld the opinions of the Portuguese clergy, then the practice of Protestantism would have been hazardous or impossible. In fact, the position of Protestants resident in Portugal was neither as secure as the treaty prescribed nor as hazardous as the Inquisitors might have preferred. The Protestants held a position somewhere in the middle of these extremes—able, much of the time, to worship quietly and unobtrusively, but subject, sometimes, to harassment.

Beginning in 1656, the defense of English freedom of worship in Portugal depended on the consul at Lisbon, who by the terms of the 1654 treaty was supposed to be a Protestant. At the time of the signing of the treaty, the English consul in Lisbon was a Catholic priest, Fr. John Robinson, of the English College of Lisbon (a seminary run by exiles for the training of Catholic missionaries for England). Robinson had been appointed consul by Charles II (about 1649), possibly on the suggestion of the Portuguese, and had been acknowledged by John IV in a letter of confirmation (13 July 1650),[28] which directed all English merchants to obey Robinson. The consul was a royalist and his appointment was not recognized in London, although the Commonwealth presented no alternative candidate of its own.

If Protestant merchants were to receive proper protection in Lisbon, it was desirable that the English consul be himself a Protestant. When Thomas Maynard became the Commonwealth's agent in Lisbon, Robinson's position, which had suffered with the decline of royalist fortunes, was undermined, and Maynard eventually succeeded in removing him altogether.[29] Maynard was not a Puritan but an Anglican, yet he possessed an almost Puritan zeal for the defense of the reformed faith. He carried on a one-man guerrilla war against the Portuguese Inquisition that discouraged that formidable institution from meddling with Protestant merchants. As he himself boasted: "I am the first protestant that ever served the office of Consul in this place, which hugely troubles the Inquisition."[30]

Maynard himself was once involved in a serious incident with the Inquisition. Late in 1659 he converted to Protestantism an English Catholic lady, Margaret Throckmorton, who had been sent to Lisbon to become a nun and join the English Brigittine sisters at their Lisbon convent. Evidently the lady changed her mind about becoming a nun, threw herself on the protection of the English consul, was sheltered at the consul's own house, and embraced the Church of England. The Inquisition issued orders for her arrest, but Maynard would not surrender her. The Queen-Regent Luisa, then at the head of the Portuguese government, suggested that the lady be placed in a private house, where the Inquisitors could reason with her. But Maynard, who claimed diplomatic immunity for himself and his household, affirmed that Margaret Throckmorton, as a Protestant Englishwoman, was entitled to the full protection of article 14 of the peace treaty.[31]

The Inquisition, arguing that consuls did not possess the diplomatic immunities of ambassadors and that article 14 did not protect English Catholics, arrested Maynard and surrounded his house with an armed guard. The consul, strongly supported by the English Protestant merchants, threatened to take the first ship to England and blow up the delicate Anglo-Portuguese negotiations then (in February 1660) taking place in London. Two agents of the Inquisition, the brothers Luís da Cunha de Ataíde and Nuno da Cunha de Ataíde—disregarding instructions that had been given to them not to attempt a forcible entry—broke down the doors of the consul's house with axes and violently intruded into Margaret Throckmorton's room. The lady, however, was nowhere to be found; evidently she had been spirited out of the consulate and hidden by friends. Queen Luisa, a pious Catholic, was both angered and baffled but felt that she had no alternative but to order the Inquisition to release Consul Maynard.[32]

In this case, as in others, Maynard was quite wrong. Nothing in article 14 authorized Englishmen to convert Catholics. In fact, his activities here were proscribed by the conditional clause: "But the English are to take care that they doe not exceed what is granted by this article." The English themselves had often complained of the proselytizing activities carried on by the Portuguese embassy in London. Portuguese priests, brought to England in numbers that exceeded the spiritual requirements of the small Portuguese community in London (which was composed mostly of Jews), ministered to English Catholics and even attempted to convert English Protestants.[33] Yet if the English wished to prevent these Portuguese activities in London, then they should have refrained from giving any comparable kind of provocation in Lisbon.

Many Portuguese may well have felt that English Protestant activities in Lisbon, simple and modest as they appear to have been by most standards, had reached an intolerable level. Queen Luisa complained to her ambassador in London that the services in the Lisbon consul's house were virtually public ceremonies, attracting more people than attended some Lisbon churches. They were highly offensive to Catholics and represented a standing danger to English Catholics and to the Portuguese employees and Negro servants of the English merchants. In Lisbon, complained the queen, there had always been Englishmen and their consuls, "but never has there been what we experience today."[34]

Queen Luisa's quarrel with Maynard was soon patched up. She claimed that he had no real grievance and that the Inquisition had treated him exceptionally well. Before he left for England in May 1660, the consul had agreed not to press any complaints in London.[35] Maynard, however, did not abandon his promotion of Protestantism but worked to recruit an English chaplain for Lisbon. In 1661 he obtained the consent of the English merchants in Lisbon to pay £250 per year, out of their own pockets, for a good minister. The chaplaincy was created under the patronage of the London merchants trading to Portugal, to be supervised by the Bishop of London, but to be supported exclusively by the merchant community in Lisbon.[36] Thomas Marsden, a protégé of Sir Richard Fanshaw (Charles II's ambassador extraordinary to the king of Portugal in 1661), received the appointment as chaplain at Lisbon. Marsden served in Portugal until 1665, when he wanted to return to England. Before his departure, Consul Thomas Maynard, Vice Consul Christopher Maynard, and twenty-four English merchants signed a certificate (31 January/10 February 1665) saying that Thomas Marsden had been "assiduous and laborious in his studies, constant and orthodox in his preaching, pious and exemplary in his life."[37] By this time, most of the English merchants may have preferred to have had no chaplain at all, because they found the tithes they had to pay quite burdensome.[38]

Anglican chaplains continued to minister to the English community in Lisbon, without interruption, using a room in the consul's house as a place of worship, until 1686 when the Inquisition intervened. On Thursday, 2/12 September 1686, the old consul was called before the Inquisitors and told that there would be no more Protestant services allowed in Portugal. A Catholic king, James II, then ruled in England, and apparently the Inquisition believed that the moment had come for restricting the activities of the English Protestants. Maynard immediately claimed the protection of article 14 of the 1654 treaty, but the Inquisitors answered that they had never heard of such an article—that "it never came to the Cognizance of the Inquisition." "To which I replyed," wrote Maynard to Henry Compton, Bishop of London, "that I had been Consul here thirty yeares, in which tyme the Kings subjects assembled to heare Divine Service and Sermons, and 'twas very improbable that in soe many yeares it should not come to the Cognizance of the Inquisition."[39]

The Inquisitors, maintaining that Protestant services had never been allowed and had only taken place because they had not been noticed, insisted that the consul should sign an order prohibiting all such services for the future. Maynard refused to sign. The Lisbon English did not secure relief from the demands of the Inquisition until after the arrival of a new ambassador, William Scarborough, who had instructions (18/28 October 1686) to insist on freedom of worship at the consul's house.[40] The incident represented an outstanding example of the Inquisition's violation of the religious guarantees in the 1654 treaty.

Relations between Inquisitors and Protestants were not always marked by tension and trouble. An Englishman's first contacts with the Portuguese Inquisition began before he had even left the ship. Before anyone aboard a visiting English ship was allowed ashore, the inspectors of the Inquisition carried out a search for forbidden books and heretical articles of worship. These inspections took place regularly and usually with little friction. The Inquisitors were often assisted by English Catholics, who served as interpreters. Protestants would hide all their religious books and articles before they came into a Portuguese port—and, indeed, the Inquisitors were not greatly concerned about Protestant Bibles and other books printed in English, a language that almost no one in Portugal could read. If such books were found, the Inquisitors sealed them and kept them in a safe place and returned them to their owners when the ship left port.[41]

The Inquisitors were much more worried about books in Latin, especially religious books owned by English Catholics that might come into the hands of Portuguese Catholics and that, although Catholic, might deviate from the strict line of Iberian orthodoxy. The Inquisitors also checked on the comings and goings of foreign Catholic clergy. In 1683 the Inquisitors at the Algarve port of Vila Nova de Portimão seized seventy-three books from the English ship *Undevar (Endeavour?),* whose captain and eighteen crew members were *all Catholics.*[42]

According to article 14 the English were permitted to have Protestant Bibles and other religious books—but the Inquisition never really accepted this provision in the treaty. The English merchants reported in 1671 that the Inquisition had prohibited the ownership of Protestant Bibles.[43] In reality, what attracted the ire of the Inquisitors was not the use of Bibles in private, but any public display of them, such as carrying them about in the streets without bothering to conceal them. The merchants could well afford to heed Catholic susceptibilities in this matter.

The English complained of certain other difficulties with the Inquisition. Despite the provisions in the 1654 treaty, the Inquisition did not pay some debts owed to English merchants by New Christians whose estates had been confiscated by the Inquisitors. The Inquisition interfered with Portuguese servants employed by English merchants and sometimes even seized and carried away Negro slaves owned by Englishmen.[44] The Portuguese also prevented the merchants from acquiring a regular cemetery. The English continued to bury their dead on their own lands (perhaps in the orchards or farms outside Lisbon owned by most of the successful merchants) or at sea or at night between the tide marks of a beach somewhere near Trafaria, across the Tagus from Oeiras. They finally obtained their Lisbon cemetery, and a proper church, early in the nineteenth century.[45]

One of the strangest incidents involving Englishmen and the Inquisition came when Samuel Palmer, an English resident of Oporto, married to a relative of Consul Maynard's, and a converted Catholic, petitioned the Inquisition (in February 1684) for an appointment as a familiar of the Holy Office. After an exhaustive investigation into his background (to determine whether he had any

Jewish, Moorish, or Negro ancestry), he was accepted as a familiar of the Portuguese Inquisition on 2 March 1686. The prolonged investigation required the cooperation of English Catholics in Portugal and England, of nine English Protestant merchants of Oporto, and of members of the Jewish Portuguese community in London.[46]

In this fashion, at least one official of the Inquisition, and he a Londoner, obtained his appointment because of a great deal of cooperation extended to him by Protestants and Jews. In the curious figure of Samuel Palmer the convert—with his Protestant ancestors, his business connections with English merchants, his Anglo-Portuguese wife related to Consul Maynard, and his religious associations with the Portuguese—in such a figure all the various strands of this story, English and Portuguese, Protestant and Catholic, seem to come together.

In the view of the London Puritans, the Protestant in Portugal was as a Christian in the land of the Turks; in the opinion of the Inquisitors, he was as a ravenous wolf in the vineyard of the Lord. Neither view had much to do with the realities of the case. The resident English Protestant in seventeenth-century Portugal went about his religious duties, possibly devoutly but discreetly, without giving offense to Catholics and without suffering much molestation from them. He was not a missionary propagating the reformed faith, nor was he called on to give the testimony of martyrdom. No Englishman tried to be the "reformer" of the Portuguese church, and none was ever victimized in the bloody drama of the auto-da-fé. In religious matters, the rule of "live and let live" governed relations between the English and Portuguese.

The Inquisition could never make its vision of the heretic the effective basis of government policy. The Inquisition could and did prevent some of the clauses in article 14 from being put into practice—but it was not successful in any of its various efforts to coerce English Protestants in the physical sense. Pressure on Protestants in Lisbon brought effective counterpressure on Portugal from London. This was as true in the days of Charles II as it had been at the time of Cromwell. The resident Protestants, supported in London and backed by the greatest fleet in the world, although unable to enjoy all the religious freedoms they might have wished, yet maintained the security of their property and their persons—most of the time and in most circumstances—and avoided the grosser forms of harassment that the Inquisition might otherwise have inflicted upon them.

In summary, during the year 1655 and the interim between the signing of the Anglo-Portuguese treaty in July 1654 and its ratification in June 1656, the church in Portugal carried out a thorough study and review of the position of the English "heretic" resident in Portugal. The chief result of this study was the emergence of a consensus of opinion, embracing the broad ranks of nobles, clergy, and people, that Englishmen ought not to be given any further religious rights and that "heretics" should remain content with the privileges they already possessed. Supported by this body of opinion, King John refused to ratify the Anglo-Portuguese treaty. Thus 1655 was a year of stagnation in the relations between the two countries. But London refused to accept the diplomatic stalemate and eventually forced on Portugal the serious, even desperate and critical, negotiations that came during the spring and summer of 1656.

8

THE RATIFICATION OF THE TREATY OF 1654

Cromwell was angered by Portuguese intransigence over the peace treaty. Early in 1656 he decided that the time had come to use force in asserting his demands. On 19/29 February 1656 the Council of State recommended that the diplomat Philip Meadowes be sent to Portugal.[1] It was planned to send him to Lisbon some ten days or two weeks in advance of a great fleet, and he would try to persuade the Portuguese to pay the promised £50,000 and to ratify the treaty before direct naval pressure was actually applied.

Philip Meadowes arrived in Plymouth on Friday, 7/17 March 1656, and wrote a letter to Thurloe on Tuesday saying that he would try to sail aboard the frigate *Phoenix* that same day. He hoped that "our frigat wil salute King John at his palace royal before our fleet be out of the Channel."[2] General-at-Sea Robert Blake was busy preparing the fleet at Ellen's Road and trying out his impressive new flagship, the *Naseby*. Aboard her he wrote his will (13/23 March 1656)[3]—and indeed the voyage he was about to start was to prove his last. The great fleet assembled at Ellen's Road numbered forty-eight men-of-war (about one-third of the effective fighting strength of the navy) and was commanded by two coequal Generals-at-Sea, Blake and Edward Montagu, the future Earl of Sandwich. The men of the Commonwealth seemed to have much faith in divided commands, in committees and commissions, and in the collective decisions that emerged from them, although during the West Indies expedition the joint commanders, Penn and Venables, had quarreled with each other, with disastrous consequences for the expedition. The joint commanders Blake and Popham had worked well together in 1650, but during 1656 there was to be some friction between Blake and Montagu, although not to the point where it affected the efficiency of the fleet. Their dispute was not over the conduct and organization of the fleet, but over the objectives of the expedition and how to interpret their instructions.

The trouble came mostly from the inexperienced Montagu, who desired, above all else, to plunder Portuguese commerce. Except in the unlikely event of John IV's immediate and complete capitulation, Montagu wanted to have a free hand to attack Portuguese shipping, especially the returning Brazil fleet, regardless of the progress or eventual outcome of Meadowes's negotiations in Lisbon. On the mainland, the agent Meadowes strove very hard to obtain an accommodation of interests, a negotiated settlement produced by persuasion. Blake had to steer a tricky course between the aggressive admiral and the well-intentioned diplomat. On the one hand, Blake required Montagu to abide by any promises made by Meadowes to the Portuguese—on the other, he tried to put pressure on Meadowes to obtain a quick decision from John IV.

Blake's own letters were so reticent and modest that it is hard to form a clear impression of what he thought about the Portuguese negotiations. It seems reasonable to say that this honest and prudent admiral sought no wars that could be avoided and that he was in favor of peace with Portugal if it could be obtained without sacrificing England's interests. London issued broad instructions for Meadowes and the navy to force the king to accept the peace but, at the beginning at least, left the crucial question of timing to the joint decision of Meadowes, Blake, and Montagu.

In the handling of the Portuguese question, the government did not speak with a single voice, since the personalities of Meadowes, Montagu, Blake, and even Cromwell pulled the negotiations in different directions. In Portugal, the king spoke for the nation, but he usually favored postponement and delay; behind him, struggling hard to influence him, were three general factions: (1) those, such as António de Sousa de Macedo (former resident in London in the days of Charles I), who favored outright defiance of the Commonwealth regardless of consequences; (2) those who wanted the main points in the peace treaty renegotiated, as did the Count of Penaguião, the original negotiator of the treaty; and (3) those few, led by the Count of Odemira, who felt that a settlement had to be made with England, if possible on good terms but if not on whatever terms could be obtained. From the tangle of English and Portuguese personalities, with divergent policies, one person emerged with extraordinary credit: Philip Meadowes, who saved the treaty and preserved the peace in spite of firm objections from the Portuguese and in the face of unreasonable demands from his English associates.

On 15/25 March Blake prepared to sail, and he was able to leave the next day. Twenty-one days later Montagu wrote to Thurloe (5/15 April 1656) that the fleet was some forty leagues from the Rock of Lisbon and the commanders were ready to send a frigate to Lisbon "with our credentialls, and to lett the kinge understand of our approach to his dominions in an amicable way."[4] The frigate carried a friendly letter from Cromwell to John IV (on the supposition, apparently, that the king was ready to ratify the treaty) and instructions to Meadowes that the frigate would await his replies for twenty-four hours and then rejoin the fleet. The fleet would continue on the way to its first objective, the Cadiz area, where it would disrupt Spanish shipping. If Meadowes had any messages for the admirals that could not be sent in time to catch the frigate, then he should remit them overland to Lagos, where a vessel would pick them up.

The admirals' dispatches reached Meadowes on Monday morning, 7/17 April 1656, by which time the envoy had already reached the conclusion that the first stage of his mission had failed; that is, Meadowes's initial effort to secure payment of the £50,000 and obtain the ratification of the treaty without any further discussion or delay had met with a firm refusal from the king of Portugal. Meadowes communicated this fact to Cromwell in a letter dated Sunday, 6/16 April, the day before the arrival of the admirals' frigate, as follows: "Am sorry after so much earnest travel and endeavour, I could not ripen this affair to a better issue; yet hope my service wil be never the les acceptable, although it has not hitherto produced that good effect, which I desired. My duty and affection have not been wanting, but the event depends upon the wil of others."[5] With this letter Meadowes enclosed the king's negative reply to the Lord Protector.

Meadowes seemed to be trying to dispel any notions London might have had that satisfaction from Portugal could be obtained cheaply and quickly; if Cromwell entertained any hopes of rapid success, then he must be undeceived. Yet only the first stage of the negotiations had failed—and these had taken place before the fleet had even arrived. The second stage would take place under the psychological threat of the fleet—a threat that was psychological and not direct and immediate, because the fleet did not linger in Lisbon waters but sailed past on its way to the straits.

Meadowes's report to Blake and Montagu (dated Tuesday, 8/18 April 1656, and sent via the admirals' frigate) was rather more optimistic than his letter to the Lord Protector had been. Meadowes reported that the king delayed accepting the treaty because he claimed he lacked jurisdiction over the religious concessions. Actually, wrote Meadowes, John IV did not want to pay the £50,000, which had to be paid before the exchange of ratifications. He acknowledged the receipt of Cromwell's letter to John IV—a sealed communication of whose contents he had had previous information—but said he did not intend to deliver it until a more auspicious occasion: "In this juncture of time and state of affaires to present letters of that nature to his majestie, giving all assureances of friendship and good offices, albeit the treaty was not yet ratified, would redound to the prejudice of the business before me."[6] As soon as the admirals' frigate had come to Lisbon (on Monday 7/17 April), Meadowes had rushed to the king and informed him of the arrival of the English fleet, in these terms: "Telling him withall, that it was now in his majestie's choise to serve himself of the best fitted and appointed fleet in the world, to be as a wall and defence to his dominions against the declared enemy of both nations . . . trusting he would never give occasion for converting that strength against him, which was designed and employed for his benefitt and advantage."[7] Meadowes used the carrot and the stick: the fleet, in its operations against the Spaniards, could render enormous service to the king of Portugal—and it could also, if the Portuguese proved uncooperative, annihilate the Brazil fleet. John IV, said Meadowes, "asked me by name concerning generall Blake, whome he had often heard so much of." The English envoy finished by informing the king that there was an English ship bound for Bristol, which would carry any messages to London that he might care to send.

In the same letter, Meadowes furnished the admirals with several items of naval intelligence. The Brazil fleet, he said, with 100 sugar ships escorted by eleven men-of-war, was expected back in May 1656. As for Philip IV's fleet, "the Spaniard is reported to be in no condition to fight you, and that if you fight him, you must breake open his dores to come at him, for he intends not to come out of his owne howse." Meadowes hoped, if only for the sake of the Lisbon negotiations, that the fleet would win a victory over Spain, for "the newes of your successe will give life to your affaires here."[8]

After this exchange of correspondence there was almost no further contact between Meadowes and the admirals during the next three weeks. In Lisbon, John IV reacted to the presence of the English ships by ordering the dispatch of four companies of infantry to defend Cascais[9] and by putting Lisbon in a condition of preparedness. The king was hard-pressed by the "fire-eaters," the *valentões* or bravos, who were eager to fight the English. The clergy were adamant against the religious articles. Dom Francisco de Sotomaior, Bishop of Targa *in partibus infidelium,* wrote (12 April 1656) from the frontier at Elvas urging the king to stand fast. The people of Portugal, said the belligerent bishop, "embrace war and hostilities with the English for the purity of the faith with joy, and peace with sadness."[10]

John IV, with his usual shrewdness, tried to find a middle ground between Portuguese opinion and the English demands. His message to Cromwell[11] went as far as he could go toward accommodating the English without giving way on the religious articles. The king ratified the treaty, *conditionally,* provided that key clauses in articles 6 and 14 were changed or else were submitted to the pope's approval.

The king's reply, coming on top of Meadowes's gloomy letter of 6/16 April 1656, caused distress in London. Cromwell was upset, and his letter (6/16 May 1656) to Blake and Montagu seethed with anger. John IV, he said, "not only refused to give us satisfaction" in the matter of the treaty "but instead thereof sent us a pretended ratification of a Treaty, so different from what was agreed by his Ambassador that it was quite another thing." As for submitting anything to the approval of the pope, the Puritan ruler of England would as soon have sought the opinion of the Devil! The king of Portugal's proposal "would bring us to an owning of the Pope, which, we hope, whatever befall us, we shall not, by the grace of God, be brought unto."[12]

The king's wish to protect seamen supposedly converted to Catholicism would furnish an excuse, thought the Lord Protector, "for any knave to leave his duty, or for the Roman Catholics to seduce our men." The English had been treated very shabbily: "Upon the whole matter, we find them very false to us, who intended nothing but what was simply honest." England had been driven into a corner; force might have to be used with the Portuguese, not from choice but from necessity. The king had to be given a time limit in which to accept the treaty; if he continued to refuse, then let war be unleashed on the Portuguese.

On the same day (6/16 May) that this letter was written, new orders were issued to the Generals-at-Sea, who were told that if they received word from Meadowes that the king of Portugal would not give satisfaction, they were to take the following course of action: "Use your best endeavours, by the fleet or such part thereof as you shall judge necessary, to take, arrest, and seize upon the fleet or fleets belonging to the king of Portugall, or any his subjects, with their guns, cash, goods, and merchandizes whatever, now expected from the East and West Indyes."[13] At the same time, Cromwell ordered Meadowes to demand ratification without subtracting from, adding to, or altering the words in the treaty as signed by Penaguião on 10/20 July 1654; Meadowes was to tell John IV that he would be given five days to return an answer; at the end of five days, if no satisfactory answer had been received, then the envoy was to leave Portugal.[14]

The Portuguese resident in London, Francisco Ferreira Rebelo—who had been left in charge of the embassy since the departure of Penaguião—had received instructions from the king to put off the English with promises and get them to delay all decisions.[15] According to Francesco Giavarina, the Venetian resident in London, Cromwell summoned Rebelo to a conference and breathed fire and defiance, threatened the resident with expulsion, and "boasted that the power of England was equal to dealing with no matter what weight of arms and with any power soever."[16]

The agent Thomas Maynard boarded the frigate *Sapphire* and took Cromwell's ultimatum to Lisbon. He arrived there on 18/28 May 1656 and presented the astonished Meadowes with these new instructions. Meadowes had little idea that Cromwell would react so strongly to his reports, which had been sent to London six weeks previously. During these six weeks Meadowes had labored, with considerable success, to achieve a negotiated settlement with Portugal and to come to an honest arrangement with John IV on the basis of principles far less violent than those embodied in the ultimatum.

The Commonwealth's agent held talks, first of all, with Dom Vasco Luís da Gama, Marquis of Niza—a man with extensive diplomatic experience[17]—and with Penaguião. Niza and Penaguião demanded guarantees against any attack being made on the Brazil fleet; otherwise they would refuse to negotiate. Meadowes replied: "Ratefy the treaty, and then you are secure. Till that be done, you must run the hazard."[18] The Portuguese replied that if no security for the safety of the Brazil fleet was given, then the Commonwealth's ships (which required the use of Portuguese harbors in the campaign against Spain) would be denied entry in Portuguese ports. Meadowes replied that the English would consider this to be a declaration of war.

Since Niza and the embittered Penaguião did not seem anxious to reach a settlement with Meadowes, they were replaced by the Count of Odemira, "a man well affected to our nation," said Meadowes.[19] Odemira headed a new body of commissioners. With goodwill on both sides, the differences between English and Portuguese were narrowed to two points: (1) the compulsory return of Catholic seamen to their ships and (2) the insertion of a *scandal clause* in article 14. As for the first point, the English merchants of Lisbon assured Meadowes that it was ridiculous that so momentous and beneficial a treaty should be held up for so small a matter; if the treaty was endangered by it, the English would be wise to drop the demand. As for the scandal clause, John IV explained the matter to Meadowes in this way: the meaning of the word *scandal,* he said, would only apply to cases of overt and deliberate blasphemy against the Catholic church, and it would not be stretched in any way; at all events, he added, if the English did not accept the scandal clause the inhabitants of Portugal would still expect them to live up to it—"for if the word *scandall* be not expressed, it is still implyed, and the practice will be one and the same."[20] The king's point was well taken, and the English envoy was willing to consider it.

The Portuguese required of Meadowes a promise that he would do his best to persuade Cromwell to accept these two changes—and they also wanted an iron-clad guarantee that the Commonwealth's ships would not engage in hostilities against Portuguese vessels. In return for these minimal concessions, Meadowes obtained: (1) a promise of immediate payment of the £50,000; (2) acceptance of the secret article fixing customs duties at a maximum level of 23 percent of the value of the goods that were dutiable; (3) the enormous privileges of free access to Brazil, Africa, and the East in article 11; (4) the favorable method for determining the amounts of compensation to be paid to the merchants for their losses in 1650, as per article 25; and (5) a host of other privileges as contained in the undamaged and unaltered text of the treaty.

Meadowes had every reason to feel pleased with himself. He had not consented to anything being submitted to the pope; rather, the religious articles were left to the decision of Cromwell. "It may wel be wondered," the envoy wrote, "how I could bring them to discend to such honorable terms."[21] He believed that the threat against the Brazil fleet had proved decisive.

This happy condition of affairs was interrupted by a dramatic incident. On Thursday, 11 May 1656, at nine o'clock in the evening, when Meadowes was traveling in a litter from the Count of Odemira's house to his own, two horsemen rode up and discharged pistols into both sides of the litter and then fled. One bullet passed through Meadowes's left hand, but otherwise he was not hurt.[22]

Englishmen in Portugal all thought that the assault on the English envoy was an attempt to avenge the execution of Dom Pantaleão de Sá e Meneses. William Mettam, John Thurloe's secret agent in Lisbon (unknown even to Meadowes himself), reported that Penaguião—or, more probably, Penaguião's brother-in-law the Count of Tôrre, "a man noted for bloodshed and murthers"—may have been behind the attack on the envoy.[23] Whether or not revenge was the motive for the assault, it came at the worst possible moment for Portugal. Meadowes and the king had virtually reached an agreement; London was very sensitive to attacks on English diplomats (because of the murder of Commonwealth envoys in Madrid and The Hague) and was certain to react with energy; and the event would furnish an excellent excuse for Montagu, and all the other mariners who were greedy for booty, to launch a general assault on Portuguese shipping.

In the circumstances, John IV had to act quickly to reassure Meadowes and the English, disassociate his government completely from this untoward event, and apprehend and punish the guilty. Within hours of the attack, on the same evening, the king summoned the chief law officers to his presence and issued instructions that all officials and judges in the Lisbon area, in all districts, were to conduct a meticulous investigation into the assault, "trying with the greatest care that can be, with all possible diligence, to discover the guilty in the said case."[24] On the days following the attack the government posted edicts and proclamations in Lisbon calling for information from any witnesses, whose identity would be kept secret, who were promised immunity from prosecution if any other crimes or charges lay against their names, and who could claim a reward of 4,000 cruzados (£800) if they contributed valuable information.

The guilty were not caught or punished. Some of the English were quick to accuse the Portuguese of having made no real effort to apprehend the felons. Montagu, who knew nothing about the Lisbon government, protested against "the horrible indignitye done to our nation in the endeavouringe to assassinate Mr. Meddowes, for which no justice hath been done (only a little flourish of regret thereat)."[25] The accusation of Portuguese half-heartedness in the pursuit of the culprits may have been legitimate, but it ignored the practical difficulties of the investigation. The assault had taken place in darkness and with great rapidity; before the victims had recovered from their surprise the assailants had galloped away—it could all have been over in a matter of seconds; Meadowes's servants did not recognize the attackers and there were no other witnesses. It was easy to charge that the Count of Penaguião, or his relatives, had instigated the assault, but proof may have been very difficult to obtain. In view of these conditions and considering that the incident disrupted royal policy, it may be wiser to assume that John IV made a sincere effort to apprehend the culprits.

The king sent his personal physicians to attend the wounded man and did everything to assure his comfort and his recovery. Both John IV and Odemira sent apologies to the Lord Protector, lamenting that the envoy had been "shot through his left hand with a bullet by some wicked man."[26] These measures helped to allay the anger of the English. Most important of all, Meadowes did his utmost to minimize the incident. In a letter to Blake and Montagu (3/13 May 1656) he spoke only of an "indisposition of body," and sent a trusted emissary, a certain merchant called Smith, to the admirals with a verbal message, relating the incident but urging caution.[27] The envoy did not permit the episode to interrupt the negotiations in any way.

On 3/13 May 1656, two days after the assault, Meadowes asked the admirals to write letters to John IV assuring him that they would not attack Portuguese ships, because the Lisbon negotiations were coming to a successful conclusion: "I must intreat your lordships, that if your intentions are not to fall upon the Brasill fleete, which for my part I must needs say God forbid, you would give his majesty all satisfaction in this particuler."[28] Meadowes urged the admirals to offer the king protection for his Brazil fleet, sincerely and effusively: "And if you intend the thing, never spare for words."

Ten days later, on 13/23 May 1656, the envoy informed the Generals-at-Sea that everything had been settled:

> I am now to salute your lordships with the good news of the conclusion of the peace; for his majesty of Portugal hath ratified the treaty, togeather with the secret article, as they were concluded by his ambassador and plenipotentiary in England; only in the two articles of religion there is soome litle diference remaiening, which yet standes refer'd unto his highnes, who, I doubt not, but upon the accoumpt and representation of afaires, which I shall give him, will rest satisfyed with what is propounded by his majestie.[29]

John IV had signified his sincerity by "a due performance of all other things agreed, and perticularly the paiement of the 50000 poundes." Meadowes suggested, in this sentence, that the £50,000 was in process of being paid, although it seems more likely that the money, as yet, had only been promised. He warned the admirals, as follows: "I have engaged my faith unto his majestie, that security shall be given him against any hostile attempt to bee made by the fleete under your command, not onely upon his fleet's from Brasile now expected, but upon any other his subjects and dominions."[30]

These letters did not please the admirals. They were particularly dissatisfied with the pledge not to attack the Brazil fleet. From the *Naseby,* near Cadiz, Montagu wrote to Thurloe (19/29 May 1656) as follows: "Your Agent at Lisbon had put us in great straights, having promised that we shall engage not to oppose their Brazile fleet or others; whereas we have no power to do so, considering the matter of the treaty that it is not granted in termes but altered."[31] The admiral declared that he would send twenty ships to Lisbon; if the Portuguese paid the £50,000 then there would be no attack—"otherwise," wrote Montagu, "I know not what."

Montagu thought that Meadowes had been duped by the Portuguese, who would promise the sun and moon as long as the Brazil fleet was at sea; once it was safely in port, the Portuguese would change their tune. Their intent was (wrote Montagu to Thurloe) "by delay to gett home their fleets and then to cheat you of the money . . . in this nicke of tyme they looke for their Brazil silver."[32] The Brazil ships, of course, carried sugar, not silver; Blake could have enlightened his colleague on that point. But had Montagu ever discussed this matter fully with Blake? Blake did not write these letters and did not seem to have shared either Montagu's distrust of Meadowes or his eagerness to attack the Portuguese.

A letter Blake did sign (together with Montagu), on the day (20/30 May 1656) the fleet sailed from the bay of Cadiz for Lisbon, and which was sent on ahead by the frigate *Phoenix,* simply invited Meadowes to confer with the Generals-at-Sea aboard the *Naseby* when the fleet reached Cascais.[33] All of this was done, it will be understood, before the fleet had received Cromwell's orders of 6/16 May 1656, sent to Portugal aboard the frigate *Sapphire.* Also Meadowes's letters to the fleet had been sent before the *Sapphire,* with Cromwell's ultimatum, had reached Lisbon.

On 18/28 May the *Sapphire* arrived at Lisbon with Cromwell's ultimatum. Then the frigate set sail immediately for the fleet to deliver London's belligerent new instructions. The *Sapphire* did not find the *Naseby* until about 23 May/2 June, after which she was sent back to Cascais with a message for Meadowes. She was supposed to stand by off Cascais in case Meadowes had to leave Lisbon in a hurry.[34]

Cromwell's unnecessary ultimatum to the king of Portugal, to pay the £50,000 and sign the ratification of an unaltered treaty within five days or else, cut the ground out from under Meadowes. The envoy's reasonable settlement with John IV—so ably, patiently, and conscientiously negotiated—was undone. Six days after he had written about "the good news of the conclusion of the peace," Meadowes was compelled to call at the royal palace, formally repudiate the previous arrangements, present the Lord Protector's new demands, and give notice that an answer was expected within five days. On 25 May/4 June 1656 the envoy reported to Blake and Montagu: "The five days are now lapsed: I have not nor am like to receive any satisfaction from his majesty to the demands, which I have made in his highnesse name, unless it be the very hower that I am goeing aboard; for what extremityes may enforce them to I know not."[35] A tone of weariness and disgust ran through the letter. Meadowes asked that a ship be dispatched for him (Blake was sending him the *Sapphire* that very day), but to come no farther than Cascais. He told the admirals that the Brazil fleet was expected "every hower."

William Mettam—Thurloe's private agent in Lisbon, who reported to London without Meadowes's knowledge—gave his own account of the situation in a letter (24 May/3 June 1656) sent "by a little herring ship for Yarmouth." Mettam had a deep prejudice against the Portuguese and their "shallow and unexperienced counsellors." He said that they believed that England could not make war on both Spain and Portugal at the same time. "If this be war, say they, the English are fooles"—fools to refuse £50,000, incite new enemies, imperil English properties in Portugal, "and all this for a punctilio in religion, which no English marchant values a straw."[36]

The king, thought Mettam, wanted to postpone all decisions, or approve only a conditional ratification, until such time as the Brazil fleet had come into port. To some extent, he believed, the Portuguese were using religion as an excuse not to ratify: "Inquisition is made much use of to apologize the king's backwardness in peace. Som difficulty, especially in protecting converted seamen, is reall, but more scruple is made than is reall."[37] Yet the tension over the religious question was genuine. A Jesuit who preached against the peace had been banished to Elvas. There was no question, thought Mettam, of any real friendship between England and Portugal, even if the treaty were ratified. Of the chances of ratification, he wrote: "I am halfe of opinion it may be concluded."

Oliver's ultimatum not only disheartened Philip Meadowes; it also discredited the Count of Odemira. A trio of men close to the king—Odemira; the king's confessor, André Fernandes; and Fernandes Monteiro—"the three chiefe and sole advancers of this peace,"[38] had argued that the English were reasonable men with whom an acceptable accommodation could be reached. These counselors felt that Portugal benefited from the Commonwealth's war with Spain and believed that the war turned England and Portugal into natural allies. Cromwell's ultimatum, with its demand for a complete capitulation, exposed the element of appeasement in Odemira's policy, strengthened the war party, hardened the resistance of the church and Inquisition, and destroyed the possibility of reaching a sincere, voluntary, negotiated compromise. For months later the Count of

Odemira spoke with great bitterness about English intransigence over the religious articles.[39]

The king and his ministers faced the immediate problem of guaranteeing the safe arrival of the Brazil fleet. The fleet in question was the largest and richest that the General Company of Brazil had ever sent to sea. From the time it sailed for Brazil until its return to Lisbon it spent over fifteen months abroad. The main unit of the fleet, thirty-six ships under Gen. Francisco de Brito Freire (who had commanded the *Nossa Senhora da Candelária* in support of Rupert in 1650), weighed anchor at Lisbon on 17 April 1655 after having been delayed for six weeks in a quarrel over the freighting of four Genoese ships. The fleet reached Madeira on 21 April, sailed from there on 15 May, and reached the Cape Verde Islands eleven days later.[40] The voyage to Brazil was slow and difficult. At six o'clock one morning, in a calm wind and sea, the flagship *São Pedro* sprang her mainmast. She was supposed to sail for Rio de Janeiro, but Brito Freire took her into Salvador da Bahia, which was reached in mid-July. Many ships had reached Bahia before the flagship, but others did not straggle in until 1 August. On 13 August 1655 the general of the armada posted notices in Bahia informing everyone that the sugar fleet would leave on 15 December 1655. The governor general of Brazil, Dom Jerónimo de Ataíde, Count of Atouguia, argued that the ships should wait until a second sugar crop had been harvested in April.[41] In the event, the fleet gathered together off Pernambuco and left the coast of Brazil on 11 April 1656, a few days after Philip Meadowes had reached Lisbon.

The armada of the Brazil Company reached the Azores on the very day, 4 June 1656, that Meadowes reported that the five-day period of waiting for the king's answer to the ultimatum had expired. The war party in Lisbon argued that Portugal could risk a naval battle with the Commonwealth. The armada in the Azores was not the weak Rio de Janeiro squadron engaged by Blake in 1650 and bore no resemblance to that ill-fated force. The Brazil fleet of 1655 included 50 ships from Bahia, 33 from Pernambuco, 24 from Rio de Janeiro, and 32 other ships—107 ships in all, including thirty-six men-of-war.[42] The warships held 4,268 soldiers and sailors and mounted 795 guns (an average of only 22 guns for each warship).

In addition, there were the seven or eight warships of the Armada Real stationed at Lisbon, which, in an emergency, could be built up to perhaps fifteen men-of-war. Mettam reported that the commander of the Armada Real—António Teles de Meneses, Count of Vila Pouca de Aguiar, "Perpetual General of the Ocean Sea"—was one of the war party, eager to fight England: "He brags with one to fight ten English. . . . Their ships are good, their soldiers ill payed, their seamen few, and unskillfull."[43]

The forty or fifty ships of Blake's fleet were scattered from the Bay of Biscay to the Straits of Gibraltar; even if all the state's ships could be concentrated against the Brazil fleet, they would have had to fight at one and the same time the Armada Real, the thirty-six warships escorting the sugar ships, and the 100-odd merchantmen of the Brazil fleet, some of which may have been powerful ships. Optimists among the Portuguese felt that these were forces sufficient to hold off Blake, perhaps even sufficient to defeat him. Realists in Lisbon held a less rosy view. The English frigates outgunned the Portuguese and were faster, better disciplined, and better led. The state's ships, which had routed Ruyter and Tromp, if they ever engaged the sugar fleet would most assuredly have brought about the destruction or capture of at least one-third of the sugar ships.

Brito Freire said that the Brazil fleet carried 53,221 chests of sugar (containing over 15,500 metric tons), as well as quantities of tobacco, amber, ivory, slaves, ginger, gold, brazilwood, Brazilian hardwood *(jacarandá),* and other products—worth, all told, some 9 million crowns; that is, according to Brito Freire, the fleet's cargoes were worth 3,600:000$000 réis or £1,700,000, a staggeringly large figure for that day.[44] The question facing King John, in this the last great crisis of his life, was: should all this wealth be hazarded, and the security of 150 ships as well, for £50,000 and "a punctilio in religion"?

During 26–28 May/5–7 June 1656, while the great Brazil fleet lay at its hazardous anchorage at Angra, Terceira, in the Azores—apprehensive about bad weather and bewildered by the lack of news from Lisbon—and while Blake and Montagu crowded on all sails for Cascais, Meadowes and John IV strained every nerve to save the peace. The English envoy probably made it clear to the Portuguese that only the immediate payment of the £50,000 would stop the admirals from attacking the Brazil fleet; the religious question was of less importance than the money, in the sense that agreement of the religious clauses, without the payment of the £50,000, would not assure the safety of the Brazil fleet.

The king began to collect the necessary money but still remained apprehensive about the religious question. The royal confessor, Father André Fernandes—who in the exercise of his confessional functions could have made it extremely awkward for the king to acquiesce in the heretics' demands—tried to find a solution. The confessor suggested that the treaty should be ratified, but the clause concerning the compulsory return of Catholic seamen should be left blank in article 6 and space should be left in article 14 for the insertion of the scandal clause. For this purpose, new Latin copies of the treaty should be drawn up, one of which would be sent to London with the King's signature. The trusted English merchant Christopher Warren would carry a confidential explanation to the Portuguese resident in London, Francisco Ferreira Rebelo, and a final diplomatic effort would be made to get Cromwell to accept these changes. In any event, troublesome ecclesiastics in Portugal could be shown the amended Latin copies of the treaty, duly signed by the king, and given to understand that the treaty, in its original form, had not been and would not be accepted.[45] The Portuguese translation of the Latin, which was all that most Portuguese not in the king's confidence would ever get to read or be capable of reading, could be made to sound as innocuous as possible.

Soothed by such high-level chicanery, John IV prepared to swallow the bitter medicine prescribed by Cromwell. On 29 May/8 June 1656 Montagu wrote to Thurloe that the English would have to receive the £50,000 in cash before any assurances could be given about the security of the Brazil fleet. If there were any doubts, then the Brazil ships would be intercepted, because it was better to detain them and then wait for instructions from London than to allow them to pass and then receive, too late, the orders to attack.[46] Montagu was most anxious to get his hands on the "Brazil silver," and his fastest frigates scouted the oceanic approaches to Portugal.

Meanwhile Meadowes informed the Portuguese that he wished an audience with the king for the purpose of bidding farewell, because he would soon be going aboard the English fleet that would come into Cascais. The Portuguese immediately indicated their willingness to ratify the treaty without further delay. Meadowes wrote to Blake and Montagu (30 May/9 June 1656) that the approach of the Commonwealth fleet, together with his request to be allowed to leave, "hath much altered the state of affaires heer." According to the envoy, by the next morning "all things are like to be agreed, and so a peace setled betweene both the nations."[47]

Meadowes, caught between the inertia of John IV and the impetuosity of Montagu, sought to hurry the former while he restrained the latter. One day later, the envoy again wrote to the admirals, informing them that instruments of ratification had been exchanged, that "the Condé de Meira [Odemira] threatens to visit his old acquaintance, as he calls him, generall Blake," and asking them not to send more than two or three frigates into Cascais, so as not to alarm the Portuguese.[48] The commanders aboard the *Naseby,*[49] now cruising off Cape Espichel, requested Meadowes (1/11 June) to confer with them: "Pray lose no time in coming to us."[50]

Admiral Montagu hoped that Meadowes's negotiations with Lisbon would end in failure. If he had found a suitable pretext, such as Portuguese dilatoriness in paying the £50,000, he would have attacked them. The better-intentioned and more experienced Robert Blake was a tired and sick man and played a less active role than Montagu, although he served as some restraint on his colleague. Montagu disobeyed Meadowes's request that only two or three warships should approach Cascais: at 7:00P.M. On 3/13 June he deliberately brought the whole fleet into Cascais.[51] The next day, Meadowes and "most of our Lisbon merchants" came aboard the great ship *Naseby.*

Meadowes knew the temper of the admirals, and he did his utmost to restrain them; he told them, not quite truthfully, that £50,000 in specie was ready for collection. The envoy's declarations prevented Montagu from carrying out any aggressive moves he may have had in mind. During the next few days, while Montagu fretted at Cascais, Meadowes in Lisbon worked assiduously to obtain the cash from the king. The Portuguese probably had little idea of what great pressures the envoy had to contend with and how hard he had to struggle to keep the navy in check.

The *Naseby* had arrived at Cascais on Tuesday evening (3/13 June 1656); on Wednesday Meadowes went aboard; on Friday the admirals sent the frigate *Colchester* up the Tagus to collect the money. On Saturday the envoy informed the admirals that he had £30,000 in Portuguese currency on hand, but that it should be changed into Spanish pieces-of-eight because the Spanish coins would fetch a better rate of exchange in London. Meadowes asked the admirals to supply the Portuguese with a written declaration that the fleet would leave the vicinity of Cascais and the Tagus when the money had been paid. The admirals gave their assurances to that effect on Sunday (8/18 June). Meadowes acknowledged their reply on Monday, spoke of difficulties in changing the money and getting it aboard the *Colchester*, and said the Portuguese Armada Real, now composed of fourteen ships, was ready to sail but wanted assurances as to the courtesies the English would use in saluting John IV's ships in his own waters.[52]

This request enraged Montagu, especially because of the delay in payment of the £50,000, a sum that had somehow turned into £30,000, and even that lesser amount could not, for some fanciful reason (as he conceived it), be placed aboard the frigate that had been sent to collect it. On Tuesday (10/20 June), one week after his arrival at Cascais, he wrote angrily to Meadowes: "The money (as we understood from yourself and some others) was paid, and in your possession in specie, and to the value of so much sterling, before we came hither. If so, surely other accommodations for the shipping of it might have been sooner prepared than we yet see done."[53] As for the saluting of the king's ships, "let all things with you be transacted, as we have desired; and then there needs no discourse of compliments with the King of Portugal's ships." Montagu sent a certain Captain Lloyd to Meadowes to obtain a personal report.

The Commonwealth's envoy did not reply until Thursday (12/22 June), when he informed the admirals, triumphantly, that the *Colchester* had set sail that morning with forty-four chests containing 60:131$450 réis—an amount worth, said Meadowes, about £29,000.[54] The rest of the money would be put aboard the frigate *Sapphire*. There had been some argument with the Portuguese about the Count of Penaguião's London debts, for which the merchants were demanding payment plus interest, but this was a small matter.[55]

Saturday, 14/24 June 1656, was the day of final settlement. The Portuguese paid another installment of the £50,000 in gold coins, which Meadowes insisted had to be changed into silver; and then the *Sapphire* took aboard a final payment of 30,000 cruzados. John IV wrote to the Lord Protector confirming the ratification of the treaty and making a desperate eleventh-hour plea for changes in the religious articles.[56]

The only Englishmen dissatisfied with the peace were Montagu and some of the more piratically minded naval officers. Meadowes, on a return visit to the *Naseby,* received quite a shock and felt quite hurt, as he explained in a letter to Thurloe (16/26 June): "I found general Blake satisfied with the peace, but general Montague somewhat scrupulous, nay, which was more, he told me, that I should have had more thank at Whitehal, if I had not concluded it. This, me thought, was cold entertainment for al my travel and care in this busines."[57] The English envoy—who had handled matters with goodwill, dexterity, and tact and who received a shabby recompense from Montagu—felt called upon to defend his policy and his attitudes. Meadowes argued that an attack on the Brazil fleet, even if successful, would have cost the English merchants more than they would have gained. For the sake of thirty or forty sugar ships they would have had to sacrifice all their Portuguese properties, forgo future opportunities for business and profit, and relinquish the many valuable concessions guaranteed to them by the treaty. And what if an attack on the Brazil fleet should miscarry or the sugar ships slip into harbor unperceived? "Consider, if the Brasil fleet had got home, and the treaty not ratified, in what condition had his highnes affairs been in?"[58]

But Montagu reported to Thurloe that "the generall Blake and myselfe have been in great straights in this businesse . . . consideringe the vile falseness of the Portugalls, and aversion to make good what he had agreed to by his plenipotentiaryes." This ungrammatical sentence was followed by a reference to the assault on Meadowes, for which Montagu seemed to blame the Portuguese government. The admiral said that the Brazil fleet of that year was the richest ever and lamented that so little had been squeezed out of the Portuguese: "You have at this time the Portugall upon his knees, and if wee had authoritye to make further demands, wee might aske what we would (almost) and he durst not but performe it, or his country would be all in rebellion."[59] This letter was Montagu's alone and did not bear Blake's signature. The joint report that the admirals made to Cromwell (19/29 June 1656), and which did carry Blake's name, was a milder statement, which noted that peace had been concluded and that "our work hath proved to be only the endeavouring to get the money on board, and to dispatch it away for England."[60]

Montagu sent the entire record of the correspondence with Meadowes to London, just to make sure that London understood that the envoy had followed a conciliatory line and therefore was to "blame" for the "loss" of the Brazil fleet. The frigates *Sapphire* and *Phoenix*—with a copy of the ratified treaty, the last portion of the money, and with Maynard in charge—left the Cascais area on 19/29 June 1656. Ten days previously Cromwell had issued orders recalling a part of Blake's fleet for operations against the privateers of Dunkirk and Ostend, who were creating havoc with English shipping. The rest of the fleet would have to resume its station in the western Mediterranean and off Cadiz.[61]

Throughout all of this time the 107 ships of the Brazil fleet waited impatiently at Angra, consuming the foodstuffs of the island of Terceira and driving up prices.[62] One of the ships, the smaller *Nossa Senhora do Rosário,* slipped her cable and had to put to sea; she was then attacked by pirates and surrendered, after a stiff fight during which twenty-nine of her crew were killed. About 14 June 1656 a caravel that had left Setúbal on 3 June arrived at the island of São Jorge with the news that there were thirty-five English ships off Lisbon. Brito Freire, who was apprehensive about the security of the fleet in the poor anchorages afforded by the islands, received no instructions from Lisbon and no official confirmation of the presence of the English ships.[63]

Finally, after waiting sixteen days, the fleet put to sea on Saturday, 1 July 1656. According to the commander's *regimento,* if the fleet returned before the end of March, it was to approach Portugal at the latitude of Lisbon and come into the Tagus immediately; if the fleet returned between April and 15 September, it was to come in at north Portugal, detach the merchantmen for Oporto, and sail south to Lisbon; if it returned later than 15 September then the fleet was to sail via Madeira (not the Azores) and sail straight to Cape Espichel.[64] The changing patterns of prevailing winds at different seasons made these various arrangements desirable. From Terceira in the Azores, Brito Freire sailed due north until he reached the latitude of forty-two degrees North and then due east for Viana do Castelo in the extreme north of Portugal (in conformity with his *regimento*). On the way he met a dispatch boat with orders from the king telling him to bring the fleet home to Portugal, because peace had been made between England and Portugal—and to disregard previous orders, which had never reached him, to remain in the Azores.[65]

Somewhere off the coast of Galicia, the sugar ships ran into a squadron of English men-of-war. Commonwealth naval officers representing four ships came aboard the general's galleon, the *São Pedro,* presented their compliments and offered their services as escorts to the fleet. Since the approach of the sugar ships always drew swarms of privateers from Dunkirk, Ostend, and Santander—as well as Dutch freebooters and North African pirates—the protection of the State's ships was most welcome. The merchantmen destined for the ports of Viana do Castelo, Oporto, and Aveiro detached themselves from the main fleet, which sailed on for the Tagus and reached Lisbon on 28 July 1656. Brito Freire's entire journey, Lisbon–Brazil–Lisbon, had taken 468 days, of which 397 had been spent at sea.[66]

On the journey from the Azores to Portugal not a single ship from the Brazil fleet was lost. In this fashion, with Blake's ships escorting Brito Freire's merchantmen, the traditional Anglo-Portuguese friendship reasserted itself, as, indeed, it so often has done over the centuries, even in unpromising situations.

Meadowes and Maynard returned to London in mid-July 1656. The Council of State, meeting on 15/25 July, thanked them, acknowledged the receipt of the £50,000, conferred a reward on Meadowes in consideration of the injury he had suffered in the attempt on his life, and arranged to pay Maynard £40 for expenses incurred by him in the careening of the state's ships at Lisbon.[67] Merchants and government officials praised Meadowes for his successful achievement of the peace. "With great ability and amid universal applause," reported the Venetian resident Giavarina to his doge (14 July 1656), Meadowes "has completed his negotiations to the entire satisfaction of the government and with considerable advantage to the country."[68] Giavarina's accurate account of the Meadowes mission and of the factors at stake concluded that England had been successful, not only because of the skill of the envoy but also because of the Lord's Protector's tenacity and determination.

On 24 July/3 August the officers of the Mint recorded the receipt, from Maynard, of 133, 642 pieces-of-eight of Seville and Mexico silver, 103,070 Portuguese cruzados, and some miscellaneous gold pieces. The exchange value of these coins on the London money market was £47,116, but £48,058 was realized on their exchange—about £1,000 above the market price—because Edward Blackwell, a goldsmith with foreign connections, purchased £20,000 of the Mexican coins (which were poorly regarded in London) above the going rate and exported them.[69]

Meanwhile, the Lord Protector received John IV's letter (24 June 1656), which, although it acknowledged the ratification of the treaty, requested that changes be made in articles 6 and 14, for they contained things that "went above our kingly authoritie,"and therefore "it was not lawefull for us to ratifie." The king told Cromwell that Meadowes had agreed to negotiate the differences over the religious articles, but that—after the arrival of Maynard with the ultimatum—Philip Meadowes insisted on the ratification of the treaty without additions or alterations. The king had complied, but only out of a desire to please the Protector:

> Wee being lovers of a good peace, that wee might gratifie your Most serene Highnesse in this thing als[o] which the saide Philip thought commodius to the business, and necessarie for himselfe, wee at lengthe subscrib'd to the treaty, with our undoubted hope that it would soo come to passe, that the businesse neverthelesse, as it was more commodiously compos'd, would be concluded; therefore, as at other time, soo now againe, and with renewed desires, sincerely, and as be[fits?] a good friend and confederate, confidently entreate your Most serene Highnesse, that you would approve and ratifie those short and easie clauses concerning religion, which noe way can be prejudiciall to the English Commonwealth.[70]

The awkward phrases of this rough translation did not conceal the king's belief that the ratification of the treaty could not commit him to articles 6 and 14 as they stood. The only treaty he was willing to uphold was that version ("as it was more commodiously compos'd") suggested during the negotiations with Meadowes. To make the ratified treaty conform with the proposed Lisbon version, Cromwell was asked to accept the "short and easie clauses concerning religion."

The "short and easie clauses" were set forth in a paper that accompanied the king's letter. In article 6, the king wanted the removal of the phrase requiring the compulsory return of seamen, claiming to be Catholics, to their ships. In article 14, the proposed changes were more complex. To the clause guaranteeing freedom of worship to the merchants "together with their families" should be added the phrase "of the same Nation and Religion." The king suggested this change "because those who have once profess'd the Catholicke religion, will ever be lyable to the iudgment of the Inquisitors, that they may not have power of revolting from theme."[71] That is, freedom of worship applied only to English Protestants who had been reared as Protestants; it could not apply to the Portuguese wives of English merchants or to Englishmen who were Catholics or had once been Catholics, all of whom remained perpetually under the jurisdiction of the Inquisition, or so the Inquisitors claimed.

The second change demanded by the king of Portugal was of less importance: the treaty said that Englishmen should practice their religion "as shall seeme good to them," and the king wanted these words replaced by the phrase "according to their owne manner and rite"—"Which is in effect the same, except that the former seems to sound more harshly and unwontedly."[72] Apparently Portuguese ecclesiastics had objected to the word *good* appearing in a sentence relating to the ceremonies of heretics.

The king's third and final change was, of course, the insertion at the end of the article of a disclaimer concerning "scandal": "But let them demeane themselves modestly and without scandale." A considerable explanation was appended to this request. By means of the scandal clause, John IV said, "the authoritie of the Church will be salv'd, and my subjects will be satisfied, whose minds in causes of religion are easilie stirr'd up." He pledged his kingly honor that the interpretation of the scandal clause would not be stretched, nor would the clause be used as an excuse whereby to deny the validity of the rest of the article: "The word Scandale shall not be extended either to pervert or weaken the sense of the Article, wee oblige our faith, and will take care for the future, that the same exercise of religion may be continu'd to the English which they now enjoy, more than which, in any reason, can neither be requir'd nor granted."[73]

At the same time the king instructed the Portuguese resident in London, Francisco Ferreira Rebelo, to press the English on the issue of mitigating the religious clauses. He told the resident to remind them that the treaty was "the most favorable that England until now had ever made with Portugal"[74] and that the religious clauses could not be accepted unless altered, because they contained unjustified innovations involving radical departures from traditional Anglo-Portuguese treaties.

Cromwell well knew that articles 6 and 14 extended the religious privileges granted in previous treaties; in his speech to Parliament on 4/14 September 1654 he had boasted of that very fact. It is probable that Cromwell, like many of the Portuguese, felt that the religious articles were the most significant provisions in the treaty; suggestions that the key phrases should be watered down must have been distasteful to him. He would not, under any circumstances, accept the reservation about scandal. With the treaty already negotiated, signed, and ratified, he stood on firm ground; only one more step remained—the proclamation of the peace.

In his letters to the king of Portugal during July and August 1656, Cromwell barely mentioned the mitigation of the religious articles. The Protector stressed the securing of the compensation for English merchants who had suffered losses in 1650 and the punishment of those guilty of the assault on Meadowes, but his sole reference to religion came at the end of the letter in which he formally acknowledged the ratification of the peace: the English copy of the ratification had been received in Lisbon, and the Portuguese copy had been received in London—"thus the instruments of the forementioned ratification being mutually interchanged on both sides in the beginning of June last, there is now a firm and settled peace between both nations." He expressed a vague willingness to discuss, either in London or Lisbon, the king's suggested changes in the religious articles but added: "However, the league being now confirmed, and duly sealed with the seals of both nations, to alter any part of it would be the same thing as to annul the whole."[75]

These were the last words Cromwell had to say about the matter. On the one hand, the king had virtually refused to abide by the terms of the religious articles as these had been signed and ratified; on the other, the Protector declined to reopen the issue. London forgot about the question, but in Lisbon it continued to rankle.

One further step remained before the treaty could become fully effective: the peace had to be proclaimed by trumpet and herald and the text of the treaty published. The Portuguese, whose wishes on the religious question had been ignored, made unexpected difficulties about carrying out these last formalities. The treaty was not published in Portugal until the spring of 1657. The delay was caused, in part, by the death of John IV on 6 November 1656.

Between the exchange of the instruments of ratification and the formal publication of the treaty, English warships visited the Tagus several times. After Montagu and Blake had spent most of July and all of August off Cadiz and the straits, they sailed for Lisbon on 2/12 September 1656 and anchored at the "Bay of Wyers" (Oeiras) in the Tagus on 11/21 September. Montagu, who seems to have mellowed toward the Portuguese, wrote to Thurloe (16/26 September 1656) that "the Kinge of Portugal hath used us with much respect, and sent a person of qualitye with complements and sweetemeates to us yesterday, and other fresh provisions."[76] The English commanders had planned to send their large ships home for the winter and ride out the season of storms in their smaller ships, which required less maintenance. But they changed their minds and decided that if they could make free use of the port of Lisbon, then they could keep the larger ships at sea and refit them in the Tagus when necessary.[77]

In October, Montagu said good-bye to Blake and sailed for England in the *Naseby,* which put in at Portsmouth on 24 October/3 November 1656. Blake moved his flag to the 900-ton, sixty-four-gun *Swiftsure,* which sailed for Cadiz on 14/24 October. Six weeks later, an acute shortage of supplies had forced Blake to return to Lisbon. With Cadiz closed to English shipping by the war with Spain, the Bay of Oeiras, half a mile up the Tagus, had become the main base for the Commonwealth navy outside England.[78]

On 27 August/6 September 1656 the Protector signed letters patent appointing Maynard as the English consul in Lisbon. In October, Cromwell wrote his last two letters to the king of Portugal: the first letter contained the credentials of Maynard, with a request that he be afforded free access to the king at all times; the second was written on behalf of Thomas Evans, former master of the *Scipio,* who claimed losses of £7,000 in the Bahia confiscations of 1650.[79] While these letters were being composed, John IV lay dying; the correspondence, in fact, did not leave England until after the death of the king.

The merchants in the Portuguese trade made special arrangements for the payment of the new consul. A tax of .5 percent was to be levied on all goods brought into Portugal by English merchants;

the sum raised thereby had to support the consul and a chaplain. On 20/30 November 1656 the Council of State ordered the frigate *Phoenix,* bound for Lisbon, to touch at Portsmouth and take Consul Maynard and his family to Portugal. At the same time, the government arranged for the construction of three small, fast frigates, equipped with oars, to carry persons and dispatches between England and Portugal. The need for swift, reliable, and frequent communications with Lisbon and the Mediterranean was becoming recognized in London.[80]

Maynard arrived in Lisbon on (or shortly before) 19/29 January 1657, after a nine-day passage from Falmouth (not Portsmouth, as in the preceding order from the Council of State). After the death of John IV, the thirteen-year-old mentally retarded Alphonso VI became king, under the regency of his mother, Queen Luisa de Guzmán. The queen allowed some of the unpopular policies of John IV (such as the protection of Jewish and New Christian properties) to be overturned and was far more liberal with money and honors than John IV had been. Maynard reported that "the common people are much better satisfied with her government, then they were with the king."[81] In foreign affairs, under the influence of the Count of Odemira, the new regime slowly developed a remarkably pro-English policy, moving in the direction of Anglo-Portuguese military collaboration.

Before Odemira began to court a military alliance with England—an alliance that would invoke energetic, active cooperation and not be merely a paper declaration or formal show—he had to deal with the old sources of friction in Anglo-Portuguese relations: the religious articles. The new regime, timidly trying out its powers and apprehensive of challenges from those who wanted a larger share in the government, greatly feared the Inquisitors and churchmen who had given the late king so much trouble. It was vaguely felt in Lisbon that many of the men in the upper ranks of the clergy and nobility were pro-Spanish at heart. The Count of Odemira could not afford to publish the Anglo-Portuguese treaty until he felt more secure of his position.

In England, the Portuguese resident Rebelo requested the government not to publish the treaty before 1 February 1657, Portuguese style (or 22 January 1657 English style)—this delay was suggested in deference to the mourning for John IV. On Saturday, 23 January/

2 February 1657, a full panoply of trumpeters and heralds proclaimed the peace with Portugal in the streets of London.[82]

Maynard reported to Thurloe (10/20 February 1657) that he had seen the Count of Odemira and asked the Portuguese to contribute 6,000 crowns (£1,200) every year toward the cost of maintaining the packetboats (the three dispatch frigates) sailing between England and Portugal. Odemira replied that he would contribute toward the expense of the boats if Cromwell confirmed the mitigation of the religious articles. Consul Maynard said that the mitigation of the treaty was not in his (the consul's) hands, whereupon Odemira "broke out into a passion, and saide, if that were not graunted, the inquisition and the common people would ruine them." Whenever the consul approached Odemira with any request or question whatever, the matter of the mitigation of the religious articles was "sure to be mentioned."

> And 'tis cleare, they delay the publication of the peace on noe other ground (whatever is pretended) but hopes, that his highnesse will at laste grante them thire desire, fearinge the inquisition beyond measure.[83]

About one month later, the Queen-Regent decided to send a new Portuguese ambassador to England, Francisco de Melo, who would seek a closer military and naval alliance. As a consequence of this move, in itself a natural outgrowth of Odemira's policies, the peace with England was proclaimed and published in Lisbon, "with a greate deale of solumnitye,"[84] on 25 March/4 April 1657. Two years and eight months had passed since Penaguião signed the treaty on that somber day of 10/20 July 1654. Over seven years had passed since Prince Rupert had provoked war between England and Portugal; the Palatine prince, if he failed in everything else, had certainly succeeded in embroiling England in a hundred difficulties and problems, of long-lasting effect, with the kingdom of Portugal.

Since the 1654 treaty contained articles that are construed as prejudicial to Portugal, Portuguese historians have commonly regarded the treaty as a whole as prejudicial to Portugal. Yet the second proposition does not necessarily follow from the first, because there always remains the question of how well the treaty, especially in its prejudicial articles, was enforced. If a Portuguese historian claims that the 1654 treaty was prejudicial to Portugal because it granted religious freedom to heretics, then he should prove that the heretics actually came into the enjoyment of the religious freedoms promised them (which, in the complete sense, they did not, as has been shown); if he claims that the treaty was prejudicial because article 11 allowed aliens to trade freely with Brazil, then he should establish that Englishmen could and did make use of this privilege (which, in fact, they were prevented from doing until the nineteenth century); or if he feels that the secret article limiting customs duties paid by Englishmen undermined Portuguese sovereignty, he should prove that the Portuguese government adhered to this provision (which, in fact, it did not).

One Portuguese critic of the 1654 treaty, aware of this difficulty, declared flatly that "the treaty was rigorously imposed on us."[85] Declarations of this kind (and this one happens to be nonsense) are not sufficient—the question requires proof. The effect of the religious articles on the lives of Englishmen resident in Portugal has already been examined. On the evidence presented, it is clear that some clauses in article 14 were observed all the time, that other clauses were occasionally violated, and that yet other clauses were never observed at any time.

Modern Portuguese critics, unlike their seventeenth-century predecessors, have shown little interest in the religious articles but concentrated their fire on the commercial articles. Yet what was true of article 14 was also true of the most important commercial articles: some clauses in the commercial articles were observed meticulously, other clauses were sometimes broken, and yet other clauses were openly violated all of the time.

The most frequently violated clauses were precisely those that most hurt Portuguese pride or which seemed to impair Portuguese sovereignty—the very clauses, in fact, that later Portuguese critics considered the most prejudicial to Portugal, although, in the strictly practical sense, they could not have been very damaging if they were not enforced. For instance, the treaty specified that English merchants and their ships were to have unrestricted access to all parts of the Portuguese empire, without any licenses, whether general or special, with one qualification: when sailing to Brazil, English ships had to join the convoys and abide by the rules of the Brazil Company.

The historical record reveals that English ships went to the Portuguese empire in the 1660s on the same terms, with the same licenses, under the same conditions, and facing the same hazards as English ships in the 1640s. English merchants wishing to send ships to Portuguese colonies always cited article 11 as conferring on them the right to do so—but they cited the article in the body of a petition requesting permission to send a ship, named in the petition, to a specific place, for a designated cargo. If the Overseas Council (or the Treasury Council) ruled favorably on the petition, then they would cite article 11 as one of the reasons for doing so. But the very process of petitioning and the issuing of special licenses were in themselves violations of article 11 and were signs that the pre-1654 procedures were being followed without change.

On 9 February 1657 the Overseas Council considered the petition of one "Guilherme Burchez" (William Birch?), captain of the *Liberty,* to convey a cargo of horses from the Cape Verde Islands to Barbados. The councillors approved the petition because "it is expedient to extend good treatment and favor to the English nation at the present time" but added the reservation that the Englishman was not to buy slaves. Queen-Regent Luisa, still very new at her duties, on reading the councillors' recommendation wanted to know "if there is any example of a license being given to a foreign ship to go and trade in the conquest of Cape Verde."[86] The Council assured the queen that there was nothing out of the ordinary in such a license and that the use of "private licenses" was in the interests of Portugal because it meant "an improvement in what was capitulated" with England.[87] That is, the issuing of private licenses meant that Portugal continued to control the access of English ships to the colonies, in the same way as formerly, and this was "an improvement" on the principle of unrestricted trade enunciated in the treaty. The Council's *consulta* of 10 March 1657 thus acknowledged that article 11 was not being observed. On 17 March 1657 the government duly issued to the captain of the *Liberty* the license he had requested.[88]

In Guinea, Angola, and the East, English ships—whatever the treaty may have said—could only visit Portuguese colonies, without special license, at their peril. Although the treaty was most specific and detailed about English rights to trade with Brazil, the provisions of 1654 were never honored by the government of Portugal. In fact, a royal letter of 21 July 1661—sent to the governor-general of Brazil,

Francisco Barreto, and circulated in all the captaincies of Brazil—laid down the rule that no foreign ship was to trade in Brazil without license and added the proviso, in the event of misunderstanding, that this also applied to all English ships.[89]

Similarly, the secret article, limiting tax duties to 23 percent of the value of the product, was also ineffective. The 23 percent maximum represented, in 1654, the legal maximum paid by English merchants at Lisbon. Shortly before the signing of the treaty, the Portuguese announced that the Lisbon duties had been raised to 26 percent. This stratagem enabled the Portuguese to argue that the secret article ought not to be observed because it conferred on Englishmen greater privileges than those enjoyed by the native subjects of Portugal. This argument, however misleading with respect to the circumstances existing in the spring of 1654, has been echoed by the latter-day critics of the treaty. The complaints of the English merchants trading with Portugal during the 1660s and 1670s suggest not only that the secret article was never enforced but also that the old extortions and abuses (most of which were specifically prohibited by the 1654 treaty) continued as before.[90]

Consul Maynard complained frequently about Portuguese violations of the 1654 treaty. In a letter to Thurloe (17/27 February 1658) he claimed that the Portuguese had broken fourteen articles in the treaty.[91] Twelve years later, in 1670, he said that they "have noe respecte at all to the treaty of peace."[92] The English merchants supported their consul in these complaints. In a document entitled "The Particular Agrievances of the English Nation"—which was delivered to Francis Parry, English resident at Lisbon, on 4/14 September 1671—they protested the systematic violation of the 1654 treaty, alleging that Englishmen had been arrested illegally, English goods had been apprehended illegally, English ships had been impounded and detained illegally, English merchants had been charged exorbitant fees and double duties and had been compelled to sell their goods at an arbitrarily low price and to purchase other goods at an arbitrarily high price, and so forth.[93]

The Portuguese violations of the 1654 treaty could be documented at considerable length; at whatever points the treaty came into conflict with fundamental Portuguese interests, or what were considered to be such, at these points it was broken—although the very existence of the irksome clauses has given Portuguese critics reasonable grounds for complaint. Yet the nonobservance of the controversial articles is not the whole story, for the basic principles of the treaty were respected and remained in force. The violations, however frequent, of certain clauses did not involve the invalidation or repudiation of the whole instrument. The great treaty, like a massive edifice, in spite of the cracks and fissures in its walls, remained erect for almost two hundred years as the most notable structure in the landscape of Anglo-Portuguese relations.

In 1736, eighty-two years after the signing of the treaty, a copy of it was published in London under the title "The Privileges of an Englishman in the Kingdoms and Dominions of Portugal Contain'd in the Treaty of Peace Concluded by Oliver Cromwell." Interest in the 1654 treaty remained high during the eighteenth century, especially when there were difficulties with the Portuguese. The text of the 1654 agreement provided a foundation for appeals against abuses of many kinds.[94] Until the time of the Napoleonic wars, the guiding principles in Anglo-Portuguese relations sprang from the treaty, and other Anglo-Portuguese agreements—notably Methuen's celebrated port-wine compact—were stimulated and shaped by its influence. The tensions following the French Revolution and Napoleon's invasion of Portugal rendered the treaty obsolete. Yet its influence endured in a general way until the 1830s in Portugal and until about the mid–nineteenth century in Brazil, where, during the three decades after Brazil's independence (1822), Englishmen enjoyed a privileged position.

The Anglo-Portuguese treaty of 1654 had a curious and paradoxical history. It was fashioned by a transitory "interregnum" regime, negotiated under coercion, signed by a Portuguese ambassador under distressing circumstances, ratified by a Portuguese king under threats and duress, and published with reluctance—only to be broken by Portugal in a hundred ways during the years immediately following its proclamation—yet it was to prove the most influential document in the modern history of Anglo-Portuguese relations.

9

THE SPANISH WAR AND THE ALLIANCE REAFFIRMED

The Cromwellian treaty with Portugal was signed in July 1654, ratified in June 1656, and published and proclaimed in Lisbon in April 1657. During the two years that elapsed between the signing of the treaty and its ratification, the Protectorate government launched a major attack on the Spanish West Indies; and in the middle of the ten-month interval between the ratification and the publication of the treaty John IV died (6 November 1656). Both the Anglo-Spanish war and the death of the king had important effects on Anglo-Portuguese relations: the former created conditions that favored closer cooperation in political, economic, and naval affairs between Lisbon and London, and the latter brought into being a Portuguese government that was more willing than the old king had been to take advantage of the situation and enlist English aid in direct support of Portugal's war of independence. Prior to the king's death, England's attack on Spain had not resulted in any great increase in Anglo-Portuguese collaboration, but after his death the Lisbon government courted the English alliance with a new vigor and earnestness. Lisbon's initiatives brought about the Anglo-Portuguese rapprochement of 1658–1660, which in turn led, quite naturally although unexpectedly, to the Stuart-Bragança dynastic alliance of 1662.

Blake and Montagu's fleet of 1656, which launched an all-out war against Spain in European waters and compelled John IV to accept the 1654 treaty, was faced with the problem of finding suitable bases near the Straits of Gibraltar. For the first time, the state's ships could not use Cadiz or any other Spanish port, and if John IV should prove difficult, they might be barred from Portuguese harbors as well. How were the ships to hold their station at the straits without any support from accessible bases on land? The attempt to revictual, repair, and reinforce a Mediterranean fleet from bases in the British Isles would prove costly, difficult, and probably dangerous, and French, Italian, and North African ports were unavailable, unsuitable, or too distant.

Ideally, a naval base for the support of English squadrons in the western Mediterranean should have met the following conditions: it should be within three or four days' sailing distance of the straits; it should allow large ships to enter and leave without navigational hazards; it should afford a safe anchorage for numerous vessels in every kind of weather; it should have excellent facilities for cleaning and repairing ships; it should have ample supplies of rigging, cordage, sailcloth, timber, pitch, and ship's stores of all kinds and should be able to furnish such difficult items as "crooked" timbers and the great masts needed for a ship-of-the-line; it should have victuals and beverage in adequate quantities, of good quality, and at reasonable prices; and it should also have a colony of English merchants who would be able to change sterling into the local currency and who could advance large sums of credit to an English fleet when necessary.

Only two ports could meet all of these conditions most of the time: Cadiz and Lisbon. English fleets, from time to time, made use of such harbors as Málaga, Tangier, and Lagos, but only Cadiz and Lisbon could even begin to supply all of their necessities. From 1649 to 1655 the state's ships had made good use of Cadiz, but when the Spanish war closed that fine harbor to the English the ships depended more and more on Lisbon. The navy, of course, would have liked to have had a purely British base in the straits area, and when Charles II married Catherine of Bragança the Portuguese were persuaded to include Tangier as a part of her dowry. Yet the Royal Navy found Tangier quite unsatisfactory: the town, which was little more than an alien fortress-garrison embedded in hostile territory, had almost no commerce and lacked facilities of every kind, and even the construction of an immense, costly, but unfinished mole could not transform the exposed and hazardous anchorage into a safe harbor.[1]

The problem of finding a reliable Mediterranean base continued to perplex British naval strategists throughout the last half of the century and only began to be solved with the conquest of Gibraltar in 1704. Even after the development of good naval facilities at Gibraltar, British men-of-war continued to put in at Lisbon—and the use of the fine Tagus River base was one of the permanent benefits conferred on the Royal Navy by the perennially renewed Anglo-Portuguese alliance.

Blake was the first English admiral to take advantage of Lisbon's facilities. After many weeks spent in patrolling Cadiz and the straits, he put in at Oeiras on the Tagus on 11/21 September 1656, aboard the *Naseby* and accompanied by most of his ships, although he left a squadron of some eight vessels to watch Cadiz and wait for the Spanish silver fleet. Although Cromwell had already approved plans to send Montagu home to England with all the larger ships, leaving Blake to hold the Spanish station throughout the winter with twenty of the smaller frigates, the admirals now began to think that the shelter and provisions afforded by the Lisbon harbor would enable them to keep many of the larger ships at sea during the winter. Their relations with the Portuguese were quite good, and the only threat to Anglo-Portuguese cordiality on the Tagus came from the Quaker crewmen of an English vessel from Newfoundland, who refused to take their hats off to the Portuguese.[2]

Montagu returned to England in the *Naseby*, with some of the less serviceable ships, and reached Portsmouth on 24 October/3 November 1656. Blake moved his admiral's flag to the sixty-gun *Swiftsure* (an old ship that had been rebuilt in 1653) and was still at Oeiras on 10/20 October 1656, a month after his first arrival at the Tagus, by which time he reported his readiness to sail with the first wind, since Oeiras had become "a prison" to him. The *Swiftsure*, accompanied by *Speaker*, *Tredagh*, and *Providence*, sailed out of the river on 11/21 October and reached the main fleet off Cadiz three days later.[3]

In the interim—while Blake and Montagu had rested at Lisbon—Capt. Richard Stayner, at the head of the eight-ship squadron guarding the straits, intercepted a small, poorly armed, and carelessly led Spanish silver fleet, the *Flota de Tierra-Firme*. The Portuguese Armada Real, under António Teles de Meneses, was also looking for the silver fleet and had put in at Angra, in Terceira (Azores), during August 1656. After the Armada Real left Angra, a Portuguese pinnace, under João Franco, tried to catch up with the king's ships. The pinnace was a Terceira-built ship, which had come from Brazil and picked up a cargo of wheat in the Azores and was bound for Lisbon. The master of the swift-sailing pinnace saw some lights at night and made haste to catch up with them, believing them to come from the ships of the Armada Real. In the morning the Portuguese were astonished to see themselves in the company of seven Spanish ships, which quickly captured the Terceira pinnace.[4]

The *Tierra-Firme* squadron eventually reached the vicinity of Cadiz but made its approach at night. The Spanish ships, with their lights shining, slowed down and waited for the dawn before entering the harbor. Late that night, Stayner detected their presence and moved toward them. At nine o'clock on the morning of 19 September 1656, some twelve miles off Cadiz, Stayner (who was able to bring only three of his ships into action, although these were three of his largest,[5] while the other men-of-war were scattered on patrol) attacked the lightly gunned Spanish ships, fought for several hours, pursued the admiral's galleon (which entered Cadiz in sinking condition, with many dead and wounded), and captured a large *urca* (supply ship) armed as a man-of-war and filled with silver. Stayner also boarded the vice admiral's galleon and the rear admiral's *urca* (which was also doing duty as a fighting ship), but both these ships were set on fire by their crews and destroyed to prevent their capture. If they carried any silver, it went to the bottom of the sea. The Englishmen also chased a private Spanish merchantman, whose captain beached her, but the three smallest vessels (two private merchantmen and the Portuguese pinnace) escaped into Gibraltar and Cadiz.[6]

Captain Stayner was raised to the rank of rear admiral and accompanied Montagu to England, where he received a triumphant reception. London was soon disappointed, however, to learn that the captured treasure, which was expected to yield over £600,000, amounted to "only" £225,000, to which could be added another £20,000 in captured cochineal.[7]

Stayner's attack on the Tierra-Firme fleet was the only notable English naval success against the Spaniards during 1656. While the Spanish men-of-war kept to their home ports and avoided combat, the state's ships plied the sea lanes off the southern Spanish coast, maintaining a constant vigilance, holding their station throughout the winter of 1656–1657, and, in the process, inaugurating a new form of naval warfare—the permanent blockade of a long stretch of hostile coast—and establishing a model for the Mediterranean campaigns of the Royal Navy for the next three centuries.

Blake watered his ships at Lagos during November 1656 and wrote letters to England complaining of the shortage of supplies—of the lack of beverage wine, beer, and victuals—and lamenting the long-standing and seemingly ineradicable abuses of the Admiralty's victualers.[8] He reported that the shortages might force him to return to Lisbon, although there was probably not enough bread and wine at Lisbon, since the supplying of the Brazil Company's new fleet to Brazil (1656–1657) had "drained the country."[9] But return to Lisbon he did, from whence he wrote to Thurloe, on 8/18 December 1656, acknowledging the arrival of three supply ships from England but still complaining of the shortage of beverage wine, of which there was only a six-week supply on hand. The fleet had been forced to buy expensive table wines with which to make beverage. In addition, 400 pipes of wine had been ordered from Madeira but would not arrive at the straits for another eight weeks, and, even then, "how they must be converted into beverage for the use of the fleet, without going to Port, is a riddle to those, who are of experience, though to others perhaps it may seem easy."[10]

Blake remained at Oeiras, near Lisbon, into January 1657, and it is difficult to conceive of how the fleet would have fared if the bases at the Tagus and at Faro had not been available. Then he returned to his station at the straits, using Lagos as his immediate base, but by March 1657 he was, in his own words, "growing every day weaker and weaker," and he hoped that God would support him "till the appointed time."[11] Fortunately for the English, the "appointed time" was still five months away, and, during the interim, Blake won his greatest naval victory in an action fought on 20/30 April 1657 at Santa Cruz in Tenerife of the Canary Islands, against the Flota de Nueva España. In this hard-fought battle, in which English tactics and performance showed nautical and fighting skills of the highest order,[12] Blake and Stayner destroyed all sixteen of the Spanish ships engaged while losing none of their own (although three of the state's ships sustained considerable damage). But unfortunately for Cromwell's empty Treasury, the English took no booty—for the Spaniards had unloaded the silver cargoes and concealed them deep inland, in the mountains of Tenerife.

The Portuguese of 1657 realized the large debt they owed to the English fleet. When Blake entered the Bay of Cascais on 26 June/6 July 1657 for an eight-day stay he was given a hero's welcome. Luisa, the Queen Regent, sent him an elaborate present of twelve oxen, 100 sheep, 400 hens, forty turkeys, twenty pipes of wine, and many canisters of sweetmeats and other delicacies. Unfortunately, the admiral was too ill to enjoy the adulation of the Portuguese; as Consul Maynard reported to Thurloe (14/24 July): "The generall is very weake; I beseech God to strengthen him."[13]

In the meantime, London ordered the admiral to return to England. Blake sailed for home on 17/27 July with the *George* and ten other ships, leaving Capt. John Stokes with nineteen men-of-war to maintain the Cadiz blockade. When in sight of Plymouth, at ten o'clock in the morning of 7/17 August, he breathed his last; the tired and ailing admiral had been at sea for over five hundred days. The city of London, plunged into gloom by the news of his death, honored him with a splendid funeral and buried him in Westminster Abbey on Friday, 4/14 September 1657.[14] In the ports and along the coasts of Portugal and Spain the name Roberto Blac was remembered for many years.

News of victories over the Spaniards was always welcomed, not only in England and Portugal but also in France. Early in 1657 the three countries seemed to have common military, naval, and diplomatic goals, but each country pursued its own war against Spain in its own way, with little consultation and no direct military cooperation. But this condition of affairs soon changed. England and France signed agreements during March and May of 1657, which eventually led to a joint Anglo-French military effort; the following year, 1658, the Anglo-French army defeated the Spaniards at the Battle of the Dunes and captured Dunkirk (14/24 June 1658). The Anglo-French arrangement could well have included Portugal as a third partner—and the Portuguese rejoiced in such a prospect—but no triple alliance was formed during 1657–1658. The Portuguese approached the French enthusiastically, but the French, although outwardly friendly and receptive, in the end always evaded commitments.[15] As for the English, their constant demands on the Portuguese for compensation for the losses suffered in 1650, made it difficult for Portuguese diplomats, already resentful about the terms of the 1654 treaty, to bring about effective Anglo-Portuguese military cooperation.

Yet, as has been indicated, the death of John IV made it both possible and necessary that Lisbon try once again to negotiate productive military alliances with other powers. The disappearance of the king by itself plunged Portugal into a political crisis, because it brought to the throne Alphonse VI, a backward, crippled, irresponsible, and perhaps mentally defective thirteen-year-old child.[16]

From contemporary accounts one senses the anxiety that possessed the king's court when John IV began to feel severe pain on Wednesday, 25 October 1656—and it was the anxiety not only of courtiers, worried about their personal positions, but also of patriots, concerned about the future of their country. On Saturday, 28 October 1656, the king took to his bed; he was suffering from severe kidney pain and had passed no urine. Very quickly the court seems to have reached the conclusion that he would not recover, and efforts were made, particularly by the Count of Odemira, to place the affairs of the kingdom in good order. In truth, the king lived for only another eight days, dying on Monday morning, 6 November 1656, in a chamber crowded with councillors, attendants, priests, relics, and images and filled with the murmurs of prayers and chants and the ringing of small bells.[17] He was fifty-two years old and died twenty-four days short of completing sixteen years on the throne of Portugal.

The king's last will and testament,[18] signed three days before his death, named Queen Luisa as regent of the kingdom but otherwise was more concerned with personal rather than public matters. The new Queen-Regent had little political experience but was not without capacity, strength of character, and energy and was only forty-three years old. But the uncertain climate of the regency, which generated a struggle among political factions, led to a dangerous political confusion that was beyond the regent's control. Moreover, her authority was weakened by the fact that she had little understanding of the military and naval operations that were necessary to maintain Portuguese independence.

As soon as John IV died, he began to be missed, for he was quickly recognized as having been both the architect and the guarantor of Portuguese independence. In spite of this, he has been widely misunderstood by historians. A hoary legend, enshrined in a hundred textbooks, depicts him in December 1640 as being dragged to the throne reluctantly, giving way to his wife's entreaties. His pretense of reluctance, a show designed to mislead the Spaniards in the event of failure, has misled historians instead; in actual fact, contemporary Spaniards were less naive, for word of John of Bragança's plots had reached Madrid as early as mid-October 1640.[19] His was the leadership that persuaded his Spanish wife and that gave stimulus to the conspiracy in Lisbon, and his was the motive power behind the legal, dynastic, and political revolution that was so smoothly disguised behind the legitimist term *restoration (restauração).*

His character has also been misrepresented. The distinguished historian João Lúcio de Azevedo wrote that King John was "pusillanimous, ungrateful, vindictive, and, in the hour of vengeance, cruel."[20] Doubtlessly incidents could be selected from the life of John IV that might justify each of these adjectives, but these incidents, so selected and so interpreted, would not add up to an accurate or convincing portrait. Other incidents of equal weight showed him to have been fair-minded, good-natured, cautious, shrewd, kindly, unpretentious, and patient. Few would deny that he was honest and careful with public money, played no favorites, fell under no evil influences, listened to everyone but made up his own mind (albeit slowly), and yet allowed able men, such as Odemira, a good deal of freedom in the conduct of affairs. And if, as ruler and administrator, he was neither bold nor brilliant, yet he was conscientious, meticulous, and able.

In the conduct of relations with England, one can see John IV's administrative qualities: a strength and stubbornness that were all the more enduring and potent for being somewhat concealed; an unwillingness to precipitate crises and a desire to live and let live, to forgive and forget; an ability, by the exercise of sheer persistence, to whittle away and minimize the demands made upon him; a prudence that would not give way to the extremists and hotheads in his own court or knuckle under to foreigners who threatened the national interest; and, on the whole, a sense of responsibility toward Portuguese interests, combined with a fundamental goodwill in his approach to the English and other aliens.

He had begun his reign by negotiating with Charles I the Anglo-Portuguese treaty of 1642 but did not allow himself to be drawn into the pro-royalist schemes of his London agent, António de Sousa de Macedo. The Rupert affair of 1650, it is true, had turned out badly for the Portuguese—but that was surely not King John's fault. Rupert had arrived in Lisbon rather like a foundling left on a doorstep: the householders, who were quite without moral responsibility toward the babe, found it unthinkable to reject him but awkward to take him in and impossible to keep him permanently. Yet even in the Anglo-Portuguese war that ensued John IV managed to save the main part of the Brazil fleet and eventually obtained peace without really satisfying English demands. His long resistance against paying the high English claims shows elements of political brilliance. Only in 1656 did he pay, and then only £50,000, and under extreme duress. The same pressures forced him to ratify the treaty of 1654, but he did so with the clear warning that he did not feel himself bound by all its articles—and, at the time of his death, he still had not published the treaty.

John IV's subjects should have had few complaints about his conduct of relations with England. His successors were less prudent—for it is hard to imagine John IV accepting the terms of the Bragança-Stuart marriage treaty of 1662, by which Portugal ceded Tangier and Bombay and agreed to pay 2 million cruzados (about £378,000) for Catherine's dowry, and harder still to imagine his undertaking, at the same time, to pay the Dutch 4 million cruzados (about £756,000) merely to bribe them to keep the peace. For during 1661–1662 John IV's successors gave up Tangier and Bombay and agreed to pay the Dutch and English an amount equivalent to well over 1 million pounds sterling!

It is evident that, from 1656 to 1662, there were considerable changes in the attitudes, goals, and methods that governed the conduct of Portuguese foreign policy. The Queen-Regent's government discarded the cautious approach that the late king had taken in his foreign policy, and, in addition, discarded some of his most cherished domestic policies. After his death, the Inquisition grew more powerful, the seizure of New Christian properties was once again permitted, and the privileges and rights of the Brazil Company (which the old king had defended, almost every month of his reign, with skill and resolution) were curbed, diminished, and even nullified. In fact, the Brazil Company, the old king's favorite project, was emasculated.

The Queen-Regent's government contained, at the very top, two bitter rivals: the Count of Odemira, nearly sixty years of age, for fourteen years president of the Overseas Council, who had wide influence on foreign policy and on colonial and maritime affairs; and António Luís de Meneses, Count of Cantanhede, Comptroller of the Treasury, eager for military glory and with a special interest in the land war against Spain. Since Queen Luisa showed no special favors to either of these powerful men, their conflicting political ambitions might well have torn the administration apart; that this did not occur was probably because Odemira and Cantanhede worked in very different administrative areas, because both were devoted to the national interest, and because the queen gathered all her chief advisers together every week in the *junta nocturna*—which was a kind of privy council that met regularly at night. Most of the members of the *junta nocturna* probably sided neither with Odemira nor Cantanhede but helped to impose a single line of policy on both.

The two holdover secretaries, Pedro Vieira da Silva and Gaspar Severim de Faria, although aging, were still important in the new regime; neither of them sided consistently with the Odemira or Cantanhede factions, but they worked closely with the queen, trying to influence her decisions and looking to her for favors. The late king's Jesuit confessor, André Fernandes, continued to exercise some influence and was a supporter of Odemira. Within the government and also outside it, a number of individuals struggled for positions of power and authority. They included the Marquis of Niza (former ambassador to Paris), Pedro Fernandes Monteiro (former secretary of state), the Count of Penaguião (former ambassador to London and a partisan of Cantanhede), the Count of Soure (a supporter of Odemira), and a number of soldiers who wanted military commands, particularly Joane Mendes de Vasconcelos, the Count of São Lourenço, the Count of Vila Flor, and the Count of Ericeira.[21]

The soldiers, when they eventually did receive their commands, had to withdraw from the court and serve on the frontier, where they usually lost their reputations (the outstanding exception being Cantanhede himself, who distinguished himself in the wars and was rewarded with the title of Marquis of Marialva). As time passed, the struggle in the court among Odemira, Cantanhede, and other factions turned into a struggle between the old officials of John IV's government and the new men. With Cantanhede absent from Lisbon much of the time and the death of Odemira on 15 March 1661, the new men came to the fore and the Queen-Regent herself was threatened. The most vigorous of the new politicians was Luís Vasconcelos e Sousa, who became Count of Castelo Melhor on the death of his father in 1658 and acquired some kind of a hold over the mind of the unmanageable Alphonse VI. In June 1662 the Count of Castelo

Melhor engineered a coup d'état and forced Queen Luisa to dissolve the regency and retire to a convent.

From the death of John IV in 1656 until his own death in 1661, Odemira was probably the dominant influence on Portuguese foreign policy. These years saw the Portuguese involved in half a dozen major diplomatic initiatives. In France, the Portuguese diplomats tried to get the French to support Portugal with troops and ships, tried to negotiate a marriage between Louis XIV and Princess Catherine of Bragança, and tried, above all, to prevent peace between France and Spain. In Sweden, the Portuguese sought naval support and a meaningful Luso-Swedish alliance. In Rome, they tried, with their usual lack of success, to win papal recognition of Portuguese independence and end the breach with the Vatican. In the United Provinces, they attempted to avoid war with the Dutch—and when war became unavoidable, they tried to end it as quickly as possible. And last, in London, Portuguese ambassadors sought to give real meaning to the Anglo-Portuguese alliance by obtaining British troops to fight in Portugal against Spain.

Anglo-Portuguese diplomacy of the period 1657–1662 was part of a larger pattern of Portuguese diplomatic initiative. The almost desperate character of the various Portuguese diplomatic offensives was the result of the continuous military threat on the Spanish border during this period and also the result of Lisbon's having sustained serious diplomatic reversals. There were three military crises on the Luso-Spanish border: (1) the Spanish invasion of April 1657, which led to the fall of Olivença on 22 May and to continued military pressure until the end of the summer; (2) the Spanish siege of Elvas, which lasted from October 1658 until January 1659; and (3) the large-scale Spanish invasion that began in May 1662 and was not beaten back until June 1663. Each of these Spanish thrusts was met and blunted, but only at great cost in men, money, and anxiety. But even more costly and worrisome were two diplomatic reversals: (1) there was a breakdown in Luso-Dutch negotiations, which led the United Provinces, in November 1657, to issue a wholly unacceptable ultimatum, whose rejection by Lisbon brought on a naval war that lasted until 1661;[22] and (2) France and Spain, despite all Portuguese efforts, signed the Peace of the Pyrenees on 7 November 1659—a move that seemed to threaten the imminent end of Portuguese independence.

The Lisbon government, in securing peace with the Dutch, committed itself to a heavy indemnity that was not fully paid until about 1710, some fifty years later. The settlement with the Dutch freed the Portuguese for the final bitter struggle with the Castilians, which took place during the mid-1660s. In legal theory, at least, no help could be expected from the French—for by article 60 of the Pyrenees treaty the French solemnly promised that after a period of ninety days during which they would try to bring about a settlement of the Luso-Spanish conflict, if their efforts ended in failure, they (the French) would give no assistance whatever to Portugal, whether public or private, open or secret, direct or indirect, or by land or sea. The Spaniards made certain that the language and intent of article 60 were absolutely clear and unequivocally binding.[23]

It is true that the French continued to press the Spanish to reach an accommodation with Portugal and that they interpreted the Pyrenees treaty almost as they pleased, but the treaty itself represented a resounding defeat for Portuguese diplomacy. Unfortunately for the Portuguese, the Franco-Spanish agreement was not their only setback: not only in Paris, but also in The Hague, in Rome, and in Stockholm their diplomatic ventures miscarried or proved disappointing. Only in London were the Portuguese, in the end, wholly successful.

Anglo-Portuguese negotiations extended from 1657 to 1661 and were beset by two major difficulties. First, the Portuguese had to adjust to great and bewildering political changes in England, to the numerous short-lived regimes that came after the death of Cromwell on 3/13 September 1658, and then to the restored monarchy of Charles II, who returned to England on 25 May/4 June 1660. With all the changes in England it was difficult for the Portuguese to maintain continuity in their diplomatic contacts. Second, the Portuguese were beset by new English demands for compensation for the losses suffered in 1650, and the issues of compensation (to whom? in what amounts?) continued to bedevil Anglo-Portuguese negotiations well into the mid-1660s.

By the terms of article 25 of the peace treaty of 1654, a committee of claims consisting of two Englishmen (John Crowther and Dr. Walter Walker) and two Portuguese (Francisco Ferreira Rebelo and Dr. Jerónimo da Silva de Azevedo) were to meet on 20/30 July 1654 and begin processing all petitions for compensation. The committee, whose decision was to be final, had to determine the validity of claims and the amounts to be paid and to whom. The Portuguese were to set aside one-half of all customs duties paid by Englishmen in Portugal[24] and hold the money in a special fund to be used to satisfy the judges' awards. But if the judges could not agree on the amounts to be paid and were still deadlocked on 1/11 September 1654, then the Lord Protector, from among the members of the Council of State, would appoint a supposedly impartial umpire, who would render a final judgement on all disputes.

The judges met as scheduled and the Portuguese accepted a number of English claims as valid, but they could not agree with their English colleagues on twenty-three specific cases and would not accept the English merchants' demands that interest, dating from the day of the sequestrations, should be paid in addition to compensation. That is, the English felt that if a merchant was awarded £1,000 in compensation, he should also receive the interest on that amount for all the time elapsed since the sequestrations. The Portuguese judges, besides objecting to paying interest, also objected to the very high rates of interest (6 percent and up) demanded.[25]

After the Portuguese and English judges had reached a deadlock on all outstanding issues, Cromwell appointed his umpire, Col. Philip Jones, who was supposed to be "assisted" by a Portuguese procurator or assessor (Ferreira Rebelo).[26] Jones wanted to begin his work in April 1655 but he could not do so and had to wait for the ratification of the treaty. Finally, in July 1656, he told the Portuguese resident that he would proceed to judgment on all disputed claims. Jones wanted the resident, Ferreira Rebelo, to furnish him with the Portuguese documents concerning the disputed cases, and the resident said he needed time to gather them. Jones gave him seven weeks. Then Ferreira Rebelo demanded to see the English merchants' evidence before submitting the Portuguese documents. Jones at first resisted but finally gave way and sent the English papers to the resident but gave him "only 14 days to see, consider, and answer them." Jones also wanted all Portuguese papers translated into English immediately.

Ferreira Rebelo, whose main intention was, if not to thwart, at least to delay action on the disputed cases, replied that he needed time to gather the Portuguese papers, translate them, and write answers to the English papers. "I sent him word," said the resident, "upon the

10/20 of October last [1656], that I was not able to do it in less than six months."[27] Jones refused to accept this delay and, during the last three months of 1656, demanded "six or seven times" that the papers be turned over to him immediately—but the resident refused all communication until his own self-chosen six-month grace period had elapsed (which would only occur on 10/20 April 1657). Finally, Jones informed the resident, on 24 January/3 February 1657, that judgment would be rendered forthwith, even in the absence of Portuguese participation. The resident then appealed to Cromwell and warned him that if Jones handed down decisions without listening to the Portuguese, "in Portugal the sentences will not be judged lawful nor binding."[28]

Although Ferreira Rebelo maintained a firm posture toward the London authorities, his reports to Lisbon showed traces of panic. He told the Queen-Regent that Colonel Jones had decided that the Portuguese should pay between 4 percent and 6 percent interest on all claims, which would cost the Portuguese at least 40,000 cruzados (£8,000). He said that the English merchants claimed 100,000 cruzados (£20,000) for the lost cargoes of the *John Adventure,* a ship that had been taken prize by Prince Rupert *before* his arrival in Lisbon—but the Portuguese judges would accept no responsibility for this ship. The Portuguese also refused to pay anything for the *Sara,* which had been lost with all hands on the return voyage to Portugal after the sequestrations and whose cargo may have been worth up to 100,000 cruzados. The merchants, reported the resident, had strong influence on the London government: if their claims were not paid, they would secure letters of marque and reprisal and wreak havoc on Portuguese shipping. This situation could lead to a new war between England and Portugal. The Portuguese were faced with an old and recurrent dilemma: either risk war or pay ruinously large sums of money for the peace.

Ferreira Rebelo suggested two positive steps that Lisbon might take. First, Colonel Jones should be heavily bribed: "It would be wise to win this third judge to our cause with an offer of such weight that it will incline him wholly to our side; for even though it might be expensive, it will still come out cheaper than the cost of the sentence he may give against us."[29] Second, a determined and strong-minded ambassador should be sent to London to resist English pressures.

Lisbon had already chosen an ambassador, Francisco de Melo (later Count of Ponte and Marquis of Sande), not simply to deal with the disputes over compensation payments but primarily to bring about a close Anglo-Portuguese military alliance. In his public instructions from the Queen-Regent, dated 10 July 1657, Melo was told to reject the unilateral decisions of Cromwell's umpire, because "if his sentences are carried out, there will be no end of payments for many, many years."[30] He was also to press for the mitigation of the religious articles. In his secret instructions (of the same date), Melo was asked to try to bribe, not Colonel Jones, but the incorruptible secretary of state, John Thurloe.

The resident in London, in the spring of 1657, was not fully aware that Lisbon had begun to place less emphasis on resistance to paying compensations. Melo, to be sure, was to reject exorbitant and unreasonable demands, but otherwise his protests may have been perfunctory and only *pro forma*. For Lisbon—in order to win English military assistance and, it was hoped, to become a partner in the English-French-Swedish alliance that seemed to be taking shape—was willing to pay and to pay heavily. The Queen-Regent ordered the Portuguese ports to begin setting aside the one-half portion of customs duties paid by Englishmen on English commodities, which were to be used to finance compensations. On the island of Madeira, for example, the following sums were placed in a special fund: in 1657, 325$283 *réis;* in 1658, 629$610; in 1659, 523$458; in 1660, 557$275; and in 1661, 514$727. The collections for these five years—amounting to only 2:550$353 réis (£1,200)—were given directly to John Carter, English consul at Madeira.[31]

The Madeira Treasury books seem to show that the collection of these funds was painfully slow and probably irregular, but some money was collected and some restitutions were made. In London, the Portuguese seem to have lost the contest with Colonel Jones—but that did not mean that they actually paid the disputed claims. In 1669, nineteen years after the original sequestrations, Sir Robert Southwell, then ambassador extraordinary to the king of Portugal, was still negotiating unpaid compensations and negotiating with none other than the same Ferreira Rebelo.[32] By that time, the Portuguese had muddled the matter by claiming that money paid toward Queen Catherine's dowry also satisfied the merchants' demands or by claiming the reverse, that money paid to merchants should be regarded as part of the dowry.

In the Anglo-Portuguese negotiations in 1657–1661, the central role was played by Francisco de Melo,[33] who was the architect of the reconstructed Anglo-Portuguese alliance and the author of the dynastic union of 1661–1662. Melo arrived in England on 24 June/4 July 1657, spent some time in Greenwich, and then lived quietly in a Portuguese house in London, although he was not formally admitted to the city until Monday, 31 August/10 September. On that day he returned to Greenwich, where he was met at 3:00 P.M. by Master of Ceremonies Sir Oliver Fleming and by a party of twenty gentlemen representing the Lord Protector (who was ill and could not receive the ambassador). Melo was taken to a barge on the Thames, and the party proceeded upriver to the Tower of London, where two members of the Council of State and the ambassadors of France and the United Provinces greeted him. The dignitaries entered the waiting state coaches, which took them, through crowds of novelty seekers, to a banqueting hall where they "found the table set, but the food not yet made."[34] This was the first of seven banquets at which Melo was to be entertained at the expense of the state.

Melo first met Cromwell at one of these banquets, on Wednesday, 2/12 September 1657. It was a splendid affair, with the ambassador's entourage trying to outdo the Protectoral court in magnificence of dress. After elaborate salutations, the ambassador delivered a speech wherein he told the Protector that the very first act of the new king, His Majesty Alphonse VI, had been to send an embassy to England to support "a friendship that brings with it so many advantages to the one and to the other nation." Melo then delivered a letter signed by Alphonse. The Lord Protector replied "very agreeably" *("com muito agrado")* and assured the ambassador that he would do "all that lay within his power" to accommodate the Portuguese.[35]

Two days later (on 4/14 September) Blake was buried at Westminster, and at 7:30 in the evening Melo went to see Thurloe to give him a jewel worth 2,500 cruzados and to offer him a personal subsidy or a lump sum of money, if he would work to include Portugal in a league with France and England. Secretary Thurloe scorned the money and rejected the jewel, but the ambassador pressed him for two hours, until Thurloe finally said that he would accept the jewel if the Protector approved. "Such are the virtuous qualities of this Secretary, with whom neither diamonds have power, nor gold value."[36] After this comic performance, Melo retired, "not very pleased."

The first business interview between Melo and Cromwell took place on Wednesday, 9/19 September, one week after they had met at the banquet. Melo asked Cromwell to keep, at all times, a strong force of the state's ships in the straits off Portugal. Portugal would provide the English ships with docks, warehouses, hospitals, and "everything else they may need, beyond the limits declared in the peace treaty." If the Anglo-Portuguese alliance was to prosper, "it is necessary that England shall not take her fleet away ever."![37] As for the peace treaty of 1654, Melo still wanted the religious articles to be amended, but the Portuguese were quite willing to confirm and adhere to the rest of the treaty. Further than that, and this was the essential point, Melo wanted an additional compact, one providing for joint military assistance, with perhaps 2,000 British troops to serve in Portugal. In return for English help, Portugal would invade Extremadura and threaten Andalusia. Neither country should make a separate peace with Spain.

What a change had come over the Portuguese approaches to England, in both style and substance, since the days of the diplomacy of João de Guimarães and the Count of Penaguião! The Protectoral government found the change gratifying and was quite receptive to Portuguese suggestions but wondered about the *quid pro quo*—how much would Portugal pay for an English military alliance? The government, when it eventually replied to the ambassador, took exception to various details in the Portuguese proposals and raised the question of a subsidy in unequivocal terms but, on the whole, answered positively and met the Portuguese halfway. The English emphasized the value of their fleet to Portugal:

> His Highness fleet having beene instructed to performe all goode offices to the Kingdome of Portugall upon all occasions, whereof his Highness hopes, that as his Majestie of Portugall hath received the good effects, soo he will not be unmindfull thereof, and that as both States are bound up in interest, in the management of this Warre, soo both will reciprocally unite their endeavors to carry it on, for the good of both, by all the meanes becomeing Confederates that beare soo sincere a friendship each to other.[38]

The Lord Protector was "well content" not only to keep the treaty of 1654 but also "to establish with his Majestie of Portugall, a further League for uniteing of their Armes against the house of Austria in generall, and the Dominions of the King of Spayne in particular."

London reminded the Portuguese that England kept "a considerable fleet" in the West Indies, a force in Flanders, "and Mayntayns ships in the Mediterranean," all of which "contracts a vast Charge to his Highness," but added: "His Highness will nevertheless oblige himselfe to keepe a fleet on the Coasts of Spayne, and Portugall, in such proportion and for such tyme as shall be hereafter agreed . . . in case his said Majestie will undertake to pay to his Highness the sum of———[left blank] towards the support of that Charge."[39] The English were willing to instruct their naval commanders to protect the ports of Portugal, willing to pledge themselves not to make a separate peace with Spain, and willing to consider sending land forces to Portugal if the Portuguese would specify the exact terms. London suggested a joint agreement with a fixed time limit with an option allowing for renewal if both sides desired it.

The English, as always, wanted money from the Portuguese. The demand had been anticipated; in her secret instructions to Melo, Queen Luisa authorized the ambassador to offer Cromwell a small annual subsidy, up to 80,000 cruzados (£15,000), toward the expenses of the English fleet.[40] But the ambassador had no sooner left for England than the queen wrote to him (24 July 1657), anxiously, that he was not to offer the English any money whatever without her prior permission.[41] Melo was told to try to obtain the alliance without making any payments for it.

Queen Luisa did not wish to make any avoidable payments to the English, since she was all too conscious of the fact that the Portuguese had already offered the French large sums of money. In Paris, the Portuguese were pressing for a Franco-Portuguese alliance with roughly the same kind of terms they asked of the English: the French were not to make a separate peace with Spain, Portugal would subsidize France, and Paris would send troops to fight in Portugal. During the Franco-Portuguese negotiations, which extended from 1655 to 1658, the Portuguese had at one time been willing to pay the French 2 million cruzados and give them Tangier if they would accept a marriage between Princess Catherine and Louis XIV and agree to make no separate peace with Spain.[42]

The French, as usual, disappointed the Portuguese; in her secret instructions to Melo the Queen-Regent complained that the French had deceived Portugal for a full seventeen years, during which time Lisbon had received "no benefits whatever" from France, only promises: "France wants to keep Portugal forever dependent on her favor." It was better, thought the queen, to deal with the Lord Protector than with the cunning Cardinal Jules Mazarin; and if, as she told Melo, the English would enter a military alliance with Portugal, then he was to write immediately to Paris to have all negotiations with the French broken off. For, as she put it, "I cannot hand out in both places [London and Paris], nor pay France for benefits I receive from England."[43]

By the middle of 1658 the Portuguese overtures to the French had failed completely. As the French and Spanish moved toward what was to become a dramatic dynastic union, the way was open for a treaty between the Queen-Regent and Cromwell. By the time Melo's negotiations with the Lord Protector had begun to reach maturity, Cromwell fell ill and died, expiring on his famed "lucky" day of 3/13 September 1658. Nowhere abroad was the news of the Lord Protector's death received with less joy than in Lisbon. Ambassador Melo had to begin his labors anew, approaching first the short-lived government of Richard Cromwell, then the succession of unstable governments that followed.

While the Portuguese were thwarted at Paris and frustrated by long delays in London, they were busy, during the years 1657–1661, trying to reach a settlement with the Dutch. In a letter to Melo (30 September 1657), the queen informed him how the Dutch had arrived in Portuguese waters with a force of some thirty fighting ships, under Admirals Ruyter and Opdam, and how they had sent ashore two commissioners, whom she received on 29 September. The commissioners confronted the queen with an ultimatum, so exorbitant in its terms that it amounted to a declaration of war. They wanted the return of formerly Dutch-occupied areas in Brazil and Angola and the island of São Tomé, coupled with a yearly indemnity of 600,000 florins, plus an annual tribute of 13,000 chests of sugar to be conveyed to Holland at Portuguese expense.[44] The queen was given fourteen days to accept the terms or else face the blockade of her ports and the seizure of the Brazil fleet, which was expected back in Portugal by 15 November 1657.

The Portuguese had no alternative but to resist, and, on this occasion at least, luck and the weather were on their side. The great sugar fleet, with about eighty-five ships, escaped with the loss of twenty-one ships. Because of exceptionally bad weather, the Dutch missed the main unit of the scattered fleet, and some sixty ships arrived in Portugal safely. In retaliation, the Portuguese seized the cargoes of seventeen Dutch vessels in Portuguese ports and issued letters of marque and reprisal against Dutch shipping but found few who were willing to take up the letters. The Netherlanders gained little from their aggression: they had lost property in Portugal and weakened their commercial position in Lisbon, their fighting ships had suffered considerable weather damage, and their prizes were badly battered by the Atlantic gales that blew for six weeks.[45]

Nonetheless, Portugal was anxious for peace. Plans for the 1658 Brazil fleet were abandoned, and Lisbon had to be content with sending out some half-dozen large English ships (which the Dutch would not attack) to Brazil instead. The Queen-Regent earnestly requested Cromwell to intervene with the Dutch, and the English diplomat George Downing was entrusted with the task of negotiating a truce between the United Provinces and Portugal. The Portuguese agent in Amsterdam, Jerónimo Nunes da Costa, reported favorably on Downing's activities (during January and February 1658), which seemed to have had the effect of relaxing Dutch pressures on Portugal, and the Queen-Regent sent Downing a formal letter of thanks.[46]

Unfortunately for Lisbon, the tense situation in the Baltic, involving England and Sweden against the United Provinces and Denmark, made England less eager for a Luso-Dutch peace. As Thurloe explained (26 March/5 April 1658) to Downing, when instructing him to reverse himself and work against the peace, it was better for Dutch ships to be diverted toward Portuguese waters than to have them in the Danish Straits.[47] But Downing's work could not be entirely undone: although the Dutch would not accept a truce with Portugal without signing a peace treaty, they had agreed to receive an ambassador from Lisbon. Early in 1659 the Queen-Regent chose a trusted and experienced *fidalgo,* Dom Fernando Teles de Faro, described by her as of "capacity, zeal, and prudence,"[48] to be ambassador extraordinary to the United Provinces. An English ship conveyed Teles de Faro to the Netherlands, but, shortly after his arrival, he defected to the Spaniards with all the embassy papers![49] This astonishing betrayal proclaimed to all of Europe that some Portuguese, especially the members of the nobility, had little confidence in the future of a country governed by a Spanish-born queen and even less confidence in the prospects of a dynastic line whose leading representative was a weak-minded cripple. A bitterly embarrassed Lisbon government avenged itself by tearing down Teles de Faro's house, sowing the ground with salt, and solemnly decapitating and burning his effigy on 7 August 1659.[50]

The ambassador's defection had repercussions in London, where Francisco de Melo managed to detain the Jesuit priest António Vaz, Teles de Faro's confessor, and hold him prisoner at the Portuguese embassy. Queen Luisa wrote to Parliament and requested that an English ship be used to convey the prisoner securely from England to Lisbon.[51] In the meantime António Vaz, by the hand of a certain Marcos Dias Brandão,[52] conveyed a petition to the newly reconstituted House of Lords, in which he declared that he had been under detention for nine months, that he lived in daily fear of being murdered, and that the Portuguese ambassador wanted to send him to Portugal to be tried by the Inquisition. Their Lordships took up the petition on 4/14 May 1660 and decided that Ambassador Melo should be asked for an explanation. Melo replied that previous governments had allowed him to keep Vaz under detention, that Vaz was a priest (a fact not revealed in Vaz's petition) accused of high treason, and that the Inquisition had nothing to do with the matter. The lords, after referring the question to their committee on privileges, ruled that the issue should be left to Charles II, who would soon be restored to his throne, but that, in the meantime, Vaz was not to leave England.[53]

For obvious reasons, Lisbon was anxious to force Vaz to return to Portugal. The queen went to great trouble in the matter but received little cooperation. She asked the Jesuit provincial Francisco Manso to order Vaz to come back and "finish his studies,"[54] but Manso refused to comply. Her effort to enlist the aid of the Inquisitor Nuno da Cunha brought only his reply that Vaz should be turned over to the "English fathers who are concealed in London" and that it "was a scandal for a religious to remain prisoner in the house of an ambassador of the king of Portugal in a land of heretics."[55] The queen could only order Melo to hold Vaz as long as possible but not to endanger relations with the English because of him. In the end, English pressure forced Melo to release Vaz, and the queen was reduced to begging the Portuguese Jesuits to punish him.[56]

If the queen was helpless in the Vaz case, she was even more helpless in knowing what to do about the political changes occurring in London. Originally Lisbon acted on the assumption that the Lord Protector Oliver would become King Oliver, and Melo had been supplied with 3,000 cruzados to be spent on the embassy's festivities at Cromwell's coronation. When Cromwell died, still uncrowned, the queen authorized Melo to spend this money, to which was added a further 1,000 cruzados, for the embassy's mourning expenses and for the festivities of the acclamation of the new Lord Protector Richard Cromwell.[57] The Portuguese had become quite happy with Oliver Cromwell during his last months; as the queen wrote to Melo (2 January 1659): "It will be very important that this Republic [England] maintains itself in the same state in which the deceased Protector left it."[58]

The queen's letter to Richard Cromwell rejoicing in his assumption of the Protectorate probably arrived in England after Richard's ephemeral regime had already collapsed. A few months later Luisa sent letters to England rejoicing in the prosperity and reinstitution of Parliament and furnishing Melo with new credentials (dated Lisbon, 12 June 1659). In a letter dated 3 July 1659 the queen admitted that Lisbon was completely confused about affairs in England and that the Portuguese government had no instructions to give their ambassador except to follow his own judgment and observe the behavior of the other ambassadors in London.[59]

It is to Melo's credit that during the various changes in English governments he still managed to hold London, as regards Portuguese affairs, to a single line of policy. Negotiations for an Anglo-Portuguese agreement proceeded slowly but nonetheless continued to make progress. The ambassador's credentials of 12 June 1659 invested him with the full powers of a plenipotentiary entitled to act in Queen Luisa's name. He used his powers to obtain from London a new treaty of alliance. By the terms of this treaty the Portuguese were authorized to raise 2,500 cavalrymen, with their horses, in the British Isles (articles 2 and 3); they were allowed to recruit up to 12,000 infantry (up to 4,000 each from Scotland, England, and Ireland), but all officers from colonels downward must be British (articles 4 and 5); and they were permitted to freight up to twenty-four warships for the defense of Portugal (article 6). The Portuguese were also given leave to purchase any quantity of arms and ammunition they wanted (article 8).[60] Lisbon, of course, was required to pay for everything—men, horses, equipment, munitions, and transport—but these various provisions of the treaty represent, nonetheless, substantial concessions by the English.

Article 1 of the new agreement explicitly confirmed and ratified the Anglo-Portuguese treaty of 10/20 July 1654 "in all its clauses, periods, and articles, in accordance with the true and genuine meaning of the said articles." There was nothing in the new compact about payments to the English government or about compensations to merchants. The subject of religion was touched upon briefly in article 13, wherein all soldiers and sailors recruited by the Portuguese were to be free to practice their religion in accordance with the guarantees of article 14 of the 1654 treaty. The final clause (article 14) specified that for the treaty to be valid, ratifications between the two powers must be exchanged within sixty days.

This document was solemnly signed by the Portuguese ambassador and by representatives of the Council of State at Whitehall on 18/28 April 1660. But it had been signed too late! Five weeks and two days later, on 25 May/4 June, Charles II landed in England, bringing with him a host of ties, debts, and obligations to Philip IV's Spain—and, in the eyes of the Portuguese, the Anglo-Portuguese alliance was once more in jeopardy. The treaty of 18/28 April 1660—which when it came into the hands of the Queen-Regent she had signed immediately, "to the great satisfaction of her ministers"[61]—remained unratified, in the limbo of diplomacy. It is still the lost and forgotten treaty; rare is the history book of today that mentions it.

In relation to the events of 1657–1660, it will be seen, in conclusion, that the Anglo-Spanish war created the conditions for a significant renewal of the age-old Anglo-Portuguese alliance. The death of John IV cleared the way for a new regime in Lisbon, with new ideas and policies. Odemira, who had long favored closer ties with England, occupied an important position in the formulation of the Queen-Regent's foreign policy. Events in other countries—particularly the new threats from Spain and the United Provinces and the rapprochement between France and Spain—drove Lisbon into closer dependence on London. Portugal's able ambassador Francisco de

Melo had worked well and closely with various English governments but had been hampered by the political instability in London and by such side-events as the Baltic crisis.

In the end, when Melo had secured from London much of what he had wanted, it was too late. The Restoration, to Portugal, came at the worst possible time—and Lisbon was forced to make a considerable readjustment to the new regime. Ambassador Melo played his part with consummate skill; in a diplomatic performance of great brilliance he was to transform what had seemed to be the unwanted accident of the Restoration into a situation of the greatest advantage and profit for Portugal.

10

THE DYNASTIC ALLIANCE OF 1661–1662

At the time that the Bragança-Stuart marriage was arranged, Secretary of State Sir William Morice declared that "this marriage is not the simple marriage of the King of England with a Princess, but a marriage of the Kingdom of England with the Kingdom of Portugal."[1] This statement succinctly expressed what was, for the Portuguese, the central significance of the marriage treaty: the fact that England, in the person of her sovereign, committed herself to the principle of sustaining an autonomous Kingdom of Portugal. Since the marriage treaty committed Charles II—morally, legally, and personally—to upholding his brother-in-law on the throne of Portugal, it also committed him to maintaining Portuguese independence. With the consummation of the Bragança-Stuart alliance, the Spanish effort to reconquer Portugal began to look hopeless, for the issue of the war was no longer in doubt, even though some of the hardest fighting along the Luso-Spanish border came after 1661. Moreover, by the principles of international law, England's commitment was perpetual. In 1935 the distinguished student of Anglo-Portuguese relations Prof. Edgar Prestage wrote that Charles II's engagement to defend Portugal "had no time limit, it has been successfully invoked by the Portuguese on several occasions and is regarded as still binding."[2] On the floor of the House of Commons, on 12 October 1943, Prime Minister Winston Churchill recognized that the mutual obligations of Portugal and Great Britain to aid each other, formally contracted in 1661, still remained in effect.[3]

The dynastic alliance of 1661–1662 also marked the culmination of over two decades of Anglo-Portuguese diplomacy. The chief provisions in the agreements of 1642, 1654, and 1660—whether negotiated by king, Parliament, or Lord Protector—were reaffirmed. In fact, Charles II made the acceptance by the Portuguese of every clause and article in the Cromwellian treaty of 1654 a precondition of the Bragança match—and thus, in the eyes of English law, legalized the results of negotiations that had been carried on during the Commonwealth and Protectorate. The great treaty of 1654 was preserved intact. The marriage agreement and military compact of 1661 might be seen, with little loss of accuracy, as but amendments and additions to the 1654 treaty. And certainly the Methuen treaty of 27 December 1703—"the shortest, simplest, and perhaps the most famous of all commercial treaties"—could be described, in the words of Prestage, as really "two supplementary clauses added on to that great treaty [of 1654]."[4]

The momentous agreement reached in 1661 did not look even remotely possible to Francisco de Melo during the spring and summer of 1660. How was the Portuguese ambassador to explain to the restored monarch the close and amicable relations that his country had enjoyed, during 1657–1660, with protectoral, republican, and parliamentary regimes? Or how was the king, who for years had been a Spanish pensioner and dependent, to receive an ambassador from the "rebel" Portuguese? Melo betrayed deep anxieties about these questions in a letter written to Lisbon six days after the king had landed in England. The ambassador—who had taken the precaution of organizing elaborate and costly festivities at the embassy on the occasion of the Restoration—carried out extensive inquiries "through my friends, through ladies, and Consul Maynard has carried out his own," with the intention of discovering what promises Charles II had made to the Spaniards and what influence they had on him, and all agreed on a melancholy conclusion: "the Court is totally Castilian" *("a Corte está totalmente Castelhana")!*[5]

The Portuguese were alarmed by the secret compact Charles II had made with the Spaniards in 1656;[6] they knew that the exiled king had spent most of his time during the years 1656–1660 in the Spanish Netherlands, where he had tried to keep up a royal court at Bruges and Brussels; they also knew that he had been present, late in 1659, on Spanish soil at the Franco-Spanish negotiations in Fuenterrabía on the Bidassoa, where there was delivered what seemed to have been a mortal blow against Portuguese independence. And, finally, it worried the Portuguese that the restored king was surrounded by English Catholics, most of them pro-Spanish, many of them educated in Spain or ministered to by priests who had been trained in Spain.

The situation, in truth, was not quite as gloomy as it appeared to Melo in June 1660. The exiled Charles's contacts with Philip IV had not been as profitable as the royalists had hoped. The Spanish seemed to be ready to drop the Stuart cause at the first sign of peace with Republican England. At Fuenterrabía, Charles II could attract no additional support from either France or Spain. Madrid's enthusiasm for Charles II began only after his restoration seemed certain; by then, it was too late. In order to escape the inconvenience of too close a Spanish embrace, Charles, from his residence in Flanders, slipped over the border (4/14 April 1660) to the Dutch town of Breda, from whence he made his preparations for the triumphant return. Most important of all, for the Portuguese, was Charles II's character—his suppleness, practicality, and lack of scruple. Regardless of past Spanish connections or of the advice proferred by faithful English Catholic followers, the restored monarch was likely to follow an independent line, to do what seemed most advantageous or expedient, even if it meant repudiating the Spaniards and embracing the Portuguese. Moreover, after years of near-penury, the king of England was impressed by hard cash; if, in the strict sense, money could not buy him, the prospect of acquiring money could influence him in important matters.

About three weeks before Charles II landed in England, the Portuguese ambassador had secured from the key political figure of the Restoration, Gen. George Monk, his explicit promise that English troops would be sent to Portugal.[7] In this fashion Melo tried to maintain the momentum of the military agreement during the transition from the parliamentary regime to the royal government of Charles II. Instructions from Lisbon (15 June 1660)—written in cipher and accompanying new credentials appointing Melo as ambassador extraordinary to Charles II—urged him to remind the restored king that Portugal had gone to war to help Prince Rupert and the royalists.[8]

Melo hardly needed to be coached from Lisbon. In his first addresses to Charles II's court, he no longer referred to the close cooperation he had enjoyed with antiroyalist regimes during the years 1657–1660. That period of time was forgotten; Melo talked only about 1650, about Cromwell's aggressions, and about how the Portuguese had been compelled, by force, to sign the treaty of 1654. For ten years Portuguese ambassadors had been explaining to London that they had not been responsible for Rupert's actions in Lisbon, but in mid-1660, in a dramatic volte-face, they now claimed to have supported Rupert heart and soul. Prince Rupert, Portugal's naval war with the Commonwealth, and Cromwell's coercion of John IV became Melo's cards with which to trump the Spanish ambassador's aces.

The Portuguese diplomat was aided by a number of allies of greater or lesser importance. Consul Maynard, a Cromwellian appointee who saw nothing but disaster ahead of him if he lost his post, made himself as useful as possible to Melo and to Charles II. A body of London merchants signed a petition, addressed to the king, that strongly favored a renewal of the Anglo-Portuguese alliance.[9] António de Sousa de Macedo, who had smuggled letters between Charles I and Henrietta Maria during the difficult days of 1645, wrote to Charles II to remind him of his services to the king's parents and to urge the advantages of friendship with Portugal. Queen Luisa also made use of certain pro-Portuguese English Catholics, particularly Fr. Richard Russell, as Portuguese agents in the English court. Russell traveled between Lisbon and London several times.[10]

Melo needed as much help as possible; the new men around Charles II were distrustful of the Portuguese and would not even let Melo see the king. The London government, which had listened to the advice of merchants, had demands of its own: First of all it insisted on the reconfirmation of the treaty of 1654 without any alterations, not even in the religious articles. Melo agreed, provided he could secure from England the rights and privileges obtained by the military treaty of 18/28 April 1660. In response to English criticisms, Melo sent Secretary of State Morice a memorial vigorously defending Lisbon's former policies. Melo hammered away at the central point that, in the hour of their greatest need, Portugal had gone to war to help the royalists: "My lord the King," wrote Melo, "was the only king who went to war for Your Majesty [Charles II], and he was the last to come to terms with the Republic, and then on such conditions that the treaty was the ruin of Portugal."[11] The Spaniards, however, had been the first to recognize the Republic and had only aided Charles II after Cromwell had attacked them. Moreover Portugal was still paying for the events of 1650, still paying English merchants for losses suffered through Rupert's seizure of ships.

For a time Lisbon feared that King Charles would not confirm the old treaties. Queen Luisa even advised Melo (on 12 August 1660) that if his mission ended in failure, he was to leave London with as much dignity as possible. By the time the queen wrote this letter, Melo had finally obtained his interview with Charles II (on 19/29 July) and had begun to lay the foundations for a renewal of Anglo-Portuguese friendship. Yet the ambassador still faced many difficulties, mostly arising from side-issues. There were the usual small annoyances, such as the claims from the Bushell brothers that Manuel Valente of Madeira owed them large sums of money. Also, there were situations that might arouse religious animosity, such as Consul Maynard's imprisonment by the Inquisition in the dispute over Margaret Throckmorton; Melo had to answer awkward English questions about this case. He also had to deal with angry Englishmen who claimed that an English ship (called *Escapado* in the Portuguese records, with John Man as master), wrecked at the bar of Setúbal, had been lost through the uncooperativeness of Portuguese harbor officials.[12]

Worst of all was the report from Angola that an English ship, the *Esperança (Hope? Hopewell?),* under Capt. John Cobb, had been seized with her cargo by the Portuguese authorities and the captain hanged (sentence passed on 18 November 1658). The ship was trading off the Benguela coast for slaves and ivory; she had come from Lisbon and was bound for the West Indies.[13] This episode dramatically illustrated the unreliability of the guarantees obtained by the English under article 11 of the 1654 treaty. A storm broke out in London that, if it had gone unchecked, could have wrecked any Portuguese agreement with Charles II. But Melo, through his diplomatic skill, through his growing influence with the king, and possibly through a judicious use of bribes, survived the crisis. On 2 September 1660 the ambassador was able to report to Lisbon that King Charles had agreed to a reconfirmation of the 1654 treaty and had accepted the terms of military assistance to Portugal.[14]

Up to this point the Portuguese had been trying only to obtain confirmation of the 1654 treaty, with the military articles of 18/28 April 1660 attached. There had been, as yet, no formal proposals for a dynastic alliance; who first raised the question of marriage between Charles and Catherine of Portugal has not been established, but the thought probably occurred to many persons during the summer and autumn of 1660. In September 1660 the question seems to have come to the surface. Certainly the possibility of a Stuart-Bragança marriage must have been apparent to the Portuguese at an early date. For ten years or more Lisbon had been searching for a suitable husband for Princess Catherine, and, indeed, Queen Luisa had made it the heart of her policy to secure a strong dynastic alliance that would guarantee the future of Portugal. She had tried hard to tempt Louis XIV with money and possessions but had failed. No suitor could be found in Spain, Austria, or the United Provinces or in any state with strong ties to the Hapsburgs or to the pope. The list of friendly first-class powers with marriageable princes was very short. To Luisa, and also to Melo (who, later in Portugal, defended the English match against all criticism), a union with the king of England looked almost too good to be true.

When the marriage question was first broached to the English government, Sir Edward Hyde, who had been created Earl of Clarendon and Lord Chancellor, declared that the king might be interested in the Portuguese princess provided she brought a dowry of 4 million crowns (or some £800,000); provided the Portuguese ceded to England the ports of Tangier, Bombay, Bassein, Mozambique, and either Recife or Rio de Janeiro and granted a number of factories at other points; and provided the Portuguese allowed English merchants to send ships directly from England and Newfoundland to Brazil without touching at Lisbon.[15]

These were impossible terms; Melo suggested more reasonable ones. Charles, although interested, refused the marriage—and, in November 1660, only some six months after the Restoration, Melo returned to Lisbon for further instructions. He arrived in Lisbon (probably on 15 November 1660) bringing with him Charles II's confirmation of the existing treaties and was joyfully received—for, as Consul Maynard remarked, with his usual exaggeration, the league with England "is the only thinge under Heaven lefte them [the Portuguese], to keepe them from dispaire, and ruine."[16] The queen immediately ordered the confirmation of the treaties to be publicly proclaimed in Lisbon. Portuguese anxiety about a possible Anglo-Spanish alliance directed against Portugal was relieved, and the sugar fleet, so often threatened by enemies, set sail for Brazil on 15 November with the hope of English protection.[17]

Melo remained in Lisbon from mid-November until the end of the following January, preparing the terms of the marriage agreement to be offered to Charles. At the end of November, Fr. Richard Russell was sent to London on a secret mission, probably to sound out the views of Charles II.[18] His reports seem to have been encouraging, for Lisbon proceeded with its plans. Melo wanted to be made a count before returning to London, but the queen would only raise him to the nobility if the marriage negotiations proved successful. (He was duly created Count of Ponte and later Marquis of Sande.)

Melo arrived in London on 13 February 1661 and was greeted enthusiastically by the merchants trading to Portugal. He spoke to Father Russell, who arranged a highly confidential interview with Charles II. Russell obtained a key to a door leading into one of the palace gardens, and there Melo saw the king at nine o'clock on the night of 17/27 February 1661. The king opened the letters from Portugal and read their contents aloud, and, in Melo's words, "he told me that they could not be more obliging."[19] Melo again saw the king, at the same place, the following night, and then held a secret interview with Secretary of State Morice (the ambassador went incognito) on 19 February/1 March. On 21 February/3 March the ambassador reported to Queen Luisa that the king had pledged his word to the match and would not go back on it, in spite of the opposition of the Spaniards, the French, and others. This was seventy-seven days before the supposedly decisive meeting of the king's council on 9/19 May and three months before Charles II formally announced to the nation that he had accepted a Portuguese bride.[20]

The chief opposition to the Stuart-Bragança match came from: (1) Cardinal Mazarin and Henrietta Maria, (2) the Spanish ambassador, (3) English Protestants opposed to a Catholic marriage, and (4) English Catholics opposed to a Portuguese marriage (because many were pro-Spanish and others did not want a Catholic princess from a country that, canonically speaking, was in a state of schism and not in communion with the pope, since the Vatican had had no formal relations with Portugal for over twenty years). Fortunately for Melo, English Protestants found it embarrassing to be on the same side as the pope, the king of Spain, the Spanish Inquisition, Cardinal Mazarin, Henrietta Maria, the recusants, and the English missionary priests while the Spanish ambassador, by too forced and strident a presentation of his case, alienated all factions. Luckiest of all for the Portuguese diplomat, Cardinal Mazarin died on 9 March 1661 and Louis XIV, taking the affairs of France into his own hands, turned French policy in a different direction.

Cardinal Mazarin, in spite of the Peace of the Pyrenees, sent two high-ranking officers, Lord Inchiquin and the Count of Schomberg, to Portugal with French infantry, cavalrymen, and artillery.[21] Schomberg arrived in Lisbon with 600 men on 11 November 1660 and immediately set about the difficult task of reorganizing the Portuguese army. Thus Mazarin, after France was at peace with Spain, effectively supported Portuguese independence—but he did *not* support the Anglo-Portuguese marriage, for he wanted Charles II to marry his niece.

After the death of Mazarin, his niece was dropped from consideration and Louis XIV became a strong supporter of the Bragança bride; in fact, the king of France even claimed that his influence was decisive in persuading Charles to go through with the marriage. Some historians have claimed the same thing,[22] although Melo's letters seem to contradict this view.

Mazarin's sending troops to Portugal and Louis XIV's advocacy of Catherine were violations in letter and spirit of the Peace of the Pyrenees. The Spaniards, for obvious reasons, were adamantly opposed to the Bragança marriage; the king of Spain, betrayed once again by the French, wondered whether Charles II would listen to him.

Philip IV sent to England an experienced diplomat, Baron Charles Vatteville, with instructions to prevent the Bragança-Stuart marriage at all costs. Vatteville had been present at the Franco-Spanish negotiations at Fuenterrabía and had probably met Charles II there. To the English Catholics, Vatteville said that it was impossible for pious and orthodox Catholics to support a marriage with a schismatic princess; that if Catholics were to derive the true benefits from a Catholic marriage, the princess chosen should be one in good standing with the pope—such as a princess from the House of Parma (the candidate favored by Spanish and Italian interests and by many English Catholics). To the Protestants, the Spanish ambassador said that it would stand to their advantage if Charles II married a Protestant princess. If the king demanded a great dowry, then Philip IV was willing to adopt one of the German or Scandinavian Protestant princesses, endow her liberally, and present her to the king of England as one of his own daughters.[23] These offers were ridiculed by Charles II in his speech to Parliament (on 8/18 May 1661) announcing his intention of accepting Catherine when he said that the Spanish ambassador "is so solicitous for the Advancement of the Protestant Religion, that he had offered several Protestant Princesses to whom his Master shall give a Portion, as with the Infanta of Spaine; and truly less than the Universal Monarch could not dispose of so many Princesses without the Least Consent or Privity of their own." And then Charles added, sarcastically, that marriage "to the First Protestant Daughter that ever any King of Spaine had, would not probably bring so great Advantages to it as was pretended."[24]

As the negotiations between Melo and Charles II progressed, during February, March, and April 1661, toward a constructive conclusion, Baron Vatteville, supported by the pro-Spanish faction in the court, desperately argued for a Protestant match. The result of Spanish diplomacy was nearly to persuade English Protestants that no harm could come to the Protestant church from a marriage opposed by the pope, the king of Spain, and the English recusants. London was treated to the almost comic spectacle of Catholics urging a Protestant match and Protestants acquiescent to a Catholic one. Charles II dealt deftly with his Hispanophile followers. He twitted Sir Harry Bennet (former royalist agent in Madrid) for his pro-Spanish sentiments: "the King jestingly told him he would cut off his Spanish beard with a paire of Portugal scissors."[25]

Finally, Vatteville threatened a resumption of war. Charles II had made peace with Spain but had refused to restore Dunkirk and Jamaica to Philip IV. The Spaniards were grateful for the peace but angry at the terms, particularly since they may have expected the restored king to disassociate himself from the "piratical" Cromwellian policy that had cost them Jamaica. Spain, it seemed, was always the victim of English policy: Philip IV, after having been unjustly attacked by Cromwell, was now to be repudiated by Cromwell's enemy, the prince he had befriended. The Bragança match was the last straw. Spain, having allied herself to France and come to terms with England, was prepared to try conclusions with the Portuguese: the reconquest of Portugal would have redeemed the long and somewhat disastrous reign of Philip IV. But now England stood in the way.

Charles II brushed aside Spanish threats, accepted Princess Catherine, informed the lords and commons of his decision (on 8/18 May 1661), sent Sir Richard Fanshaw to Lisbon to arrange the details, and dispatched Edward Montagu, Earl of Sandwich, to take possession of Tangier and bring the princess to England. Montagu weighed anchor in the Downs aboard the *Royal James* on 19/29 June 1661, spent a few weeks in the area of the straits, and on 6/16 September, sailed into Oeiras where he was greeted by the jubilant Ambassador Melo, now back in Lisbon and graced with the title of Count of Ponte. On 22 September/2 October the Brazil fleet with fifty-two sugar ships, under the protection of the Royal Navy, arrived safely at Lisbon. On 3/13 October the English commander sailed for Tangier, where he spent the next four months. He then returned to Lisbon and, on 1/11 March 1662, anchored "right against Belem Monastery." The Portuguese ratified the marriage treaty and sent a copy to Montagu by the hand of Melo. After several weeks' delay, Catherine boarded the magnificent HMS *Royal Charles*—which was none other than the former state's ship *Naseby*, under a new name—and sailed for England on 14/24 April. After a difficult passage, the new queen arrived at Portsmouth a month later, on 14/24 May, but did not meet her husband until six days had passed. For better or for worse, the dynastic alliance had been accomplished.[26]

It would be needless to dwell on the further details of events, treaties, and circumstances that have been described, many times, by English, Portuguese, and other authors. The intention here is to assess, in general terms, the significance of the dynastic alliance of 1661–1662—which can be seen, glancing backward, as the summary and resolution of many trends that had characterized Anglo-Portuguese diplomacy during the period 1642–1660, or which can be looked at, glancing forward, as a fresh start, with important consequences for the future of both countries.

The dynastic alliance affected Englishmen in five different areas: (1) it strengthened the position of English merchants trading in Portugal, particularly in relation to the guarantees contained in the reaffirmed treaty of 1654; (2) it influenced the role of the Royal Navy in the straits; (3) it secured a port for the British East India Company in Western India; (4) it brought dowry monies into Charles II's Treasury; and (5) it brought a Portuguese queen to England.

About English merchant privileges, as contained in the 1654 treaty, enough has been said. Despite the clear language of the treaty, English merchants did not obtain all the privileges that had been legally granted. Nonetheless, as one ponders the cumulative effect of the events of 1642, 1654, 1656, 1660, and 1662, one senses a steady strengthening of the position of the merchants in Portugal. The position of the Dutch merchants became more uncertain at the very time that English merchants were reaching out for a larger share of Portuguese trade. By the end of the century, the English alone began to dominate Portuguese trade.

Second, the dynastic treaty, in ceding Tangier to England, affected the position of the Royal Navy in the straits. The demand for Tangier arose, of course, because of needs developed by the navy during the western Mediterranean operations of 1650–1660. Unfortunately, Tangier proved to be impractical as a naval base and was abandoned in 1684—but its very possession during the years 1662–1684 helped to draw the Royal Navy towards the straits and foreshadowed the eventual British occupation of Gibraltar.

Third, the treaty gave to the British East India Company the island and harbor of Bombay, with certain rights of access to the Portuguese trading centers at Goa, Diu, Cochim, and elsewhere. In 1662, Bombay was a neglected and undeveloped naval base, and even the most sanguine visionary could hardly have foreseen that it was destined to become the greatest city in India. Its possession gave the East India Company a key position on the west coast, thus matching its base of Madras on the east coast. The actual transfer of Bombay to English hands only took place after interminable delays and great difficulties.[27] In truth, Anglo-Portuguese relations in the East were less cordial than in any other part of the world, although the Convention of Goa (signed on 10/20 January 1635), which was reaffirmed in 1642, 1654, and 1661, assured a certain amount of cooperation. In 1662, the East India Company was still very weak, with only a few ships, forts, and men in India; the Portuguese, although considerably stronger, had been steadily losing ground to the Dutch. By the end of the century the British had become the chief rivals of the Dutch in Eastern waters, and the once-proud Portuguese imperial ventures in the East had shrunk to a half-dozen small enclaves (chiefly Goa, Diu, Damão, Timor, and Macau).

Fourth, the marriage was supposed to bring Charles II a dowry of 2 million cruzados, which, according to Queen Luisa, was the largest dowry in history. In 1662, 2 million cruzados, or 800:000$000 réis, was worth rather less than £400,000 in Lisbon, but when taken to London, the Portuguese coins, if in mint condition, would have fetched a maximum of £378,000 sterling.[28] One-half the money was supposed to accompany Catherine to England, and the other half was to be paid a year later. Strenuous efforts were made in Portugal and Brazil to collect the cash. The Queen-Regent raised about 80:000$000 réis, one-tenth of what was required, by forced loans in Lisbon; other money came in through the doubling of selected taxes and from the withholding of certain amounts from the salaries of civil servants.[29] Yet once these sums had been raised, the Queen-Regent, characteristically, "borrowed" from them to pay and supply the Portuguese army. When the time came to place the first one-half installment of the dowry aboard the English ships, the Portuguese included Catherine's jewels, plate, furniture, and even personal clothing as sums paid on the dowry and also included large cargoes of sugar and smaller amounts of other commodities as contributing toward the required sum. Silver cruzados made up perhaps one-half or more of the whole. Even so, with the queen's jewels and personal effects, sugar chests, silver coins, and the rest, all added together, the stipulated one-half portion of the dowry was not met.

According to Catherine's treasurer, the immensely wealthy New Christian merchant Duarte da Silva, the total paid to the English amounted to 760,000 cruzados, which represented 38 percent and not 50 percent of the dowry.[30] That left 240,000 cruzados owing on the first installment, plus the 1 million that was supposed to be paid in one year's time—or 1,240,000 cruzados in all. This large sum was either not paid directly to Charles II or paid very slowly. When British soldiers went to Portugal to help fight the Spanish, the value of the wages, equipment, and accommodations supplied to them by Lisbon was deducted from what was owed on the dowry. Even with these expedients, the Portuguese still had 669,093 cruzados to pay in 1669. Ten years later, in 1679, the Portuguese had paid two-thirds of this sum, but there was yet a balance of 220,616 cruzados owing.[31] By that time, the debasement of Portuguese coinage had further reduced the value of the amounts still owed.

In 1662, using the promise of the dowry monies as collateral, Charles II had raised large loans among the London bankers.[32] He may have had little thought, then, that the collection of the dowry would take over eighteen years and that much of it would be paid in forms that were of no direct profit to his Treasury.

Last, the dynastic alliance brought to England the person of Catherine of Bragança. Catherine[33] arrived in England as an inexperienced twenty-four-year-old woman, poorly educated, unable to speak English, but with certain tastes in dress, appearance, furniture, music, and the arts that were somewhat more sophisticated than those of the ordinary upper-class Englishwoman. Catherine's most difficult task was adapting herself to English ways and identifying herself with England's interests, just as her mother, Queen Luisa, although Spanish-born and -bred, identified herself with Portuguese interests (although Luisa never learned to speak or write Portuguese). That Catherine failed, particularly in religious matters, to accommodate herself to the major trends and forces in English life and never succeeded in passing herself off as someone fully committed to the welfare of her adopted country helps to explain why her thirty-year stay (1662–1692) in England was often unhappy and why her impact on the nation was so small.[34]

Catherine's characteristically Iberian commitment to advancing the cause of Catholicism was the main reason for her failure in England. It has been the complaint of Portuguese historians that the English, particularly the English Protestants, did not understand her, but it would be truer to say that, in matters of religion, the English Protestants understood her only too well. If Catherine had taken a pragmatic view of the English political situation, she would have practiced her religion as quietly and unobtrusively as possible. But she did precisely the opposite; even before she left Portugal it had been agreed between her and her extensive ecclesiastical retinue that their main task in England was to provide a base for the restoration of Catholicism.[35] In their negotiations with London, the Portuguese insisted that Catherine should have a large staff of priests, friars, and nuns, because such was the Portuguese custom—and to diminish the number of her religious attendants would be to derogate from her status as a Portuguese Infanta. Yet the true function of her religious establishment was not simply to minister to the queen but to secure the conversion of influential persons in the court (such as the members of the royal family), to meet the needs of the English Catholic community, and to afford cover, protection, and support for Catholic missionaries.

If Catherine's ecclesiastical retinue had been entirely Portuguese, there would have been less English criticism—but, instead, her retinue included many English, Irish, and Scottish Catholics. In 1678, for instance, she had eleven British chaplains on her payroll (costing her £2,600 per annum), including Philip Thomas Howard, Cardinal of Norfolk and vicar-apostolic of the English Catholic Church; Richard Russell, Canon of the English Catholic Chapter of London and Portuguese Bishop of Portalegre; and Dr. Thomas Godden, former president (1655–1662) of the English College at Lisbon.[36] Catherine's extensive involvement with English recusancy explains, but does not excuse, the strong attacks made on her during the years (1678–1681) of the Titus Oates anti-Catholic hysteria. The net effect of Catherine's advocacy of Catholicism was to accentuate those pro-Catholic proclivities of certain members of the royal family that contributed so much to the fall of the House of Stuart. If she had had children, her influence would have been greater, but whether the result would have been better or worse for England is hard to say.

Yet there is another and more creative side to Catherine's historical role: she became the living embodiment of the principles of the Anglo-Portuguese alliance. If in England she was unpopular for pushing Catholicism too hard, in Portugal she was often criticized for being too pro-English. In England she tried to obtain maximum support for Portugal, while, in her letters to her brother, the Prince-Regent Pedro, she stressed the value to Portugal of the English connection.[37] Even after Portugal made peace with Spain (1667–1668), when the alliance became less vital for Portugal, she worked hard for continued Anglo-Portuguese friendship. After her return to Portugal in 1693, she became the chief spokesperson in Lisbon for the traditional policy. The success of John Methuen and his son, Paul, in negotiating the Methuen Treaty of 27 December 1703 may have owed something to her influence.[38] Also, after thirty years in England, she had become English in her habits and found it difficult to adapt herself to the restricted pattern of behavior expected of a Portuguese lady.

In viewing the general effects of the dynastic alliance upon England, one can detect many advantages and few disadvantages for the English. But, from the other point of view, looking at its effects upon Portugal, opinion is divided. Among the Portuguese, criticism of the dynastic union began quite early. Some three months after Catherine had left Lisbon, the Queen-Regent Luisa was forced out of office and soon retired to a Carmelite convent, where she died on 28 February 1666. As soon as the old queen lost power, criticism of her policies became open, and people complained that she had "exhausted the wealth and aliened the flowers of the crown for the advancement of that one child [Catherine]."[39] This view has been echoed many times during the last three centuries. In the middle of the nineteenth century, one of the Portuguese critics of the Anglo-Portuguese alliance wrote of the marriage treaty in vitriolic terms: "It was in this manner that those infamous governments, at their own good pleasure, disposed of the fortune, honor, lives, and property of their subjects, whom they called vassals, that is, slaves, in this way augmenting the wealth of a foreign nation, contributing to her aggrandizement, and giving her arms with which she could afterwards insult us and reduce us to vassalage!!!!"[40]

The view that Luisa set aside the interests of Portugal in favor of advancing the fortunes of Catherine cannot stand examination. The whole object of the match was to guarantee the independence of Portugal, and Catherine was, in a very real sense, sacrificed to the national interest (and not the reverse). It would not be difficult to think of places where the princess would have been much happier than in England. If her comfort and happiness had been prime considerations, then surely a marriage with the prince of a Catholic country would have been arranged.

The nub of the criticism is that in paying a large dowry and ceding Tangier and Bombay, Portugal gave up too much. The dowry, as has been seen, was less onerous a payment than it appeared to be on the surface. The "loss" of Tangier was a blessing in disguise; the barren garrison town, with no wealth of its own and little commerce, had constantly drained men, money, ships, and resources from Portugal, with no adequate return. Nevertheless, Tangier has been the subject of myth-making by Portuguese historians, both amateur and professional, who have represented it as a place of great wealth and importance. As for Bombay, the Lisbon government, at least initially, felt no difficulty in surrendering it.[41] When the English arrived to take possession of Bombay, they acknowledged the excellence of the anchorage but otherwise thought the island was hardly worth possessing.[42]

The cession of Bombay has given Portuguese critics another angle of attack: by the terms of the treaty of 1661, England was to assist the Portuguese in India against the Dutch, and, very clearly, there was almost no English assistance given to them during the critical decade of 1661–1670, when the Portuguese Eastern empire underwent a fatal decline. Yet the blame for this lack of cooperation rests squarely on the shoulders of the Portuguese viceroy, António de Melo de Castro, who had quarreled bitterly with the English commanders of the five-ship squadron that conveyed him to India.[43] Melo de Castro made it impossible for the English to take possession of Bombay (which he withheld for five years), although its transfer had been the chief object of the Anglo-Portuguese expedition; he rejected English help and did everything to antagonize his supposed allies.[44] While British troops, for lack of proper shelter and accommodations, died like flies on the coasts of western India,[45] the Dutch drove the Portuguese out of most of their positions on the Malabar coast and badly defeated them at Cochim. By the time the transfer of Bombay had been effected, it was too late; the British expeditionary force had been frittered away, and the Dutch were everywhere triumphant.

For the purposes of making a case against the Anglo-Portuguese alliance, the questions of the dowry, and of Tangier and Bombay, have often been misrepresented or misunderstood. Errors of interpretation have arisen from lack of knowledge. The hard facts about these issues are not to be found in the secondary literature and are not easy to unearth elsewhere.

The central significance of the marriage treaty, to the Portuguese, lay in the British guarantee of Portuguese independence. London gave meaning to this guarantee by supporting Portugal in three ways: (1) at sea, (2) on the land, and (3) through diplomacy. At sea, London supported Portugal strongly during the years 1660–1663, but, thereafter, the Royal Navy took a battering during the Second Anglo-Dutch War (1664–1667) and was not always able to maintain ships in the Mediterranean or the straits or off Portugal with regularity. The lack of British warships stimulated the Portuguese to rebuild their own fleet, beginning in 1663, when they began to construct frigates of the foreign type, instead of turning out their traditional galleons. By the end of the Spanish war the new Portuguese frigates had taken the offensive in Iberian waters. Yet British ships returned to Portuguese waters in greater and greater numbers, particularly at the end of the seventeenth century and all during the eighteenth, and the presence of the friendly Royal Navy was usually an important factor in Portuguese strategic and political calculations.

More significant to the Portuguese was the English help given to them by land. During the years 1662 to 1665 Portugal had to repel several large-scale Spanish invasions. In May 1662 a Spanish army of 14,000 men, under the command of Don Juan José of Austria, Philip IV's natural son, invaded Central Portugal and ravaged the province of Alentejo, without meeting effective Portuguese opposition.[46] Don Juan retired at the end of the summer but came back in May 1663 with even more men, some 18,500, including a large and excellent cavalry unit. The Portuguese army lay at Estremoz, not far from the frontier, with some 19,000 men under the command of Dom Sancho Manuel de Vilhena, first Count of Vila Flor, assisted by the experienced German soldier, the Count of Schomberg.

The Portuguese forces at Estremoz included 1,500 British infantry, 350 British cavalry, 300 Italian infantry, and 300 French cavalry.[47] All the foreign troops together made up only about 13 percent of the total force (the British alone a little under 10 percent of the total); the British and French cavalry units comprised about 20 percent of the total cavalry force of 3,150, and the British and Italian infantry made up about 10 percent of the total force of 15,800 infantry. The small numbers of British and other foreign troops has led Portuguese historians into almost ignoring them—and has given Anglophobes an opportunity to charge that Portugal gave up "a princess, Tangier, Bombay, Ceylon[!], an immense dowry in money, and many privileges for . . . two thousand infantry and one thousand horse!!!"[48]

The numbers and percentages, however, are very deceptive. The French and British cavalry were the heart of every cavalry operation, because the Portuguese horse was so inferior as to be almost useless. The Portuguese infantry contained two or three excellent veteran regiments, particularly the regiments of Cascais and Almada, but the bulk of the forces was made up of raw militia units—poorly trained and virtually unpaid, pressed into service for the summer—who sometimes deserted at the rate of hundreds a night. In these circumstances the brigade of British redcoats, trained in the high traditions of Cromwell's New Model Army, played a key role in the Portuguese victories of 1663–1665. The redcoats were in the van in every advance, formed the rear guard in retreat, were the preferred troops in assaults on fortified positions, manned the most exposed positions, and, from first to last, bore the brunt of the Portuguese campaigns.[49]

In the battle of Ameixial (8 June 1663), which drove Don Juan out of Portugal, the English cavalry lost its commanding colonel, two captains, and half its force in three charges on the Spanish right wing. The survivors were saved by the prompt and intelligent intervention of the regiments of Cascais and Almada, who left their center position when the Portuguese infantry on the left wing failed to support the English cavalry. In the center, the redcoats won the battle without much help from anyone, giving no quarter and slaughtering Spaniards by the hundreds with murderous efficiency.[50]

The same courage, efficiency, and disregard for their own lives was displayed by the English soldiers in the campaigns of 1664 and 1665. In June 1664 the Portuguese army attacked the walled and fortified Spanish town of Valencia de Alcántara. Although a breach was made in the walls, the Portuguese infantry hesitated to advance over the exposed ground to the foot of the walls. As usual, the decisive assault was delivered by the redcoats. A Lisbon newspaper described the storming of the breach admiringly: the English "formed ranks at the foot of the wall, and with bared breasts fought admirably with those inside, as if the struggle were of equals on an open field; and 150 of them were killed, falling in the same ranks as they found themselves, without losing an inch of ground."[51] The losses were made up by new troops that landed in Lisbon that same month. At the decisive battle of Montes Claros (17 June 1665), the last major engagement of the war, the British contingents again distinguished themselves.

Contemporary Portuguese recognized the value of England's assistance and were very appreciative. British troops were cheered to the echo in the streets of Lisbon, and the Lisbon press heaped lavish praise on the foreigners.[52] In the light of contemporary Portuguese opinion, which recognized the fact that much English blood was shed on behalf of Portuguese independence, it is unfortunate that a number of later Portuguese authors have belittled the extent of English assistance, denied it altogether, or misconstrued the function of the English brigade in the campaigns of 1663, 1664, and 1665. One prominent Portuguese scholar once wrote that he was not aware of any assistance given to Portugal under the marriage treaty.[53] Another stated that English troops were promised but never actually came to Portugal.[54] Still another remarked that Charles II gave no help to Portugal at all.[55]

Toward the end of the long Luso-Spanish war the English helped the Portuguese in yet another way: through diplomacy. In the summer of 1664 Charles's ambassador to Spain, Sir Richard Fanshaw, labored to negotiate a treaty between England and Spain that would also include a peace between Spain and Portugal. Until the reverses suffered on the field of battle during the campaign of 1665, the Spanish continued to nurture faint hopes of conquering Portugal. On 17 September 1665, Philip IV died, still unreconciled to the loss of Portugal. A sickly four-year-old boy, Charles II, the last of the Spanish Hapsburgs, became king of Spain, and the attention of Spanish statesmen turned inward toward their own domestic problems. At this time, when Spain entered what was to become a prolonged period of dynastic stress, in Portugal the young, ambitious, and able Prince Pedro was moving slowly toward the achievement of complete power. The time had come for peace between Portugal and Spain.

At Madrid, on 17 December 1665, Fanshaw signed an Anglo-Spanish treaty. In it the king of Spain was still referred to as king of Castile, León, Aragon, the Two Sicilies, Jerusalem, and Portugal, but, by the terms of various secret articles, the Spaniards accepted the mediation of the king of England in the Luso-Spanish dispute (article 25), accepted in principle that a thirty-year truce should be declared between Spain and Portugal (article 36), and stipulated that no article in the Anglo-Spanish agreement should in any way inhibit the Anglo-Portuguese alliance (article 45).[56] In the secret articles of the Anglo-Spanish treaty of 1665, Queen Luisa's well-laid plans in arranging the Stuart-Bragança marriage had finally come close to fulfillment.

At this stage of events the Portuguese, victorious on the land and strong at sea, delayed the peace. They demanded from the Spaniards not a truce, but a peace, with full legal recognition of the House of Bragança as the legitimate rulers of Portugal. The arrival of a French princess on Portuguese soil (she married first Alphonse VI and then Pedro), the signing of a Franco-Portuguese alliance in

March 1667, and continued English diplomatic pressure in Madrid induced the Spaniards to give way. On 13 February 1668, by which time Pedro had become Prince-Regent of Portugal, the Luso-Spanish peace was signed on terms favorable to the Portuguese.

The Portuguese war of independence lasted from 1 December 1640 to 13 February 1668, or twenty-seven years, two months, and thirteen days. During that span of time one can perceive several distinct phases in the development of Anglo-Portuguese relations: (1) Initially, during 1641–1642, there were friendly diplomatic contacts that led to the treaty of 1642. (2) But during the period of acute English domestic disturbances (1642–1649), Anglo-Portuguese relations fell into a state of quiescence, the treaty of 1642 had few important consequences, and diplomatic contacts between the two countries became infrequent. (3) Then there were two years, 1649–1650, marked first by ill-feeling and then by open warfare. (4) This was followed by years (1651–1654) of difficult negotiations, leading to the treaty of 1654. (5) Two further years (1655–1656) were spent in the struggle over the ratification of the treaty. (6) During the next phase, 1657–1660, the Portuguese brought about a growing rapport between the two nations, which led to the military treaty of 1660. And (7), last, after the crisis of the Restoration, the Portuguese capitalized on the trends of 1657–1660 to build the dynastic alliance of 1661–1662 that dominated the subsequent decades.

Throughout the whole period, except for a few difficult months in 1650, English merchants transacted business in Portugal, trading particularly in Brazilian sugar. Also, throughout most of these years, the Portuguese desired and sought English naval and military assistance. These two circumstances help to explain why the alliance existed, why it was regularly renewed, and why it seemed to prevail over every vicissitude and adversity.

In general terms, when Englishmen thought about the Anglo-Portuguese alliance they were concerned with commercial advantages; but when the Portuguese thought about it they were concerned with obtaining military, naval, and political advantages. It was perhaps the fondest dream of English merchants in the Portuguese trade to secure somehow a monopoly position in the Portuguese commercial world—such as control over Setúbal salt (which the Dutch had long engrossed), over Brazilian sugar, Madeira wines, and Angolan slaves. What the Portuguese wanted was English help in the long war against Spain and support in the struggle against the Dutch (particularly in the East), and they also wanted the stationing of a protective squadron off the Portuguese coast and, in general, the defense of Portuguese shipping, property, and colonial possessions by the Royal Navy at all times and in all waters.

The demands made by Englishmen and Portuguese of each other were not wholly contradictory or impossible of achievement but afforded room for compromise; although neither side could gain all, or even most, of what it wanted, there remained the possibility of a growing collaboration that might prove desirable and rewarding for both parties. This study maintains that such a possibility began to be realized as early as 1657 and was fulfilled abundantly by 1662. This study also maintains, as its central thesis, that the granting of commercial benefits by the Portuguese to the English, in return for implicit British guarantees of the independence of Portugal in Europe and of the integrity of her empire overseas, was the essence of the Anglo-Portuguese alliance.

If the Portuguese never really conceded the fundamental English demand for freedom to trade, throughout the empire, in all commodities, at all places, and at all times, they did grant the English in the 1650s a considerable position in the marketing of Brazilian sugar and eventually an all-important position in the marketing of Portuguese wines. And if the British failed to do much for Portugal in the Indian Ocean and the China Sea, they did give the Portuguese enough naval and military assistance (from 1656 to 1665) to enable them to win their war of independence against Spain. Also, from the long-range point of view, it might be said that the Royal Navy helped to ensure that the Portuguese empire, as it existed in 1670, survived almost intact until 1822, when Brazil became independent.

The chief friction between the allies was over religion. The Portuguese objected more to article 14 of the 1654 treaty than to the commercial concessions. Even though John IV was forced to sign the treaty, he never had any real intention of permitting the religious privileges guaranteed to English Protestants under article 14 to go into effect. Indeed, the Englishmen never obtained their church and cemetery at Lisbon until the time of the Napoleonic wars, when the intellectual climate had changed. Similarly, the chief obstacle to the fulfillment of that Anglo-Portuguese friendship that the dynastic marriage seemed to promise was the obtrusive Catholicism of Queen

Catherine. The royal union only accentuated religious misunderstandings.

Apart from religion, serious friction between Portugal and England was somewhat infrequent, except for the naval war of 1650–1651, which perhaps should be viewed, against the wider pattern of Anglo-Portuguese contacts, as an unexpected and untypical incident. Prince Rupert exported to Lisbon a quarrel that the Portuguese had no real interest in entering. As soon as it was decently possible, Portugal sent Guimarães to London to sue for peace. After he failed, the Count of Penaguião was dispatched on the same mission. The execution of Penaguião's brother, the harsh terms of the 1654 treaty, and the even harsher manner in which its ratification was forced on John IV—none of these deeds seemed to interrupt, for more than a season, the important trends that were bringing about understanding between Lisbon and London. England's aggressive foreign policy, which resulted in wars with both the United Provinces and Spain, redounded to Portugal's interest. The Anglo-Spanish war created a favorable environment for Luso-British cooperation, and, after the death of John IV in 1656, the Queen-Regent Luisa and the Count of Odemira sought to turn England's strength to Portugal's advantage.

Francisco de Melo, the Portuguese ambassador in London, survived the changes in English government that occurred after the death of Cromwell in 1658 and obtained the long-sought military alliance in 1660. The Restoration of Charles II was a setback for the Portuguese but opened up new opportunities, for Charles II had suddenly become one of the most eligible bachelors in Europe. The Portuguese exploited their opportunities and ignored the wreck of the 1660 military treaty. Melo, by combining the restored 1654 treaty with a new military compact and adding a large dowry, plus Tangier and Bombay, enticed Charles II into marrying Catherine. Melo transformed failure into triumph and maintained the rhythm of Anglo-Portuguese friendships that had marked the years 1657–1660. Portuguese independence was saved.

The marriage treaty brought benefits to both parties, with little real damage to either. In fact, it could be said of the Anglo-Portuguese alliance as a whole, across large periods of time, that it harmed neither Britain nor Portugal but brought significant advantages to both. Although some Portuguese students have defended the Anglo-Portuguese alliance[57] and others have taken a fairly dispassionate and neutral position,[58] a numerous and sometimes noisy majority have depicted the alliance as a system of economic and political exploitation in which Britain, with her strength, reaped all the profits and benefits while Portugal, in her weakness, was always the loser. The conclusions of this study, dealing primarily with the seventeenth-century situation, do not support this view. The Brazilian sugar trade, in which English merchants took a prominent part, furnishes an important example of how each party helped the other, to the benefit of both. By using well-gunned English ships, the Portuguese—who were not primarily concerned with the enrichment of the English—more than doubled the fighting strength of the Brazil fleets, thereby making the sugar trade possible in the face of persistent threats from privateers, pirates, and the Dutch and Spanish. The greater security thus afforded to the Brazil fleets enabled Portuguese merchants to carry on and expand their own trade with more safety, and the resultant increase in commercial activity brought a larger flow of cash into the king of Portugal's Treasury, which depended heavily on income from import and export duties. Moreover, the English merchants—considering their capital investments, the risks they took, and the high taxes they paid to the Portuguese—usually made only moderate profits.

The logic of historical reasoning would suggest that when an alliance between two nations persists over the course of centuries, it is because it meets common needs and confers mutual advantages. The extant records from the period 1642–1662 seem to support this logic. This does not mean that there were no conflicts between the allies and no intensity of ill-feeling—such as was aroused when the English merchants in Portugal were jailed and had their property confiscated or when Cromwell used brute force to impose his will on John IV in 1656. England and Portugal, in truth, were uneasy allies. But, uneasy or not, Francisco de Melo was close to the truth when he declared that the Anglo-Portuguese alliance brought with it "advantages that are more reciprocal than those of any other alliance."[59]

NOTES

Chapter 1

1. *De Expugnatione Lyxbonensis,* ed. and trans. Charles W. David (New York, 1936). H. A. R. Gibb, "English Crusaders in Portugal," *Chapters in Anglo-Portuguese Relations,* ed. Edgar Prestage (Watford, 1935), pp. 9–36.
2. *De Expugnatione,* p. 178. Gilbert served as Bishop of Lisbon until his death in 1166.
3. Alwyn A. Ruddock, *Italian Merchants and Shipping in Southampton 1270–1600* (Southampton, 1951), pp. 12–19.
4. Eduardo Brazão, *Anglo-Portuguese Alliance* (London, 1957), p. 12.
5. Thomas Rymer, *Foedera,* vol. 5 (London, 1708), pp. 763–764.
6. See P. E. L. Russell, *The English Intervention in Spain & Portugal in the Time of Edward III & Richard II* (Oxford, 1955).
7. BM, Add. MSS. 27344, fols. 65–70.
8. Or 452½ tons, since four *pieces* made up one ton.
9. *Port Books of Southampton 1427–1430,* ed. Paul Struder (Southampton, 1913), pp. 10, 103, 132, 134.
10. V. M. Shillington in V. M. Shillington and A. B. Wallis Chapman, *Commercial Relations of England and Portugal* (London, 1907), p. viii.
11. BM, Harleian MSS. 1855, fols. 1–15; PRO, S.P. 14/21; charter printed in Pauline Croft, *The Spanish Company* (London, 1973), pp. 95–113, and see her discussion, pp. xxix–xxxix.
12. Margarita, or Margherita, was the daughter of Duke Carlo Emanuele of Savoy, the granddaughter of Philip II of Spain and the widow of Vicenzo Gonzaga, third Duke of Mantua. The Count of Olivares entrusted her with the government of Portugal (1636) as his instrument in the execution of unpopular policies. In the critical first moments of the Portuguese revolt, she conducted herself with courage and resolution and had to be threatened with physical restraint. The Portuguese did not blame her for their troubles but held her in respect. Eventually John IV arranged for her safe conveyance to the Spanish border.
13. Francisco Manuel de Melo, *Tácito Portuguez* (Rio de Janeiro, 1940), p. 65.
14. BM, Add. MSS. 25227, fols. 51–52.
15. PRO, S.P. 89/4, fols. 18–19.
16. Carlos Roma du Bocage, *Subsídios para o estudo das relações exteriores de Portugal 1640–1644,* vol. 1 (Lisbon, 1916), pp. 186–188; *Relação da embaixada do Padre Mestre Inácio de Mascarenhas à Catalunha em 1641* (Coimbra, 1926); Ferran Soldevila, *Història de Catalunya,* 2d ed. (Barcelona, 1963), pp. 1024–1041.
17. Quirino da Fonseca, *Os Portugueses no mar* (Lisbon, 1926), 1:468; BM, Add. MSS. 25227, fol. 51.

18. PRO, S.P. 89/4, fol. 48. Chandler's estimates of tonnage were somewhat exaggerated; see Quirino da Fonseca, vol. 1, pp. 712–14.
19. PRO, S.P. 89/4, fol. 48; *Relaçam verdadeira de huma assinalada vitoria que a armada do Rey de França teve na Costa de Catalunha* (Lisbon, 1641); Cesáreo Fernández Duro, *Armada Española,* 9 vols. (Madrid, 1895–1903), 4:270–72; C. R. Boxer, "M. A. de Ruyter, 1607–1676," *Mariner's Mirror* 44 (1958): 5–6.
20. Fernando de Meneses, Conde de Ericeira, *Historia de Tangere* (Lisbon, 1732), pp. 163–69.
21. There are four pages of signatures in the register of the *auto* entered into the books of the municipal chamber of Funchal: Arq. Dist. Funchal, "Livro de vereações, 1641," fols. 7–9.
22. Arq. Dist. Funchal, "Livro de vereações, 1641," fol. 10; and the unpublished history of Madeira in the Arq. Dist. Ponta Delgada: Henrique Henriques de Noronha, "Memorias seculares e eclesiasticas para a historia da dioçesi do Funchal," fol. 210.
23. Arq. Dist. Angra, Manuel Luís Maldonado, "Fênix Angrense" (a valuable history of Terceira that still remains to be published), years 1640–1642, fols. 242–295; Francisco Ferreira Drummond, *Annaes da Ilha Terceira,* 4 vols. (Angra, 1850–1859), 2:1–61; Miguel Cristóvam de Araújo, "A Restauraçáo na Ilha Terceira, 1641–1642," *Boletím do Instituto Histórico da Ilha Terceira* 18 (1960): 38–116.
24. Diego de Saavedra Fajardo, *Obras completas* (Madrid, 1946), p. 1212.
25. María de Jesús de Ágreda, *Correspondencia con Felipe IV,* 2 vols. (Madrid, 1942), 2:149.
26. Roma du Bocage, 1:50; H. V. Livermore, *History of Portugal* (Cambridge, 1947), pp. 281–288.
27. Ajuda 51-V-5, fols. 38–40. See Edgar Prestage, *Diplomatic Relations of Portugal with France, England, and Holland 1640–1668* (Watford, 1925).
28. PRO, S.P. 89/4, fols. 28–29. The phrase "old nobility of England" refers to the fact that the Almada family was founded by an English Crusader who assisted the first king of Portugal in the Lisbon campaign of 1147 and then remained in Portugal. Two of Almada's fifteenth-century ancestors served under English kings and were both created knights of the Order of the Bath.
29. PRO, S.P. 89/4, fol. 38; Earl of Clarendon, *State Papers,* 3 vols. (Oxford, 1767–1768), 2:84–89.
30. *Articles of Peace and Commerce between Charles, King of Great Britain, and John the 4th, King of Portugal* (London, 1642). There is a manuscript copy of the official Latin text in Ajuda 49-X-22, fols. 144–150.
31. José de Almada, *Aliança Inglesa,* 2 vols. (Lisbon, 1946–1947), 1:25.
32. Englishmen in Portugal entered into many contracts with Portuguese *New Christians,* the most active native merchant class, whose property was liable to seizure by the Inquisition at any moment, and outside claims against confiscated property were seldom allowed.
33. Protestants could not make valid wills in Portugal, and hence their estates, after death, could be legally forfeited to the Portuguese crown. The Judge Conservator of the English *(Juiz Conservador dos Ingleses)* was a Portuguese lawyer, usually a magistrate in the customs house, appointed to have exclusive jurisdiction in legal disputes affecting Englishmen.
34. House of Commons, *Journals,* 2:495–496.
35. "As ingresas tem tal conceito do aperto q̃ em Portugal sofrem as molheres, q̃ difficultoso será a hum Portugues achar aquy quem o queira por marido" (the

tone of the passage suggests that Macedo did not believe that Portuguese women were really in an *aperto*—"plight" or "fix"). Arq. Dist. Évora, Codex XVI/2-8, fol. 34.

36. *Documents Relating to the Civil War 1642–1648,* ed. John R. Powell and Edward K. Timings (London, 1963), p. 24; Arq. Dist. Évora, Codex CVI/2–8, fols. 33, 42; *Commons Journal,* 2:775; *Cal. S.P. 1641–1643* (London, 1887), p. 343.
37. Edgar Prestage, *Dr. Antonio de Sousa de Macedo, Residente de Portugal em Londres, 1642–1646* (Lisbon, 1916).
38. Arq. Dist. Évora, Codex CVI/2–8, fol. 120.
39. Ibid., fol. 32, *et passim.*
40. Ibid., fol. 354.
41. Ibid., fol. 34.
42. Ibid., fols. 49, 65.
43. *Cal. S.P. 1644–1645* (London, 1890), p. 605; Prestage, *Macedo,* pp. 30–33, 73–75; *The Kings Cabinet Opened* (London, 1645).
44. Macedo's major work was the 800-page *Lusitania liberata ab injusto Castellanorum dominio,* a Latin work published by Richard Heron in London in 1645. He also engaged in a pamphlet war with one Juan Caramuel Lobkowitz, author of *Ioannes Bragantinus Lusitaniae illegitimus rex demonstratus, (Louvain, 1642),* to which Macedo replied in *Juan Caramuel Lobkovvitz. . . . Convencido* (London, 1642). Prestage, *Macedo,* p. 69; Arq. Dist. Évora, Codex XVI/2–8, fol. 174.
45. The English Jewish scholar Alfred M. Hyamson wrote that Macedo "was himself a Marrano or Crypto-Jew, and it was in the chapel of his embassy that the small colony of Spanish and Portuguese merchants used to assemble weekly, apparently to hear mass, in reality, however, it seems, to join in divine service in accordance with Jewish rites." *A History of the Jews in England* (London, 1908), p. 171. This speculation is far-fetched. Some kind of Jewish rites may have taken place at the embassy, but they could not have taken place under the masquerade of a Catholic mass, since this would have involved the connivance of devout English and alien Catholics. At certain times during the years 1640–1660 the mass at the Portuguese embassy was the only regularly scheduled public Catholic service held in London, and at such times many of the faithful would have attended.
46. The embassy gave its name to the street now called Portugal Street—see Prestage, *Chapters,* p. 138.
47. Arq. Dist. Évora, Codex CVI/2–8, fols. 74, 83; Richard Challoner, *Memoirs of Missionary Priests* (London, 1924), pp. 460–461.
48. Arq. Dist. Évora, Codex CVI/2–8, fols. 82–83, 93, 99–100, 113–14, 134, 210; Prestage, *Macedo,* p. 44.
49. Arq. Dist. Évora, Codex CVI/2–8, fols. 120–121; Prestage, *Macedo,* p. 51.
50. Arq. Dist. Évora, Codex CVI/2–8, fols. 125–126, 135.
51. PRO, S.P. 89/4, fol. 55; Prestage, *Macedo,* pp. 24–25; HMC, *Manuscripts of the Duke of Portland,* 1 (London, 1891): 202.
52. Arq. Dist. Évora, Codex CVI/2–8, fol. 195; Prestage, *Macedo,* pp. 24–26; PRO, S.P. 89/4, fols. 60–61.
53. *El Príncipe vendido* (Barcelona, 1643); Prestage, *Macedo,* p. 26. After nine years as a prisoner, the Infante Duarte died in a castle at Milan on 3 September 1649 at the age of forty-four. Ajuda 50-V-37, doc. 29.

54. Ajuda 51-II-18, fols. 15–16.
55. Arq. Dist. Évora, Codex CVI/2-8, fol. 251.
56. BM, Add. MSS. 4155, fols. 250–251.
57. PRO, S.P. 89/4, fols. 62, 66.
58. Prestage, *Chapters*, p. 140.
59. Ibid., p. 139; Prestage, *Macedo*, pp. 78–79; Arq. Dist. Évora, Codex CVI/2–8, fols. 228–229, 252–254.
60. *Cartas de El-Rei D. João IV ao Conde da Vidigueira*, 2 vols. (Lisbon, 1940–1942), 2:279–280.
61. *Cartas de El-Rei D. João IV para diversas autoridades do Reino* (Lisbon, 1940), p. 276. (Cited hereafter as *Cartas de D. João IV;* the collection in the preceding note, *Cartas de D. João IV ao Conde da Vidigueira,* will not be cited again.)

Chapter 2

1. BM, Add. MSS. 19399, fols. 142, 144–147; Michael Geddes, *Several Tracts against Popery* (London, 1715), pp. 374–382.
2. These biographical details emerged in the course of an inquiry by the judges of the Court of Admiralty into the conduct of English Lisbon merchants during the Anglo-Portuguese crisis of 1650. PRO, S.P. 89/4, fols. 88–95.
3. Richard Flecknoe, *A True and Faithful Account of What Was Observed in Ten Years Travels* (London, 1665), pp. 50–52, 56.
4. CU *cons.* 18 May 1649, AHU, Bahia, Caixa V (Bancroft m/f, Caixa VI, frames 232–233); AHU, Codex 278, fols. 253–254, Codex 92, fol. 109.
5. PRO, S.P. 89/4, fols. 93–94.
6. Ibid., fol. 95.
7. CU *cons.* 16 September and 16 October 1647, AHU, São Tomé, Caixa I.
8. Bahia sequestrations, September 1650, AHU, Bahia, Caixa V (Bancroft m/f, Caixa VI, frames 282–302).
9. *Cal. S.P. 1661–1662* (London, 1861), p. 456.
10. "The Complaints of the English Merchants Resident in the Kingdom of Portugall," PRO, S.P. 89/5; *Heathcote MSS.* (Norwich, 1899), pp. 68–69, 79.
11. J. C. Whitebrook, *Edward & John Bushell, Puritans and Merchants* (London, 1915), genealogical table between pp. 9 and 10.
12. At this rate John Bushell made a profit of about 10 percent; *Cal. S.P. 1650* (London, 1876), pp. 128–129.
13. "Declaration of Prince Rupert to the Kingdom of Portugal," *Cal. S.P. 1650,* pp. 115–116.
14. This was a larger quantity than may be apparent at first glance. At twenty *arrobas* per chest, the 181 chests would have come to 117,179 pounds (53, 152 kilograms), or fifty-three metric tons. That much sugar, retailing at a price of eighteen pence per pound, would have fetched £8,788 on the London market.
15. Bahia sequestrations, September 1650, AHU, Bahia, Caixa V (Bancroft m/f, Caixa VI, frames 286–288, 290–291).
16. The word *Portugal* (usually spelled *Portugall*) served as both noun and adjective in the mid-seventeenth century, had the convenient plural form *Portugals,* and was used ten times as often in 1650 as the then new and literary-sounding word *Portuguese.* There was no word for the language, which was referred to as

"the Portugal tongue" (or by some other circumlocution)—but a scribe at the Prerogative Court of Canterbury noted, ingeniously, that a will had been translated "out of the Portingalltory"! *Index to Wills,* vol. 7 (London, 1925), p. 296.

17. John Thurloe, *State Papers,* 7 vols. (London, 1742), 1:155.
18. CU *cons.* 3 October 1653, AHU, Bahia, Caixa VI; AHU, Codex 45, fol. 166.
19. *Cal. S.P. 1658–1659* (London, 1885), p. 242.
20. Biblioteca Nacional de Lisboa, Chancelaria de D. Afonso VI, livro 24, fol. 80.
21. PRO, S.P. 89/5.
22. *Report on the Manuscripts of F. W. Leyborne-Popham* (Norwich, 1899), p. 167.
23. Edward Bushell was the most influential member of a jury that refused to convict William Penn and William Mead of the crime of preaching in the street. The members of the jury were arrested and fined and subjected to heavy pressure from the Lord Mayor and aldermen of London, but they held firm. The Court of Common Pleas, upon appeal, ruled in favor of the jury and established, for all time, the principle of the independence of the jury. Whitebrook, pp. 9–10.
24. Whitebrook, p. 8; *Original Lists of Persons of Quality Who Went from Great Britain to the American Plantations 1600–1700* (New York, 1874), p. 439.
25. BM, Add. MSS. 35099, fol. 165.
26. Virgínia Rau, "Subsídios para o estudo do movimento dos portos de Faro e Lisboa durante o século XVII," *Anais da Academia Portuguesa de História,* series 2, vol. 5 (Lisbon, 1954), p. 225.
27. Thurloe, 6:582–583.
28. Ajuda 44-XIV-1, doc. 29.
29. For a full account of the Portuguese islands and their merchants, see T. Bentley Duncan, *Atlantic Islands* (Chicago, 1972).
30. Charles Sellers, *Oporto Old and New* (London, 1899), pp. 1–4; André L. Simon, *History of the Wine Trade in England,* vol. 3 (London, 1909), pp. 351–354; A. D. Francis, *The Wine Trade* (London, 1972), pp. 99–139; H. E. S. Fisher, *The Portugal Trade: A Study of Anglo-Portuguese Commerce, 1700–1770* (London, 1971).
31. For an angry catalog of English grievances against the Dutch, see *The Advocate, or a Narrative of the State and Condition of Things between the English and Dutch Nation, in Relation to Trade* (London, 1652); this, with a companion piece titled *Free Ports,* was reprinted in R. W. K. Hinton, *Eastland Trade* (Cambridge, 1959), pp. 203–218, briefly discussed (pp. 89–94), and the author identified as Benjamin Worsley.
32. Tôrre do Tombo, "Corpo Cronológico," Parte III, Maço 30, doc. 103. The fact that Dutch-Iberian trade flourished even during the most bitter phases of the Dutch-Spanish struggle of 1572–1648 can be documented; for the underlying explanation, see Boxer, *Dutch Seaborne Empire 1600–1800* (New York, 1965), pp. 21–22.
33. For a thorough analysis of the Dutch situation, see the fine book by Charles Wilson, *Profit and Power: A Study of England and the Dutch Wars* (London, 1957).
34. Wilson, p. 45. Wilson says that the Dutch had probably five or six times as many ships as the English (p. 46), that in 1650 they outnumbered the English in the Baltic by 15 to 1 (p. 42), and that in 1648 of thirty-one ships trading to Virginia, twelve were Dutch (p. 44).
35. Officers of the Inquisition came aboard every foreign ship to search for heretical or prohibited books and prevent their import into the country; records of these

visits were kept and are known as the "Livros para as visitas das naus" (housed in the Tôrre do Tombo, as part of the Inquisition archives). Statistical information from them has been abstracted by Virgínia Rau in her valuable study "Movimento dos Portos de Faro e Lisbôa" (see note 26). All the figures cited by me are derived from this work.

36. By *British* ships are meant all ships owned by subjects of the king of England, including Scottish, Irish, New England, Virginian, and British West Indian owners.
37. Figures based on Rau, "Movimento dos Portos," *Anais,* 5:220.
38. Ibid., 5:224.
39. Tôrre do Tombo, Arquivo da Alfândega do Funchal, Codices 1233, 1234, 1503, 1506, and 1507.
40. Arq. Dist. Ponta Delgada, "Livros da Alfândega de Ponta Delgada," arranged and numbered by their year-dates.
41. For the vicissitudes of the English trade in the Azores, see Duncan, *Atlantic Islands,* chap. 5.
42. Thomas Willsford, *Scales of Commerce and Trade* (London, 1660), pp. 44–47.
43. *Records Relating to the Society of Merchant Adventurers of Bristol in the Seventeenth Century* (Bristol, 1952), pp. 172–173.
44. A *flyboat,* in the parlance of seventeenth-century English seamen, or *flute,* was an inexpensively built, easily handled, lightly manned, almost unarmed merchantman, first designed and constructed by the Dutch. The flyboat had to be escorted by warships in time of danger but was ideal for bulk cargoes, and her cheapness helped to make the Dutch supreme in maritime commerce. See Ralph Davis, *The Rise of the English Shipping Industry* (Newton Abbot, Devon, 1962), pp. 47–54.
45. Tôrre do Tombo, Arquivo da Alfândega do Funchal, Codex 1233, fols. 77–84.
46. *Bristol Deposition Books,* vol. 2 (Bristol, 1948), pp. 19–20, 22–23.
47. Bahia sequestration papers, AHU, Bahia, Caixa V (Bancroft m/f, Caixa VI, frames 286–291).
48. CU *cons.* 21 January 1655, AHU, Bahia, Caixa VI (Bancroft m/f, Caixa VII, frame 63); AHU, Codex 45, fols. 283–284; Codex 46, fol. 95; Codex 92, fols. 263, 311.
49. *Collecção chronológica da legislação portugueza 1603–1612* (Lisbon, 1854), pp. 108–109.
50. AHU, Codex 15, fols. 127–128. During the years 1649–1658, the AHU papers show that foreign merchants received over forty licenses to send foreign ships to the colonies. To these must be added the unknown number of licenses issued by the Conselho da Fazenda (whose records have mostly been lost), as well as the foreign ships freighted by the Brazil Company.
51. Tôrre do Tombo, Arquivo da Alfândega do Funchal, Codex 1146, fol. 40.
52. AHU, Codex 92, fols. 131–132.
53. Ibid., fols. 298–323.
54. See Duncan, *Atlantic Islands,* pp. 61, 65–68.
55. Tôrre do Tombo, Arquivo da Alfândega do Funchal, Codex 1232, fol. 22.
56. Petition by Thomas Maynard, read on 17 May 1658, Ajuda 51-V-17, doc. 71.
57. Shillington and Chapman, p. 189. The cumbersome system of consular fees was not abolished until the reign of George IV, in an act passed on 5 July 1825: A. R. Walford (ed.), *British Factory in Lisbon* (Lisbon, 1940), p. 122.
58. Shillington and Chapman, pp. 326–29; *British Factory in Lisbon,* pp. 25–26; *Collecção chronológica da legislaçáo portugueza 1648–1656* (Lisbon, 1856),

p. 65; *Calendar of the Manuscripts of the Marquess of Ormonde, New Series,* vol. 1 (London, 1902), p. 258.

59. HMC, *Fifth Report* (London, 1876), p. 22.
60. *Cal. S.P., Venetian Series,* vol. 30 (London, 1939), pp. 266–267; PRO, S.P. 89/4, fols. 161–167.

Chapter 3

1. For technical information on cane sugar, see Noël Deerr, *Cane Sugar,* 2d ed. (London, 1921), and Andrew Van Hook, *Sugar: Its Production, Technology, and Uses* (New York, 1949).
2. Adriaen van der Dussen, *Relatório sôbre as capitanias conquistadas no Brasil pelos holandeses, 1639,* trans. José António Gonsalves de Melo Neto (Rio de Janeiro, 1947), pp. 94–96.
3. Edmund Oskar von Lippmann, *História do açúcar,* 2 vols. (Rio de Janeiro, 1941–1942), 2:16—this is Rodolfo Coutinho's annotated translation of *Geschichte des Zuckers,* 2d ed. (Leipzig, 1929).
4. Richard Ligon, *A True and Exact History of the Island of Barbadoes,* 2d ed. (London, 1673), p. 92.
5. An *arroba* weighed thirty-two Portuguese pounds, or 14.686 kilograms.
6. Dussen, p. 95.
7. *Engenho Sergipe do Conde: Livro de contas 1622–1653* (Rio de Janeiro, 1956), pp. 286–292.
8. Ibid., p. 457.
9. "Briefe Considerations Touching the Trade that May Bee Expected Hereafter between England and Portugall," PRO, S.P. 89/4, fol. 68.
10. *Cal. S.P., Venetian Series,* 30:242.
11. James Hart, *Klinike, or the Diet of the Diseased* (London, 1633), p. 96.
12. Ibid., p. 124.
13. Ibid., p. 97.
14. PRO, S.P. 89/4, fol. 68.
15. *Acts and Ordinances of the Interregnum,* 2:1211.
16. Herbert I. Bloom, *Economic Activities of the Jews of Amsterdam in the Seventeenth and Eighteenth Centuries* (Williamsport, PA, 1937), pp. 36–37; J. J. Reesse, *De Suikerhandel van Amsterdam van het Begin der 17e Eeuw tot 1813* (Haarlem, 1908), p. 32.
17. See the Bristol figures (December 1670 to December 1671) for white sugar imports in *Merchants in Seventeenth-Century Bristol,* p. 295.
18. Ralph Davis, "English Foreign Trade 1660–1700," *Economic History Review,* 2d series, vol. 8 (1954–1955), pp. 150–166.
19. Afonso d'Escragnolle Taunay, "Na Bahia Colonial: 1610–1764," *Revista do Instituto Histórico e Geográfico do Brasil,* vol. 90 (1921), pp. 248–254.
20. Azevedo, *Épocas de Portugal económico* (Lisbon, 1929), p. 271. Azevedo reckoned on the basis of thirty-five *arrobas* per *caixa,* which is rather high; a safer ratio of 20 *arrobas* per caixa would yield a total of 420,000 *arrobas,* which, at 2$000 réis per *arroba* (instead of Azevedo's odd 2$041 per *arroba*) would amount to 840:000$000 (£566,800), which is still a large sum.
21. Dussen, pp. 31–64, 71–80.

22. Boxer, *Salvador de Sá and the Struggle for Brazil and Angola 1602–1686* (London, 1952), p. 180.
23. *Manuscritos do Arquivo da Casa de Cadaval,* 2 vols. (Coimbra, 1955–1958), 1:92.
24. Francisco de Brito Freire, *Relação da viagem que fez ao Estado do Brazil a armada da Cõpanhia, anno 1655* (Lisbon, 1657), p. 252. The 53,221 chests, at twenty *arrobas* per chest, would have come to 1,064,420 *arrobas* (15,632 metric tons), with a value, at 2$000 réis *per arroba,* of 2,128:840$000 (a little over 1 million in sterling).
25. Tôrre do Tombo, Arquivo da Alfândega do Funchal, Codex 40.
26. *Engenho Sergipe do Conde,* pp. 286–290.
27. Bahia sequestration papers, AHU, Bahia, Caixa V (Bancroft m/f, Caixa VI, frames 283–291).
28. By the 1670s and later, the *caixas* became much larger; some *caixas* of white sugar, by the end of the century, contained as much as thirty-five *arrobas.*
29. *Engenho Sergipe do Conde,* p. xi.
30. Attached to letter from the governor of Brazil to John IV; Bahia, 15 June 1655; AHU, Bahia, Caixa VI.
31. Paper dated 29 November 1655, AHU, Bahia, Caixa VI.
32. Noël Deerr, *History of Sugar,* 2 vols. (London, 1949–1950), 2:528.
33. A. H. Taylor, "Carrack into Galleon," *Mariner's Mirror* 36 (1950): 144.
34. Certificate dated Lisbon, 23 December 1652; AHU, Pernambuco, Caixa IV (Bancroft m/f, Caixa III-A, frames 110–111).
35. Thomas Fuller, *History of the Worthies of England,* 3 vols. (London, 1840), 2:118.
36. L. G. Carr Laughton, "Gunnery, Frigates, and the Line of Battle," *Mariner's Mirror* 14 (1928): 339–363.
37. In 1650, John IV ordered two frigates of between four and five hundred tons to be built at the works of the Ribeira do Douro in Oporto, for service in the Lisbon-Madeira trade. *Cartas de D. João IV,* p. 427.
38. Facts taken from the Lisbon newssheet *Mercurio Portuguez,* issues of December 1663; March, April, June, July, and October 1664; and September 1665.
39. *Mercurio Portuguez,* March and May 1665.
40. Jaime Cortesão, "Economia da Restauração," *Congresso do Mundo Português,* 7:683.
41. These figures, although taken from the manuscript itself, are not scrupulously accurate, because the document was badly drafted and contains numerous duplications and errors. CU *cons.* 2 May 1651, AHU, Bahia, Caixa IV (Bancroft m/f, Caixa I-A, Roll 1, frames 526–535). Boxer reproduced the list and attempted to clarify its difficulties in an appendix to his *Dutch in Brazil* (Oxford, 1957).
42. *Legislação antiga,* 1:130-41.
43. *Manuscritos de Cadaval,* 1:43–44.
44. *Alvarás* of 15 March 1648 and 25 January 1649, *Collecção chronológica 1648–1656,* pp. 3, 25–26.
45. W. Chapman, *Topographical Chart of the Entrance of the River Tagus* (London, 1810).
46. *Light of Navigation* (Amsterdam, 1612), pp. 64–75.
47. Peniche, with its quite well sheltered deep-water harbor, was the only exception.
48. The strained relations between the king and the Inquisition are discussed in António Baião, *El-Rei D. João IV e a Inquisição* (Lisbon, 1942).

49. Ajuda 49-IV-20, doc. 4. See Boxer, "Padre Antonio Vieira and the Institution of the Brazil Company in 1649," *Hispanic American Historical Review* 29 (1949): 474–497.
50. Ajuda 49-IV-20, doc. 5. There is a manuscript copy in BM, Add. MSS. 20951, fols. 15–18.
51. Ajuda 49-IV-20, doc. 6. There is a manuscript copy in BM, Add. MSS. 20951, fols. 19–24.
52. AHU, Codex 14, fol. 134.
53. *Manuscritos de Cadaval,* 1:71–73, 82–83.
54. João Lúcio de Azevedo, *História de António Vieira,* 2 vols. (Lisbon, 1918–1920), 1:136, 161–163. Silva was accused not of heresy but of having violated the secrets of the Inquisition in having talked about another person's case, revealing confidential details. The king was unable to secure Silva's release, and he was put to the torture on 23 November 1652, penanced at an *auto* held on 1 December 1652, and sentenced to a five-year exile in Brazil. At this point the king intervened and issued a royal pardon. Silva and his sons retained the high confidence of the royal family. He eventually went to London, as manager of the monies in Queen Catherine's dowry, and then to Antwerp, where he died circa 1688. See Antônio Baião, *Episódios dramáticos da Inquisição Portuguesa,* 2d ed., 3 vols. (Lisbon, 1936–1953), 2:299–401.
55. Lúcio de Azevedo, *Vieira,* 1:161.
56. Ajuda 49-IV-20, doc. 10; *Alvará de 6 de Fevereiro de 1649,* printed in *Collecção chronológica 1648–1656,* pp. 27–29.
57. Ajuda 49-IV-14, doc. 59.
58. Ajuda 49-IV-20, doc. 15.
59. A manuscript copy of the *alvará* of 8 March 1649, "Instituição da Companhia Geral para o Estado do Brazil," is in Ajuda 49-IV-20, doc. 12. The printed version, *Instituiçam da Companhia Geral para o Estado do Brazil* (Lisbon, 1649), can be found in Ajuda 51-V-10, doc. 4; and in BM, Add. MSS. 20951, fols. 36–47; or reprinted in *Collecção chronológica 1648–1656,* pp. 31–40.
60. Ajuda 49-IV-20, doc. 13.
61. Printed broadsheet dated "Lisbon, 16 March 1649," without title or publisher, in Ajuda 44-XIII-42, doc. 34.
62. As recorded in forty pages of manuscripts in Ajuda, 49-IV-20, doc. 16.
63. Dom Francisco de Castro to Innocent X; Lisbon, 17 October 1649; Ajuda 49-IV-20, doc. 18.
64. Ajuda 49-IV-20, doc. 19 (Latin text) and doc. 69 (Portuguese translation).
65. Ajuda 49-IV-20, docs. 23, 25–27.
66. *Conselho Geral da Inquisição, consulta* of 10 October 1654, Ajuda 49-IV-20, doc. 47.
67. Évora inquisitors to John IV; 31 October 1654; Ajuda 49-IV-20, doc. 48.
68. Ajuda 49-IV-20, doc. 49.
69. Ibid., doc. 53.
70. Ibid., doc. 62.
71. Ibid., doc. 68.
72. *Alvará de 2 de Fevereiro de 1657:* MS. copy in Ajuda 49-IV-20, doc. 71; and printed copy in BM, Add. MSS. 20951, fols. 136–137.
73. Ajuda 44-XIII-42, doc. 34, a printed one-page announcement, without a title, beginning "Os Deputados da Ivnta da Companhia Geral do Estado do Brasil. . . ."

74. Ajuda 44-XIII-42, doc. 34.
75. Lúcio de Azevedo, *Vieira,* 1:162. Azevedo cited a letter dated twenty-four years after the event: Fr. Manuel Fernandes to Prince Pedro the Regent, 15 June 1673, Tôrre do Tombo, Papéis dos Jesuitas, Caixa I, doc. 32. See also Gustavo de Freitas, "A Companhia Geral do Comércio do Brasil 1649–1720," *Revista de História,* vol. 3 (São Paulo, 1951), pp. 87–88—the only full-length account of the Brazil Company, but covering only the period 1649–1660 in detail.
76. AHU, Codex 92, fols. 121–123; Codex 278, fols. 253–254; CU *cons.* 18 May 1649, AHU, Bahia, Caixa IV (Bancroft m/f, Caixa VI, frames 232–233).
77. AHU, Codex 14, fol. 157.
78. AHU, Codex 92, fol. 169.
79. Luisa da Fonseca, "O Brasil e os estrangeiros: Mercadores," *International Colloquium on Luso-Brazilian Studies: Proceedings, 1950* (Nashville, 1953), pp. 274–275.
80. Boxer, "English Shipping," *Mariner's Mirror,* 37:204.
81. Letter attached to CU *cons.* 8 July 1649, AHU, Pernambuco, Caixa III (Bancroft m/f, Caixa I, reel i, frames 682–683).
82. AHU, Codex 92, fols. 121–123; Codex 278, fols. 253–254; CU *cons.* 23 April 1649, AHU, Maranhão, Caixa II.
83. The *Sara,* which made two journeys to Brazil in 1649, has been counted twice.
84. Boxer, *Dutch in Brazil,* pp. 223–228; "Relaçam dos sucessos da Armada," *Annaes da Bibliotheca Nacional do Rio de Janeiro,* 20:158–166 (a reprint of an account published in Lisbon in 1650 and attributed to Dom Francisco Manuel de Melo); Freitas, "Companhia Geral," *Revista de História,* 3:93.
85. Ajuda 52-X-2, doc. 85; Freitas, "Companhia Geral," *Revista de História,* 3:328; Bahia sequestration papers, AHU, Bahia, Caixa IV (Bancroft m/f, Caixa VI, frames 291–302).
86. See Castelo Melhor's correspondence in "Correspondência dos Governadores Geraes, 1648–1672," *Documentos Históricos* (Rio de Janeiro, 1928): 3:31, 37–39; 4:461–462, 465–466.

Chapter 4

1. R. C. Anderson, "Royalists at Sea in 1648," *Mariner's Mirror* 9 (1923): 35–38—the first of a series of articles on the royalist fleet, extending from 1923 to 1935 and appearing in vols. 9, 14, 17, and 21 of *Mariner's Mirror.* The third article, "Royalists at Sea in 1650," 17 (1931): 135–168, has the best account of Rupert in Lisbon currently available. Also good is John R. Powell's summary in Robert Blake, *Letters* (London, 1937), pp. 8–96. See also Samuel R. Gardiner, *History of the Commonwealth and Protectorate,* vol. 1 (London, 1894), pp. 331–337, which includes a map of the mouth of the Tagus; and his edition of "Prince Rupert at Lisbon," *Camden Miscellany,* vol. 10 (London, 1902), containing documents from BM, Add. MSS. 35251. Rupert's biographer, Eliot Warburton (*Memoirs of Prince Rupert,* 3 vols., London, 1849), is inadequate for the Lisbon episode (3:299–313) but is better on Rupert's later voyages. The biography includes many documents reproduced verbatim. The only good biography of Blake is by J. R. Powell, *Robert Blake, General-at-Sea* (London, 1972). There are useful details about the movements of Portuguese ships in

Boxer, "Blake and the Brazil Fleets in 1650," *Mariner's Mirror* 36 (1950): 212–228.

2. Prince Rupert (1619–1682), a son of Elizabeth Stuart (daughter of James I) and of the unfortunate Frederick, Elector of the Palatinate, "Winter King" of Bohemia. While a young man Rupert offered his sword to his uncle Charles I and became a distinguished cavalry commander. He served the royalists at sea for five years (1648–1653) and, after the Restoration, was one of Charles II's admirals in the naval wars against the Dutch.
3. Blake, pp. 8–11, 47, 71–72; Oliver Cromwell, *Writings and Speeches,* 4 vols. (Cambridge, MA, 1937–1947), 2:155; Charles H. Firth, "Sailors of the Civil War," *Mariner's Mirror* 12 (1926): 248.
4. BM, Add. MSS. 35251, fol. 30.
5. Ibid.
6. *Cartas de D. João IV,* p. 304.
7. *Constant Reformation* (forty-six guns), flagship with Prince Rupert as admiral; *Convertine* (forty guns), with Prince Maurice, Rupert's brother, as vice admiral; *Swallow* (thirty-six), with Sir John Mennes as rear admiral; and the *Blackamoor Lady, Mary, Scott,* and *Black Knight.* Blake, pp. 10–11.
8. BM, Add. MSS. 35251, fols. 26, 30; Anderson, "Royalists," *Mariner's Mirror,* 17:135.
9. AHU, Codex 45, fol. 155.
10. BM, Add. MSS. 35251, fols. 26–29.
11. Warburton, 3:299–301—where Oeiras is called Weyrs and the tower of Belém called the fort of Belleisle.
12. BM, Add. MSS. 35251, fols. 26–29.
13. The "Rock of Lisbon" is the sailor's chief navigation mark near the mouth of the Tagus, but it is not a "rock" and is not near Lisbon. It is a promontory, the Cabo da Roca, extending westward from the high and rugged Sintra mountains, and visible far out to sea.
14. Thurloe, 1:132; BM, Add. MSS. 35251, fol. 32.
15. Thurloe, 1:131; BM, Add. MSS. 35251, fol. 33; Arq. Dist. Évora, Codex CV/1-17, fol. 244.
16. BM, Add. MSS. 35251, fols. 26–29.
17. Thurloe, 1:136; BM, Add. MSS. 35251, fol. 36; Rymer, *Foedera,* 20:577.
18. Warburton, 3:301.
19. Thurloe, 1:138–139; BM. Add. MSS. 35251, fol. 34.
20. Blake, p. 11; *Cal. S.P. 1649–1650* (London, 1875), pp. 435, 482.
21. *Commons Journal,* 6:353.
22. Thurloe, 1:134–136.
23. Milton, *Works,* vol. 13 (New York, 1937), pp. 14–15, 22–25. Correspondence between England and other countries was conducted in Latin. The poet John Milton, the finest English Latinist of his day, served as secretary for Latin and foreign languages from 1649 to 1659 and drafted many of the Latin letters sent to Portugal.
24. John Hasclock, *Letter from Lysbone* (London, 1650), p. 4; Thurloe, 1:138; Blake, p. 11.
25. *Portland MSS.,* 1:521–522.
26. *Cartas de D. João IV,* pp. 355–356.
27. Capt. Charles Thorowgood's letter, 31 March/10 April 1650, in *Prince Ruperts Declaration to the King of Portugall* (London, 1650), pp. 10–12. There is a Portuguese translation in Ajuda 50-V-36, doc. 200.

28. Latin text in *Portland MSS.*, 1:519; English text in Blake, pp. 54–55.
29. AHU, Codex 92, fol. 144; *Ruperts Declaration,* pp. 10–12.
30. *Ruperts Declaration,* pp. 10–11.
31. Parts of this fort seemed to have been made of wood, but it is unlikely that the base was anything but stone, built on the supporting rocks. In the sixteenth century it was a triangular fort; in the eighteenth century it was a round stone fortress with two tiers of guns and a lighthouse.
32. The forts of Lisbon during the reign of John IV and the problems of defending the Tagus are discussed in Ajuda 50-V-36, docs. 135, 138, 141 (which has a drawing of the Tagus defenses), 145, and 173; BM, Sloane MSS. 3665, fols. 4–5, contains an excellent drawing and map of the entrance to the Tagus circa 1688–1690 (though the map is all wrong for everything upriver beyond Belém). The *Topographical Chart of the Entrance of the River Tagus* (London, 1810), surveyed in 1806 by W. Chapman of the Royal Navy, gives a precise idea of forts, shoals, and distances before the use of dredging and of efficient artillery. There is additional information in Mário de Sampaio Ribeiro, "A Tôrre e a Fortaleza de Belém," *Anais da Academia Portuguesa de História,* series 2, vol. 5 (Lisbon, 1954), pp. 143–195.
33. For guns and gunnery between 1600 and 1750, see Leblond, *Treatise of Artillery* (London, 1746); Robert Norton, *Of the Art of Great Artillery* (London, 1624); and Robert Norton, *The Gunner: Shewing the Whole Practise of Artillerie* (London, 1628).
34. Ajuda 50-V-36, doc. 173.
35. *Ruperts Declaration,* pp. 10–12; Hasclock, p. 4; Blake, pp. 56–58, 78–84.
36. BM, Add. MSS. 35251, fols. 26–29.
37. *Ruperts Declaration,* also printed in *Cal. S.P. 1650,* pp. 115–116.
38. Richard Ell was captain of the *Prosperous* and Peter Tatam captain of the *Hannibal*—two English merchantmen in Lisbon that were freighted by the Brazil Company for a voyage to Brazil.
39. Printed in *Ruperts Declaration,* pp. 6–9, MS. copy in BM, Add. MSS. 35251, fols. 37–38.
40. Papers attached to CU *cons.* 21 January 1651, AHU, Bahia, Caixa V (Bancroft m/f, Caixa VI, frames 304–313).
41. Blake, pp. 56–58; *Ruperts Declaration,* pp. 10–12.
42. *Cartas de D. João IV,* p. 356.
43. Blake, pp. 76–78.
44. Warburton, 3:302.
45. Blake, pp. 56–58; Hasclock, p. 5.
46. Blake, pp. 74–76; *Ruperts Declaration,* pp. 10–12.
47. Blake, pp. 56–58.
48. *Portland MSS.*, 1:522–523.
49. *Cal. S.P. 1650,* p. 97.
50. Thurloe, 1:141.
51. Ibid., pp. 139–140.
52. BM, Add. MSS. 35251, fols. 26–29.
53. BM, Add. MSS. 20902, fol. 153; Alfredo Botelho de Sousa, *Subsídios para a história das guerras da Restauração,* 2 vols. (Lisbon, 1940), 1:254.
54. BM, Add. MSS. 18982, fols. 206–209; Thurloe, 1:141–142, 145–146; *A Perfect Diurnall* (London), issue for 3 June–10 June 1650.
55. Ajuda 50-V-36, doc. 201. My text is my translation of a Portuguese translation of Rupert's original letter, and therefore my English may vary somewhat from the English of the original.

56. Ajuda 50-V-36, doc. 202.
57. Thurloe, 1:147.
58. *A Perfect Diurnall,* 3–10 June 1650; Thurloe, 1:145–146; Warburton, 3:304–305; Anderson, "Royalists," *Mariner's Mirror,* 17:142.
59. Thurloe, 1:156. The galleon ("carrack" in the English accounts) was the Indian-built *Santo António de Mazagão* under the command of António da Costa de Lemos, and the value of her cargo was probably closer to £50,000 than to £250,000, for she mounted only eighteen guns and was probably a three-decker of not more than 500 tons. CU *cons.* 22 November 1650, AHU, India, Caixa XXI; Boxer, "Blake," *Mariner's Mirror,* 36:218.
60. Ajuda 50-V-36, doc. 205.
61. Ibid., doc. 204.
62. Ibid., doc. 203.
63. Boxer, "Blake," *Mariner's Mirror,* 36:219.
64. Manuel Luís, *Theodosius Lusitanus* (Évora, 1680), chaps. 22–23.
65. BM, Add. MSS. 20936, fol. 10; Arq. Dist. Évora, Codex CV/1–17, fol. 244.
66. Arq. Dist. Angra, "Fenix Angrense" codex, section on year 1665, fol. 225. António Luís de Meneses (d. 1675), third Count of Cantanhede and first Marquis of Marialva, was president of the Treasury Council and one of the most important Portuguese ministers.
67. Eduardo Freire de Oliveira, *Elementos para a história do Município de Lisboa,* vol. 5 (Lisbon, 1899), pp. 200–207.
68. Thurloe, 1:141–142.
69. PRO, S.P. 89/4, fols. 88–95.
70. Ibid., fol. 92.
71. *Heathcote MSS.,* p. 79.
72. PRO, S.P. 89/4, fols. 92, 95.
73. Ibid., fols. 89–94; Boxer, "Blake," *Mariner's Mirror,* 36:221.
74. Edward Popham's diary, "Narrative of a Voyage," in *Report on the Manuscripts of F.W. Leyborne-Popham,* pp. 61–64. The diary runs from 16/26 April 1650 to 22 July/1 August 1650 and breaks off in the middle, stopping, unfortunately, at a vital point.
75. Thurloe, 1:142–143; *Cal. S.P. 1650,* pp. 102–103.
76. Thurloe, 1:144–145; *Cal. S.P. 1650,* pp. 104, 122–123.
77. *Leyborne-Popham MSS.,* pp. 64–65; Blake, p. 13.
78. Warburton, 3:306.
79. PRO, S.P. 89,/4, fols. 72–73, 88; AHU, Codex 92, fol. 144.
80. *Leyborne-Popham MSS.,* p. 65.
81. *Cartas de D. João IV,* p. 372.
82. PRO, S.P. 89/4, fols. 93–94, 100.
83. *Leyborne-Popham MSS.,* p. 66.
84. *Collecção chronológica 1648–1656,* p. 62.
85. *Cartas de D. João IV,* pp. 373–377.
86. Ajuda 51-VI-22, fol. 225.
87. Ibid., fol. 245.
88. *Leyborne-Popham MSS.,* p. 66.
89. Ibid.
90. *Cartas de D. João IV,* p. 378.
91. *Leyborne-Popham MSS.,* pp. 66–67.
92. *Cal. S.P. 1650,* p. 200.

93. *Leyborne-Popham MSS.*, p. 67; Blake, p. 14; *A Perfect Diurnall,* 1–8 July 1650.
94. *Cartas de D. João IV,* p. 381.
95. *A Perfect Diurnall,* 19–26 August 1650.
96. *Leyborne-Popham MSS.*, p. 67.
97. Ibid., pp. 67–68.
98. Ibid., pp. 68–69.
99. *Collecção chronológica 1648–1656,* p. 64.
100. Botelho de Sousa, *Guerras da Restauração,* 1:70; Arq. Dist. Évora, Codex CV/1–17, fol. 245. The Lisbon squadron of 1650 was an improvised force; many units of the Armada Real, in an unusual move, had been sent to Brazil in 1649 and had not returned.
101. Botelho de Sousa, 1:70; Anderson, "Royalists," *Mariner's Mirror,* 17:145, 157; Boxer, "Blake," *Mariner's Mirror,* 36:221; Blake, pp. 14, 60–63.
102. *Leyborne-Popham MSS.*, p. 71. The MS. of Popham's diary breaks off at this point.
103. Portuguese and English sources do not record the names of the Frenchmen or of their ships. The standard French naval histories do not mention the Lisbon episode.
104. Arq. Dist. Évora, Codex CV/1–17, fol. 245.
105. Ibid.
106. BM, Add. MSS. 20846, fol. 52.
107. Attack, not escape, seems to have been what Rupert had in mind, for he probably hoped to bring about a general engagement between the Portuguese and the parliamentary fleets. The *Constant Reformation* had Portuguese Catholic chaplains and three companies of Portuguese infantry aboard her (Arq. Dist. Évora, Codex CV/1–17, fol. 244), and it is unlikely that Rupert intended to take all these Portuguese to the Mediterranean with him, if an immediate escape had indeed been his aim.
108. Details in Blake, pp. 14, 60–63; Anderson, "Royalists," *Mariner's Mirror,* 17:145–150; *Severall Proceedings in Parliament,* 29 August–5 September 1650; Warburton's version (3:308–310) is rather muddled.
109. BM, Add. MSS. 20846, fol. 52.
110. The "weather gauge" is the wind advantage that a ship possesses over any ship downwind from her. By abandoning the weather gauge Blake offered Rupert the advantage of maneuver and the opportunity to choose the time, place, and position of attack.
111. *Severall Proceedings in Parliament,* 29 August–5 September 1650.
112. "Demaziadamente inclinados a continuar na explendida hospedagem da grandeza Real." Arq. Dist. Évora, Codex CV/1–17, fol. 246.
113. *Commons Journal,* 6:437; Thurloe, 1:155–156.
114. *Cal. S.P. 1650,* p. 405; Whitebrook, p. 7.
115. *Cartas de D. João IV,* pp. 404–406, 410–412; Boxer, "Blake," *Mariner's Mirror,* 36:221; Ajuda 51-V-13, fol. 279.
116. Blake, p. 15; PRO, S.P. 89/4, fols. 119–120.
117. *Severall Proceedings in Parliament,* 26 September–3 October 1650; CU *cons.* 24 November 1650, AHU, Índia, Caixa XXI; Boxer, "Blake," *Mariner's Mirror,* 36:222.
118. Blake, p. 15.
119. Blake, pp. 63–65. Brito Freire said that Rupert's ship was repaired at Cascais.
120. *Cartas de D. João IV,* pp. 413–415.

121. AHU, Bahia, Caixa V (Bancroft m/f, Caixa VI, frames 279–280).
122. Papers attached to CU *cons.* 21 January 1651, AHU, Bahia, Caixa V (Bancroft m/f, Caixa VI, frames 278–279); Biblioteca Nacional (Rio de Janeiro), Codex I-4-1-62; for a discussion of Temudo's instructions and his movements, see Boxer, "Blake," *Mariner's Mirror,* 36:217–225. Temudo defended his conduct in a letter to John IV, Lisbon, 10 December 1652; AHU, Rio de Janeiro, Caixa I.
123. CU *cons.* 21 January 1651, AHU, Bahia, Caixa V.
124. Arq. Dist. Évora, Codex CV/1–17, fol. 247; *Severall Proceedings in Parliament,* 17–24 October 1650.
125. *A Brief Relation,* 1–22 October 1650; BM, Add. MSS. 4192, fols. 98–102, 187; *Severall Proceedings in Parliament,* 31 October–7 November 1650; *A Perfect Diurnall,* 14–21 October 1650; Anderson, "Royalists," *Mariner's Mirror,* 17:156.
126. Tôrre do Tombo, Arquivo da Alfândega do Funchal, Codex 1232, fol. 5.
127. The vice admiral was probably António Abreu de Freitas and the rear admiral Vitório Zagalo.
128. BM, Sloane MSS. 1039, fols. 115–116; Blake, pp. 63–65; *Severall Proceedings in Parliament,* 31 October–7 November 1650; PRO, S.P. 89/4, 115.
129. Anderson, "Royalists," *Mariner's Mirror,* 17:156; *Cartas de D. João IV,* p. 415.
130. *Cartas de D. João IV,* pp. 416–418.
131. Ibid., p. 420.
132. Anderson, "Royalists," *Mariner's Mirror,* 17:157–158.
133. Warburton, 3:313.
134. Anderson, "Royalists," *Mariner's Mirror,* 17:158–166; Blake, pp. 67–70; William Penn's journal, *Portland MSS.,* 2:72.
135. Anderson, "Royalists," *Mariner's Mirror,* 17:168.
136. Warburton gives a good account of Rupert's voyages during 1651–1653, as does Anderson in the articles in *Mariner's Mirror.*
137. Thurloe, 2:426.

Chapter 5

1. *Portland MSS.,* 3:311.
2. Ajuda 50-V-36, doc. 203, shows that John IV was so advised.
3. After 1662 the question of compensation payments was overshadowed by, and mixed up with, the payment of the dowry of Queen Catherine of Bragança.
4. Castelo Melhor to John IV, Bahia, 3 September 1650, AHU, Bahia, Caixa V (Bancroft m/f, Caixa VI, frames 279–280); *Cartas de D. João IV,* p. 375.
5. AHU, Bahia, Caixa V (Bancroft m/f, Caixa VI, frames 280–283.). The confiscations were carried out under the direction of the Council of State, whose papers have mostly been lost; the Bahia sequestration papers survive only because they were attached to an Overseas Council inquiry into whether or not Castelo Melhor had obeyed his instructions.
6. They were: the *Sara* (twenty-six guns, 400 tons) under Thomas Grant, replaced as master by the Portuguese Valentím Cardoso; *Sampson* (twenty-four guns, 650 tons) under John Lynde, replaced by Bernardo Lopes; *Nicholas* (twenty

guns, 300 tons) under William Maple, replaced by Manuel Rodrigues; *Scipio* (twenty-eight guns, 400 tons) under Thomas Evans; *Three Brothers* (twenty-two guns) under John Wilkes, replaced by Domingos Barrados; *Thomas and Lucy* (twenty guns) under Andrew Rand, replaced by José Gomes; *Talbot* (twenty-four guns) under Joseph Rohot (?), replaced by Manuel Vieira; and the *Blessing* under Robert Moore (armament, tonnage, and name of Portuguese master not recorded).

7. BM, Add. MSS. 4192, fols. 215–217.
8. "Diligençia q̃ se fes o Guilherme Maple Capitam da nao Sam Niculao," AHU, Bahia, Caixa V.
9. "Inventario da Nao Samsam," AHU, Bahia, Caixa V.
10. Ibid.
11. BM, Add. MSS. 4192, fols. 86–87.
12. Ibid., fols. 215–217.
13. Milton, 13:272–275, 422–425.
14. AHU, Codex 92, fol. 112.
15. AHU, Bahia, Caixa V; Ajuda 50-V-36, doc. 190.
16. AHU, Codex 92, fols. 131–132; *Bristol Deposition Books,* 2:100; Milton, 13:460–463.
17. Tôrre do Tombo, Arquivo da Alfândega do Funchal, Codex 1232, fols. 4–5, 8–9; Codex 1233, fols. 87–91.
18. Ibid., Codex 1232, fols. 4–9; Codex 1233, fols. 65, 70–72; BM, Add. MSS. 4192, fol. 242; *Cal. S.P. 1655* (London, 1881), p. 195.
19. *A Perfect Diurnall,* 7–14 October 1650; *Portland MSS.,* 1:567.
20. When a contractor delayed a vessel beyond the period of time stipulated in the contract, he was usually obliged to pay a surcharge in addition to the freightage; this extra charge was called demurrage.
21. BM, Add. MSS. 4192, fols. 218–221.
22. *Cartas de D. João IV,* p. 421.
23. BM, Add. MSS. 4192, fols. 86–87.
24. *Cartas de D. João IV,* pp. 318, 382.
25. *Bristol Deposition Books,* 2:109–110.
26. Ibid., pp. 18–23, 97–100.
27. BM, Add. MSS. 4192, fols. 86–87; Shillington and Chapman, p. 193.
28. BM, Add. MSS. 25227, fols. 143–144; Ajuda 51-V-16, doc. 16.
29. Tôrre de Tombo, Arquivo da Alfândega do Funchal, Codex 1232, fols. 4–5.
30. *Cartas de D. João IV,* p. 453.
31. Ibid., p. 458.
32. The London merchants trading with Spain suffered losses in the *John Adventure* and *Hopeful Adventure,* taken by Rupert, and they claimed the extravagant sum of £68,000 for the ships. Eventually the claim was reduced to £20,000, but the Portuguese government refused responsibility for these losses. BM, Add. MSS. 4192, fol. 84; Ajuda 50-V-36, doc. 190.
33. *Cal. S.P. 1650,* pp. 285, 287; *Commons Journal,* 6:467, 473.
34. BM, Sloane MSS. 1039, fols. 115–116.
35. PRO, S.P. 89/4, fol. 115.
36. Ibid., fols. 119–20; BM, Sloane MSS. 1039, fols. 115–116; Add. MSS. 4192, fols. 98–102.
37. Freire de Oliveira, 5:216–217, 256–259; *Cartas de D. João IV,* pp. 382–384.
38. Angola, Caixa III, folder 445; AHU, Codex 278, fol. 341. The AHU papers from the period 1649–1658 contain about fifty petitions requesting permission to employ foreign seamen aboard Portuguese ships.

39. CU *cons.* 7 December 1650; AHU, Bahia, Caixa V (Bancroft m/f, Caixa VI, frame 457); Codex 278, fol. 341.
40. *Cal. S.P. 1655,* p. 392.
41. CU *cons.* 10 July 1653; AHU, Bahia, Caixa VI.
42. CU *cons.* 9 November 1652; AHU, Bahia, Caixa V (Bancroft m/f, Caixa VI, frame 451).
43. *Cal. S.P. 1650,* pp. 330, 347. It was proposed that George Gage, a Catholic priest held prisoner in London, be exchanged for Beare and Bushell. Gage was to post bond for £20,000 and go to Lisbon. If he could not secure the release of Bushell and Beare within three months, then he was to return to London and surrender himself to the authorities. Nothing came of the scheme. See Whitebrook, pp. 6–8.
44. *Cartas de D. João IV,* pp. 421–423.
45. *Collecção Chronológica 1648–1656,* p. 64; *Bristol Deposition Books,* 2:97.
46. *Cartas de D. João IV,* pp. 422–423.
47. Ibid., p. 424.
48. Ibid., pp. 425–426.
49. Ibid., p. 428.
50. Ibid., pp. 430–432.
51. *Acts and Ordinances of the Interregnum,* 2:449–451.
52. *Portland MSS.,* 2:70.
53. *Cal. S.P. 1650,* p. 468.
54. *Portland MSS.,* 1:546.
55. Ibid.; Milton, 13:46–47.
56. *Commons Journal,* 6:510.
57. Ibid., p. 513.
58. *Portland MSS.,* 1:547.
59. Ibid., 1:540–541, 550.
60. *Commons Journal,* 6:516.
61. Ibid., pp. 519–520; *Portland MSS.,* 1:551.
62. *Commons Journal,* 6:522–523; *Portland MSS.,* 1:552.
63. Thurloe, 1:168.
64. *Portland MSS.,* 2:71; Boxer, *Dutch in Brazil,* p. 232.
65. Boxer, *Dutch in Brazil,* p. 232.
66. *Portland MSS.,* 2:71, 82; Blake, p. 19.
67. *Portland MSS.,* 1:551–552, 555; BM, Landsdowne MSS. 827, fol. 41; *Commons Journal,* 6:525, 529.
68. Since most of the leading members of the "Rump" Parliament were also members of the Council of State, they had the habit of referring business back and forth from one body to the other.
69. Council meetings of 5/15 and 8/18 February 1651; *Cal. S.P. 1651* (London, 1877), pp. 36, 38.
70. *Cal. S.P. 1651,* p. 40; *Portland MSS.,* 1:565–566.
71. *Cal. S.P. 1651,* pp. 138–140.
72. *Portland MSS.,* 1:565.
73. Ibid., p. 566.
74. *Cal. S.P. 1651,* pp. 122, 128–129.
75. *Commons Journal,* 6:556, 558.
76. *Cal. S.P. 1651,* p. 138.
77. *Commons Journal,* 6:558–560; *Cal. S.P. 1651,* pp. 138–140.

78. *Cal. S.P. 1651,* p. 140.
79. *Portland MSS.,* 1:569; *Cal. S.P. 1651,* p. 158.
80. *Cal. S.P. 1651,* p. 161; *Commons Journal,* 6:565.
81. *Portland MSS.,* 1:570–571.
82. Ibid., pp. 571–572; *Cal. S.P. 1651,* pp. 165–166.
83. *Cal. S.P. 1651,* pp. 182, 197; *Commons Journal,* 6:570, 573; *Portland MSS.,* 1:572–573.
84. *Portland MSS.,* 1:573; *Cal. S.P. 1651,* p. 201.
85. *Commons Journal,* 6:575; *Cal. S.P. 1651,* pp. 201–202.
86. *Cal. S.P. 1651,* p. 203.
87. *Portland MSS.,* 1:574; *Cal. S.P. 1651,* p. 211.
88. *Portland MSS.,* 1:574.
89. *Cal. S.P. 1651,* p. 245.
90. *Portland MSS.,* 1:567.
91. *Cal. S.P. 1651,* pp. 234, 562.
92. *Cartas de D. João IV,* p. 443.
93. Ibid., p. 450.
94. Ibid., p. 459.
95. Cromwell, 2:477.
96. *Cal. S.P. 1651,* p. 485.

Chapter 6

1. BM, Lansdowne MSS. 190, fol. 78.
2. *Portland MSS.,* I, 655.
3. *Commons Journal,* 7:165; PRO, S.P. 89/4, fol. 121; *Portland MSS.,* 1:656; *Cal. S.P. 1651–1652* (London, 1877), pp. 368, 370.
4. *Cal. S.P. 1651–1652,* p. 409.
5. Ibid., p. 417.
6. *Portland MSS.,* p. 658.
7. This was a quibble. Blake's "attack" on the Brazil fleet was only his detention of nine *English* ships freighted by the Brazil Company, and took place on 31 May 1650; the general sequestrations followed on 11 June; the real attack on the sugar fleet did not come until 24 September.
8. *Portland MSS.,* 1:658–659.
9. *Commons Journal,* 7:188.
10. *Cal. S.P. 1651–1652,* pp. 431–432, 436.
11. *Portland MSS.,* 1:662–663.
12. BM, Add. MSS. 4192, fols. 98–102, 187.
13. *Portland MSS.,* 2:82; *Cal. S.P. 1652–1653,* pp. 70–71.
14. *Cal. S.P. 1651–1652,* p. xxiv.
15. BM, Add. MSS. 4192, fols. 131–132.
16. Ibid.
17. *Portland MSS.,* 1:664–665; *Cal. S.P. 1652–1653,* p. 13; *Commons Journal,* 7:230.
18. *Cal. S.P. 1652–1653,* pp. 51, 77.
19. By my estimates one pound equalled 2$117 rëis during 1643–1663; see note 28 in chap. 10.

20. BM, Add. MSS. 4192, fols. 90–94, 189–190.
21. *Commons Journal,* 7:243, 245; BM, Add. MSS. 4192, fol. 96.
22. Carlo Prayer (ed.), *Oliviero Cromwell dalla Battaglia di Worcester alla sua morte: Corrispondenza dei rappresentanti Genovesi a Londra* (Genoa, 1882), p. 71.
23. BM, Add. MSS. 4192, fol. 136.
24. Ibid., fols. 182–185.
25. "A Particular of the Articles of Peace Desired by the English Marchants to Be Graunted Them by His Majestie of Portugall," BM, Add. MSS. 4192, fols. 43–46.
26. BM, Add. MSS. 4192, fol. 139.
27. Ibid., fol. 142.
28. "Articles Proposed by the Portugall Ambassador, with the Answer of the Councell," BM, Add. MSS. 4192, fols. 17–41, 141.
29. BM, Add. MSS. 4192, fols. 17–41, 139–142.
30. Ibid., fols. 141–142, 174–177.
31. Ibid., fol. 208.
32. Ibid., fols. 168–169, 281.
33. *Cal. S.P. 1652–1653,* pp. 382, 399, 402.
34. *Cal. S.P. 1653–1654,* p. 23.
35. BM, Add. MSS. 4192, fols. 248–250.
36. *Cal. S.P. 1653–1654,* pp. 168, 483.
37. *Cal. S.P., Venetian Ser.,* 30:303.
38. Thurloe, 1:316–317.
39. Cromwell, 3:34, 44, 52.
40. Ibid., 3:106–107.
41. BM, Add. MSS. 4192, fols. 285–288.
42. *Cal. S.P. 1653–1654,* pp. 427, 434, 439.
43. Ibid., pp. 432, 437, 443, 444, 446.
44. Accounts of the incident can be found in: *Mercurius Politicus,* 17–24 November 1653; *Severall Proceedings of State Affaires,* 17–24 November 1653; *The Faithful Scout,* 18–25 November 1653; Pantaleão de Sá e Meneses, *A Narration of the Late Accident in the New-Exchange* (London, 1653); Frances Clarke, *A Briefe Reply to the Narration of Don Pantaleon Sa* (London, 1653); Bulstrode Whitelock, *Memorials of the English Affairs* (London, 1732), p. 569; Thurloe, 2:222–223; Cromwell, 3:127–128.
45. Clarke, *Briefe Reply,* p. 2.
46. Thurloe, 2:222–223; *Severall Proceedings of State Affaires,* 17–24 November 1653; *The Faithful Scout,* 18–25 November 1653; Pantaleão, *Narration,* pp. 9–12; Cromwell, 3:127–128.
47. *Cal. S.P. 1653–1654,* p. 266; Whitelock, p. 569.
48. *The Faithful Scout,* 18–25 November 1653.
49. *Cal. S.P. 1653–1654,* p. 281.
50. Ibid., p. 269.
51. *Commons Journal,* 7:355.
52. *Cal. S.P. 1653–1654,* pp. 276–277.
53. *Quadro Elementar,* 18 vols. (Paris/Lisbon, 1842–1876), 7:85.
54. Clarke, *Briefe Reply,* p. 4.
55. *Cal. S.P., Venetian Ser.,* 29 (London, 1929): 160–162; *A Perfect Account of the Daily Intelligence from the Armies in England, Scotland, and Ireland,* 14–21

December 1653, 28 December 1653–4 January 1654; *Cal. S.P. 1653–1654,* pp. 447, 449.

56. *Severall Proceedings of State Affairs in England, Ireland, and Scotland,* 22–29 December 1653.
57. Ibid., 29 December 1653–5 January 1654; Prayer, p. 135.
58. Cromwell, 3:162; Prayer, pp. 138–141.
59. *Cal. S.P. 1653–1654,* pp. 360–362.
60. Ibid.; *Portland MSS.,* 1:677–678. See also the "Justification of the Proceedings against the Portuguese for the Murder of Mr. Greenway, notwithstanding Their Relation to Their Embassador," Thurloe, 2:428–429—a weak attempt to find legal precedents for the action against Pantaleão.
61. *Cal. S.P. 1653–1654,* p. 419; Thurloe, 2:222–223.
62. The official treaty was in Latin—English and Portuguese translations were unofficial. Printed versions can be found in many places: Cromwell, 3:915–925; *British and Foreign State Papers, 1812–1814,* vol. 1 (London, 1832), part 1, 480–492; *Collection of Treatys* (1732), 3:97–111; José de Almada, *Aliança Inglesa,* 1:31–38 (extracts)); *Collecção Chronológica 1648–1656,* pp. 353–363; *Quadro Elementar,* 17:88–98; Eduardo Brazão, *Uma velha aliança,* pp. 95–115; Borges de Castro, *Collecção dos tratados,* 1:169; Jerónimo da Câmara Manuel, *Portugal e Inglaterra,* p. 80. There are also many manuscript copies. The British Museum has at least eleven separate versions (in Latin, English, and Portuguese): Lansdowne MSS. 190, fols. 81–90; 1152, fols. 7–25, 27–38 (the official Latin text); Stowe MSS. 192, fols. 3–20, 22–34, 36–61; Add. MSS. 4192, fols. 8–12, 64–75; 27344, fols. 43–59; 34329, fols. 18–34, 38–46. See also PRO, S.P. 103/57; 108/386; Tôrre do Tombo, Miscelâneas de Graça, Caixa II, Tomo II-C, fols. 145–155 (an official copy in Latin), and Gaveta 18, Maço 18, No. 2; Ajuda 51-V-5, fols. 40–51; Biblioteca de Vila Viçosa, Codex LXXXVIII, fols. 1–16; and Academia das Sciencias de Lisboa, Códices, Série Azul, MSS. 464, 762, 1458. The manuscript copies are more interesting than the printed versions, and those written in Portugal should be checked for alterations, omissions, or additions—or spaces left for additions—in the religious articles (6 and 14) and for the presence or absence of the secret article. Manuscript copies written in England should be checked for alterations in the words *Protector* and *Commonwealth,* which were often changed, later to *King* and *Kingdom.* Versions copied out in Portugal, whether in Latin or Portuguese, usually adhered to the original language ("Most Serene Protector," "The Commonwealth of England," etc.).
63. Cromwell, 3:240–242.
64. Thurloe, 2:113.
65. *Cal. S.P., Venetian Ser.,* 29:216.
66. Thurloe, 2:247; Cromwell, 3:276.
67. Thurloe, 2:248.
68. BM, Add. MSS. 4192, fols. 285–288.
69. *Cal. S.P. 1654* (London, 1880), pp. 151, 156.
70. Ibid., pp. 218–219.
71. BM, Add. MSS. 4192, fol. 357.
72. Whose names the extant accounts fail to mention.
73. Cromwell, 3:358.

74. Later, in 1667, he became Judge Conservator of the English, as well as a *desembargador da Casa da Suplicaçao* (BM, Add. MSS. 27344, fols. 186–187). Because João Milis de Macedo could speak both English and Portuguese and because of his name, I am tempted to think that he was a son of the English merchant John Mules (always called João Milis by the Portuguese) and acquired the surname Macedo from his Portuguese mother.
75. *The Weekly Intelligencer of the Commonwealth,* 4–11 July 1654.
76. Ibid.; Whitelocke, p. 592; Cromwell, 3:358; *Mercurius Politicus,* 29 June–6 July 1654.
77. Cromwell, 3:303.
78. Thurloe, 2:447.
79. Ibid., 2:429.
80. Cárdenas to Philip IV, London, 9/19 July 1654; in Simancas MSS. 2529, quoted by Gardiner, *History of the Commonwealth,* 2:386, note 1.
81. Prayer, p. 171; *A Perfect Diurnall of Some Passages and Proceedings of and in Relation to the Armies in England and Ireland,* 3–10 July 1654.
82. *Cal. S.P. Venetian Ser.,* 29:238–239; *Quadro Elementar,* 17:99.
83. *Weekly Intelligencer,* 4–11 July 1654; Whitelock, p. 593.
84. Philippa Mohun (b. 1623), daughter of John Mohun (d. 1641), first Baron Mohun of Okehampton, may have helped Pantaleão in both of his efforts to escape; she had to flee to Holland to evade Cromwell's wrath—see *Nicholas Papers,* 4 vols. (London, 1886–1920), 2:83–86. She should not be confused with her mother (also called Philippa) or with Philippa, wife of Charles Mohun (1645–1677), the third Baron Mohun.
85. *Weekly Intelligencer,* 4–11 July 1654; Whitelock, p. 595; *Mercurius Politicus,* 6–13 July 1654.
86. *The Weekly Intelligencer* (4–11 July 1654) said about Pantaleão: "His indeavour to escape last Night out of Newgate in a Womans Habit did hasten his Execution." See Prayer, p. 171; Gardiner, *History of the Commonwealth,* 2:386, note 1.
87. Newberry Library (Chicago), Greenlee MSS. 158.
88. Thurloe, 2:439; BM, Add. MSS. 4192, fol. 75.
89. *The True and Perfect Speeches of Colonel John Gerard upon the Scaffold at Tower-hill. . . . Likewise, the Speech of the Portugal Ambassadors Brother upon the Scaffold* (London, 1654).
90. *A Perfect Account of the Daily Intelligence,* 5–12 July 1654.
91. Whitelocke, p. 595.
92. *A True and Impartial Narration of the Death of M. John Gerhard* (London, 1654).
93. *Mercurius Fumigosus, or the Smoking Nocturnall,* 5–12 July 1654.
94. Prestage, *Chapters,* p. 146.
95. Ericeira, *Historia de Portugal Restaurado,* 2 vols. (Lisbon, 1679–1698), 1:804–806.
96. *Quadro Elementar,* 17:99–101.
97. *Cal. S.P. 1654,* pp. 250–251; Thurloe, 2:517.
98. BM, Add. MSS. 19399, fol. 79.

99. Cromwell, 3:375, 381. The unfortunate ambassador died four years later. He participated in the frontier wars with Spain, was captured by the Spaniards under Don Luis de Haro, and retired to a Franciscan convent outside Elvas, where he died on 21 December 1658 when only thirty-nine years of age.
100. Milton, 13:210–213; Cromwell, 3:381–382.
101. Cromwell, 3:438.
102. Ibid., 3:441.

Chapter 7

1. C. R. Boxer, *Golden Age of Brazil 1695–1750* (Berkeley, 1962), p. 133.
2. Ajuda 49-IV-20, fols. 184–208.
3. Ibid., fol. 208.
4. Ibid., fol. 186.
5. Ibid., fols. 188–193.
6. Ibid., fol. 198.
7. Roma du Bocage, 1:200.
8. Ibid., p. 203.
9. BM, Add. MSS. 4192, fol. 43.
10. Ibid., fols. 17–41.
11. BM, Lansdowne MSS. 1152-A, fols. 7–25.
12. Ajuda 49-IV-20, doc. 84, fols. 210–211.
13. Ibid., doc. 85, fols. 211–213.
14. Ibid., doc. 92, fol. 217.
15. Ibid., docs. 90–91, fols. 214–216.
16. Cromwell, 3:379; Blake, pp. 268–269.
17. Ajuda 49-IV-20, doc. 94, fol. 230.
18. Ibid., fol. 241.
19. Ibid., fol. 243.
20. Ibid., fol. 244.
21. AHU, Bahia, Caixa VI.
22. Cromwell, 3:711, 747, 754–755.
23. Blake, pp. 299–302; Freire de Oliveira, 5:527.
24. Blake, p. 309.
25. Hill's wife was the sister of Peter Sterry, preacher to the Council of State, and of Nathaniel Sterry, a strong Cromwellian. Through the Sterrys, who were close to Cromwell, Hill could obtain favors from London. Details about Maynard's early career can be found in BM, Add. MSS. 35099, fols. 165–167.
26. *Cal. S.P. 1655,* p. 334.
27. See the next chapter.
28. *Collecção chronológica, 1648–1656,* p. 65.
29. Heathcote MSS., pp. 66–68.
30. PRO, S.P. 89/4, fol. 199.
31. Vila Viçosa, Codex XCI, doc. 136; copy in Tôrre do Tombo, Coleção de São Vicente, Livro XXIII, fol. 211; Baião, *Episódios dramáticos,* 3:43–48; Ericeira, *História de Portugal Restaurado,* new ed., 4 vols. (Oporto, 1945), 3:311.
32. Vila Viçosa, Codex XCI, docs. 143–144.

33. See, for instance, Council of State meetings, 4/14 November 1652 and 4/14 January 1653, *Cal. S.P. 1651–1652,* p. 474, and *Cal. S.P. 1652–1653,* pp. 78–79.
34. Vila Viçosa, Codex XCI, doc. 145.
35. Ibid., doc. 164.
36. PRO, S.P. 89/5; *Heathcote MSS.,* p. 81.
37. *Heathcote MSS.,* pp. 176–177.
38. Ibid., p. 81.
39. BM, Add. MSS. 19399, fols. 146–147; Geddes, *Several Tracts,* pp. 374–382.
40. BM, Lansdowne MSS. 1152-B, fols. 41–42.
41. Baião, *Episódios dramáticos,* 3:50–51; Rau, "Movimento dos Portos," *Anais,* 5:204–205, 207, 210.
42. Rau, "Movimento dos Portos," *Anais,* 5:262–263.
43. BM, Add. MSS. 34332, fols. 1–2.
44. "The Complaints of the English Merchants," PRO, S.P. 89/5; BM, Add. MSS. 34332, fol. 28.
45. Walford, pp. 115–118; A. D. Francis, *Methuens and Portugal* (Cambridge, 1966), p. 21.
46. The events are described at length in Baião, *Episódios dramáticos,* 3:240–250.

Chapter 8

1. Thurloe, 4:546.
2. Ibid., p. 598.
3. Blake, pp. 342–345.
4. Thurloe, 4:592, 620, 679; Blake, p. 324.
5. Thurloe, 4:681.
6. Ibid., p. 682.
7. Ibid., p. 683.
8. Ibid.
9. Freire de Oliveira, 5:547.
10. Ajuda 50-V-36, doc. 188; 49-IV-20, doc. 95. The rupture between Portugal and the Vatican had made Sotomaior a very important man. Although he was a mere titular bishop of a nonexistent North African diocese, he was for eleven years the only living canonically instituted Portuguese bishop, and hence a key part of the Portuguese ecclesiastical machinery. All other bishops were merely bishops-designated, not recognized by Rome.
11. The contents of his letter can only be inferred from Cromwell's reaction to them; see Cromwell, 4:154–155.
12. Cromwell, 4:154–155.
13. Ibid., 4:153–154.
14. Thurloe, 5:59–60.
15. *Quadro Elementar,* 17:104–106.
16. *Cal. S.P., Venetian Ser.,* 30:242.
17. He had been Portuguese ambassador in Paris during 1642–1649.
18. Thurloe, 4:758.
19. Ibid.
20. Ibid.

21. Ibid.
22. Ibid., 5:144.
23. Ibid., 5:113–115.
24. Ajuda 44-XIII-32, doc. 110-F.
25. Thurloe, 5:124–126.
26. John IV to Cromwell, Lisbon, 26 May 1656 (a translated English copy), BM, Add. MSS. 4192, fol. 76; Latin original Add. MSS. 4157, fol. 62; printed versions in Thurloe, 5:28, and *Quadro Elementar,* 17:103.
27. Thurloe, 4:759.
28. Ibid., 4:758–759.
29. Ibid., 5:14.
30. Ibid.
31. Ibid., 1:726–727.
32. Ibid., 5:67–70.
33. Blake, p. 351.
34. Ibid., pp. 351–352; Thurloe, 5:59–60.
35. Thurloe, 5:59.
36. Ibid., 5:55.
37. Ibid.
38. Ibid., 5:113.
39. Ibid., 6:49.
40. Brito Freire, pp. 14, 17, 19, 30–32.
41. Ibid., pp. 60–68, 72, 74, 94–98.
42. Ibid., pp. 178–180.
43. Thurloe, 5:113.
44. Brito Freire, pp. 252–253.
45. Ajuda 50-V-36, doc. 187. For an example of the tampering with the Latin text of the treaty, see article 6 in BM, Stowe MSS. 192, fol. 6.
46. Thurloe, 5:67–70.
47. Ibid., 5:77.
48. Ibid., 5:79–80.
49. Both Montagu and Blake, at this time, used the *Naseby* as their flagship.
50. Blake, p. 353.
51. Thurloe, 5:125.
52. Ibid., 5:97–98; Blake, pp. 353–354.
53. Blake, pp. 355–356.
54. This works out at a rate of 2$073 réis per £1.
55. Thurloe, 5:113.
56. Ibid., 5:116, 118–119, 123.
57. Ibid., 5:123.
58. Ibid.
59. Ibid., 5:125.
60. Blake, p. 361.
61. Ibid., p. 363; Cromwell, 4:183–184.
62. For instance, prices of chickens at Angra rose from under $100 to over $200 réis each. Arq. Dist. Angra, "Fénix Angrense," year 1656, fols. 169–170; Drummond, 2:130–131.
63. Brito Freire, pp. 200, 207–208, 223–241.
64. Paragraph 15 of the *regimento,* Ajuda 51-VII-43, fol. 119.
65. Brito Freire, pp. 242–244.

66. Ibid., pp. 248–257.
67. *Cal. S.P. 1656–1657* (London, 1883), pp. 22, 317, 394; Cromwell, 4:205, 207.
68. *Cal. S.P., Venetian Ser.*, 30:242.
69. *Cal S.P. 1656–1657*, p. 319.
70. The original letter in Latin is in BM, Add. MSS. 4157, fol. 64; a printed version in Thurloe, 5:118–119. I have quoted from a contemporary English translation, roughly done but used by the government officials themselves, in BM, Add. MSS. 4192, fols. 76–77.
71. BM, Add. MSS. 4192, fol. 78.
72. Ibid.
73. Ibid.
74. *Quadro Elementar*, 17:106–110.
75. Cromwell, 4:216–217, 241–242; Milton, 13:226–229, 244–249.
76. Thurloe, 1:730.
77. Ibid., 1:729–730; Blake, p. 373.
78. Cromwell, 4:313; Blake, pp. 331, 375–380.
79. Cromwell, 4:239, 322–323; Milton, 12:268–269, 272–275.
80. Thurloe, 5:374–375; *Cal. S.P. 1656–1657*, p. 167; *Cal. S.P., Venetian Ser.*, 30:266–267.
81. Thurloe, 6:3–5.
82. Thurloe, 5:612; *Cal. S.P. 1656–1657*, p. 244.
83. Thurloe, 6:49.
84. Ibid., 6:118–119, 152.
85. João V. Claro, *Aliança Inglesa* (Lausanne, 1943), p. 90.
86. AHU, Codex 46, fol. 39.
87. Ibid., fol. 47.
88. AHU, Codex 92, fol. 298.
89. *Documentos históricos*, 4:101.
90. See for instance, BM, Add. MSS. 34329, fol. 36; 34332, fols. 1–2; and 35099, fols. 89–94.
91. Thurloe, 6:808–809.
92. BM, Add. MSS. 35099, fol. 85.
93. BM, Add. MSS. 34332, fols. 1–2. Francis Parry, however, believed that the merchants' complaints were exaggerated: "I doe what I can to procure a remedy for the merchants grievances, but really I find that in some things they make heavy complaints without reason, and in others without proof." Of twenty-seven specific grievances, he thought seven were valid, six possibly valid, and fourteen not proved (fol. 5). A Portuguese version of these complaints is in BM, Add. MSS. 35099, fols. 89–94, with Lisbon's answer on fols. 95–97.
94. PRO, SP. 65; Sir Richard Lodge, "English Factory at Lisbon," *Transactions of the Royal Historical Society*, 4th Ser., 16 (1933): 211–247.

Chapter 9

1. The Portuguese conquered Tangier in 1471; the British took possession of the town in 1662 but abandoned it in 1684 (without giving the Portuguese a chance to reoccupy it). For further information see Edward Montagu, *Journal*, ed. R.C. Anderson (London, 1929), pp. 102–121; Ericeira, *Historia de Tangere* (Lisbon,

1732); W. B. T. Abbey, *Tangier under British Rule 1661–1684* (Jersey, Channel Islands, 1940).
2. Cromwell, 4:239–240; Thurloe, 1:730 and 5:421–422; *Cal. S.P., Venetian Ser.*, 30:250.
3. Cromwell, 4:313; Blake, pp. 331, 375–376.
4. Arq. Dist. Angra, "Fénix Angrense," year 1656, fol. 172.
5. *Speaker* (sixty-four guns), *Plymouth* (fifty-four), and *Bridgewater* (fifty-two).
6. My account is a composite woven from various (unsatisfactory) English, Spanish, and Portuguese sources and agrees with no single one of them, though it is closest to the version in Arq. Dist. Angra, "Fénix Angrense," year 1656, fol. 172, which was probably based on the accounts of the Azorean sailors aboard the Terceira pinnace. See the following: Charles H. Firth, *Last Years of the Protectorate,* 2 vols. (London, 1909), 1:50–51; *A True Narrative of the Late Success . . . of the Fleet of this Commonwealth upon the Spanish coast, against the King of Spain's West-India Fleet* (London, 1656), of which there is a French translation: *Narration veritable du dernier succes* [etc.] (Paris, 1656); Thurloe, 5:399–400; *Cal. S.P., Venetian Ser.,* 30:273–275; Jerónimo de Barrionuevo, *Avisos 1654–1658,* 4 vols. (Madrid, 1892–1893), 3:85; Duro, 5:22–24.
7. Firth, 1:55–56.
8. Blake, p. 378.
9. The sugar fleet of eighty ships or more left Lisbon during the autumn of 1656 and arrived at Bahia on 20 March 1657. On its return journey part of the fleet was attacked by the Dutch. AHU, Codex 15, fols. 288–289; AHU, Bahia, Caixa VI (Bancroft m/f, Caixa VIII, frame 14); *Cal. S.P. 1657–1658* (London, 1884), p. 154.
10. Blake, pp. 379–380.
11. Ibid., pp. 383–384.
12. For descriptions of the battle, see the following: *An Order of Parliament . . . for a Day of Publike Thanksgiving . . . for the Great Success God Hath Been Pleased to Give the Navy of this Commonwealth under the Command of General Blake Against the Spaniard* (London, 1657); Thurloe, 6:152–154, 184, 312–313; Blake, pp. 333–334; Cromwell, 4:537–538; Duro, *Armada Española,* 5:24–27, and his *Bosquejo biográfico del Almirante Don Diego de Egues y Beaumont y relación del combate naval que sostuvo con Ingleses in Santa Cruz de Tenerife año 1657* (Sevilla, 1892), pp. 14–17.
13. Thurloe, 6:401.
14. Cromwell, 4:538, 600, 615; Blake, pp. 334–335.
15. Accounts of Franco-Portuguese relations of this period can be found in Prestage, *Diplomatic Relations of Portugal with France, England, and Holland from 1640 to 1668* (Watford, England, 1925), and in his *Frei Domingos do Rosário* (Coimbra, 1926).
16. Alphonse VI was nominally king of Portugal from 1656 until his death in 1683, but he was never in control of the country. Queen Luisa remained regent until 1662, when the third Count of Castelo Melhor forced her into retirement and ruled the country himself for five years (1662–1667). Alphonse's brother, the Infante Pedro, ousted Castelo Melhor, virtually deposed his brother, married Alphonse's French wife (after the annulment of the previous marriage), and ruled Portugal as Prince-Regent during 1668–1683 and in his own right as Pedro II during 1683–1706. The unfortunate Alphonse was kept in confinement, first in Lisbon, then in the Azores, and finally in a small room in the royal palace at Sintra, where he died (12 September 1683).

17. A full account of John IV's death can be found in Vicente de Guzmán Soárez, *Ultimas acções del Rey D. João IV,* ed. Edgar Prestage (Lisbon, 1918). Two manuscript sources add some additional details: BM, Add. MSS. 20933, fols. 214–215, and Add. MSS. 15189, fols. 169–170.
18. Manuscript copies in Ajuda 51-V-7, fols. 39–40; BM, Add. MSS. 20933, fols. 216–219, and Add. MSS. 15189, fols. 191–194.
19. The evidence of John's active role in the conspiracy of 1640 comes from declarations made by Francisco de Sousa Coutinho (John's agent in Madrid during September and October 1640) in a letter to Queen Luisa, dated "Rome, 20 April 1659," in Vila Viçosa, Codex XC.
20. "Pussillanime, ingrato, vingativo e, na hora da vingança, cruel"; Azevedo, *Vieira,* 1:57. For a more balanced appraisal, see Ângelo Ribeiro's essay in Damião Peres, *História de Portugal,* vol. 6 (Barcelos, 1934), p. 76.
21. The fundamental source for Portuguese politics of the period 1656–1662 is the 400-page account in Ericeira, *Portugal Restaurado*—although it is far from accurate in details and pays excessive attention to minor military campaigns. Most later Portuguese histories seem to be derived from Ericeira. In English, a brief sketch of the main events can be found in Livermore, *History of Portugal,* pp. 302–312.
22. For details see Boxer, *Dutch in Brazil,* pp. 249–255.
23. *Tratado entre esta Corona y la de Francia* (Madrid, 1660), pp. 15–16.
24. As interpreted by the Portuguese, this meant the setting aside of half the customs duties *only on English merchandise brought into Portugal by English merchants on English ships*—that is, the goods, the ship, and the merchant all had to be English before any money was set aside. No such money was held separately until 1657, well after John IV's death. Tôrre do Tombo, Arquivo da Alfândega do Funchal, Codex 1232, fols. 30, 71.
25. Copy of Ferreira Rebelo's memorandum to Queen Luisa (1657), Ajuda 50-V-36, doc. 190; and his letter to Cromwell, 10/20 February 1657, Thurloe, 6:51–52.
26. Ferreira Rebelo tried to advance the argument that the English umpire was bound by the advice of the Portuguese procurator.
27. Thurloe, 6:51–52.
28. Ibid.
29. Ajuda 50-V-36, doc. 190.
30. Tôrre do Tombo, Miscelâneas de Graça, Caixa II, Tomo II-C, fols. 53, 58.
31. Tôrre do Tombo, Arquivo da Alfândega do Funchal, Codex 1232, fol. 30. The Portuguese Council of State, in its *consultas* of 15 and 20 October 1659, declared that all sums owed to the English would be paid on time, through the collection of the one-half percent customs. By that time, Lisbon was interested in quickly securing an Anglo-Portuguese military agreement. Vila Viçosa, Codex XCI, doc. 114.
32. Southwell to merchants formerly sequestered in Portugal; Lisbon, 4/14 May 1669; *Portland MSS.,* 3:311.
33. Melo's private papers (which I have not seen) still belong to his descendants. Unfortunately, those who have examined the papers state that a volume of the earlier papers has been lost—precisely those dealing with the most obscure phase of Melo's activities, the years 1657–1660. There is a shortage of archival sources for the Anglo-Portuguese diplomacy of this period, particularly for the two years extending from February 1658 to March 1660. For a statement of

this problem and an evaluation of the Melo papers, see Guernsey Jones, "Beginnings of the Oldest European Alliance: England and Portugal, 1640–1661," *American Historical Association: Annual Report for the Year 1916,* 2 vols. (Washington, 1919), 1:413–414. Jones was not aware, however, of the collection of original letters (many of them in cipher) from Queen Luisa to Melo, which help to bridge the gap and which can be found in Vila Viçosa, Manuscritos, Codex XCI.

34. In the words of João Milis de Macedo, Portuguese embassy interpreter, in a letter to Odemira, London, 18 September 1657, Ajuda 50-V-36, doc. 181; Cromwell, 4:567, 615.
35. Ajuda 50-V-36, doc. 181; Vila Viçosa, Codex XCI, doc. 12.
36. The words were intended by Milis de Macedo as sarcasm, for their supposed exaggeration, but they might better be understood in their literal sense; Ajuda 50-V-36, doc. 181. Tôrre do Tombo, Miscelâneas, fol. 58.
37. Tôrre do Tombo, Miscelâneas, Caixa II, Tomo II-C, fols. 49–50; Cromwell, 4:620.
38. Copy of an undated document sent (by Thurloe? the Council of State?) to Melo, with a Latin translation attached, in Tôrre do Tombo, Miscelâneas, fol. 182. I know of no other version of this text, in manuscript or in print, in English or Portuguese.
39. Tôrre do Tombo, Miscelâneas, fols. 183–184. The sum of money demanded is also left blank in the Latin text.
40. Ibid., fol. 58.
41. Vila Viçosa, Codex XCI, doc. 4.
42. The Portuguese ambassador in Paris was the Irish Dominican friar Domingos do Rosário, once known as Daniel O'Daly, who established an Irish Dominican school in Lisbon and served as Queen Luisa's confessor. Prestage, *Frei Domingos,* pp. 9, 13, 18, 21.
43. Tôrre do Tombo, Miscelâneas, fols. 57–58.
44. Vila Viçosa, Codex XCI, doc. 7.
45. Ibid., doc. 11; Thurloe, 6:582, 631–634; *Cal. S.P. 1658–1659,* pp. 152–154, 167, 174–175, 185; Boxer, *Dutch in Brazil,* pp. 249–250.
46. Thurloe, 6:808–809, 7:18; Cromwell, 4:726; BM, Add. MSS. 4158, fol. 120.
47. Cromwell, 4:770. After Charles II's restoration, Downing remained in Holland and continued to oppose the Luso-Dutch peace, because the Dutch sought great trading privileges from the Portuguese, privileges that Lisbon finally granted and which might have damaged the English merchants trading with Portugal. The peace treaty was signed on 6 August 1661 and ratified by Alphonse VI on 24 May 1662. Boxer, *Dutch in Brazil,* pp. 252–254; Tôrre do Tombo, Miscelâneas, fols. 121–139.
48. Vila Viçosa, Codex XCI, doc. 34.
49. An important Portuguese nobleman, the Duke of Aveiro, defected at about the same time. There is a full account in Ericeira, *Portugal Restaurado,* 3:267–281.
50. Ajuda 51-V-7, fols. 68–69.
51. *Portland MSS.,* 1:684–685.
52. A Portuguese resident in London who may have been in the pay of the king of Spain. Ericeira, *Portugal Restaurado,* 3:312–315.
53. HMC, *Seventh Report* (London, 1879), p. 80; *Lords Journal,* 11:14, 17–18, 24.
54. Vila Viçosa, Codex XCI, doc. 138.
55. Ibid., doc. 175.

56. Ibid., doc. 185.
57. Ibid., doc. 68.
58. "Muito importará que essa Republica se conserve no estado em que o defunto Protector a deixou." Vila Viçosa, Codex XCI, doc. 67.
59. Ajuda 50-V-36, doc. 177–178; Vila Viçosa, Codex XCI, doc. 81.
60. The official Portuguese copy, written on parchment in Latin, can be found in Tôrre do Tombo, Miscelâneas, fols. 145–155; there is an official Portuguese translation in Ajuda 50-V-36, doc. 182; the full text can be found printed, in Portuguese, in Borges de Castro, *Colecção dos tratados,* 1:226; and there is a summary in *Quadro Elementar,* 17:118.
61. Ericeira, *Portugal Restaurado,* 3:312. An English merchant carried to Lisbon the news of the treaty (probably during May 1660); the treaty itself, in the hands of João Milis de Macedo, arrived a little later. By 14 July 1660 the queen had ratified the treaty and given a copy to the English vice consul in Lisbon (probably Christopher Maynard; Consul Thomas Maynard, at this time, was in London, where he supported Queen Luisa and Melo in pressing for an Anglo-Portuguese agreement). The English merchant Robert Parker—described by the queen as "one of the Englishmen in whom my ministers have great confidence"—was sent to London on 15 June 1660 with highly confidential dispatches for Melo. Vila Viçosa, Codex XCI, docs. 170–174, 192.

Chapter 10

1. My translation of his words as reported, in Portuguese, in a letter to Melo, 9/19 May 1661, BM, Add. MSS. 20933, fols. 328–329.
2. Prestage, *Chapters,* p. 149.
3. House of Commons, *Parliamentary Debates,* vol. 392, no. 106, col. 716.
4. Prestage, *Chapters,* pp. 165, 169.
5. Ajuda 50-V-36, doc. 183.
6. Clarendon, *State Papers,* 3:303–304.
7. Vila Viçosa, Codex XCI, doc. 181.
8. Ibid., docs. 170–174.
9. Ibid., doc. 207.
10. Ibid., doc. 183; Joseph Gillow, *Bibliographical Dictionary of English Catholics,* 5 vols. (London, 1885–1902), 5:455–457.
11. Ajuda 50-V-36, doc. 185.
12. Vila Viçosa, Codex XCI, docs. 136, 143–145, 164, 177, 190, 196, 202, 213.
13. Ibid., docs. 168–169.
14. Ibid., docs. 204, 205, 210.
15. Jones, "Beginnings of Oldest Alliance," *American Historical Association: Report 1916,* 1:415.
16. PRO, S.P. 89/4, fols. 189–190.
17. Ibid., fols. 188, 198–199.
18. Ibid., fol. 198.
19. Copy of letter, Melo to Luisa, London, 17 February 1661, Vila Viçosa, Codex XCIII, fols. 1–4. Luisa's public instructions (18 January 1661) to Melo can be found in Tôrre do Tombo, Miscelâneas, fols. 23–27, and secret instructions on fols. 35–44.

20. Vila Viçosa, Codex XCIII, fols. 5–6, 8–12. The statement "between February and April 1661 the Portuguese hopes sank to zero" (Keith Feiling, *British Foreign Policy 1660-1672* [London, 1930], p. 46) is incorrect. Feiling's account of the marriage negotiations (pp. 37–46) needs to be rectified and supplemented by Portuguese sources.
21. Murrough O'Brien (*circa* 1614–1674), first Earl of Inchiquin, was an exiled royalist and a converted Catholic who rose to the rank of lieutenant general in the French army. On his way to Lisbon he was captured, with his son William, by Algerian pirates, who held him for ransom. Queen Luisa ransomed O'Brien and also paid him ten months of back salary, but, on arrival in Portugal, he wanted to join the restored Charles II in England immediately. Luisa took the opportunity to entrust him with a confidential diplomatic mission to London (Biblioteca de Vila Viçosa, Codex XCI, doc. 203). In June 1662, Inchiquin was back in Lisbon, where he stayed for a while in Consul Maynard's house (Maynard's letter, 30 June 1662, in PRO, S.P. 89/5).

    Friedrich Hermann von Schönberg (1615–1690), Count and then Duke of Schönberg, was born in Heidelberg but served so many years in the armies of Louis XIV that he was usually called Frédéric-Armand, duc de Schomberg. He was sent to Portugal by way of England, in order to maintain an official pretense that the French were not sponsoring his mission. He spent seven and a half years in Portugal and could claim major credit for the victories achieved by the Portuguese armies over the Spaniards. See the biographical essay in the *Dictionary of National Biography.*
22. Clarendon, *State Papers,* 3: appendixes 1–2, 4–6; Prestage, *Chapters,* p. 147; Jones, "Beginnings of Oldest Alliance," *American Historical Association: Report 1916,* 1:417; Melo's report (8 August 1661) to Lisbon in BM, Add. MSS. 15202.
23. HMC, *Fifth Report,* p. 159; Clarendon, *State Papers,* 3: appendix 7; BM, Add. MSS. 20933, fols. 323–324. Melo reported to Luisa (Vila Viçosa, Codex XCIII, fol. 11) that the Spaniards "are making the strangest efforts that can possibly be imagined, resorting to ignoble and indecent ways" of preventing the marriage.
24. *Lords Journal,* 11:244.
25. HMC, *Fifth Report,* p. 151.
26. Montagu, pp. 89–99, 102–124, 132–140; *Relaçam diaria da jornada que. . . . D. Catherina fez de Lisboa a Londres* (Lisbon, 1662); BM, Lansdowne MSS. 1236, fols. 124–125, 130–131; Ajuda 51-V-7, fols. 63–64.
27. For details, see Shafaat Ahmad Khan (ed.), *Anglo-Portuguese Negotiations Relating to Bombay 1660–1677* (London, 1922).
28. One pound sterling in English silver coin, in mint condition, contained as much fine silver as could be found in 2$117 réis of Portuguese silver coin in mint condition. Thus 800:000$000 réis in good coin contained enough silver for the minting of £377,893 4s 9½d in English silver coin (at the standard of £2 1s 4d per mark of silver). But on 22 March 1663 the Portuguese reduced the amount of silver in their coins—a move that was designed partly to ease the burden of payments that Portugal had assumed toward England and the United Provinces. After 22 March 1663, 800:000$000 réis was worth only £302,228 18s 7¼d. See Duncan, *Atlantic Islands,* p. 265. Gertrude Z. Thomas, *Richer than Spices: How a Royal Bride's Dowry Introduced Cane, Lacquer, Cottons, Tea, and Porcelain to England* (New York, 1965), p. 14, states the value of the dowry at half a million in sterling, which is too high. The article on Catherine

in the *Dictionary of National Biography* cities the figure of of £300,000, which is correct after the devaluation of 22 March 1663.

29. Freire de Oliveira, 6:272–285.
30. *Heathcote MSS.*, p. 80.
31. BM, Add. MSS. 35099, fols. 228–229.
32. *Heathcote MSS.*, p. 34.
33. The article on Catherine in the *Dictionary of National Biography,* although brief, is accurate and annotated. Three full-length popular biographies all have the deficiencies of the genre: L. C. Davidson, *Catherine* (London, 1908); J. Mackay, *Catherine* (London, 1937); and M. B. Jones, *Restoration Carnival: Catherine at the Court of Charles II* (New York, 1937). Virgínia Rau, *D. Catarina de Bragança* (Coimbra, 1941), although a scholarly biographical essay, lacks English sources.
34. Some say that her most permanent contribution to English life was in having made tea drinking fashionable. Manoel Cardozo wrote that her "sole contribution to English artistic life was the introduction of Italian songs and singers" but added that "she may have also had a hand in making popular the most popular of all Christmas hymns, the 'Adeste Fidelis,' said to have been composed by her father, who was indeed a fine composer of sacred music." "England's Fated Ally," *Luso-Brazilian Review* 7 (1970): 53.
35. Indications of this can be found in Ajuda 51-VI-20, fols. 179–207.
36. Davidson, *Catherine,* p. 311; C. F. R. Palmer, *Life of Philip Thomas Howard* (London, 1867); Edward Petre, *Notices of the English Colleges and Convents Established on the Continent* (Norwich, 1849), pp. 18–23; Gillow, 2:9–10, 442–451, and 5:455–457.
37. Letters in BM, Egerton MSS. 1534.
38. See A. D. Francis, *Methuens and Portugal 1691–1708.*
39. Heathcote MSS., pp. 68–69.
40. Francisco Assís de Castro e Mendonça, *Memória histórica* (Oporto, 1840), p. 26.
41. Tôrre do Tombo, Miscelâneas, fol. 25.
42. The Portuguese "fortress" at Bombay consisted of "onely two small Bulworks, some Earth and Stones"; as for the island, "the King of Portugall (as they say) hath neither house, Fort, Amunition nor foote of Land on it" (letter from Bombay, 3/13 March 1665; *Anglo-Portuguese Negotiations Relating to Bombay,* p. 466). Bombay "doth not answer our Kings expectation by four-fifths of what was represented to him" (letter from India, 26 September/6 October 1662); "I must confess that Bombain of it selfe will yeild His Majesty little benefitt, because there is little land belonging to it" (letter from Goa, 31 December 1662/10 January 1663; *English Factories in India 1661–1664,* ed. Sir William Foster [Oxford, 1923], pp. 134 and 143).
43. In an unprecedented move, the Portuguese viceroy went to India aboard an English warship, the *Leopard,* accompanied by the *Convertine, Dunkirk,* and *Mary Rose* and the pinnace *Chestnut.* The squadron, under the command of James Ley, third Earl of Marlborough, sailed from Lisbon on 10/20 April 1662 and reached the coast of India on 18/28 September. Montagu, *Journal,* pp. 124, 130; "Treslado dos primeiros papeis que o Governador Antonio de Mello de Castro remeteo de Bombaim," AHU, India, Caixa XXV; *English Factories 1661–1664,* pp. 123–132.
44. The viceroy not only revealed these facts in his letters to Lisbon (AHU, India Caixas XXV–XXVI), but he also boasted of them. Lisbon disassociated itself from Melo de Castro's policies and was compelled to recall him in disgrace.

45. Within one year's time, a force of 450 men had shrunk to 150. *English Factories 1661–1664,* pp. 224–225.
46. Livermore, *History of Portugal,* pp. 312–314.
47. BM, Harley MSS. 6446, fol. 2.
48. No words have been left out—the three periods of the ellipsis are but a stylistic device of the author to indicate a momentous pause. Claro, *Alianca Inglesa,* p. 102.
49. Harley MSS. 6446, fols. 4, 8, 11, 13 *et passim.*
50. Ibid., fols. 13–20; Col. James Apsley of the English army in Portugal, relation dated 29 May/8 June 1663 (the day of battle), *Heathcote MSS.*, pp. 101–105; António Álvares da Cunha, *Campanha de Portugal pella Provincia do Alentejo na primavera do anno de 1663* (Lisbon, 1663), pp. 50–54.
51. *Mercurio Portuguez,* July 1664. Actually the English brigade lost 178 men killed, including one lieutenant colonel, one major, four captains, two lieutenants, three ensigns, nine sergeants, and 158 common soldiers. *Heathcote MSS.*, pp. 160–161.
52. Harley MSS. 6446, fol. 21; Álvares da Cunha, pp. 50–51; *Mercurio Portuguez,* issues for July 1664 and November 1665; *Mercurio Portuguez Extraordinario,* [June] 1665.
53. Freire de Oliveira, 6:273.
54. Claro, p. 102.
55. F. P. da Cunha Leal, *Portugal e Inglaterra* (La Coruña, 1932), p. 178.
56. Copy of the treaty, BM, Add. MSS. 34329, fols. 77–104. This codex contains dozens of documents dealing with the Anglo-Luso-Spanish negotiations of 1666.
57. José d'Arruella, *O imperativo geográfico de uma aliança: a vitória da Inglaterra e a independência de Portugal* (Coimbra, 1945); Pedro de Tovar, *A aliança ingleza* (Lisbon, 1914).
58. Fidelino de Figueiredo, *Pyrene* (Lisbon, 1935), pp. 64–69.
59. "Alianças tão continuadas, entre as nações Ingleza e Portugueza, em todos os tempos, que alem da amizade destas duas naçoens, são mais reciprocas nellas as conveniençias q̃ em nenhuãs outras." Copy of letter, Melo to Charles II, Ajuda 50-V-36, doc. 176.

Index

Abbreviations used in the Index:
Eng. = English k. = king pr. = prince
Pt. = Portugal, Portuguese q. = queen